VITA
NOSTRA

VITA NOSTRA

MARINA & SERGEY
DYACHENKO

TRANSLATED BY JULIA MEITOV HERSEY

HARPER
Voyager

Published by Harper*Voyager*
An imprint of HarperCollins*Publishers* 2018
1

www.harpercollins.co.uk

A catalogue record for this book is available from the British Library

HB ISBN: 978-0-00-827285-2
TPB ISBN: 978-0-00-827286-9

Printed and bound in Great Britain by
CPI Group (UK) Ltd, Croydon CR0 4YY

MIX
Paper from
responsible sources
FSC™ C007454

This book is produced from independently certified FSC™ paper to ensure responsible forest management.

For more information visit: www.harpercollins.co.uk/green

To our daughter, Anastasia

PART ONE

The prices—oh, the prices were simply ludicrous! In the end, Mom rented a tiny room in a five-story building twenty minutes from the shore, with windows facing west. The other room in the one-bedroom apartment was occupied by a young couple, with whom they would have to share the kitchen, bathroom, and toilet. "Those two are on the beach the whole day," reasoned the landlady. "They are young . . . They don't need much. The sea is right there, you can almost see it out of your window. Pure paradise."

The landlady departed, leaving behind two keys: one for the main entrance and one for the door to their room. Sasha dug her faded, last year's swimsuit from the bottom of the suitcase and changed quickly in the bathroom, where someone else's underwear was drying on the space heater. She felt joyful and giddy: just a few more minutes, and hello sea, here we come. Waves, salt on her lips, deep khaki-colored water—all that was forgotten during the long winter. Transparent water changing the color of her skin to yellow-white. Swimming toward the horizon, feeling the sea glide over her stomach and back, then diving deep down, staring at the rocks on the bottom, seaweed and tiny speckled fish . . .

"Should we eat first?" Mom asked.

She was exhausted by the long trip in the stuffy economy class seats, the apartment search, negotiations with potential landlords—none of it was easy.

"But, Mom . . . we came to spend time at the beach."

Mom lay down on a couch, a pack of fresh linen under her head substituting for a pillow.

"Want me to run down and get some doughnuts?" Sasha aimed to be a dutiful daughter.

"We're not going to live on doughnuts here. We have a decent kitchen."

"Can't I at least take one little dip?"

"Fine." Mom closed her eyes. "Get some eggs and yogurt on the way back. Oh, and bread, and some butter."

Not hesitating—lest her mother change her mind—Sasha threw a sundress over the swimsuit, slid her feet into a pair of sandals, grabbed a beach bag and one of the towels provided by the landlady, and ran outside, into the sunshine.

She had no proper names for the blossoming trees that grew in the yard, but decided to call them "peacock trees." Behind the unevenly trimmed bushes began the street that led to the shore. Sasha decided it was going to be called just that—the Street That Leads to the Sea. The street sign bore the real name, but it was plain and insignificant. It happened so often—beautiful things had stupid names, and the other way around.

Swinging her bag, she walked—no, *ran*—down the street. People moved in a thick throng, some carrying inflatable mattresses and large sun umbrellas, others burdened only with a beach bag. Children, as expected, were covered by melting ice cream, and their mothers scolded them, wiping faces and shirts with their crumpled handkerchiefs. The sun had toppled over the zenith and now hung above the distant mountains, choosing a place to land. A languid smile on her lips, Sasha walked toward the sea, hot asphalt burning through the soles of her sandals.

They'd made it.

They'd made it despite the lack of money, despite Mom's problems at work. They'd made it to the seaside, and in only fifteen, no, ten minutes, Sasha would dive into the water.

The street twisted. The sidewalk was almost entirely blocked by advertisements for tourist attractions—the Swallow's Nest, Massandra, Nikitsky Botanical Garden, Alupka Palace . . . The din of video games filled the air. A mechanical voice coming from a metal contraption in front of the arcade offered palm reading. Sasha ignored it all and instead stood on tiptoes . . .

And finally saw the sea.

Restraining herself from breaking into a gallop, she ran down a steep hill toward the high tide, toward the happy squeals of children and the music of beachside cafés. *So close.*

Of course, the closest beach had an entrance fee. Not letting herself be annoyed by a simple fee, Sasha ran around the fence, jumped off a low concrete railing, and felt the pebbles crunch under her feet. She found a spot on the rocks, threw her towel and sundress down on her beach bag, took off her sandals and made her way down, wincing from the gravel biting into her feet. As soon as she got to the water, she dove in and swam.

This was happiness.

In the first second, the water seemed cold; in the second, warm, like freshly drawn milk. Right near the beach, seaweed and fragments of plastic bags swayed gently in the waves, but Sasha swam farther and farther away, and the water became clear, leaving behind inflatable mattresses and children with bright-colored floaties. The sea opened all around her and a scarlet buoy flashed like a sign of perfection between two stretches of turquoise cloth.

Sasha dove, opened her eyes, and saw a school of gray elongated fish.

On the way back she ran—Mom was probably worried. The uphill road seemed unexpectedly long and steep. She stopped at a store, where a harried saleswoman sold bread, eggs, and potatoes, and the queue was long and solemn. After enduring the line for nearly half an hour, Sasha filled up her bag with groceries and ran down the Street That Leads to the Sea into the garden with the "peacock" trees.

A man stood near a rental agency, a green booth with permanently closed shutters. Despite the heat, he wore a dark denim suit. Under the peak of his dark-blue cap his face had a jaundiced, waxy tint. Dark glasses reflected the sun's rays, but Sasha managed to catch his glance. She cringed.

She looked away from the strange man, entered the hallway that smelled of many generations of cats, and walked up to the second floor, to the door upholstered in black faux leather with a tin number 25 on it.

Every morning Sasha and her mother woke up at four, when their neighbors, the young couple, returned from a nightclub. The neighbors stumbled up and down the corridor, made tea, made the bedsprings creak, and eventually fell quiet; Sasha and her mother dozed off again and woke up next around seven thirty.

Sasha made instant coffee for both of them (the kitchen sink brimmed with dirty plates—the neighbors apologized profusely for the mess, but never did the dishes), and they headed for the beach. On the way to the shore, they bought little cups of yogurt or freshly steamed corn sparkling with salt crystals or jam doughnuts. They rented one plastic lounge chair to share, spread their towels over it, and ran toward the water, stumbling on the sharp gravel and hissing from pain. They plopped into the water, dove in, and lingered in the waves.

On the second day, Sasha got a sunburn, and Mom smeared yogurt on her shoulders to calm the sting. On the fourth day, they went on a harbor cruise, but the waves were choppy, and both of them felt a touch of motion sickness. On the fifth day, there was a real storm, and half-naked lifeguards strolled around the beach, announcing: "Can't swim—alligators abound," as Sasha's mother quoted from an old children's rhyme. Sasha played with the waves and managed to get slammed by an errant rock; the painful bruise took a long time to heal.

In the evenings, the whole town was drowned in music streaming from the nightclubs. Clusters of guys and girls armed with cigarettes stood near the kiosks or box office windows, or sat around old iron benches and participated in social engagements expected of adolescent mammals. Occasionally, Sasha caught their appraising looks. She did not like those guys with their obnoxious, overly made-up girlfriends, yet she felt uneasy—it was embarrassing for a normal sixteen-year-old to be vacationing with her mother like a little girl. Sasha would have liked to stand just like this, in the center of a noisy group, leaning on a bench and laughing with everybody else, or to linger in a café, sipping gin and Coke from a tin can, or to play volleyball on a square patch of asphalt, split by long cracks like an elephant hide. Instead she would just walk by, pretending she had some urgent, much more fascinating business to attend to, and spend her evenings strolling around with her mother in the park or along the boardwalk, gazing at the creations of the never-ending street artists, haggling over lacquered shells and clay candleholders, doing all these rather nice and not-at-all-boring things—but the peals of laughter coming from the teenage clusters sometimes made her sigh heavily.

▪▪▪

The storm subsided. The water had been freed of the mud that clung to it, the sea regained its transparency, and Sasha caught a crab, as tiny as a spider. She let it go right away. Half of their vacation had already dissolved into nothingness; it seemed as if they'd just arrived, and now only eight days remained.

She met the man in the blue cap at a street market. Moving along the rows, Sasha was pricing black cherries, when, rounding the corner, she saw him in the midst of the shoppers. The man stood nearby, his dark glasses turned toward Sasha. She was sure he was watching her, and her alone.

Sasha turned and pushed toward the market exit. After all, she could buy the cherries at her street corner; it was more expensive, but not so much that it was worth sticking around. Swinging her plastic bag, she entered the Street That Leads to the Sea and strode up to her apartment building, trying to stay in the shade thrown by the acacia and linden trees.

She looked back after half a block. The man in the dark denim suit was following her.

For some reason, she'd believed he had stayed at the market. Of course, there was the possibility that he needed to go in the same direction, but she was not that naïve. Staring into the impenetrable lenses, she felt unutterable terror.

The street was packed with beachgoers and vacationers. Ice cream was melting down children's fronts in the same way as before, open-air kiosks were just as busy selling bubblegum, beer, and vegetables, the afternoon sun was just as scorching, but Sasha's instant chill felt like a lining of frost in her stomach. Not really aware of why she was so afraid of the dark man, Sasha shot up the street, her sandals drumming a feverish rhythm and passersby hastily moving out of her way.

Gulping air, not daring to look back, she burst into the yard with the "peacock" trees. She leapt into the hallway and rang the doorbell. Mom took a long time to open the door; downstairs, in the entrance hall, a door opened, and Sasha heard footsteps . . .

Mom finally made it to the door. Sasha dove into the apartment, nearly toppling her mother. She slammed the door closed and turned the key.

"Are you crazy?"

Sasha clung to the peephole. Looking distorted, as if through a funny mirror, their next-door neighbor walked up the stairs, carrying a bag of cherry plums, and went farther up to the third floor.

Sasha started breathing again.

"What happened?" Mom's voice was tense.

"Nothing, really." Embarrassment moved in. "Somebody was following me . . ."

"Who was?"

Sasha began to explain. The story of the dark man, when narrated logically, did not seem frightening, only ridiculous. Nothing she said made any sense, and Mom clearly wasn't alarmed.

"I assume you did not buy any cherries," Mom concluded.

Sasha shrugged guiltily. The right thing to do was to pick up her bag and return to the market, but the very idea of opening the door and walking out into the yard made her knees shake.

"I suppose I might as well do it myself." Mom sighed. She picked up the bag and money and left for the market.

Next morning, on the way to the beach, Sasha saw the dark man again. He stood by the tourist center, pretending to examine the offered tours and prices, but in reality he was watching Sasha from behind his dark mirrored lenses.

"Mom, look . . ."

Mom followed Sasha's gaze. Her eyebrow lifted. "I don't understand. Some guy standing there. And?"

"You don't see anything weird?"

Mom continued walking, each step bringing her closer to the dark man. Sasha slowed down.

"I'm going to walk to the other side of the street."

"Go ahead, if that's what you want. I think you have been getting too much sun lately."

Sasha crossed the asphalt, wrinkled and covered by tire tracks. Mom passed the dark man, but he didn't pay her any attention. He watched Sasha, and only her. His gaze followed her.

Once settled on the shore, they rented a beach chair and placed it in the usual spot, but for the first time, Sasha did not feel like swimming. She wanted to return home and lock herself up in the apartment. Although, if she thought about it, the door in the apartment was flimsy, made of plywood, a mere illusion covered with ancient faux leather. It was safer here, on the beach, crowded and noisy, with inflatable mattresses floating in the water; a little boy stood knee-deep in the water, and the floatie around his belly was shaped like a swan with a long neck, and the boy was squeezing its pliant white throat.

Mom bought some baklava from a street seller clad in a white apron. Sasha took a long time licking her sticky-sweet fingers, then strolled over to the water to rinse her hands. She walked into the waves, still wearing her plastic flip-flops. The red buoy, a sign of perfection halfway to the horizon, moved gently in the water, the sun reflected in its opaque side. Sasha smiled, shrugging off her tension. And really, such a funny story. Why should she be afraid? In a week she'll be going home, and, seriously, what can he do to her?

She moved deeper into the water, took off her flip-flops, and tossed them onto the beach, aiming far to avoid losing them to a chance wave. She dove, swam a few feet under water, resurfaced, snorted, laughed, and made a beeline for the buoy, leaving behind the shore, the din, the baklava seller, her fear of the dark man . . .

In the afternoon they discovered that they'd forgotten to buy oil to fry their fish.

Pink blossoms swayed on the "peacock" trees. Farther down, in the bushes, something else blooming and aromatic was trying to attract bees. An old woman dozed off on the bench. A boy of about four dragged colored chalk over the concrete ridge of the sidewalk. The usual throng of people poured down the Street That Leads to the Sea.

Sasha entered the street and took another look around. She ran to the store, to get her errand over with as quickly as possible.

"Excuse me, are you the last one in line?"

She nodded to the person behind her. The queue moved not too fast, but not too slowly either. Sasha had only three people in front of her when she felt his gaze.

The dark man appeared in the store entrance. He took a step inside. Ignoring the queue, he moved to the counter and stopped, pretending to examine the produce. His eyes, covered by sunglasses, bore into Sasha. Bore right through her.

She did not move. First, because her feet stuck to the floor. Then because she thought it through and decided that here, in the store, she wasn't in danger. There was no danger at all . . . and dropping everything, losing her place in line, and running home would just be stupid. He'd catch her in the hallway.

Maybe she could yell for her mother from the yard. Make her look out the window. And then what? Caught in the indecision—

"Excuse me, is it your turn?"

She asked for some oil, then spilled her change when paying for it. An old man behind her in line helped her pick it up. She considered asking someone for help with the dark man.

He stood at the counter, watching Sasha. His stare made her thoughts scramble in her head. Embarrassing, but she really needed to use the bathroom now.

Should she scream for help?

Nobody would understand. Nobody knew why Sasha felt terrorized by this rather ordinary person—nobody seemed to notice him much at all. So his face was pale—what of it? Then the dark glasses—but many people wore those, too. How could she explain what was happening to her when he stared through those opaque lenses?

Squeezing the handle of the shopping bag bulging with butter and oil in her fist, Sasha stepped out of the store. The man followed her. He did not bother pretending. His movements were direct, determined, and businesslike.

Once out of the store, she sprinted. Gray pigeons flew from underneath her feet. She crossed the street and dashed toward home, wind screaming in her ears, to her mother, into the familiar courtyard . . .

She had never seen this place before. Sasha looked around—the "peacock" trees bloomed as before and the sidewalk was covered by random designs in colored chalk, but the entrance was completely different, and the bench was in the wrong place. Was it a different courtyard?

The dark man did not run—he simply walked, each step bringing him five feet closer. Losing her head in sheer terror, Sasha threw herself into the entrance hall; she should not have done that and she knew it, but she ran inside anyway. A door slammed downstairs. She sprinted up the stairs, but there were only five stories. The staircase ended in a row of locked doors. Sasha rang someone's doorbell; the sound could be heard clearly inside—*ding-dong*—but no one opened the door. It was empty.

And then the man stood next to her, blocking the exit, blocking her escape.

"It's a dream!" She screamed the first thing that came into her head. "I want it to be a dream!"

She woke up in her foldaway bed, in tears, her ear painfully pressed against her pillow.

They left the house around eight, as usual, and bought some yogurt on the street corner. Skillfully, Sasha made her mother cross onto the other side of the street, the opposite of the one with the tourist booth.

And she was right to do so—the dark man stood under the large poster of the Swallow's Nest Palace. He watched Sasha from behind his impenetrable lenses.

"I can't take it anymore. It's psychotic . . ."

"Now what?" her mother said.

"There he is again, he's watching me . . ."

She wasn't quick enough to stop her mother, who turned and crossed the street. She walked right up to the dark man and asked him something; the man answered, still staring at Sasha. Yet at the same time his face was turned toward her mother, and his mouth looked natural and quite friendly . . . if there were such a thing as a friendly mouth.

Mom returned, simultaneously pleased and annoyed.

"Relax; he's on vacation, just like you and me. I don't know what your problem is. He's from Nizhnevartovsk. He's allergic to direct sun rays."

Sasha was silent. It made sense . . . and yet it didn't. *Why does he follow me, then? And why doesn't Mom care?*

At lunchtime, coming back from the shore, they stopped at the market, and Sasha took great care to make sure they didn't forget anything. They returned to the empty apartment, heated up water, and took turns with an improvised bucket shower (water was scarce during the day), and started making their lunch.

That's when they realized they were out of salt.

The dark man was sitting on the bench in the courtyard. Sasha saw him as soon as she poked her head out of the building.

She withdrew her head.

An orange cat with a damaged ear was lapping up cream in a small bowl left by some nice person. The cat slurped and licked its chops. Its yellow eye stared at Sasha; the cat continued licking the bowl.

Sasha did not know what to do. Turn back? Proceed as if nothing was wrong? It was crazy . . .

The hallway darkened. The man in the blue cap stood in the doorway blocking the light.

"Alexandra."

She jerked as if shocked by electricity.

"We need to talk. You can run from me forever, but there is no joy or point in it."

"Who are you? How do you know my name?"

Immediately, she thought of all those times her mother called her by her name, on the street, on the beach, everywhere. There was nothing surprising about him knowing her name. It wasn't really difficult.

"Let us sit down and talk."

"I am not . . . if you don't stop following me, I will . . . I will call the police."

"Sasha, I am not a thief or a murderer. We need to have a serious discussion, which will influence your entire life. It will be better for you to listen to me."

"I am not going to. Leave me alone!"

She turned and ran up the stairs. Toward the black faux leather door numbered 25.

All the doors on the second floor were dark brown. The numbers on the small glass plates were completely different. Sasha froze.

Behind her back, unhurried steps were getting closer. The dark man moved up the stairs.

"I want it to be a dream!" Sasha screamed.

She woke up.

"Mom, what's today's date?"

"The twenty-fourth. Why?"

"But yesterday was the twenty-fourth!"

"Yesterday was the twenty-third. It always happens on vacation—the dates get all mixed up, days of the week slide by . . ."

They came down into the courtyard, into the windless and fragrant white-as-milk morning. The "peacock" trees stood still like two pink mountains covered with apricots. A happy multitude of beachgoers poured down the Street That Leads to the Sea. Sasha walked on, more or less convinced it was yet another dream. A young married couple stood by the kiosk studying the routes and prices. Their little boy—bubble-gum-filled mouth, knees painted by disinfectant—was trying on scuba-diving goggles. The dark man was nowhere in sight, but she still felt the presence of a dream.

Sasha and her mother bought a few ears of corn. Sasha held the warm corn while her mother pulled their beach chair out of the hut and placed it on the rocks. The soft yellow ear of corn tasted salty, delicate kernels melted on their tongues. Sasha placed the trash into a plastic bag and carried it to the bin near the beach entrance.

The dark man stood far away, in the midst of the crowd. Even in the distance, though, he looked only at Sasha through the impenetrable glasses.

"I want it to be a dream," she said out loud.

She woke up in bed.

"Mom, let's go home today."

Shocked, her mother nearly dropped a plate.

"What? Where?"

"Home."

"But you were so anxious to get to the beach . . . Don't you like it here?"

"I just want to go home."

Mom touched Sasha's forehead to check for fever.

"Are you serious? Why?"

Sasha shrugged.

"Our tickets are for the second," said Mom. "I had to reserve it a month in advance. And this place is all paid until the second. Sasha, I don't get it, you were so happy."

She looked so confused, so upset and helpless, that Sasha felt ashamed.

"Never mind," she mumbled. "It's just . . . nothing."

They came down into the courtyard. The "peacock" trees spread their scent over the sandbox and benches, over somebody's old car. Down the Street That Leads to the Sea the beachgoers marched heavily, carrying their inflatable devices. The tranquil, scorching, unhurried summer morning of the twenty-fourth of July continued.

The tourist booth was deserted. At a nearby café, under the sickly palms, a group of teenagers drank beer and argued over their next trip. All of them were tanned and long-legged, both boys and girls. All wore shorts. All carried half-full backpacks. Sasha wanted to leave with them. She wanted to throw on a backpack, lace up a pair of sneakers, and hitch rides along the dusty Crimean roads.

Sasha and her mother walked by the teenagers. They bought some pies, placed their beach chair on the rocks, and sat on it sideways. The sea was a little choppy, the red buoy jumped in the waves, and water scooters' motors sputtered in the distance. Sasha chewed her pie, not really tasting it. Perhaps everything will turn out fine, and the dark man will never appear again, and tomorrow will finally be the twenty-fifth of July?

After lunch, Mom lay down for a nap. The room felt stuffy, the sun leaning west shot right through the closed curtains that used to be green and were now sun-bleached into something vaguely pistachio-colored. The neighbors came home; they chatted happily in the kitchen, there was a sound of poured water and tinkling dishes. Sasha held a book in her lap, stared at the gray symbols, and understood nothing.

The metal alarm clock on the bedside table ticked deafeningly, counting seconds.

"So, shall we talk, Sasha?"

Evening. Mom leaned on the balustrade, chatting with a man of about forty, fair-haired and pale, clearly a new arrival. Mom smiled, and her cheeks dimpled. It was a special smile. Sasha was used to a different one from her mother.

Sasha was waiting on the bench under the acacia tree. A second ago the dark man sat down between her and a street artist at the other end of the bench. Even the southern twilight did not force him to lose his dark glasses. Sasha sensed his stare from beneath the black lenses. Out of complete darkness.

She could probably call for her mother. She could simply cry for help. She could tell herself it was just a dream. And it would be a dream. A never-ending dream. She needed the dream to end.

"What . . . What do you want from me?"

"I want to give you a task to perform. It's not hard. I never ask for the impossible."

"How . . . What does it have to . . . ?"

"Here is the task. Every day, at four in the morning, you must go to the beach. You will undress, go into the water, swim one hundred meters, and touch the buoy. At four in the morning the beach is empty, there won't be anyone to hide from."

Sasha felt as if someone had hit her on the head. Was he crazy? Were they both crazy?

"What if I won't do it? Why would I . . . ?"

The black lenses hung in front of her like two black holes leading nowhere.

"You will, Sasha. You will. Because the world around you is very fragile. Every day people fall down, break their bones, die under the wheels of a car, drown, get hepatitis or tuberculosis. I really don't want to tell you all this. But it is in your best interest to simply do everything I ask of you. It's not complicated."

Near the balustrade, Mom was laughing. She turned, waved, and said something to her companion—they may have been talking about her, about Sasha.

"Are you a pervert?" asked Sasha hopefully. A pervert she could understand.

The black glasses tilted.

"No. Let's just settle this right away before we incapacitate ourselves here: you're healthy, and I'm not a pervert. You have a choice: dangle forever between a scary dream and a real nightmare. Or you can pull yourself together, calmly perform the task that is asked of you, and continue living normally. You can say 'This is a dream,' and wake up again. And then we'll meet once more, with certain variations. But why would you want to?"

People strolled along the boardwalk. Mom exclaimed: "Look! Dolphins!" and pointed toward the sea, her companion broke into a series of excited interjections, passersby stopped and looked for something in the blue cloth of the shore, and Sasha, too, saw the distant black bodies that looked like upside-down parentheses, flying over the sea and disappearing again.

"Do we have a deal, Sasha?"

Mom chatted, watching the dolphins, and her companion listened attentively, nodding. Mom's teeth sparkled, her eyes shone, and Sasha suddenly saw how young she still was. And how—at that moment in time—happy.

"Tomorrow is your first official takeoff." The dark man smiled. "But remember: every day, at four in the morning. Make sure you set the alarm. It's crucial for you not to oversleep and not to be late. Try hard. Got it?"

▪▪▪

Sasha tossed and turned on her cot, wide awake. The curtains were pushed aside, and the songs of nightingales and sounds of a distant disco music poured into the open window. At two in the morning, the music stopped.

A noisy gang walked by. The voices died down in the distance. Three motorbikes, one after another, roared by. A car alarm went off. Mom stirred, turned over, and fell back asleep.

At three in the morning, Sasha dozed off. At three thirty, she jumped up as if someone had shoved her. She pulled the alarm clock from under her pillow. In twenty minutes, the short black hand would join the long yellow alarm hand.

Sasha pressed down the button and rotated the yellow hand. The alarm clock squeaked and went limp.

Sasha got up. She pulled on her swimsuit and a sundress, picked up her keys, and gingerly, trying not to wake up Mom, left the room. She stopped in the empty kitchen, tiptoed out to the balcony, and grabbed a still wet towel from the rope. With her keys in one hand and the towel in the other, she crawled out onto the staircase.

A single lightbulb was on.

Her neighbors, the blissful young couple, were coming up the stairs, shushing each other. Four bewildered eyes stared up at Sasha.

"What happened?"

"Nothing." Sasha was shaking, and her teeth chattered. "I just wanted to go for a swim. See the sunrise."

"Wow, that's cool!" The guy was clearly impressed.

Sasha let them pass and hurried out of the building. It had to be a quarter to four. She was going to be late.

Streetlights still burned on the empty street. Sasha ran—running down turned out to be easier than she thought—and she warmed up and stopped shivering. The dark sky was getting lighter. Sasha sprinted by the fence of the official town beach and reached her favorite secluded spot. The sharp white of plastic cups stood out in piles of trash. Five or six windows were lit in the hotel closest to the beach. A large clock in the front of the building showed three minutes to four.

Sasha took off her dress. Stumbling on the gravel, she walked into the high tide. Standing neck-deep in the water, she unhooked her top and crumpled it into a ball. She pulled off the bikini bottom. Holding her swimsuit in her balled fist, she swam out to the buoy.

In the mottled light of the sunrise, the buoy seemed gray, not red. Sasha slapped its iron side. The buoy responded with a dull echo. Sasha looked back at the shore—no one. It was utterly deserted.

She started back. The cold water caused her to shiver again. Barely managing to reach the rocks with her feet, she rose, balancing in the waves, and realized that the ties of her wet swimsuit were hopelessly tangled.

With a short sob, she threw the crumpled ball of faded fabric onto the shore, got on all fours, and half crawled, half ran toward her towel. She wrapped herself in it and looked around again.

No one. Not a single soul. The sea played with her discarded swimsuit, and the sky was becoming lighter with every minute. Nightingales crooned in the park.

Sasha picked up her bikini, sundress, and sandals. She staggered over to the blue changing cabin. She dried herself and suddenly felt well. She straightened her shoulders. Her skin glowed, becoming firm and radiant from the inside, like the skin of a ripe apple. Taking her time, Sasha got dressed, put on her sandals, and found the keys in her pocket. She squeezed water out of her swimsuit, walked out of the changing cabin . . . and almost immediately doubled over, retching.

She fell on her knees and vomited on the gravel. It was mostly seawater, but along with it, strange yellow disks splashed out of her. Sasha coughed and tried to calm her breathing. The retching disappeared as quickly as it came.

Three tarnished gold coins lay on the gravel.

At home, she locked herself in the bathroom and studied the coins. Three identical disks, an unfamiliar symbol consisting of rounded interconnecting lines on one side—a face, or a crown. Or, perhaps, a flower: the longer Sasha stared at it, the more three-dimensional the symbol appeared, as if it were slowly rising above the surface of the coin.

She rubbed her eyes. On the reverse side, a smooth oval resembled a zero or the letter O. Of course, there was no stamp of gold content, and Sasha was not exactly an expert on precious metals, but somehow she had no doubt that the coins were made of pure gold.

The first beachgoers appeared on the Street That Leads to the Sea. It was about six in the morning. Hearing them, Sasha stretched on her cot, covered her head with a blanket, and squeezed the coins in her fist, thinking hard.

Her throat felt sore, but the nausea had disappeared completely. Of course, one could assume that Sasha's stomach couldn't handle yesterday's baklava, and that the coins were simply lying in the exact place on the gravel where she became sick. And that the man in the dark sunglasses was simply a pervert who used a very convoluted way of spying on naked girls on the beach. In the dark. In the wee hours of the morning.

She squeezed her irritated eyes shut.

No. One could not *assume that.*

Sasha felt removed, thrown out of the normal world into the unreal. If one believed what one read in books, it did happen to people, and happened quite frequently.

Or was it really a dream?

Surprisingly, she fell asleep. And when she woke up, it was a perfectly normal morning of July 25. Mom came in from the kitchen, wiping her hands on a towel, and gave Sasha a worried look.

"Did you go somewhere?"

"I went for a swim."

"Are you crazy?"

"Why?" Sasha croaked. "It was really cool. The sun was rising. There was no one in sight."

"It's dangerous," Mom said. "There are no lifeguards or anything. What if something had happened to you? And why didn't you say something to me?"

Sasha shrugged.

"We should go to the beach." Mom looked at the clock. "It's almost nine. Let's hurry up."

Sasha sucked in her breath.

"Mom . . . Do you mind? Can I just lie down for a while? I didn't sleep well."

"Are you sick?" Mom touched Sasha's forehead in a familiar gesture of concern. "No, you don't feel hot. You are asking for it with your night swimming. It'll spoil the entire vacation."

Sasha did not reply. She squeezed the coins so hard the edges bit into her palm.

"I boiled some eggs." Mom seemed worried. "Mayonnaise is in the fridge. Those lovebirds, the neighbors, ate half of our mayonnaise already, but oh well. What can you do?"

She kept wiping her perfectly dry hands.

"I made plans to meet up with Valentin at the beach; it would be rude not to show up, you know . . . I promised we'd be there today."

Sasha thought of yesterday. Valentin was the name of Mom's new acquaintance, the light-skinned, fair-haired man who seemed so interested in the dolphins. Sasha remembered how Mom had introduced her by her full name: "This is Alexandra." Mom's voice had a special note of importance, but Sasha did not pay any attention to it yesterday. This was before the dark man rose and left, leaving behind a task for Sasha to perform—and fear. Sasha had felt chilly in the middle of a warm stuffy evening. The flower beds smelled sweet; Valentin's cologne was pleasantly woodsy and fresh. Sasha remembered the scent, but could not think of his face.

"Sure, go ahead." Sasha pulled the blanket up to her face. "I'll just stay in bed for a little, and then I'll join you guys."

"We'll be in the same place," Mom said quickly. "The eggs are on the table. I'm off."

She grabbed her beach bag and hurried to the door. At the threshold, she stopped and looked back.

"Don't forget your swimsuit when you leave. It's on the balcony, drying off."

She left.

The second time Sasha woke up, the metal clock showed half past eleven. At that time of the day, the sun was scorching, and the sea was boiling with the mass of swimming bodies, like matzo ball soup. It was too late to go to the beach, or maybe it was too early. It depended on one's point of view. Maybe around four o'clock.

Sasha was shocked by her own mundane thought process. She stared at the coins in her hand. She'd never loosened her fist in her sleep—the moist skin kept the outline of the round coins. Sasha gingerly moved them from her right hand to her left.

What should she do with them? Throw them away?

The doorbell made her jump. One coin slid off her palm and rolled underneath the cot. Nervous, Sasha found it on the dusty rug, threw on Mom's cotton housecoat, and stepped into the dark hallway.

"Who is it?"

Theoretically, it could be her mother, forgetting her keys. Or a postman. Or . . .

"It's me. Open the door."

Sasha staggered back.

The apartment was empty—the neighbors were at the beach. The door was locked. A flimsy door, made of pressed wood shavings, covered with cheap faux leather.

The coins stuck to her sweaty palm. Holding them in one hand, Sasha used the other hand to open the door—a difficult task that took a while.

"Good day to you," the man in dark sunglasses stepped over the threshold. "I'll just be a minute. Let's go to the kitchen."

He led the way down the corridor, as if he'd been to this apartment many times before, as if he were its actual owner. Of course, the building was standard enough.

Sasha followed him like a dog on a leash.

"Sit." The man pushed a chair toward the middle of the kitchen. Sasha fell onto the chair—her legs gave out from under her. The dark man sat down in front of her. "Coins?"

Sasha opened her fist. Three gold disks lay on her red palm, moist, covered with drops of sweat.

"Very good. Keep them. Please retain all of them, all that you will get. Don't bother with the swimsuit—you must enter the water naked, it's not dangerous, no one is watching you. Continue swimming, don't be late, and don't miss any days. Tomorrow. The day after tomorrow. And the day after that."

"I'm leaving on August second," Sasha said, and was surprised by how thin and pitiful her voice sounded. "I . . . we have train tickets. I don't live here, I . . ."

She was convinced that the dark guest would command her to move to this small town forever and ever, and enter the sea at four in the morning in January, and in February, and until death do us part.

"Didn't I say that I won't be asking for the impossible?" He stretched his lips slowly, and Sasha realized that he was smiling. "On August second you will go for a swim in the morning as usual, and you can leave after breakfast."

"I can?"

"You can." The man got up. "Remember: Don't oversleep."

He walked over to the door.

"Why do you need this?" Sasha whispered.

The only answer was the closing door.

▪ ▪ ▪

"Where are you going?" Mom sat up in bed.

"For a swim."

"Have you lost your mind? Get back to bed!"

Sasha took a deep breath.

"Mom, I really need to do this. I'm . . . building character."

"You're what?"

"You know, building character! I'm building up stamina. In the mornings . . . Sorry, I'm late."

Gasping for air, she stepped onto the beach. Nervously, she looked behind her—not a soul; even all the windows in the nearby hotels were dark. She took off her sundress, pulled off her underwear, threw herself in the water, and swam, broad front crawl strokes, as if trying to swim out of her own skin.

She was having difficulty breathing. Sasha switched to an easy "beach" breaststroke, scooping up water with her feet, holding her chin high above the water.

Swimming made her happy. She'd had no previous experience of skinny-dipping and had no idea how good it felt. Cold water prickled her skin, warmed up her body, and seemed to be getting warmer with every stroke. With both hands, Sasha grabbed the buoy and kept still, swaying gently, invisible from the shore.

Perhaps she didn't have to go back at all. She could just keep swimming, across the entire sea, toward Turkey . . .

Sasha shook her head at that. She flipped onto her back and, lazily moving her arms, swam toward the shore. Sparse morning stars dissolved slowly, like sugar crystals in cold water.

In the changing cabin, Sasha rubbed herself dry with a towel and got dressed. She stepped outside and listened to herself—nothing was happening. She walked toward the beach entrance; the spasms started when she reached the little shack where the lounge chairs were kept under a barn lock. Coughing, sputtering, and holding her throat, Sasha vomited four gold coins.

On the third morning of swimming exercises, she threw up back in the apartment, in the bathroom. The coins clanked into the iron tub. Sasha gathered them up, her hands shaking—the coins were exactly the same, all with the round three-dimensional symbol. Worth zero point zero kopecks. She smirked at her reflection in the mirror, pocketed the coins, washed up, and left the bathroom.

Mom was putting her hair up in curlers. There was absolutely no point to it, since the curls would dissipate in the water, but nowadays Mom spent a lot of time doing her hair, putting on makeup, and ironing her outfits.

"Would you mind if Valentin and I go to a café tomorrow night? Just the two of us?" As Mom asked the question, she carefully avoided Sasha's eyes. "You can go to the movies," she continued. "What's playing right now, in that theater on the wharf?"

"I don't know." Sasha fingered the coins in her pocket. "Go ahead. I'll stay home and read."

"But what to do about the keys?" Sasha's compliance clearly took a load off Mom's shoulders. "In case I'm late . . . I don't want to wake you up. But if I take the keys—what if you want to go for a walk?"

"Take the keys. I'll read," Sasha repeated.

"But what about fresh air?"

"I'll sit outside on the balcony. With a table lamp."

"But tomorrow, maybe tomorrow you will want to go to a club?"

"No."

The next day Valentin took them out to lunch. He seemed like a nice person, with a sense of humor, with a certain charm; Sasha watched her mom's happiness and counted the days in her head, the twenty-seventh, twenty-eighth. Five days remained. Actually, only four, on the fifth day they were leaving. And it would be all over. She would forget everything. Only five more times . . .

She swam the next morning, and the morning after.

And then she overslept.

The sun woke her up. It beat into the window that had been left ajar, and Mom's bed was empty; the alarm clock had twisted from underneath her pillow and lay on the rug.

Refusing to believe, Sasha picked it up. The yellow hand stood on half past three. The coil was disengaged. Why didn't it ring?

"Mom! Did you touch my alarm clock?"

Mom, content, benevolent, and fresh after her shower, brought in coffee on a tray.

"I did not. It fell down; I didn't pick it up. I don't want the landlady to think I broke it. Don't worry about it, you got practically no sleep in the last few days, and you need rest—you're on vacation, after all. What is it with you?"

Sasha slumped at the edge of the cot, laden with the firm conviction that something terrible had just happened. Something unidentifiable, inexplicable, some unknown threat—and thus, her terror grew in a geometric progression.

The dark man stood next to the tourist booth, studying a photo of the Swallow's Nest. Sasha slowed her step. Mom turned to her.

"Go ahead," Sasha said. "I'll catch up."

Under different circumstances, Mom would argue and start asking questions. But by now, Valentin must have already reserved their lounge chairs; Mom nodded, told Sasha not to dawdle, and walked down to the shore.

The asphalt had softened under the morning sun. The tires of passing cars and trucks pressed over a puddle of spilled motor oil and left fancy tracks on the road.

"My alarm did not go off," Sasha said, not knowing what she was apologizing for, or to whom. "It fell . . ."

His eyes could not be seen through the dark glasses. The lenses reflected nothing, as if they were made of velvet. The dark man was silent.

"My alarm did not go off!"

Sasha burst into tears right there, on the street, from fear, from the unknown, from the emotional strain of the past few days. The passersby turned their heads, staring at the weeping girl. Sasha felt as if she'd dived deep into the sea and was watching a school of pale fish through a thick layer of water.

"It's very bad, but not terrible," the man in the dark glasses said finally. "As a matter of fact, it's even good for you—it'll teach you some discipline. The second such blunder will cost you a lot more, and don't say I didn't warn you."

He turned and departed, leaving Sasha sobbing and vigorously shaking her head to all the questions from the sympathetic passersby. Hiding in a park alley—deserted at this hour—and pulling a handkerchief out of her bag, she was finally able to clean up her tears and snot. Still, she did not manage to calm herself down.

Her own dark sunglasses, the ones she'd had for over a year, with a thin frame, hid the redness of her eyes and her swollen lids. Pushing her hat low on her forehead, Sasha walked down the street, avoiding looking at people, keeping her eyes from the pavement. In front of her, a girl of about four stomped her red sandals on the ground, holding her mother's hand.

An ambulance stood in front of the beach entrance. Sasha stopped, and her shoes stuck to the softened asphalt.

Almost immediately, she saw her mother. Mom wobbled on the gravel, a towel thrown over her shoulders, holding on to a stretcher. The very pale man lying on the stretcher vaguely resembled a cheerful, sanguine Valentin.

Sasha sat down on the balustrade.

The stretcher was loaded into the ambulance. The medic said something to Mom; she nodded several times and asked something in return. The medic shook his head and climbed into the ambulance. The ambulance beeped at the crowd, pulled back, reversed in a small parking lot in front of the hotel, and drove up the Street That Leads to the Sea.

His words echoed in her head.

"Very bad, but not terrible."

"What happened to him, Mom?"

Mom turned around. Panic and grief swam in her eyes.

"Hospital Number Six," she chanted, like an incantation. "I'm just . . . I need to change, and then I'll go. It's a heart attack, Sasha. A heart attack. Oh god, oh god . . ."

Like a blind person, she moved through the throng of intrigued beachgoers. Sasha watched for a second, and then followed.

Mom spent the night at the local hospital. Almost all of their cash went to the doctors and nurses, and Mom had to go to the post office and call one of her coworkers, who promised to wire them some more money. Sasha spent a sleepless night alone in their room. The alarm clock was no longer reliable.

At three in the morning she left the house. Somewhere the nightclubs were still going strong, and the cafés were still lit. Sasha walked down to the dark sea and sat down on the gravel at the water's edge.

Far away, a ship appeared on the horizon. Cicadas shrieked in the gardens behind Sasha's back. The sea licked the beach, stole tiny rocks and brought them back, polished them, rubbing together their surfaces. The sea had time. And patience enough for two.

At quarter to four, Sasha pulled off her clothes and stepped into the water, shivering. She swam, constantly looking back as if expecting a monster in dark glasses to rear its ugly head out of the waves.

She slapped the buoy and looked up at the sky: the sun was rising. She glanced into the depth of the sea and saw the barely distinguishable metal anchor chain.

She returned to the shore and, barely managing to throw a towel over her shoulders, doubled over retching. Five coins flew out one after another, leaving a sharp pain in her throat and diminishing spasms in her stomach. The coins rolled on the gravel, hiding between the rocks.

Mom came back in the afternoon, exhausted and very focused. Valen-tin felt better—it was not a heart attack, the ambulance had come quickly, and the patient was in no danger.

"Everything will be fine," Mom repeated with an air of detachment. "I am so sleepy, Sasha, I can't tell you how sleepy I am. If you want, go to the beach by yourself, I'm going to sleep."

"How is he, anyway?" Sasha asked. "Should we send a telegram? To his relatives or whatever?"

"The relatives are here already," Mom informed her with the same air of detachment. "His wife flew in from Moscow. Everything will be just fine. Just go now, please?"

His wife . . .

Sasha took her swimsuit off the balcony and left the apartment. She did not feel like going to the beach, so she strolled aimlessly around the park, meager and dusty, but still offering a minimum of shade.

"Very bad, but not terrible."

Fear, stress, ruined vacation . . .

On the other hand, who is Valentin, anyway? Only a week ago he was simply Mom's chance acquaintance. Of course, Mom seemed so happy, but their relationship was doomed from the beginning. It was just a summer fling, a beach affair . . .

Sasha sat down on a bench. Black acacia pods littered the narrow alley. Bitterness and resentment on behalf of her mother ate at Sasha like acid. A summer fling, such a cliché. What was he thinking? And why would he bother with a nice respectable woman, when he could have had any of those girls—a navel ring, jeans cut off right up to the butt cheeks.

"It would be better if he were dead," Sasha thought glumly.

"Very bad, but not terrible."

And Sasha *did* believe that something awful would happen to her mother; her premonition was tangible. From the first moment she saw the man in the dark glasses, fear had gripped her and held her in its fist, just like she herself held her gold coins. It would let go for a minute—only to squeeze again. "This will teach you some discipline." That's for sure. From now on she would get up without any alarm clocks, and always at half past three. Or maybe she just wouldn't sleep at all. Because at the moment when she saw the ambulance in front of the main beach entrance, she'd had a feeling that all in the world was lost forever, all of it . . .

She took a deep breath. Tomorrow morning she would swim out to the buoy, and the day after tomorrow, right before their departure, she would do the same. And then she would return home and forget everything. School, routine, senior year of high school, college entrance exams . . .

She sat on the bench, staring at the handful of coins in her hands. Twenty-nine disks, with the same round symbol, with a zero on the reverse side. Heavy and small, their diameter was the same as the old Soviet kopecks.

On the train, Sasha spilled the coins on the floor.

She was lying on the top berth staring out the window. The pocket of her denim shorts must have been unbuttoned; the coins spilled out and rolled around the entire carriage, clanking joyfully on the floor. Sasha flew off her berth in a split second.

"Wow!" said a little girl from the compartment across from Sasha's. "Look, money!"

Kneeling, Sasha gathered the gold disks, picking them up from underneath somebody's suitcases, and nearly collided with the train attendant, who was carrying a tray of tea.

"Careful there!"

The little girl picked up one of the disks and examined it with interest.

"Mommy, is it gold?"

"No," answered her mother, still staring at her book. "It's some kind of an alloy. Give it back."

Sasha was already standing there with her hand outstretched. The little girl returned the coin reluctantly. Facing the window, Sasha counted the coins; she was supposed to have thirty-seven, but had only thirty-six.

"Excuse me, have you seen any of these coins?"

People in the neighboring compartments shook their heads. Sasha ran up and down the carriage, and again nearly collided with the attendant; a man in a red warm-up suit sat at the very end of the carriage, right near the exit, studying the round symbol on the missing disk. She knew that staring at the symbol long enough made it seem three-dimensional—she wondered if that's what he saw.

"It's mine." Sasha stretched out her palm. "I dropped it."

The man lifted his head and gave Sasha an estimating glance. He looked back at the coin.

"What is it?"

"A souvenir. Please give it back."

"Interesting." The man was in no hurry. "Where did you get it?"

"It was a gift."

The man smirked.

"Listen, I want to buy it from you. Is ten dollars enough?"

"No, it's not for sale."

"Twenty dollars?"

Sasha was nervous. A woman sitting right next to them was listening to the conversation.

"It's my coin." Sasha made her voice sound determined and hard. "Give it back to me, please."

"I had a friend." The man glanced from Sasha to the coin and back. "He was a tomb raider. He did some illegal stuff. Dug up some things in the Crimea. And then someone stabbed him. You see, he probably dug up something he wasn't supposed to."

"I didn't dig anything up." Sasha stared at his hand. "It was a gift. It's mine."

They stared at each other. The man wanted to say something, in the same measured and patronizing manner, but he bit his tongue. At this point, Sasha was ready to fight—sob, scream, shriek, scratch his face—for her coin; this readiness of hers must have been obvious in her stare.

"As you wish."

The gold disk fell into her hand. Sasha clamped her fingers shut and, holding her breath, walked back to her mother.

Mom sat in the same spot, staring out the window, having noticed nothing.

Autumn came in October, suddenly and irrevocably. Red maple leaves stuck to the wet asphalt like flat starfish. Sasha existed between school and preparatory courses at the university: there were tons of homework, essays, reports, tests. She had no time for anything else—even Sundays were filled with work—but Sasha did not mind. She discovered that her brain, overburdened by studies, flatly refused to believe in mysterious strangers and their tasks, in gold coins produced by one's stomach. And even the sea, the kind summer sea with a swaying red buoy, seemed surreal, and everything that happened there, by the seaside, seemed just as surreal.

And Mom was back to normal. With the end of summer came the end of her depression, especially considering that her office was very busy, as usual. Both of them, locked in the vicious cycle of everyday routine, forbade themselves from thinking of the surreal—each had her own reasons. And up to a certain moment they both succeeded.

Then the letter came from Moscow. Mom took it out of the mailbox, aimlessly played with it for a few minutes, and then she opened and read it.

"Valentin divorced his wife," she said, addressing their television set.

"So what?" Sasha said, not exactly politely.

Mom folded the letter and went to her room. Sasha turned off the TV and sat down with a history textbook; she reread the same paragraph about ten times, without understanding anything. Polabian Slavs, Polabian-Pomeranian . . . They must have studied them in fifth grade, and here we go again, they are back in the program.

Clearly, though, her mind was on other things.

Maybe it'll still work out? People have all sorts of issues in their relationships. Of course, his divorce is not a good thing. And it is even worse that he's writing to Mom about it.

The phone rang. Trying to think about the ancient Slavic tribes, Sasha picked up the receiver.

"Hello?"

"Good evening, Sasha. It's me."

The desk lamp was on. It was raining outside. A textbook lay open. Everything was so normal, so real. And—that voice on the phone.

"No," said Sasha softly. "You . . ."

She almost let "You don't exist" slide off her tongue, but she stopped just in time.

"How many coins?"

"Thirty-seven."

"And how many were there?"

"Thirty-seven, honestly."

"I'm waiting downstairs. Come down for a minute."

She heard the short beeps in the receiver.

She kept the coins in an old wallet, in the depths of her desk, behind a stack of books and notepads. Sasha unzipped the wallet and poured the contents onto her desk. She counted them again—still thirty-seven.

She put the wallet in the pocket of her raincoat and slid her feet into a pair of old rain boots. She put the raincoat right over her bathrobe. She grabbed an umbrella, still wet, and picked up her keys.

The door to her mother's room remained closed. With that voice . . . she wasn't sure it would have mattered if her mother had been standing in front of her.

"I'll be right back," Sasha said to no one in particular. "I'm . . . I'm going to get the mail."

She walked down the steps without waiting for the elevator. The neighbor from the fifth floor was entering the hall, all wet, with a huge wet dog on a leash.

"Hi," said Sasha.

The neighbor nodded. The dog shook vigorously, drenching everything with rainwater.

Sasha went outside in the rain. It was dark already, the windows in the neighboring houses were lit, and maple leaves lay on the black asphalt like colored patches.

A man in a dark blue raincoat, similar to Sasha's and shiny with rain, sat on a wet bench. The lenses in his glasses were smoky rather than dark, but the dusk of an autumn evening made them completely impenetrable.

"Hello, Sasha. Did I scare you?"

She did not expect his friendly, joking inflection. She swallowed. Cold wind crawled underneath her clothes, licked her naked knees.

"Give me the coins."

She handed him the wallet with the coins. He weighed the wallet in his hand and nodded, putting the wallet away in a pocket.

"Good. I have a task for you to perform."

Sasha opened her mouth.

"It's a simple task. Very simple. Every morning, at five o'clock, you will go to the park for a jog. Run as much as you can—two laps in the alleys, three laps. When you've jogged enough, find thick bushes and urinate on the ground. It's better if you drink enough water beforehand to avoid any sort of issues. Every morning at five o'clock."

"Why?" Sasha whispered. "Why do you need this?"

Rain slid down her cheeks, mixing with tears. The dark man did not answer. Drops of rain hung on his glasses, reflecting the distant streetlights, which made his eyes seem multifaceted.

"Once a month you can have some time off during your period. Four days . . . is four days enough?"

Sasha was silent.

"Watch the alarm clock. Missing a day or being late even once is a tremendously bad idea. The sequence of actions cannot be altered: plan ahead, drink enough water."

"For the rest of my life?" Sasha burst out suddenly.

"What?"

"Do I have to run . . . for the rest of my life?"

"No." The man seemed surprised. "I'll tell you when to stop. Well, now go home, you're freezing."

Sasha *was* shaking.

"Come on," her companion said gently. "Everything will be just fine . . . Of course, as long as you demonstrate enough discipline."

A lone streetlight burned near the park entrance. Under the iron pole where a town clock hung a long time ago, an old man with a dog lingered, the first and only passerby at this time of day. His eyes slid indifferently over Sasha.

She ran through the pouring water. Jogging paths curled around the central flower bed in the middle of the park. Sasha chose the shortest path. Not watching her feet, she flew right into the puddles; cold water splashed from under her sneakers and washed over her sweatpants, right up to the knees. Sasha gritted her teeth and kept running. Water under her feet gurgled just like the contents of her stomach: she had drunk more than a quart of water before leaving the house. The feeling was unbearable. One more lap. One more.

She slowed down and stopped. The park was completely deserted. A lone streetlight shimmered through the half-naked branches. Stepping over wet leaves, Sasha crawled into the bushes that drenched her with raindrops and, cursing everything under the moon, fulfilled the last obligation of the ritual. She bitterly thought of herself as a dog being taken for a walk.

The short crawl into the bushes brought relief, a quite legitimate one, considering the amount of liquid she had poured into herself. She felt a bit less miserable and even managed to stop crying. At half past five she unlocked the door of her apartment with her own key, crept into the bathroom leaving wet footsteps, hid her jogging suit and squishy sneakers under the sink, and turned on the hot shower.

A minute later she threw up. The coins flew onto the bottom of the bathtub, yellow disks on white enamel. Sasha washed her face, took control of her breathing, and collected the coins in her hand. Four coins, the round symbol on one side and a zero on the reverse. They looked very old, as if for many years they were kept in locked chests, an unidentified treasure . . .

Fifteen minutes later Sasha fell asleep in her bed, a deep, dreamless sleep, the kind she hadn't experienced in a long time. When Mom came to wake her up an hour later, she claimed to be sick and stayed in bed.

. . . And why would she bother with school?

Her tutor called in the afternoon, and Sasha lied about being sick. The tutor, displeased, asked to warn her in advance should that happen again.

Later that evening she was supposed to attend prep courses at the university. Sasha did not go. She lay on her bed, textbooks thrown aside, and thought, *What's the point?*

Because clearly the world did not work the way she imagined before. The visible connection between different events—objective laws, consistent patterns, accidents, and regular days—all this simply served as a Chinese screen for another existence, invisible and incomprehensible. If the man in the dark glasses exists—really, truly exists—if his hands hold dreams, reality, accidents . . . What is the purpose, then, of going to school? Entering a university? When at any moment everything could disappear, be destroyed, simply because Sasha's alarm clock did not go off on time?

Mom returned from the office; she asked worried questions, took Sasha's temperature, and shook her head in despair.

"Did you overexert yourself already? It's a bit early, it's only October, and the school year is just starting. I told you to go for a walk on Sunday! Go to the movies, call your classmates. You do have friends, don't you?"

"Don't worry." Sasha's answer sounded prerecorded. "I'll be fine."

She added to herself, "Of course, as long as I demonstrate enough discipline."

Before bed, she set up three alarm clocks: her own, Mom's electronic one, and one more, an old one, her grandmother's. Throughout the night she fell into chunks of sleep, woke up in cold sweat, and glanced at their faces: one in the morning, quarter to two, half past two . . .

At half past four she was almost glad she could get up.

In November the weather suddenly improved. Unexpected, condition-ally autumnal, but quite tangible warmth returned. The sun came out every day—not for long, but it was generous enough. Dried-up leaves rustled underfoot and smelled fresh and tangy, sad but not without hope.

Sasha would wake up at four twenty-nine, one minute before the alarm clocks' roll call. She deactivated them one after the other, like mines, pulled on a warm jogging suit and a jacket, and walked to the park. In one month, she'd learned all the minute details of the path. She knew where the asphalt was touched by erosion, the places where puddles collected after the rain, knew all the slopes and all the flat spots. Running along the dry alleys, jumping over the piles of leaves gathered by the park rangers, she used the time to repeat her English dialogues, plan that day's chores, and silently sing a song that she'd heard on the radio the day before. Finishing the third and then the fourth lap around the flower bed, she knew for sure that nothing bad could happen to her, or to Mom. From that, she derived bitter, detached, autumnal joy.

Unexpectedly, "the days of rest" spent without the morning jog turned out to be the most excruciating in the last few weeks. Sasha continued to wake up at half past four, and lay without sleep until seven, listening to the waking-up sounds of her building: the rumbling of the dump truck, the din of the elevator, fights between the street cleaners. The ritual was broken; Sasha imagined her fate stretched out like a thread, pulling, drying, about to break. Every day she got more and more nervous, until the morning finally came when she could pull on her sneakers and, leaving footsteps on the frosted grass, walk into the November sunrise.

Then Valentin arrived.

Sasha came back from school for a minute, to drop off her bag, grab a bite to eat, and run to her lesson. A stranger sat on the bench near the entrance to her building. She said hello (she always said hello to anyone sitting on that bench) and only then recognized the pale-skinned, thin nonstranger.

"Hello," said Valentin. "I noticed no one was home."

"Mom will be back by six," said a bewildered Sasha. "And I . . . um."

"I'll wait."

It was half past two. Sasha glanced at her watch, then at Valentin.

There was no hope that he would leave. She did not feel too optimistic about Mom chasing him away. Plus, how could she make any decisions regarding Mom's fate according to her own desires?

"You can call her at the office," she said frostily. And added, a little too late, "How are you feeling?"

She woke up at four twenty-nine, turned off the alarm clocks, shuffled over to the kitchen, and gulped some tea from a thermos. She got dressed and went into the hall; then she left and locked the door.

Last night Mom and Valentin had stayed up in the kitchen, talking softly for a long time. Sasha had gone to bed early (she always did these days, the lack of sleep was getting to her), covered her head with a pillow to avoid inadvertent eavesdropping, shut her eyes, and tried to fall asleep. But sleep had evaded her. Sasha thought of life as a collection of identical days. To her, existence consisted of days, and each day seemed to run like a circular ribbon—or, better yet, a bike chain, moving evenly over the cogs. Click—another change of speed, days became a little different, but they still flowed, still repeated, and that very monotony concealed the meaning of life . . .

She was probably falling asleep. Never before had she had thoughts like that, not in a conscious state.

A long time ago, when Sasha was little, she wanted to get herself a daddy. Not the one who left and now lived someplace else, without a care in the world, but a real one, one who would live with them, in the same apartment. Audaciously, Sasha tried to convince her mother to date any one of the more or less suitable men they encountered; to her, life "with a mommy and daddy" symbolized true happiness.

That was years ago. Now Sasha's heart ached when she thought of her mother and Valentin. He'd lied to her once, he would probably do it again. Mom realized it, but she still spoke softly to him in the kitchen over a cup of cool tea; they sat, heads almost touching, and talked, even though it was already past midnight . . .

Nocturnal frost made the puddles sparkle. Through her woolen socks and the soles of her sneakers, Sasha could feel how cold the ground had become overnight. Her daily training made running easy. A lone streetlight burned near the park entrance. The old man with the dog lingered, and Sasha nodded to him, as if greeting an old acquaintance. He nodded back.

Somebody was in the park. That somebody stood on the path, shifting from foot to foot, wearing a jogging suit, a windbreaker, and sneakers, like Sasha herself. She had to come almost face-to-face with him before she recognized him.

It was Ivan Konev—Kon—a classmate.

"Hey. Shall we run?"

Sasha did not reply. Kon fell into step with her, almost touching her sleeve with his own. When their jacket sleeves did touch, the fabric made a harsh swishing sound—*shhikh-shhikh*.

Sasha ran, skillfully skirting the familiar puddles. Ivan slipped a couple of times; once he broke through the thin ice and stepped into the water, but kept up.

"Do you run every day?" he asked, panting. "My grandpa, he's got insomnia, he walks the dog early, and he said, 'A girl from your class runs every day like crazy, at five in the morning.'"

"Oh!"

He stumbled on a tree root and almost fell. She didn't slow down, and he rushed to catch up.

"Are you into sports now? I've never thought that about you. Or are you training your willpower?"

"Training willpower." It was the first time she acknowledged him.

"That's what I thought . . ." They had completed only two laps, but he already seemed out of breath.

"And you?" Sasha deigned to ask. "What are you working on?"

"Willpower," Kon said seriously. "I could be in my nice warm bed right now, sleeping soundly."

He slowed down.

"Think it's enough?"

Sasha stopped.

The sky was peppered with stars, bright like crystals illuminated by spotlights. Red-cheeked and out of breath, Ivan looked at her with unabashed humor.

"You're a strange creature, Samokhina. A transcendental object. A closed book. Now you're running. My grandpa says, every day, five in the morning. Are you some kind of a coded princess?"

He babbled nervously, smirking a little, afraid of appearing ridiculous. She wanted to tell him it was too late. He himself was a closed book, and yet one she'd peeked into. A boy geared toward success. A winner of competitions and a glutton for science fiction, with high cheekbones and dark curls, dressed in shirts always neatly ironed by his mom or sister, a dandy who at sixteen knew three different tie knots.

Sasha watched him and thought of one thing: she had to go into the bushes. Immediately. Otherwise the ritual would be broken; plus, to be honest, she wasn't going to make it home anyway.

"Kon, wait for me at the entrance."

He did not understand. He kept talking, smiling coyly in the half-light, kept sputtering nonsense about an encrypted princess, and how she must be deciphered.

"Kon, go and wait for me! I'll be right there!"

He did not get it. Idiot. Conceited chatterbox. Time was running out, the run was completed, but the ritual was not.

"I have to pee!" Sasha snapped. "Do you get it?"

When she left the park, the entrance was deserted. No old man with a dog, no Ivan Konev. Only a chain of footsteps stretched over frosted grass.

Valentin left. Sasha hoped for good, but it was not to be. The three of them celebrated the New Year together—like a family, with champagne and a little fir tree that Mom decorated herself, rejecting Sasha's help.

All night fireworks rumbled outside. At half past four, when Mom and Valentin were still watching *The Irony of Fate* on one of the local channels, Sasha pulled on her boots (she did not dare run over the snow in sneakers) and wound a scarf around her neck.

"Are you actually going for a run?" Valentin asked. "That's some willpower you have, Alexandra. I envy you . . ."

Sasha left without replying. The snow in front of the building was covered with confetti; here and there the stubs of sparklers poked out of the melting piles. Sasha started jogging.

The windows were lit. Groups of happy drunks lingered on street corners. Empty champagne bottles lay on the snow. Sasha ran, listening to the crunch of the snow, feeling the bite of the frost on her moist nostrils, watching the cloud of her breath dissolve in the air. "That's some willpower you have, Alexandra. I envy you . . ." Anybody would toughen up under these circumstances. Because although the connection between Sasha's twilight nightmare and a precoronary condition in a stranger was not obvious and could never be proven . . .

But no, not *really* a stranger at that point. Something had happened to Mom, something had changed; she was still young, but she wouldn't always be . . .

So that was it. While the connection could not be proven, it existed. Sasha knew that for sure, and she knew she had no room for mistakes. That's how the first circle locked onto itself.

Sasha ran over her own footsteps. She aimed carefully, placing a foot into each footstep, first subconsciously, then with interest. Circle after circle, step after step. She hadn't seen Ivan's grandfather with his mutt in a long time. Was he cured of his insomnia? Or sick, and not allowed outside? Since their romantic morning rendezvous ended in such a cringingly vulgar manner, Sasha and Kon almost never spoke. They were civil to each other, reserved, indifferent. As if nothing had ever happened. The princess remained undeciphered.

Sasha came to. Which lap was it, eighth, tenth? Her footsteps, repeated endlessly in the white powder, became large and deep, as if the Abominable Snowman had run by planting his enormous feet in the snow.

The dark sky released a multitude of snowflakes. An ambulance drove by, sirens wailing. Not for us, Sasha thought with gloomy satisfaction. No need. Nothing can happen to us.

Relieving oneself in the freezing cold is a dubious pleasure. Sasha crept out of the bushes, buttoning her clothes, patting off the snow that had fallen from the branches. It would be so nice if no one else ever saw the goddamn coins. But it couldn't be helped. The day before yesterday Mom saw that day's "income" and asked what it was. Sasha had lied, said it was brass, tokens for a game. No, of course it's not a casino, what are you talking about! It's a game like checkers, everyone plays it at school. A fad.

Mom had believed her. Sasha had never lied to her before. Well, almost never.

She arrived back home. The door to Mom's room was shut. Heavy silence hung in the apartment, and only snow swished outside, hitting the tin awnings.

Sasha went to the bathroom; she turned on the hot water and took a long time watching the running stream.

Then she vomited money. And, paradoxically, she immediately felt better.

▪▪▪

The heap of coins grew. Sasha stuffed them into an old sock and kept it in the bottom desk drawer, under a pile of old essays. Who knew what Mom would say if she ever found this treasure, but lately Mom had a lot of other things on her mind.

A shaving kit was now comfortably placed on the bathroom shelf, an extra toothbrush poked out of a glass, and Sasha no longer dared to roam around the house in her underwear. The smell of men's cologne overpowered all the other familiar smells. And Mom, who, as long as Sasha could remember, had always belonged to her and her only, now shared her attention between her daughter and Valentin—and the latter, the new kid on the block, got the lion's share.

It was obvious that Valentin intended to establish "close contact" with Sasha. He initiated long meaningful conversations at the dinner table, and Sasha's upbringing prevented her from leaving right away. Waiting for her were numerous textbooks, many unread chapters, and unfinished papers; then, on the border of night and day, there was her run, a humiliating trip to the bushes, and the clanking of coins hitting the bathroom sink. Yet Valentin asked detailed questions regarding her life, her plans for the future, questioned her desire to become a philologist, inquired whether she'd ever considered literary translation from English, and spoke at length about some business colleges that offered stipends and all sorts of stimulus programs for students with a high grade-point average. Sasha swallowed these conversations like spoonfuls of fish oil, then hid in her room and sat there at her writing desk, mindlessly doodling in her notebooks.

Valentin worked in the field of medical technology, something that had to do with research, or testing, or maybe sales, or perhaps all the above. Sasha memorized nothing of his detailed stories about himself. He had two children, either two boys or a boy and a girl, and he spoke of them at length and with gusto, stressing how much he loved them. Stunned by the hypocrisy, Sasha took her cooling tea into her room and sat there, leafing through the college brochures. She struggled to keep her eyes open. In the heart of winter, when the days were short and dark, the lack of sleep felt like torture.

In the beginning of February a thaw set in, and then—in one single night—everything was frozen again. Sasha went for a run, completed the ritual, and on the way home, right near the entrance to her building, she slipped, fell, and broke her arm.

She sat quietly, enduring the pain, until Mom woke up. Mom saw Sasha's forearm, panicked, and called for an ambulance. Valentin emerged, volunteered to accompany Sasha, frowned, commiserated, babbled all sorts of nonsense like "All things are difficult before they are easy," and his stream of consciousness made Sasha feel five hundred times worse. The ambulance took her to the trauma center, where an old surgeon, gray from a sleepless night and cigarette smoke, silently rolled Sasha's arm into a cast.

"Like apples from a tree," he said to the nurse. "They just keep falling. We should expect more harvest today. And you"—he nodded to Sasha—"you need to make an appointment with your physician. And don't worry, stuff happens. You young ones heal fast."

Valentin took Sasha home in a taxi. The pain was almost gone. Valentin ruminated on how lucky it was that Sasha had broken her left arm, which meant that she could continue attending school and her college prep classes, and she could still take notes, because her right arm was just fine! Sasha felt as if her head had ceased to be round, had turned into an aerodynamic tunnel, with Valentin's words getting sucked into one ear and, whistling and roaring, flying out of the other.

Mom called from the office, worried, asking how things were going. Deadly calm, Sasha assured her everything was fine; then she went into her room and lay down on the couch, neglecting to remove her sweater.

What was she going to do now? It was fourteen degrees outside. How was she supposed to pull her sleeve over the cast? How was she going to manage getting dressed and undressed by herself?

Three alarm clocks stood in a row. Two ticktocked quietly, one winked electronic numbers. Every day, every day, and Sasha had two months in the cast . . .

". . . People fall, break their bones, die under the wheels of a car . . ." But Sasha had done everything, met all the conditions! Why did this have to happen to her?

Don't worry, said the old surgeon. Stuff happens. And really, had Sasha been about seventy years old or so, then, yes, it would be truly terrible. And this, this was simply an inconvenience, an unpleasant accident, nothing tragic . . .

Unpleasant, but not tragic. If Valentin had not had his heart spasm on the beach, how would his relationship with Mom have developed? Would it have developed at all?

Sasha crept into the kitchen. She poured herself some of Mom's valerian root mixture, gulped it down—absolutely disgusting!—crawled under the blanket, and fell asleep.

At twenty-nine minutes past four Sasha flew up, as if on a trampoline. She sat up, her mind muddled by sleep, and tried to stretch her arm but jerked with sudden pain.

She remembered; shook her head—did this mean she'd slept for almost twenty-four hours?

Her mouth was dry. Sasha stood up, drank some water from the teapot, managed to pull on her sweatpants, and stuck her feet into her boots. She poked her right arm into a sleeve, grunting, and heaved her jacket over the left shoulder. Holding a ski hat, she went outside.

The sky had cleared up again. The stars burned brightly. Icy patches in the courtyard were cleared haphazardly; some spots were heavily covered with sand and salt. The cast grew cold on her arm, a strange, unpleasant sensation. Only a few minutes remained until five o'clock. Sasha walked faster. She went down into the underground crossing, holding the railing with her good arm. Her steps echoed in the dark tunnel. Only seconds remained.

A lone streetlight burned at the park entrance. A man stood leaning on its pole.

Sasha marched by with bulletlike determination. And only having stepped onto a snowbound path, she startled and glanced back.

The streetlight reflected in the smoky lenses. Two bright yellow dots.

"Go home," said the man who stood under the streetlight. "Get some rest. Starting today, you don't have to run anymore."

Strangely enough, the absence of her morning runs proved to be excruciatingly difficult. It felt as if life had lost meaning. Valentin's presence aggravated her more and more. Once he even left to stay at a hotel, and Mom did not speak with Sasha for several days. All alone, Sasha roamed aimlessly along the streets, hating school and college prep courses. The tutor ended up canceling their sessions.

Valentin reasoned with Mom to be patient. He convinced her that Sasha's issue was that Sasha was no longer taking painkillers by handfuls. He had a good point.

In March, the cast was removed. Mom suggested that now, finally, Sasha's nerves would get back to normal, and her "weirdness" would cease.

And Mom was right as well. Having shed the cast and regaining the use of her arm, Sasha calmed down almost immediately. The chain of everyday existence again settled over the familiar cogs, and it turned and turned again, counting the days: morning. School. College prep. Homework. Evening. Night . . .

A collection of identical days. A settled rhythm. Sasha learned not to jump at seeing passersby in dark glasses; spring came, and more and more people wore shades. At school, money was being collected for the prom. Many arguments ensued, and many disagreements—some parents, like Sasha's mother, suggested having a modest celebration, and some insisted on expensive gifts for the teachers and a river cruise.

Sasha wrote a test essay for her college prep courses and, to her dismay, got a B.

"Don't choose a free topic," her instructor insisted. "Pick a standard theme and elaborate on it just like you were taught. Free topics are for geniuses and idiots—don't make the same mistake twice!"

Sasha listened, nodded, and knew that sooner or later the man in the dark glasses would appear again . . . and essays just didn't seem all that important. He would come, and then he would ask for something again, and Sasha would not be able to refuse.

Or could she try? What if Valentin's heart scare was just a coincidence?

Every time she even allowed this thought, Sasha glanced over her shoulder in fear. She knew she could never rebel. She would not even try. It was too frightening.

Sasha did not quite make it to the highest graduation rank, but she was not really disappointed. She had known for a while that that was not going to happen. The prom passed her by: Sasha kept falling asleep amid the happy crowds and was pleased that at least there was no river cruise.

Ivan Konev danced with Irina, who was in a parallel class. Sasha almost did not care. Kon graduated with highest honors and by the time the prom rolled around, had already been accepted into the School of Mechanics and Mathematics.

Sasha went to submit her application for the School of Philology; she went by herself. Mom wanted to accompany her, but Sasha insisted on going alone.

Linden trees were beginning to blossom. The rain came down in light sprinkles. Sasha walked and smiled. This year a trip to the seaside was not going to happen, but she was fine with that. If she did not get into the university on the first try . . . It was an unpleasant thought, but oh well. She could get a job as a secretary, perhaps even at the School of Philology. She could work, make some connections. She could break out of this vicious circle—notes, homework, notes . . .

"Sasha!"

She turned around, still smiling. The man in the dark glasses sat on the bench that she'd just passed, lost in her thoughts. Reflecting her smile, he stretched his lips and patted the bench next to him in a welcoming gesture. No longer smiling, she dutifully went over and sat down, putting her bag neatly in her lap.

"How's the arm?" the man asked.

"It's good."

Sparrows fidgeted in the wet linden tree above their heads. Their chirping deafened Sasha.

"How many coins do you have?"

"Four hundred seventy-two," she answered without thinking.

"You have the passing score."

"I haven't taken any exams yet . . ."

"Oh, but you have." He grinned again. "Here you go."

He offered her a yellow piece of paper, some sort of an official letter, with Sasha's first and last names typed in neatly:

`Congratulations! Samokhina Alexandra, you are hereby accepted as a first year to the Institute of Special Technologies in the town of Torpa. Classes begin on September 1.`

And below, in small print:

`Regarding placement in dormitories, please contact . . .`

Sasha tore her eyes away from the paper. She stared at the man sitting next to her. For a couple of minutes she couldn't say anything.

"What is this?"

"This is the school you're going to. It's a very good school."

"I don't understand," Sasha managed. "The university . . . I . . ."

The man sitting next to her took off his glasses.

Sasha expected just about anything. That he had no eyes at all. That his eyes were drawn on the pale, stuck-together eyelids. That his eyes were sewn shut with a coarse thread, that his eye sockets were empty . . .

He had eyes. Brown. Serene. Perfectly ordinary at first glance.

"My name is Farit," he said softly. "Farit Kozhennikov. If you would like to know."

"I *would* like to know," Sasha said after a pause. "I'd also like to know: Can you . . . let me go, *Farit*?"

He shook his head.

"Sasha. You passed the preliminary testing, you were accepted into a good school, and you have almost an entire free summer ahead of you. Enjoy your summer—swim, take walks. Gather your strength before school. By August thirty-first, though, get a ticket to Torpa. You can get there a couple of days in advance, get into the dorm, get acquainted—"

"But how am I supposed to explain it to my mother?" Sasha almost screamed it. A woman passing by glanced at her with surprise.

"You'll find a way," Farit said. "Come up with something. You never know, it might happen that you may not need to explain anything to anyone. Embrace the freedom—do whatever you want."

He put his glasses back on. Sasha clutched the bench; the serene face of her companion swam in front of her eyes.

"But I've already applied to the university—to the School of Philology . . . I have to . . . ," she began shrilly. "You can't . . . You can't do anything. Nothing. I don't believe in you. You . . . I want it to be a dream!"

Nothing happened. The sun peeked through the clouds and was reflected in the puddles.

Sasha wanted to say something else, but instead she broke down sobbing—terrified, vulnerable, and ashamed.

"Quiet," Farit said. "Calm down. Didn't I say I would never ask you to do the impossible? I would never do that."

Sasha wept. Tears dripped onto the typed lines on the yellow paper.

"What is wrong with you?" Farit said tiredly. "Do you really need your university? No. It's not really important. Are you enjoying living in a one-bedroom hole with the newlyweds? You, a newly minted stepdaughter? No, Sasha. But you insist on keeping to the beaten path. Are you afraid of changing things?"

"I'm afraid for her!" Sasha screamed through her tears. "She must be . . . She *will* be fine, won't she? Tell me!"

"Obviously. She'll be healthy and even happy. Because you're an intelligent girl, and you will do everything as I tell you. Don't ask me what will happen if you do not."

He rose gracefully.

"Bring the coins with you—all of them. The address of the institute is on this form. Try not to lose it. Sasha, are you listening to me?"

She sat, hiding her face in her hands.

"Everything will be fine," said the man who called himself Farit Kozhennikov. "You can even take the university entrance exams if you'd like. If you don't want to enjoy your summer—that's up to you. There's just one condition: by September first, you must be at Torpa. You will be assigned to a dorm. The meals are free. You will be getting a stipend, too—a small one, but enough to buy some chocolate or whatever.

"Just stop crying. I'm ashamed of you, honestly."

Sasha remained on the bench until her tears dried up and her breath grew steady. The rain stopped, then started again. Raindrops struggled through the leaves of the linden tree. Sasha opened her umbrella.

She had not thought to ask what sort of special technologies were taught at the Torpa Institute. Frankly speaking, she was not at all interested. What mattered to her was that at seventeen years old, most of her life was now wasted, especially this last year. Notes, textbooks, tutors, studying . . . what was it all for, if this institute in Torpa was all that was in store for her?

Perhaps worse, she had no one to talk to, no one to complain to about a man in dark glasses who called himself Farit Kozhennikov. She had no friends. And Mom had switched her love to Valentin, the same way railroad points are switched from one track to another.

She got up. The rain had stopped a while ago, the sun was shining again, but Sasha still held an open umbrella, unaware of the surprised glances as she made her way to the administration building. She stepped up to the entrance, stood in line with the other applicants, handed in her application form, high school diploma, and medical records. Just as she had planned all along.

She returned home, gathered all her textbooks and notepads, admired the heap for a few minutes, and then stuck them deep inside her desk.

But she quickly pulled them out again. What could she have done, if this—all this!—had been her life for many months? The man who called himself Farit Kozhennikov was right: she could not get off the beaten path. She would sit and study, knowing that all her efforts were in vain, but hoping deep inside that someday it would come in handy, perhaps while learning the "special technologies . . ."

She found a list of places that offered higher education, a reference book for prospective students, and studied it from cover to cover. No town of Torpa, no Institute of Special Technologies.

She was not surprised.

All her life she had been a good student. Letting things slide during the entrance exams turned out to be harder than she thought.

Around her, everyone acted nervous: kids hid cheat sheets in their pockets and their mothers sucked on Valium. Dust floated around in huge echoing rooms, the air smelled of old libraries, and outside it was hot, a real scorcher. Sasha did not care. She felt translucent and indifferent, like a Christmas ornament.

The written essay was easy. Taking the oral history exam, she nearly died of shame: she confused all the dates and completely blanked out on one of the questions. She got a B. Leaving the classroom, surrounded by sweaty throngs of people, she asked herself, astonished: What am I doing here? Why do I still care about the Battle of Kulikovo?

Mom inquired about the grade and, having heard, was visibly disappointed.

"What do you mean, a B? In history, of all things? But what about the preparatory courses? You went there for an entire year . . ."

"There is no point in applying without a bribe." Valentin shared a profound thought.

Mom's eyes turned fierce.

"Without a bribe . . . she hasn't opened a textbook in the last few days! As if she couldn't care less! She skulked around somewhere from morning to night . . . Were you at the beach? I passed the exams without a bribe, and you did," she said to Valentin, "and we all did it the first time around!"

"The times were different," Valentin said philosophically. "And now . . ."

"In the worst-case scenario," Sasha said, surprising herself, "I'll just apply someplace else."

"What do you mean, 'someplace else'?"

"The world is full of good colleges," Sasha blurted out and withdrew quickly to her room.

Mom and Valentin continued talking for a long time. They were arguing.

Of course, she failed the entrance exams. It's not like anyone was sur-prised. When the lists of the accepted students were posted, Sasha's name was not included.

Mom was not caught off guard. It had been clear from the beginning that Sasha was not going to get a passing grade, and that her straight-A high school diploma made absolutely no difference.

"You were right," her mother said to Valentin with stoical bitterness. "No matter how much you spend on a tutor . . . We should have bribed someone. It's my fault. I should have. The times have changed."

"It's not like she has military duty," answered Valentin with histrionic optimism. "She's not a boy. She'll get a job for a year, get a taste of grown-up responsibilities . . ."

Sasha opened her mouth and inhaled deeply—and said nothing. She decided to wait a few more days.

August came. The heat was replaced with rain. Mom took a few days off; she and Valentin had finally decided to get married.

"Just a small ceremony," Mom said, brushing her hair in front of the mirror, her eyes sparkling. "We'll get married, and then go to the old resort for a few days. We've been there before, remember, they have these wooden cabins and a river very close, a forest . . ."

"Rain," said Sasha.

"Well, not all the time. Plus, it's kind of nice there even in the rain. They have these canopies. And you can use the fire pits, have a barbecue."

"Mom," Sasha said, as if plunging into icy water. "I've been accepted to this college. It's called the Institute of Special Technologies. It's in the town of . . . Torpa."

Mom turned to face her. Two hairpins stuck out of her mouth, like thin vampire fangs.

"I've already been accepted," Sasha repeated. "Since things did not work out with the university, I figure I'll stay in Torpa for a year. And then maybe I'll transfer."

She came up with the idea of a transfer just then, staring into Mom's darkening, wide-open eyes.

"What town?" Mom spat out the pins.

"Torpa."

"Where is it?"

"It's not far," Sasha lied. "The room and board are free. And I'll have a stipend."

"The Institute of what?"

"Special Technologies."

"What technologies? You wanted to be a philologist!"

"Specialized . . . Mom, it's a normal, decent college. It's not in the capital, fine, it is in the provinces, but . . ."

Sasha faltered. Mom stared at her like an ant would stare at a burning anthill.

"Sasha, tell me you're joking."

Sasha took out the yellow printed letter, warped and wrinkled by rain and tears some time ago, but since then smoothed out with a warm iron. Mom glanced over it and looked at Sasha.

"It's dated last June! Where did you get it?"

"It was mailed to me."

"When?"

Sasha held her breath. Lying to her mother's face was difficult, not something she was used to.

"A couple of days ago."

"Sasha, you're lying."

"Mom, it's a real document! I was accepted! To the Institute of Special Technologies! And I will be a student there!" Sasha's voice trembled. "I need this, do you understand?"

"I understand." Mom leaned on the table. "I understand. You're jealous. You—a grown woman—behaving like . . . like a nasty, spoiled child. Since I . . . You can't forgive me, can you? You can't forgive me and you are being demonstrative about it."

"What? No!" Sasha choked on her tears. "This has nothing to do with him! It's just that, well . . . It just happened that I was accepted. I am going to Torpa, and . . ."

"You are not going anywhere." Mom's voice was packed with February ice. "You will be a normal student, under normal conditions, at a normal college. I'm very sorry that I raised such a selfish creature, but I will not allow any more extreme behavior. Thank you for a pleasant chat."

And she turned back to face the mirror.

After two days of cold, tense communication, Mom came home unusually cheerful, pink-cheeked, and happy. It turned out that the university had opened a part-time evening option, and Sasha could be accepted there.

"And you can work in our office," Mom chattered, setting the table, doling out the stew. "I've already made the arrangements. You can work during the day, then go to your evening classes. And then you can transfer to the regular department. I'm sure you can. Your sophomore year, or maybe junior."

Sasha was silent.

"Tomorrow morning you need to go talk to the admissions office. Room 32. Are you listening?"

"I'm going to Torpa," Sasha's voice was barely audible. Dead silence hung over the dinner table.

"Sasha," Valentin said with reproach. "Why are you doing this?"

Escaping, Sasha got up. She left her food untouched, went to her room, crawled under the blanket, and pretended to be asleep. Mom and Valentin spoke loudly, and snippets of their conversation carried over to Sasha through the walls and blankets.

"Calm down," Valentin was saying. "Just calm down. Independence . . ."

"She's underage!"

"They get older . . . They want . . . It's not at the ends of the earth . . ."

The voices grew softer, the intensity subsided. Sasha closed her eyes. Everything was coming together beautifully. Mom and Valentin would enjoy being alone in the apartment. Right now they were going to talk it over, and then they would agree to let Sasha go to the unknown Torpa, where who knows what was expecting her . . .

She felt torn in half. If Mom agreed easily, Sasha would be mortally offended. If Mom put up a fight—and that's what it sounded like—though . . .

No. She would not. They were already laughing softly in the kitchen. Now they were having tea. They must have decided: the girl has her own destiny, she's independent, let her go wherever the hell she wants. They were pleased. Look at us, we're so modern. What's wrong with this? Tons of high school graduates move out after the first summer, looking for grown-up life.

Sasha pulled the blanket off her face. Outside her window with its tightly drawn curtains, it was still light. It was eight o'clock. Half past eight. August. Three weeks before school started.

Sasha heard a soft knock on her door.

"It's me," said Valentin. "Could we talk?"

They found the town of Torpa in the road atlas. A transparent circle lay right where the faded paper folded in half.

"Town of Torpa." Valentin chuckled. "I'd say it's more of a village. What kind of an institute are they supposed to have there?"

Sasha handed him the yellow sheet. He studied it for a while, flipped it over, then frowned.

"Did you apply there?"

"No. I mean, yes, I did."

"But your documents were submitted to the university!"

"They accept copies. Plus, I didn't get into the university anyway."

"Torpa Institute of Special Technologies," Valentin repeated. "What sort of technologies? And who are you supposed to be when you graduate?"

"An expert in special technologies," Sasha said.

Valentin glared at her. "Are you making fun of me?"

"No." Sasha squirmed. "You don't have to declare your major until junior year. Or senior. I don't know for sure."

"You don't know for sure, yet you insist on going?"

"If I don't like it, I'll come back," Sasha almost whispered. "Honestly. If it turns out to be a bad place, I'll come back. Just tell Mom not to worry. I need to go there. I really do. It's not about . . . I just *need* to."

She kept repeating the same thing in different words, and Valentin sat in front of her, confused, disoriented, and for the first time Sasha thought of him as no longer a stranger.

"Get up, miss. We get to Torpa in half an hour."

"Wha . . . ?" Sasha jumped up and hit her head on the luggage shelf.

She'd spent the entire night in a twilight zone between sleeping and waking, and only just recently managed to fall asleep. The train was old and shaky, and somewhere a teaspoon jingled in an empty glass.

Shadows and lights swam by, transfusing the open-plan carriage, where half-naked bodies dripped with sweat. Bedsheet corners hung from the cots. Somebody snored, somebody rustled a piece of cellophane, and Sasha lay on a top berth and tried to convince herself: I'll be back in one week. The condition Farit had laid out was to be there when classes start.

No one said anything about staying in Torpa for the entire year.

Valentin had wanted to come with her. He'd insisted, actually, and even gone so far as to buy two tickets at the railroad office. He'd intended to check the accreditation of the Torpa Institute, conditions at the dormitory, make sure everything was normal. And deep inside, Sasha felt grateful for his concern. The dark man who called himself Farit Kozhennikov had not specified that Sasha must show up alone.

But the day before their departure Valentin received a call from Moscow: his son from his first marriage had been run over by a car, and while he had not suffered any serious injuries, the hospital wasn't cheap, and Valentin's presence—with his connections in the medical field—was required to work through the bureaucracy. Valentin, having almost immediately forgotten about Sasha's issues, dashed away to Moscow. Sasha ended up returning his ticket before the train departed, somehow finding a way during that time to convince Mom that she would be perfectly fine.

Mom saw her off. She stood by the train window for a long time, looking through the glass pane, waving, and dispensing last-minute advice. Sasha had wished fervently for the train to start moving. But when the locomotive gave the initial tug, she felt her heart drop down into her knees, and she nearly jumped out of the moving train, into Mom's arms.

This was her first time traveling alone by train. She kept glancing over at the luggage shelf, where her suitcase was stowed. She palpated the little bag full of coins on the bottom of her purse and checked the documents in the inside pocket—passport, high school diploma, medical records, letter of acceptance, and some other papers, all neatly folded into a plastic envelope. She felt unbearable loneliness; she kept thinking how a while back she and Mom had traveled to the seaside in a train just like this one, and poppies had blossomed outside their windows, and she had been happy, peaceful, and safe.

She cried, hiding her tears from her fellow travelers, and placed a tremendous blame on herself for giving in to the man in the dark glasses that very first time. Even if she were forever subjected to the eternal nightmare, even if she would have had to wake up on the folding cot in the rented room every morning for the rest of her life, Mom would always be there with her. And there would always be the sea. If one's life were forever to consist of half of the summer day of July 24, it would still be a pretty good life. At least, it would be a life without gold coins, or Valentin, or a long road to Torpa.

The sun went down. Sasha's fellow passengers were having supper, crunching half-sour pickles, peeling lusterless hard-boiled eggs. Sasha took out Mom's sandwiches and nearly burst out crying again: this little plastic bag held a piece of home. Without touching the food, she put it away again, had a cup of tea, and crawled onto the top berth.

And now she was almost there.

"Miss! Are you awake? I'm telling you, Torpa is close."

"Yes, I'm ready."

They reached the border between night and morning. It was around four o'clock, maybe four thirty. After so many months, Sasha was used to getting up this early. She knew that morning would bring relief. Now, gathering her things, lacing up her shoes, dragging the suitcase off the shelf (carefully, trying not to wake up the other passengers, and still accidentally touching people's arms hanging off the berths), she almost forgot the previous night's sorrow. The winds of exotic travels, of unexpected discoveries—one had to take all that into account. She was an adult now, an independent person, traveling by herself, without supervision, and this was all part of the journey.

She'd just have to see what this Torpa is all about.

Sasha dragged her suitcase into the hallway. The train attendant snoozed on a cot covered by a thin blanket.

"How long is the stop?" Sasha asked.

"In Torpa? One minute. Do you have a lot of luggage?"

The train slowed down. The carriages clanked. In the darkness of the August morning Sasha saw nothing, only a blue streetlight barely visible in thc sky.

The train jerked, clanked, and stopped. The attendant, yawning, started fiddling with the key.

"I'm not going to make it!" Sasha was terrified. "Please hurry up!"

The attendant swore under her breath.

The train jerked again. The attendant finally unlocked the door. The train started moving slowly; Sasha threw her bag over her shoulder, dragged the suitcase behind her, and tumbled down the iron steps. She landed on the low platform and saw the train attendant yawn once more before locking the door behind her. She looked around.

This was it.

The train was gathering speed. Sasha hauled her suitcase farther away from the edge of the platform. The last car rambled by, and two lights on its tail end quickly melted away in the dark.

The green light of the semaphore turned red. Sasha stood alone on the empty platform . . .

But she was not alone. Out of the darkness appeared a scrawny shadow with a large suitcase. The shadow stopped in front of her. A boy Sasha's age—pale, sleepy, bewildered.

"Hey," he said after a moment's silence. "Is this Torpa?"

"Hey," said Sasha. "So they say."

"I've never been here before," said the boy.

"Me neither."

The boy paused, and then asked tentatively, "The Institute?"

Sasha, who was fervently hoping for this very question, nodded enthusiastically:

"Uh-huh. You too? Special Technologies?"

Visibly relieved, the kid smiled. "Is there another one in this dump?"

"I don't know," Sasha admitted. "Do you see any kind of town around here?"

The kid looked around and put his hands over his eyes, imitating binoculars.

"A kick-ass megalopolis. An impressive train station. And there, look, a shed with huge potential!"

Sasha laughed.

And just like that, they felt better. Hauling their suitcases and trying to outdo each other in wit, the new students walked over to the "shed with huge potential," which turned out to be the actual train station. In a spark of inspiration, Sasha called it a "chicken coop refurbished to the highest European standards." Sasha's new acquaintance appreciated the joke and laughed uproariously.

Of course, the station was completely empty. All the cashier windows were locked. Elongated blinking ceiling fixtures lit up the empty cafeteria table, wooden chairs with graffiti scratched here and there, a self-service storage unit with six compartments, all open. The floor, relatively clean, was covered with white and black tiles.

"Looks apocalyptic," said Sasha, glancing around her.

A cloud of August flies flew off one of the lighting fixtures and filled the small room with optimistic humming.

"Hello!" the boy called out. "Is there anyone here?"

The only reply he got was the droning of the flies.

"I don't like it here," Sasha said.

The boy didn't say anything, and she took that as agreement.

They stepped back outside, onto the platform. It was getting a little lighter. Under the lone streetlight they found a "Train Station—Center" bus schedule, blurry from the rainwater. If the schedule was to be trusted, the first bus would depart for the mysterious "Center" in one hour.

"We'll wait," the boy said decisively. "And if we get lucky, we can always grab a cab. I have money."

His name was Kostya. Perhaps in Sasha's presence he felt especially manly, or maybe it was just his personality, but he kept trying to take charge. Sasha did not protest. Kostya's energy, and even his amateur vigor, gave her an illusion of safety.

They left their suitcases in storage (the compartments did not require tokens, just a code) and found a comfortable bench on the platform, then unwrapped their provisions. Sasha's sandwiches, which had made her so sad the night before, disappeared within minutes. She shared with Kostya, he shared with her; a bottle of mineral water was opened, and Kostya brought out a thermos almost full of coffee. Sasha's nostrils quivered; breakfast put her in a very good mood. A freight train rolled by the station, the rumble died down in the distance. Silence reigned, disturbed only by the birds.

"The bus is coming in half an hour," Kostya said with certainty. "The address of this place is 12 Sacco and Vanzetti Street."

"Do you know who they are, Sacco and Vanzetti?"

Kostya shrugged. "Italians, I think."

Another freight train rolled by in the other direction.

"Can you please tell me," Sasha began carefully, "what made you decide to apply to this . . . Special Technologies thing? Who gave you this . . . this idea?"

Kostya's face darkened. He looked at her suspiciously, folded dirty napkins and oily paper, and dropped them all into an empty trash barrel next to the bench.

"I'm just asking," Sasha added quickly. "If you don't want to tell me, don't, and accept my apology."

"I was forced," Kostya admitted reluctantly.

"You too!"

For a minute they stared at each other, both waiting for the other one to speak.

"That's strange," Kostya said finally. "You're a girl. You don't have military duty."

"What does it have to do with military duty?"

"Everything," Kostya said harshly. "Do you think every man should serve in the army?"

"I don't know," Sasha said. "I guess so." And, just in case, she added: "But if someone doesn't want to serve, then he shouldn't have to."

Kostya sighed and shook his head.

"My own father gave me an ultimatum. I didn't get accepted to law school, twice, actually. I was supposed to get drafted this fall. But my father . . ." Kostya fell silent. He gave Sasha a side glance, as if wondering why he was sharing intimate details of his life with a chance fellow traveler, whom he'd known for all of an hour.

"So you didn't want to go to this institute?"

Kostya shrugged.

"Whether I wanted to or not . . . it doesn't matter anymore."

They fell silent. The platform was still deserted; not a single person showed up—not an equipment inspector, not a street cleaner, no one. The reddish August sun was rising from the bushes. Birds were chirping. The high blades of grass along the railroad were covered by morning dew, each drop a colorful gem.

"And you don't even have to serve in the army . . . ," Kostya said pensively.

Sasha did not reply. She really did not feel like telling Kostya the story of her meeting with Farit Kozhennikov. She had hoped that Kostya himself was in a similar situation, but his turned out much more banal: failed exams, military summons in the fall, a stern father . . .

"Is it time to go?" she asked nervously, hoping to change the subject.

Kostya glanced at his watch. "I guess. Might as well walk over—there's another bench near the bus stop."

Despite Sasha's concerns, the metal doors of the storage unit opened easily. Kostya grabbed both suitcases. A crumpled piece of paper was stuck to the bottom of Sasha's suitcase.

"Trash," Kostya murmured and held the paper gingerly with two fingers.

It was a note—large penciled letters could be easily read even now, after the note had gotten wet and dirty:

"Leave now."

There was no signature.

Half an hour later they sat in a small bus that Kostya called "a hearse." The stupid piece of paper had spoiled their mood, even though they both tried to pretend it meant absolutely nothing.

In a way, it *didn't* mean anything to Sasha—she knew she could not leave. Tomorrow was September 1; she had to be there. She had to do what Farit Kozhennikov requested, and only after that she would have to figure it out.

Kostya was quiet. His zeal disappeared without a trace. The bus came at five of seven, its driver a perfectly average, solid middle-aged man, wearing a worn denim jacket thrown over a black T-shirt. Sasha and Kostya bought their tickets and settled in the backseat. The driver started the engine, and then suddenly they were joined by an old lady with a basket, a woman carrying a shovel wrapped in sackcloth, and two young empty-handed men. It seemed to Sasha that the young men took particular notice of her and Kostya. Again, she felt lonely and helpless.

First, the bus drove among the fields, dotted here and there with tiny human figures. Then they drove into Torpa "proper." It was not exactly a village as Sasha had imagined: five-story brick buildings mixed with single-family homes. Rather, it was very much a town, albeit one that was very old and not at all modernized: heavy buildings made out of stone, with occasional columns and molding on the facades. These abutted curved streets, in some places paved, but more often covered with black cobblestones. Windows were hidden behind green shutters. Sloping timbered roofs. Steps touched by erosion.

"Would you look at this," Kostya said softly. "You could film a movie here. Not too shabby, is it?"

Sasha did not reply.

The bus stopped at a small square, the bus stop under a simple awning.

"Torpa," said the driver. "We're here."

Sasha waited until the two suspicious guys left, and only then did she follow Kostya out. The driver passed them their suitcases, settled back in his seat, stepped on the gas, and the bus disappeared from view before Sasha and Kostya had a chance to look around.

Again, they were left alone. The old lady, the woman with a shovel—even the suspicious guys—were all gone.

"And whom are we supposed to ask for directions?" Kostya inquired sarcastically.

"There is a sign," Sasha said, looking around. "Here—'Sacco and Vanzetti, one point five kilometers.'"

They started walking.

It took them almost half an hour to walk a kilometer and a half; pant-ing, Kostya dragged both suitcases. Surprisingly long, Sacco and Vanzetti Street began at building number 114, then the numbers descended. The sidewalk in turn widened and disappeared entirely. The street expanded like an overflowing river, turning into a boulevard, then narrowed again, turning into a gorge.

"Elegance galore," Kostya murmured.

Stone and peeling plaster. Ivy and grapevines stretched over the gutters. Geraniums hung in pots. Sasha kept turning her head in all directions: here was a three-story brownstone stylized as a castle, with cozy-looking alabaster Chimeras. Over there was an uninspiring concrete building with old-style commercial air-conditioning units. And over there a tumbling-down wooden shack, a young birch tree growing on its roof.

Each awning housed a swallow's nest. The birds streaked through the air, covering the street with a moving black net, drawing large complicated circles, diving occasionally into the broken attic windows.

Sparrows shrieked above the chestnut and linden trees.

"Seems like a decent kind of place." Sasha rubbed her aching neck.

Kostya snorted as the stores were beginning to open.

In front of a bakery stood a dignified little queue—three old ladies with shopping bags. Three men in overalls were smoking in front of a liquor store. On the other side of the street a team of workers were fixing a roof: a pulley strained, an enormous vat filled with resin passed above the heads of passersby, and faded, quivering warning flags strewn on a wire protected the danger zone into which one could not, under any circumstances, take even a tiny step . . .

Building number 12 emerged as a large house, clearly redesigned several times: two stories boasted colorful bricks—almost like a gingerbread house—the third story was built out of simple white limestone brick, and the fourth floor was of plain wood. A stone porch, its steps slightly sloping and worn out, led to the main entrance. A black door of impressive height looked haughty and stern. A small plaque shined dully to the left of the entrance:

MINISTRY OF EDUCATION. INSTITUTE OF SPECIAL TECHNOLOGIES

"We're here," said Kostya, dumping the suitcases onto the pavement.

Sasha stared at the door. A black rectangle with a shiny brass handle. Four steps leading up.

Kostya was out of breath. He had hauled two huge suitcases along the entire Sacco and Vanzetti Street and now had a good reason to be sweaty and clearly short-winded. It was more complicated for Sasha. Trying to control her breathing, she could have sworn that both she and Kostya were thinking the same thing: it was not too late to get out of here. They had one more chance to escape before stepping over the threshold. The moment this door closed behind them, there would be no way back.

Kostya was silent, not wanting to seem cowardly in Sasha's presence, not realizing she was worried about seeming scared in front of *him*.

What am I doing here? thought Sasha in sheer panic. *Why am I not home? Why did I go where I have no desire to go, like a passive sheep, an obedient dog on a leash?*

Why is this my *life?*

Kostya looked around.

"I wonder if there is a café or something like that," he said seemingly to himself. "Would be nice to get a cup of coffee, I'm really thirsty. Look, there is a place!"

And in fact, right across from the institute, they saw the entrance to a ground-level cellar with a wooden sign: PASTRY, COFFEE, TEA. A single table with an open striped sun umbrella stood on the sidewalk.

Sasha sighed and glanced back to the institute's building. The windows—small on the first two floors, large on the third, dull on the fourth—watched them with faceted eyes.

"Let's go in," Sasha croaked. "We can't sit here with our suitcases all day anyway."

The vast half-lit entrance hall seemed deserted. The glass reception booth was empty. Staircases stretched left and right, and in the center of the hall, under a ray of light coming from above, rose an equestrian statue of stunning proportions.

"That's a stallion." Kostya stifled a giggle.

Mesmerized, Sasha came closer. It certainly was a stallion: the horse's belly and legs were carved with a great degree of anatomical precision, as were . . . *other* things. Colossal bronze hooves trampled upon the granite pedestal. Immense boots hung from the stirrups. The face of the horseman was impossible to see—it was lost far above, and no matter what angle Sasha tried, she could see only a huge upturned chin and a prominent Adam's apple.

"First years?"

The voice echoed in the deserted hall. Sasha and Kostya spun around. A short concierge in a printed dress stood by the entrance, her fat finger with a candy-pink nail motioning for them to approach.

"You need the dean's office. Behind the staircase, to the right, you can't miss it, just look for the sign. You can leave your suitcases, no one will take them."

The long corridor smelled of dust and fresh whitewash. On both sides stretched doors, just like in a high school, but taller and somehow more important looking. The DEAN'S OFFICE sign left them no chance of getting lost.

Sasha entered and immediately had to squint.

The office was full of light—sunshine burst through the windows. Right in front of Sasha was a wooden partition with an opening. Two women sat on the other side of the partition, one skinny, one corpulent, both wearing white blouses, both with equally impenetrable impressions on very different faces.

"First years?" asked the fat onc. "Documents."

Sasha fumbled with the inside pocket's fastening and the pin she'd added for safety.

"Hurry up," said the fat woman. "Young man, if you are ready, you can go first."

Kostya stepped up to the barrier. The woman glanced at his diploma, then opened his passport and checked it against the long list on her desk.

"Congratulations, you have been accepted," she stated lifelessly. "Sign here. This is your dormitory assignment, and here are the tickets for the dining hall. Textbooks will be distributed by your professors. Please wait in the hall while I register the girl."

The skinny woman said nothing. She glanced at the list over her colleague's shoulder, then stared up at Kostya with a great deal of attention, squinting slightly. Under her watchful eye, Kostya left the room, gripping a gray stamped envelope.

Sasha approached the barrier. It was old and worn; time had made its surface grainy and three-dimensional. Sasha couldn't resist caressing the wood with her palm.

"Your name?" asked Ms. Corpulent, not in a rush to open Sasha's passport.

"Samokhina, Alexandra."

"Samokhina." A long-nailed finger slid down the list. "Samokhina . . ."

"Farit's girl," Ms. Skinny mumbled to herself. Sasha flinched; her sudden move caused the opening of the partition to snap closed.

"Is Kozhennikov your advisor?" Ms. Corpulent asked, not looking at Sasha.

"I guess . . ."

"Be careful," said Ms. Corpulent. "He's a good man, but he can be harsh. Here's your dormitory assignment, your dining hall tickets. Do you have your coins? You're supposed to have four hundred and seventy-two."

Sasha reached into her bag. The combination of this perfectly ordinary office space and this perfectly ordinary bureaucratic procedure with gold coins of obscure denomination, obtained during bouts of vomiting, made her lose her sense of reality. Even the sun outside the windows now appeared illusory.

The woman took the heavy plastic bag out of her hands. She placed it somewhere under her desk; the gold jingled.

"All set," said the fat woman. "Go, move in. Tomorrow morning all the first years are expected to meet at nine in the morning in the assembly hall, straight in front of the main entrance, by the statue, there is a small staircase—you'll see. Hello, who's next? Come in!"

"Where is the dorm?" Sasha asked, regaining her senses. But they were already done with her.

She eventually found the dormitory—it was buried inside a courtyard, accessible only from the institute itself, or from a narrow, dark, and smelly alley off Sacco and Vanzetti. Peeking at the alley from a distance, Sasha vowed to avoid it entirely after dark.

From the outside, the dorm appeared to be a long, peeling, rundown, two-story barrack. The main door was locked. Kostya knocked with a bent finger, then banged on it with his fist, then kicked it (rather gingerly).

"That's strange," Sasha said. "Are they asleep? What time is it?"

Kostya turned to answer her, but at that moment the door squeaked and opened. Kostya stepped back, nearly falling off the steps.

In the doorway stood a tall, basketball player–sized guy with a black eye patch on his right eye. He was painfully thin and sort of lopsided, as if an entire half of his body was crippled by a permanent seizure. His blue eye looked at Kostya and immediately switched to Sasha. Sasha shrank back.

"First years?" the guy asked in a hoarse strained voice. "Moving in? Got the assignments? Come in . . ."

He disappeared in the dark, leaving the door ajar. Sasha and Kostya exchanged glances.

"Are we going to be like him?" Kostya inquired with an exaggerated meekness. Sasha did not respond; she found the joke uncalled for.

She also wasn't so sure it *was* a joke—and was afraid he might be prescient.

They entered the barrack, which from the inside was not much more exhilarating than from the outside: brown linoleum, walls painted blue on the bottom and white above eye level, a staircase with metal railings. Steam rose from somewhere, accompanied by the hum of water in a shower.

"Here." The one-eyed guy appeared at the reception desk, over which hung a plywood board with several sets of keys. "The girl is going to room 21, second floor. The boy, room 7, it's down the corridor, to the right. Here's the key for room 21. There are two second-year students in room 7—they have already arrived."

"I'm not 'the boy,'" Kostya muttered.

"Do you work here?" Sasha inquired tentatively, ignoring Kostya.

"I'm subbing for someone. I'm a third year, actually. Name's Victor."

The guy winked with his only eye and laughed. Half of his face remained immobile, while the corner of his mouth slid way down. His laughter looked so frightening that Sasha nearly burst into tears.

She yanked her heavy bag up the stairs, along a similar corridor, floor covered by the same dull linoleum, with room numbers barely visible on the doors painted white. Sasha reached number 21, fumbled with the key due to her trembling hands, and, after a short struggle, managed to open the door.

Three wire bed frames with striped mattresses. Three desks, three bedside tables. Built-in wardrobe. A large window, small, hinged pane slightly ajar, with a dusty windowsill. Sasha hauled her suitcase inside, sat down on the nearest bed, and wept.

She had about five minutes to lament over her life and her troubles before she heard steps in the corridor. Sasha barely managed to wipe her tears; there was a short knock on the door, but almost immediately the door opened and two girls walked in. Sasha had seen them briefly in the hallway, on her way from the dean's office to the dorm. Both were about seventeen, a blonde in a blue denim outfit and a brunette, plump and round, in a knee-length skirt and a jersey top.

"Hello." The brunette had a low basso voice.

"Hello," said the blonde; with one quick glance at Sasha's red eyes, she inquired,"What's wrong?"

"Nothing." Sasha looked away. "Homesick."

"Right." The blonde threw a disinterested look around the room. "Got it."

"I kind of like it here," the brunette said, pulling her luggage closer to the window. "No one hanging over your shoulder. Do whatever you want. Freedom."

Farit had said something similar to her when she'd been told about her acceptance to Torpa. But Sasha couldn't see where the "freedom" part came in. All she could think was that she would not be able to do what she wanted for the rest of her life. In fact, the chances were she would have to do what she desperately did not want to do. Stare into

Kozhennikov's eyes, hidden behind the dark glasses, and execute all of his whims under the pain of cruel punishment . . .

Out loud she said nothing. Her voice wasn't really cooperating anyway.

The blonde briefly looked in her direction before saying, "Actually, I am not going to live here myself. I think I'm better off renting an apartment somewhere nearby. It's better for you, too—you'll have more space."

Sasha did not respond. The brunette shrugged, her meaning clear: *You're the boss.*

"My name is Lisa," the blonde told Sasha. "And this is Oksana."

"Alexandra," croaked Sasha. "Samokhina, Sasha."

"Looks like we're classmates." Lisa kept her blue appraising eyes on Sasha.

"Looks like it."

"All this dust," grumbled Oksana, sliding her plump finger over the desks and the windowsill. "And where are we supposed to get the bed linen, does anyone know? Has anyone seen the superintendent? Easy to get along with?"

Lisa took her eyes off Sasha. She walked around the room, touching the door of the wardrobe, which emitted a hoarse squeak.

"We should celebrate," Oksana suggested. Immediately, not waiting for anyone's consent, she began to take out jars, containers, and packages from her bag. She took out paper plates and peeled three white paper cups off an accordion-pleated snake, then filled each with some liquid from a murky plastic bottle.

"Here, girls. We're roommates now. Help yourself: the sausage is homemade, and here are some pickles. And the bread, well, whatever is left."

"Drink—this early in the morning?" Lisa said.

"We'll have just a drop." Oksana picked up a thick slice of the sausage. "To good grades, to easy living. Cheers!"

Sasha held the cup; whitish liquid splashed on the bottom. It smelled of yeast.

"What is it?"

"Moonshine." Oksana gave her a cheerful grin. "Come on, bottoms up!"

She bumped her glass with Lisa's, then with Sasha's, drank, widened her eyes, and bit into the sausage. Lisa took a small sip. Sasha wanted to refuse, but then thought, *Why shouldn't I?* She held her breath and swallowed the murky liquid like medicine.

She's never tasted anything worse. All the alcoholic beverages she'd tasted before—champagne on New Year's Eve and her birthday, the occasional dry red wine—had had a pleasant taste and a nice smell. The moonshine remained stuck in her throat, preventing her from breathing.

"Eat!" Oksana yelled at her. "Have a pickle."

Letting tears stream down her face, Sasha bit into a pickle and then into a fatty sausage and black bread with caraway seeds. Now she was thirsty, but no one had any water. Efficient Oksana assured them that there should be a kitchen, and the kitchen should have a teakettle, and she was going to find everything out. The door closed behind her.

Sasha took a deep breath. The room swam in front of her eyes, and she felt not exactly happy, but a little easier, and now she wanted to talk.

She wanted to ask Lisa how she ended up at the Institute of Special Technologies. And whether Farit Kozhennikov was part of her life as well. And what she was thinking of doing next. She wanted to tell Lisa about her terror, and the coins, about Valentin with his precoronary, and Mom, and about the note found by accident in the storage compartment at the train station. Sasha opened her mouth, but then stopped.

What if Lisa, unlike Sasha herself, is not mad? What if she applied to the institute like a normal student? What if she wants to be here? Who knows *what* she wants? Maybe she ran away from an odious family situation? Or maybe she's hiding from a scandal? Or something else, something normal, human, and here was Sasha with her fairy tales?

On the other hand, the coins . . .

"Did anyone . . . did you have to pay anyone?" Sasha asked curtly.

"No one accepts bribes here," said Lisa distractedly. "And if you mean *those* coins . . . I gave them to my advisor earlier. If that's what you are talking about."

The door opened, Oksana burst in with a hot teakettle in one hand and a package of tea in the other.

"Girls, there is a decent kitchen there, even pots and pans! Do you want to have tea here, or in the kitchen?"

"I don't want any tea." Lisa got up. "I'm going for a walk. Don't forget, lunch is at two. Bring your lunch tickets."

▪ ▪ ▪

Lisa returned when Sasha and Oksana were almost done with the cleanup; all they had left to do was take out the trash and wash the floor. At first, Sasha, drowsy with the aftereffect of the moonshine, flatly refused to participate, but Oksana turned out to be quite pushy: they weren't expecting to live in a pigsty, were they, and really, the thing to do was to clean up, and then they could relax. She poked and prodded, and soon Sasha discovered a rag in her hand and then found herself standing in line for bed linen in front of the superintendent's office. The first years were flowing in, some nervous and frightened, some cheerful and noisy. Sasha met tons of new classmates, and their names immediately flew out of her head. Pale and disheveled, Kostya showed up and disappeared again, looking punch-drunk. Sasha carried three sets of grayish sheets, smelling of detergent, to the second floor; meanwhile, Oksana managed to dust the insides of the wardrobe, the tables, windowsill, and even the legs of the three beds.

Lisa came back, stepped over the mound of trash in the doorway, sighed, and proceeded toward her bed with the stack of sheets set on the mattress.

"Nice walk?" Oksana inquired cheerfully.

Silently, Lisa lay down on the striped mattress and turned her face to the wall.

The dining hall was located in the basement. Before September 1, the official start of school, only the self-service station was open, but even there one could get clear soup with round meatballs in shining enamel bowls and chicken with vermicelli. One was even allowed an unlimited amount of fruit compote, three or four glasses, if one wanted.

"Good grub," Oksana stated.

Sasha noticed Kostya at a nearby table. Her traveling companion hunched over his plate, crumbling a piece of bread into tiny pieces and looking through the other diners without seeing them.

Sasha went over with a firm conviction: if he wasn't happy to see her, she would leave immediately.

Kostya *was* happy. A lot happier than Sasha had anticipated. He moved out a chair for her to sit down and offered her his portion of compote. Sasha did not refuse.

"So, you settled in?" and immediately, without any transition: "Listen, they are crazy."

"Who?"

"Those guys they put me in with. The second years. One stutters so much his eyes pop out, and he giggles constantly. And the other one gets stuck."

"What do you mean?"

"Well, he stretches his hand to get a book off the shelf, and then he . . . he gets stuck, like he's rusted all over. He stands in this really stupid pose, and he pulls, and twitches . . . and he even sort of squeaks. And then it lets him go. He gets the book and starts reading, as though nothing happened. And they keep looking at each other behind my back, winking . . . Freaks. What am I supposed to do, sleep in the same room with them?"

Kostya stopped short. He suddenly realized that he was spilling his guts—complaining!—to the girl he had only just met that morning. Evidently, according to Kostya's internal code of honor, this behavior could not be considered masculine. Embarrassed and upset, he lowered his eyes to his plate.

"My roommates are first years," Sasha said. "They seem normal. Relatively."

Kostya looked up, saying, "Just have a look around. The entire second year, and third, they are all crippled. Just look!"

Sasha turned around. A group of third years maneuvered between the rows of tables, one-eyed Victor in the lead. Tall, gangly, and lopsided, Victor's left leg was lame, and the dishes on his tray jumped and jiggled, threatening to fall off. Behind Victor, a square-shouldered guy in a bright red T-shirt and faded jeans directed himself to the empty tables in the back, smiling and constantly bumping into chairs. The chairs rattled, some fell on the floor, but the guy paid no attention and kept moving. Next to him, a girl wearing incredibly high heels took tentative steps. She gazed at the floor, seeing something completely inaccessible to others. Every now and then she aimed her heel at the floor, as if hammering in a nail, froze for a second, lifted her foot with visible effort (her heel seemingly piercing through the floor), and kept walking, swaying slightly.

"Panopticon," Kostya murmured. "Where do they get these people from?"

Sasha gave him a fleeting look. "The first years seem normal," she said, echoing her earlier statement.

"Hmm." Kostya twirled his spoon in the bowl of soup. "Yeah. I'm all set. D'you want to go?"

The post office smelled of sealing wax; a young mother with a stroller was mailing a large package tied up with string. There was only one postal worker on duty, so Sasha waited while she helped the young mother, and then she asked the middle-aged purple-haired woman to connect her with a long-distance phone number. She entered an echoing phone booth, and, stifling her heartbeat, listened to the long beeps, then jumped with joy when Mom picked up the phone.

"Hello!"

Mom was yelling into the receiver, probably having trouble hearing. Sasha yelled too:

"Mom! It's me! Everything is fine! I'm all settled in! They feed us here! Tomorrow is the first day of school! How are you?"

She screamed it out, like a team's fight song, and listened to Mom's reply: Everything is good, Valentin called from Moscow, everyone is healthy . . .

"I'll call you again soon. Bye!"

Sasha browsed through the postcards and chose one: "For you, from ancient Torpa." The postcard pictured the fountain square, swans swimming in the water. Sasha bought the postcard, wrote her mother's address, and tossed it into the huge blue box with a mail symbol on top. The envelope hit the tin bottom with a dull thud.

The post office was located about fifteen minutes' walking distance from the dorm. On the way back, the weather got worse and it started to drizzle. Sasha pulled her head into her shoulders and ran up the concrete porch, yanking the squeaky door open.

An unfamiliar boy was walking along the first-floor corridor. He took a couple of steps, and then froze in the middle of his move, like a captured video frame. He stood still for a few seconds, then, with visible effort, forced himself to move and continued walking. Then he turned and walked into the wall near the door. He stepped back. On the second try he grabbed the doorknob and pulled the door open . . .

Sasha flung herself up the stairs.

Lisa and Oksana were smoking, sitting on their beds. The window was open wide, but the smoke refused to leave; instead, cold wind burst into the room, adorned with shiny beads of rain.

"Could you possibly smoke in the bathroom?" Sasha asked hesitantly.

All she got in response was ice-cold silence.

"Good morning, first years."

The assembly hall was a large dusty room. Only the last three or four rows of chairs were occupied. Dark curtains covered the windows, letting in half of the necessary light. A screen glowed white behind the stage. *Looks like a community center,* thought Sasha.

"The coolest people sit in the back of the bus, like in middle school?" A man stepped up onto the low platform and glanced around the room. "That's not going to fly." He added in the same low voice: "Lights, please."

The chandelier was lit immediately, and now the room was filled with bright lights, like an opera theater during intermission.

"Everyone move to the front of the room," the man on the stage commanded. "Hurry up."

The first years began to move, exchanging glances, slowly creeping up closer to the stage. Sasha and Kostya found a spot at the end of the second row, and everyone trying to get to the center seats kept stumbling over their feet. She didn't care—it seemed incredibly important to be able to leave as quickly as possible if necessary.

The man on the stage waited. He looked nothing like Sasha's image of a college professor: instead of a suit, he wore jeans and a striped sweater. His straight blond hair was pulled into a ponytail, and he wore glasses, long and narrow like razor blades, that seemed specially designed to allow him to look over the lenses.

"My name is Oleg Borisovich. Oleg Borisovich Portnov. Young man in the fifth row, yes, you. Don't be shy, come closer. There are not that many of us, we have plenty of space. I would like to extend my congratulations to you, ladies and gentlemen, on this significant event in your lives: your admission to the first year of Torpa's Institute of Special Technologies. You are to expect an interesting life and plenty of hard work. Miss"—his finger pointed at Lisa, who leaned over to whisper something to Oksana—"when I speak, everyone else is silent. Please remember that in the future."

Lisa choked. The room was very quiet. Portnov took a few steps along the platform, his eyes traveling from face to face, slowly, like the ray of a flashlight.

"Congratulations, you are now students. In honor of your initiation, the student hymn will be performed. If you know the words, please sing along."

A triumphant chord burst out of the sound system. Portnov motioned for everyone to rise. An invisible chorus sang with an appropriate solemnity:

Gaudeamus igitur,
Juvenes dum sumus!
Post jucundam juventutem,
Post molestam senectutem
Nos habebit humus!

Sasha quickly observed the audience. Only a few people were singing along. Lisa stood with her lips tightly shut. Oksana strained to hear the words—her Latin did not seem very strong. Sasha herself knew the text, she'd learned it a while ago in her prep course. The translation of this seemingly joyful song never struck her as happy:

After a pleasant youth
After a troubling old age
The earth will have us.

Such a lovely beginning. But then:

Vita nostra brevis est,
Brevi finietur;
Venit mors velociter,
Rarit nos atrociter,
Nemini parcetur!

This part she particularly disliked: in this verse, all men were promised an imminent death that spares no one. Vita nostra . . . "Our life is brief, / It will shortly end; / Death comes quickly." *Maybe the medieval students didn't give a hoot,* Sasha thought darkly. *Maybe if I were listening to "Gaudeamus" at home, at our university, I wouldn't give a hoot either, and I wouldn't have any of these thoughts. But I am in Torpa.*

Vivat Academia,
Vivant professores!
Vivat membrum quodlibet,
Vivat membra quaelibet
Semper sint in flore!

The song ended. The students sat down, as if ending a moment of silence. Portnov stood at the very edge of the platform, hanging over the first rows, studying their faces. Sasha caught his gaze and lowered her own.

"And now we're going to watch a short film—our school's official presentation. I would like to ask you to pay attention and refrain from talking and interrupting your neighbors' viewing. Enjoy the film."

The lights went out. The dark curtains on the windows twitched and moved closer together. Behind the stage, a light rectangle appeared on the screen, reminding Sasha of newsreels of her early childhood: something very archaic was in the black-and-white image displayed on the screen.

"Welcome to the ancient town of Torpa," announced the deep voice of the narrator. "The Institute of Special Technologies salutes you!"

A bright logo swam out of the darkness, a rounded symbol, the same as on the front of the gold coins Sasha had collected. Sasha stopped breathing.

Last night she'd analyzed everything. She'd whispered: "I want it to be a dream," squeezing her eyes shut. She'd lain staring at the ceiling. She'd seriously believed that she'd been taken into a secret laboratory, where young boys and girls were subjected to experiments that turned them into cripples. Then she'd calmed down and was able to see some benefit in her situation: what if she were to be taught something amazing, what if Farit Kozhennikov was an alien, and she would have a chance to see other planets . . .

All night the dormitory had been awake: people yelled, sang songs accompanied by guitar chords, listened to a boom box that thundered somewhere. Every now and then somebody stamped down the corridor, this way and then the other. Somebody called for his friends out the window. Somebody laughed uncontrollably. Going mad with insomnia, Sasha had finally plunged into unconsciousness and dreamed strange dreams. At half past six Oksana had started rustling her plastic bags, filling the room with the smell of pickles, and that rustling and the smell forced Sasha wide awake.

And now she watched the screen. The film was ancient, older than Sasha herself; the narrator's voice in the old sound system made her ears pop, but no matter how hard she tried, Sasha heard nothing new or at least informative. Torpa is a beautiful ancient city. Tradition of higher education. Youth stepping into the adult life. Et cetera, et cetera. Black-and-white frames replaced each other: the streets of Torpa (which really were quite picturesque, she had to admit). Swans in the fountain. The institute's facade, the dormitory's facade, the glass dome over the equestrian statue. The voice preached the importance of a properly chosen higher education facility, and how this affects one's employment and career, talked about young specialists who graduate from the school annually, about life in the dormitory, about glorious traditions—the words were familiar and amorphous, they could be placed in any desired combination without losing any meaning. Sasha was caught off guard when the film ended suddenly, the screen darkened, and the lights came back on.

The first years squinted, exchanged glances, and shrugged. Portnov took a long stride across the stage, stopped at its edge, and laced his hands behind his back.

"This concludes the official part of the proceedings. Let's start our work. This year, thirty-nine first-year students were accepted, which makes two groups. Let's call them Group A and Group B. Understood?"

The first years were silent.

"Students whose mentors are Liliya Popova and Farit Kozhennikov, please come up."

Sasha swallowed and remained seated. Lisa walked up the squeaky stairs, nervously smoothed out her very short skirt, and stood to the side. A tall guy whom Sasha had seen at the dining hall stood next to her. A student elbowed his way out of the center seat and stumbled over Sasha's feet.

"Should we go?" Kostya asked quietly.

Sasha got up.

The stage was wide; nineteen people could have spread out from curtain to curtain, holding hands. But everyone huddled together, as if trying to hide behind one another's backs.

"Allow me to introduce first years, Group A," Portnov motioned toward the stage. "Please welcome Group A."

Someone in the audience clapped a few times.

"Your schedule will be posted right after the first block. Group B, which is now sitting in the audience, will be going to Physical Education—the gym is on the third floor, class starts in five minutes. Your second block is Specialty; we'll meet then and have a chance to chat. Group A has Specialty during the first block in auditorium number 1. Everyone, please proceed to your assigned blocks. You now have four minutes—tardiness is not appreciated."

Portnov stepped down the squeaky steps and left the hall through the side entrance. Lisa moved back and smoothed out her miniskirt again. Sasha was shocked by the length of Lisa's legs.

"Sasha!"

Sasha looked back. Oksana, still wearing the same jersey sweater, was waving to her from the audience.

"We're going to be in different groups, that's a shame, isn't it?"

"Off to the gym . . . ," somebody mumbled.

"I don't even have any sneakers, just regular shoes . . ."

Group B slowly pulled out of the hall. Sasha turned to Kostya.

"Who's this Liliya Popova?" she whispered.

Kostya shook his head.

"I have no clue."

"What do you mean?" Sasha was surprised. "But you are . . . how did you get here, anyway? You said your father . . ."

"Yes." Kostya nodded. "My father is Farit Kozhennikov. Why?"

Auditorium number 1 was located on the first floor, off the hall with the equestrian statue. The sun was beating from the outside, the glass dome shined like a projector's lens. The light was washing over the stallion and equestrian's sides and rolled off them like water off a seal's back. Precise shadows of enormous feet in stirrups lay on the floor.

"Why didn't you tell me he was your father?"

"How was I supposed to know you knew him too? I thought . . ."

"If he . . . if you are his son, how could he stick you into this hole?"

"How do I know? I hadn't seen him for many years. He divorced my mother when . . . that's not important. He showed up and gave me an ultimatum, and . . ."

"But is he really your father?"

"Well, I suppose so, considering that my full name is Kozhennikov, Konstantin Faritovich!"

"Holy shit," said Sasha, utterly astonished.

Group A flowed into the small auditorium, similar to a middle-school classroom. A blackboard with a dusty rag and a piece of chalk made the similarity all the more obvious. They barely had time to choose their seats and place their bags on the floor when the bell rang dismally in the hall, and immediately—that very second—Portnov entered: a long blond ponytail down his back, glasses perched on his nose, and an intense stare over the narrow lenses.

He pulled his chair away from the massive teacher's desk. Sat down. Laced his fingers together in front of him.

"All right . . . Good morning again, students."

He was answered by dead silence; only a spaced-out fly kept throwing itself against the windowpane. Portnov opened a thin paper logbook and glanced over the list.

"Biryukov, Dmitry."

"Here."

"Bochkova, Anna."

"Here," said a plump girl with a pale, sickly face.

"Goldman, Yulia."

"Here," a voice said from the back row.

"Korotkov, Andrey."

"Here."

"Kovtun, Igor."

"Here."

"Kozhennikov, Kostya."

A chill moved over the auditorium. Many heads turned. Kostya visibly tensed up.

"Here," he croaked.

"Myaskovsky, Denis," Portnov continued as if nothing had happened.

"Here!"

Sasha listened to the roll call, doodling on the side of the page of her notebook. Nineteen people. Her high school class had almost forty students . . .

"Pavlenko, Lisa."

"That's me," said Lisa.

"Samokhina, Alexandra."

"That's me," Sasha breathed out.

"Toporko, Zhenya."

"Here," murmured a small, very young-looking girl with two long braids.

"Everyone is present," Portnov admitted with satisfaction. "Take out your notebooks. On top of the first page, write 'Portnov, Oleg Borisovich.' In case somebody missed it, my subject is Specialty."

The first years fumbled around. Kostya did not have a notepad, and Sasha supplied him with a sheet from her own notepad.

"In the future you must bring your textbooks and notepads to every class. Regarding textbooks . . ." Portnov unlocked a wooden cabinet and took out a stack of books. "Samokhina, give these to your classmates."

Sasha, an eternal straight-A student, got up before she had time to be surprised. Even the most intelligent teacher usually required a few days to memorize the first and last names of his students. Portnov memorized everyone's name from the first try; or did he pay special attention to Sasha?

She accepted a heavy stack of books that smelled like an old library. The books looked identical and not very new. Sasha walked through the auditorium, placing two books on each desk.

The cover had an abstract pattern of colored blocks. Black letters folded into two words: "Textual Module." Underneath was a large number "1."

"Do not open the books," said Portnov quietly, before one of the first years curiously lifted the cover.

Hands jerked back. Again, silence prevailed. Sasha placed the last two books on the desk she shared with Kostya and sat down.

"Attention, students," continued Portnov just as softly. "You are at the beginning of a journey, during which all of your strength will be required. Physical *and* mental. What we will be studying is not for everyone. Not everyone can handle what this does to a person. You have been carefully selected, and you all have what it takes to make that journey successfully. Our science does not tolerate weakness and takes cruel revenge on laziness, on cowardice, and on the most infinitesimal attempt to avoid learning the entire curriculum. Is that understood?"

The fly threw itself at the glass for the last time and fell limply on the windowsill.

"To everyone who puts their best effort into the process of learning and does his or her absolute best, I will guarantee: by the time the process is completed, these students will be alive and well. However, negligence and indifference bring students to a sorry end. An *extremely* sorry end. Understood?"

A hand flew up to the left of Sasha.

"Yes, Pavlenko," said Portnov without looking.

Lisa got up, convulsively tugging on her skirt.

"You see, no one asked our opinion when we were sent here," her voice trembled.

"And?" Portnov looked at her with interest.

"But can you expect us . . . Request that we study so hard . . . if we don't want to?" Lisa tried hard not to allow her voice to squeal.

"Yes, we can," Portnov stated lightly. "When a toddler is being potty-trained, no one asks his or her opinion, right?"

Lisa remained standing for a moment, and then sat down. Portnov's answer took her aback. She wasn't the only one. Sasha and Kostya exchanged glances.

"Let us continue," went on Portnov, as if the interruption didn't particularly faze him. "You are Group A of the first year. I will be your Specialty professor, responsible for lectures on theory and individual studies. With each new semester, your work will get more complex, and other special subjects will be added. I want you to understand that Physical Education is considered one of the primary subjects in your curriculum. Do remember that. Aside from that, during the first semester you will be studying Philosophy, History, English, and Mathematics. Most of you were good students, so it will be enough to simply do your homework in those subjects. The situation with Specialty is different. It will be difficult. Especially in the beginning."

"You've already put the fear of God into us," someone said from the back row.

"Hand, Kovtun—first get your hand up, then share your thought. In the future, a breach of discipline results in an extra Specialty assignment."

Silence.

"Good. We have gotten through the introduction. Let's begin. Kozhennikov, do me a favor: take the chalk and draw a horizontal line on the blackboard."

"In the middle?" Kostya specified.

Portnov glanced askance at him over the glasses. Kostya shrugged, looked down, picked up the chalk, and carefully drew a straight line from one edge of the blackboard to the other.

"Thank you, you may sit down. Class, look at the board. What is it?"

"Horizon," said Sasha.

"Perhaps. What else?"

"A stretched rope," Lisa suggested.

"A dead worm, view from the top!" Igor Kovtun quipped.

Portnov smirked. He picked up the chalk and drew a butterfly in the top part of the blackboard. Underneath, below the horizontal line, he drew another butterfly, just like the first one, but in a dashed line.

"What is that?"

"A butterfly."

"A swallowtail."

"A cabbage white!"

"Projection," Sasha said after a short pause.

Portnov glanced at her with interest.

"Very good. Samokhina, what is projection?"

"It's an image of an object on a flat surface. Reflection. Shadow."

"Come here."

Sasha disentangled herself from her desk clumsily. Rather unceremoniously, Portnov grabbed her by the shoulders and turned her to face the group. Sasha glimpsed a surprised look on Yulia Goldman's face, a slightly contemptuous one on Lisa's, a curious one on Andrey Korotkov's; in the next second, a black scarf descended upon her face, and darkness came.

Somebody gave a nervous giggle.

"Samokhina, what do you see?"

"Nothing."

"Nothing at all?"

Sasha paused, afraid of making a mistake.

"Nothing. Darkness."

"Does it mean you are blind?"

"No." Sasha was offended. "It's just if you cover a person's eyes, the person won't be able to see."

The audience was by now laughing openly.

"Attention, students," Portnov said drily. "In reality, each one of you is in the same situation as Samokhina. You are blind. You stare into the darkness."

The giggling subsided.

"The world, as you see it, is not real. And the way you imagine it—it does not even come close. Certain things seem obvious to you, but they simply do not exist."

"And you, do you not exist?" Sasha couldn't help herself. "Are you not real?"

Portnov removed the scarf from her face. Under his gaze, she blinked confusedly.

"I exist," he said seriously. "But I am not at all what you think."

And, leaving Sasha standing there in a state of complete shock, he crumpled the scarf into a little ball and threw it carelessly on his desk.

"Samokhina, you may sit down. Let's continue."

Sasha held up her hand. The hand trembled, but Sasha continued to hold it stubbornly. Portnov half-closed his eyes and said, "What now?"

"I wanted to ask. What are you going to teach us? What specialty? And who are we going to be when we graduate?"

An approving whisper fluttered through the audience.

"I am going to give you a notion of how the world is structured," Portnov explained, with a huge emphasis on his alleged leniency. "And, what is even more crucial, a notion of your—every one of you—place in this world. I cannot tell you more at this point, since you will not understand. Any other questions?"

The girl with the braids, Zhenya Toporko, held up her hand.

"Excuse me . . ."

"Yes?" Irritation could be easily discerned in Portnov's voice. Zhenya quivered, but made herself go on:

"If I don't want to study here, and I want to cancel my enrollment . . . May I do it today?"

It became very quiet. Kostya gave Sasha a significant look. Lisa Pavlenko's eyes lit up.

"It is very important to dot all the *i*'s," Portnov stated unemotionally. "You have passed a very difficult and competitive selection process. You have been accepted into a well-established learning institution that does not tolerate doubt, uncertainty, and other forms of idiocy. So no, you may *not* cancel your enrollment. You will study here; otherwise, you will be dismissed and simultaneously buried. Your advisors, Liliya Popova and Farit Kozhennikov, will remain in that role until your fifth year. Their responsibilities include stimulating your excellent academic performance. I hope all of you have had a good chance to meet your advisors so you have an idea of how effective they can be in that regard."

A minute before Sasha thought the auditorium was quiet, but now the silence was absolute. It was deadly.

"Open your books to page three," Portnov continued nonchalantly.

"Read Section 1, slowly, carefully, paying attention to each letter. You may begin." He sat down and gave the students one more piercing look.

Sasha opened the book. The inside cover was clear of text: no author's name, no publishing data. "Textual Module 1, Section 1." The yellowing pages were worn at the corners; the font was absolutely typical, just like any normal textbook . . .

Until Sasha began to read. There was nothing typical about that.

She stumbled on the very first line. Word after word, paragraph after paragraph, the book consisted of complete gibberish.

Her first thought was "printing error." She threw a quick glance at Kostya's textbook, and at the same time he peeked at hers.

"Is yours the same garbage?"

"No talking," Portnov said quietly. "Continue reading. Pay attention. I warned you: you will have to work hard."

"It's not in Russian," Anya Bochkova squealed softly.

"I did not say it was going to be in Russian. Read silently to yourself. You do not have a lot of time left in this class."

Sasha lowered her head.

Somebody laughed. Giggles spread over the class, like an epidemic, but Portnov ignored it. The laughter died down on its own. Sasha forged through the long, senseless combinations of letters, and her hair stood on end. She imagined that somebody was repeating those sounds after her in a dark room with mirrors instead of walls, and each word, after reflecting over and over in the mirrors, finally gained meaning, but by then Sasha had moved two sections ahead, and the meaning flew away from her, like smoke from a fast-moving locomotive . . .

When she finished reading the relatively short section, she was dripping with sweat. She labored to catch her breath. Five paragraphs at the very end were underlined with a red pen.

The bell rang outside.

"Homework," Portnov said. "Read Section 1 three times, from beginning to end. The underlined paragraphs are to be memorized. By heart. Tomorrow we have one-on-one practice during the third block. Kozhennikov will compile the list."

"Why me?" Kostya jumped up.

"Because you are now the prefect," stated Portnov matter-of-factly. "Class is dismissed. You next class is Physical Education."

Group A, unusually silent, stopped in the hall, at the foot of the massive staircase. Group B was walking down, chatting happily; the gym class seemed to have put them in a good mood. Oksana walked down the stairs, her cheeks burning bright red in the semidarkness, like two slices of watermelon.

Upon seeing the other group, Oksana slowed down. "Any reason you look so miserable?"

"You'll find out," Lisa promised darkly.

"We should get to the gym," Kostya suggested. "No point in standing here until midnight . . ."

"Prefect," said Lisa with an unidentifiable modulation. "Is your last name Kozhennikov?"

"Yeah, why?"

"And who is Farit . . . Sorry, I don't know his full name?"

Kostya clenched his fists.

"He's my father. So?"

"Leave him alone, it's not his fault," Sasha said softly. "He's in the same situation as the rest of us. He was forced into it as well."

Lisa turned sharply and started walking up the stairs. The miniskirt clung to her butt, and her long tanned legs flashed in the semidarkness.

"Hmm, isn't it all so much fun," said Andrey Korotkov, a tall, square-shouldered guy older than most of them—he probably ended up in Torpa after his military service.

Sasha, trying not to look at anyone, followed Lisa up to the third floor, to the door with a modest sign: SPORTS CENTER.

The gym teacher was a gorgeous dark-haired creature around twenty-five years of age. A thin yellow shirt clung to his powerful chest and back muscles; bare shoulders and arms demonstrated an impressive physique. In front of the lineup, Dmitry Dmitrievich (that was his name) shared his entire life story with the group: he used to be a professional wrestler, enjoyed considerable success, got hurt during a match, was forced to leave professional sports and become a coach, and since he had no teaching experience, he was happy to be employed by a regional college. While telling them all the minute details, the gym teacher smiled shyly; Sasha understood immeditately why Group B seemed so happy, especially the girls. Dima Dimych—because how else but informally, like a good buddy, could one address him?—resembled a powerful but naïve tiger cub, and the thought that their schedule included four gym classes a week now made them deliriously happy, instead of depressed as it should have. Dima reminded them to wear athletic uniforms and sneakers to each class and promised to teach special classes, wrestling for boys and table tennis for girls. Yulia Goldman, feisty and lively, immediately claimed discrimination—Why, she asked, did he think wrestling was only for boys? Why couldn't girls wrestle? To the vast amusement of the audience, Dima blushed and promised "to think of something." By way of warm-up, he suggested they take off their shoes, split into three teams, and play a game of basketball.

A very recent thick layer of paint covered the gym floor. Bright green and bright yellow fields, thick white lines, thuds of the orange basketball, the smell of rubber and sweat; Sasha ran between the baskets, imitating action rather than really playing. What was happening then was a perfectly normal, joyful, juicy slice of life, and she had trouble believing that half an hour ago she was reading Section 1, bending under the will of a sadistic professor with elongated glasses on the tip of his nose.

As she played, she let her mind wander, and it became clear that here, at this college, they were being bullied. How else could one see it? Forced to read absolute gibberish and commit it to memory. The same senseless process as having to scrub a cobblestone plaza with a toothbrush. Or sort out grains that would later be all mixed together again, and again, and again . . . Senseless. Punishment. Humiliation.

But *why*? Who needs this Institute of Special Technologies with its entire staff, dining hall, dean's office, dormitory? What is it, other than a nest of sadism?

Kostya passed her the ball over Yulia's head. Sasha caught it, dribbled a few feet, and threw it toward the hoop, but at the last moment Lisa aimed a heavy blow at her arm. The ball bounced off the hoop, landed in the hands of someone on the other team, and—*thump-thump-thump*—ended up at the opposite end of the gym; Lisa followed, tugging on her miniskirt, which, frankly speaking, was not the best attire for a basketball game.

Sasha's team lost.

"I can't memorize it! I just can't!"

The textbook flew into the corner, hit the dresser door, landed on the floor, and stayed there, its yellow pages splayed open. Oksana hit the desk with both fists, making the table lamp hop.

"I can't! I am not going to study this! They are making fun of us!"

"That's what I am thinking." Lisa sat on the windowsill, smoking, a glass jar in front of her full of lipsticked cigarette butts.

"What will happen if we don't learn it?" Sasha asked.

All three girls fell silent. The question that had tortured them all day was now out in the open.

It was evening. The sun was setting outside their window. Somewhere someone was strumming a guitar. Behind them was the first day of classes—Specialty, Physical Education, Philosophy, and World History. Neither the third, nor the fourth block brought any surprises. Sasha wrote down the definition of the principal point of philosophy and how materialism differs from idealism, took notes on the dwellings of primitive peoples and their customs, and received two perfectly ordinary textbooks. An excellent dinner was consumed in dead silence. First years returned to the dorm, began to study, and soon found out that the homework assigned by Portnov was an impossible task to accomplish.

One *could* read this nonsense, forcing oneself every step of the way. But *memorizing* the underlined passages—that was unfeasible. The brain refused to function, and spots swam before their exhausted eyes. Oksana was the first one to crack, and now her textbook was crumpled on the floor.

"I can't memorize it!" Oksana sniffled. "Even if he kills me!"

Lisa looked like she wanted to say something, but at that moment someone knocked on the door.

"Come in," Sasha said.

Kostya entered and closed the door behind him.

"Hey. I am . . . I need to . . . the schedule for tomorrow. I mean, the individual workshops, they're during the third and fourth blocks."

"Prefect," said Lisa with a degree of disdain that had no equal.

"It's not like it was his idea, you know," Sasha snapped.

"Considering whose son he is . . ."

"What difference is it whose son I am?" Kostya burst out, drops of saliva flying in all directions. "What is the difference? Did I ask who your father is? Did I bother you *at all*?" And before anyone could answer him, he left the room, slamming the door and running down the corridor, Sasha flying behind him.

"Kostya. Wait. Don't pay attention to her. Just wait!"

Not answering, Kostya dashed into the men's bathroom. Sasha

slowed down. She considered the situation and perched on the windowsill, prepared to wait.

A third year was walking down the corridor, taking each step carefully. He slowly turned his head, as if his neck were made of rusty metal. Now and then he would freeze, as if listening to something, and even his eyes stopped moving, fixed on some unknown point. Then he would start walking again, and this way, step after step, he approached Sasha, perched at the window.

Despite the unusually warm, sunny, and almost summery day, he wore woolen gloves. A wide knitted headband covered his forehead, and either it was a fashion statement Sasha didn't understand or a cure for a headache.

"Hello."

Sasha had not expected him to speak and so answered automatically: "Hello."

"First years? Nightmares? Hysterics?"

Sasha licked her lips. "I guess so . . ."

"I see," said the third year. "Were you a straight-A student in high school?"

"Why?" Sasha frowned.

The guy took a step toward her. He stood swaying, then with an unexpected ease he hopped onto the windowsill next to her.

"You should get a haircut, bob your hair. And a brighter lipstick."

"What's it to you?" Sasha was deeply offended.

"I am older than you—I can give you all sorts of advice." The guy smirked. "Valery." He extended a gloved hand.

Sasha had to force herself to stretch her own hand in return and touch the pilling black wool.

"Alexandra . . ."

She took a deep breath and then began talking rapidly, quietly.

"Valery, tell me, explain to me, you must know by now . . . What are they teaching us here?"

"To explain is to simplify," Valery informed her after a short pause.

Frustrated at the nonanswer, Sasha jumped off the windowsill. "See you."

"Wait." Something in Valery's voice made her stop. "I am not . . . making fun of you. Laughing at you. Jesting. Having fun at your expense. Needling you. Taunting you . . . I . . ."

He fell silent, surprised and even confused, his own words like cockroaches running from the bright light.

Finally he said, "You see. It really is difficult to explain. The first semester is the hardest. Just survive this semester, that's all. Then it's going to get easier each year."

"Do I have a choice?" Sasha asked bitterly.

Still sitting on the windowsill, Valery shrugged.

"Listen," Sasha said drily. "Can you please go into the bathroom and tell this guy—the first year—that I'm waiting for him. Tell him to stop hiding."

At half past midnight Sasha gave up. She closed the book and dropped it under the bed, closed her eyes, and fell asleep almost immediately.

The smell of a burning cigarette woke her up. Lisa was smoking, sitting by the window, and Oksana was not in the room.

"Ugh." Sasha waved the thick cloud of smoke away from her face. "Can you please smoke in the bathroom?"

"Anything else?" Lisa inquired calmly.

Sasha forced herself to get up. Half an hour remained before the first block; the corridor was filled with the sounds of running, stomping, laughing, and yelling.

She took a shower in the steamy shower room, taking squeamish steps on the waterlogged wooden planks. It was too late to dry her hair. Sasha poked her nose into the kitchen—it was packed with the sound of clanking dishes and loud people waiting for their turn with the electric teakettle—and left immediately. She went back to her room, pulled on a pair of jeans and a shirt, and jogged over to the back entrance of the institute.

Group A was nearly bursting with emotion. Some people were flaunting their indifference, some balanced on the verge of hysterics, some were still trying to memorize the nonsensical text, staring at the accursed *Textual Module* with the abstract pattern on the faded cover. It was readily apparent that no one had managed to do as Portnov requested: the text refused to be memorized.

"It's going to be just fine," Andrey Korotkov crooned in basso profundo; from the first day Andrey had played the role of everyone's older brother. "What could he possibly do to us?"

Lisa, thin and haggard looking, watched him through squinted eyes, as if through a cloud of tobacco smoke. Sasha did her best to avoid Lisa.

The first block was Mathematics, which Sasha disliked and had hoped to avoid after high school, but it was not to be: standard textbook, review of previous material, trigonometry, triangular coordinates . . .

Despite her initial abhorrence, Sasha found herself deeply interested in half-forgotten high school subjects. The textbook was logical, it was consistent, and each task had meaning. The thin book printed on lousy paper suddenly provoked a bout of nostalgia; Sasha placed it in her bag with a warm, almost tender emotion.

The second block was English. The class was held in auditorium 1, and that auditorium, even the blackboard, which the English professor cheerfully covered with English grammatical constructions, elicited some unpleasant memories from many of the students. Listening to the familiar dialogs about the weather, London, and pets, Sasha watched Kostya reread the nonsensical section from the *Textual Module*. He shook his head hopelessly.

Sasha ended up liking the English class as well: the professor, a sarcastic woman with an intricate hairdo, and the textbook, and even what she had to do during the class. Language was logical. The efforts were clear. Even the process of memorization, the learning of new words, was reasonable.

They broke for lunch.

On the bulletin board where the generic schedule was posted, Kostya hung up a separate list: one-on-one Specialty workshops. Sasha found herself in the first time slot, right after the bell for the third block.

"How come you put me first?"

"What, you don't like it?"

"Calm down," Sasha said apologetically. "I'm just asking, no subtext."

"I just thought you'd prefer to get it over with," Kostya said after a pause. "Plus, you know that idiotic text better than everyone else."

"What the heck makes you think that?"

"If you don't want to go, I'll take your slot!"

The bell rang.

Auditorium 38 was hidden behind the dean's office, a little pigeonhole of a space. Why the auditorium had this high number—or was called an auditorium at all—Sasha had no idea. She knocked on the door and entered. The classroom was tiny, had no windows, and fit only a desk and a few chairs. A single bare bulb hung from the ceiling on a very long cord. The piercing light made Sasha squint.

"You are two minutes late, Samokhina."

"I couldn't find number 38. I thought it was on the third floor."

"I am not interested in that."

Sasha lingered by the door, not knowing where to go or what to do. Portnov beckoned her with a bent finger. She approached; Portnov, in the same striped sweater, sat behind the office desk, watching her intently. His gaze—over the glasses—made Sasha even more uncomfortable.

"Just look how bogged down we are," said Portnov, perhaps to Sasha, perhaps to himself. "Up to our ears. Pure jelly. Why don't you come here?"

He got up, his chair squeaked lightly, and a moment later he was right next to her. Very close. She smelled his cologne—and had a split second to wonder why. For some reason, she didn't think someone like Portnov would use cosmetics.

Above, almost over her head, the bare lightbulb burned brightly. Round black shadows lay on the linoleum floor. Projections. Shadows . . .

"I am listening. Tell me what you have learned."

Sasha began, losing her way, stumbling, absolutely sure that she would never get close even to the end of the first paragraph. And further—after the first ten lines—it was hard to imagine, there existed a black hole, and the gibberish melted into a solid gray hum . . .

"Look in here."

He lifted a hand to her face; she saw a ring on his finger, a ring that was not there before. A large pink stone diffracted the light of the bulb, became bright blue, then green; Sasha held her breath. She felt dizzy, took a step, trying to maintain equilibrium . . .

"Hold it."

She blinked. The ring was no longer there. Portnov stood beside her, holding her shoulders.

"Good job," he said with unexpected kindness. "I can see you worked hard. But it is only a minuscule step. You must work like this every single day. For your next practice, read Section 2. Everything that is underlined in red must be memorized."

"But what about . . . ?"

"Good-bye, Samokhina. You are already cutting into somebody else's time. Go."

Sasha stepped into the hallway, where Andrey Korotkov waited, leaning against the wall.

"So?" he asked impatiently. "Did he yell a lot? What happened, anyway?"

"I—"

"Korotkov, I am waiting," said Portnov.

The door closed behind Andrey. Sasha shook her head, completely bewildered. She lifted her watch to her nose.

Fifteen minutes had passed since she entered auditorium 38.

"I told you, I did not see him for many years. He showed up in August. I failed the law school entrance exams . . . And in September I was turning eighteen, so I would be drafted soon. My mother was in shock. And then he shows up! Sort of a savior. Made everything work out . . . Do you think I wanted to come here? I wanted to enlist! Well, not so much wanted to, but . . ."

Sasha and Kostya were walking down Sacco and Vanzetti Street, and then down Peace Street, and one other street, farther and farther from the town center, not really knowing the destination. At first, Sasha told him about the morning swimming sessions, about the gold coins, about running in the park and the trip to Torpa. Then Kostya spoke. His story was much simpler.

"He literally *made* me. Had I known what it was like here, I'd definitely have enlisted."

"No, you wouldn't," Sasha said.

Kostya threw her a surprised glance.

"My father left when I was a little girl," Sasha said. "He had another family. And he never showed up again. My entire life it was just Mom and me. Always, just the two of us. And my biggest fear—do you know what it is? That something will happen to her. I remember now what Farit did and said to me. No, he never threatened me openly. He just allowed my fear, all by itself, to break loose and spread all over me. All of me. And my fear brought me here—and is holding me down. And will continue holding me."

The street suddenly ended. Sasha and Kostya went by the last two deserted-looking houses and unexpectedly found themselves on the bank of a narrow but relatively clean river. Grass crept close to the stream. A fisherman in a roomy jacket with a hood stood on the wooden dock.

"Would you look at that," Kostya mused. "I didn't even know there was a river. Think we can even swim here?"

Sasha followed him down to the water. Grass clung to their feet. Cattails swayed gently, and frogs croaked on the opposite bank. Kostya sat down on a fallen tree trunk, old, barkless, mossy in places. Sasha lowered herself next to him.

"I wonder if there are any fish here." Kostya lowered his voice. "I used to love this stuff. I even went fishing in the winter once . . ."

The fisherman gave his line a strong pull. A silver fish the size of a man's palm flew up over the water, escaped the hook, and fell at Sasha's feet, then hopped on the grass. The fisherman turned to face them.

This time he was not wearing glasses. The brown eyes of Farit Kozhennikov were perfectly friendly.

"Good evening, Alexandra. Good evening, Kostya. Sasha, please hand me the fish."

Sasha bent down. The fish trembled in her hand; taking a wide swing, Sasha threw it into the water. Circles stayed on the surface for a few seconds. A few scales stuck to Sasha's palm.

"Have fun catching it," Sasha's voice rang out. "Just keep your feet dry."

Kozhennikov smirked. He placed his fishing rod on the grass, unbuttoned his jacket, and sat down on the tree trunk next to his son. Sasha remained standing. Kostya tensed up, but chose to sit still.

"How's everything? Classmates, professors? Are you settling down?"

"I hate you," Sasha said. "And I will find a way to make you pay for it. Not now. Later."

Kozhennikov nodded abstractedly. "I understand. We shall come back to that conversation . . . in a little while. Kostya, do you also hate me?"

"What I want to know," Kostya said, anxiously rubbing his knee, "is do you really—*can* you really turn reality into a dream? Or is it hypnosis? Or some other trick?"

Still smiling, Kozhennikov spread his hands wide, as if saying—well, that's just how it works.

"And do you have power over accidents?" Kostya continued. "People get sick, die, get run over by cars . . ."

"If one directs the sail, does he direct the wind?"

"Cheap sophistry," Sasha interjected.

"The question *is*"—Kozhennikov glanced at her—"what should be considered a tragic accident, and what should be considered a happy occurrence? And this, my friends, you cannot possibly know."

"Because you keep this knowledge from us," Sasha cut in again.

Kostya asked, "What exactly are the coins?"

Kozhennikov absentmindedly stuck his hand into his pocket. He took out a gold disk, and Sasha saw the familiar rounded three-dimensional symbol.

"Look. This is a word that has never been pronounced. And it never will be." Kozhennikov flipped the coin; it flew up and landed back on his palm. "Do you understand?"

Sasha and Kostya were silent.

"Of course you don't understand. But you *will*," Kozhennikov nodded reassuringly. "Are you interested in fishing? Kostya?"

"No," said Kozhennikov junior with disdain. "We have a lot of work for tomorrow. See you."

Without a backward glance, he walked away from the river, and Sasha quickly followed.

Sasha could deal with the mornings and afternoons. She was busy, she had lectures, classes, all sorts of worries. But in the evenings, and especially during the nights, she cried. Every night. Turning her face to the wall.

She missed her home, longed terribly for Mom. Dozing off, she would see Mom enter the room, stand right next to her bed . . .

Sasha would wake up—and cry again.

She barely managed to fall asleep by the time the alarm clock went off.

Sasha had always taken pleasure in learning. Shuffling between courses and tutors, polishing the seat of her skirt at the library, poring over textbooks in advance, she never quite comprehended how lucky she was back then to be learning things that were logical, comprehensible, and elegant, like a geometry problem.

But now, when nothing she had to learn was ever logical or comprehensible, even the very sight of the *Textual Module,* with its pattern of blocks on the cover, made her unbearably bored.

A week passed. Then another. Every day she had to read sections, memorize, cram, and grind at snippets of nonsensical, unpleasant text. Sasha herself did not understand why this gobbledygook caused more and more revulsion with each passing day. Reading the barbaric combinations of half-familiar and alien words, she felt something brewing inside her: within her head, a wasp nest was waking up, and it droned and hummed in distress, searching in vain for an exit.

People started playing hooky in the second week of school. Andrey Korotkov stopped attending Math, claiming he used to work on problems like this in ninth grade. Lisa Pavlenko occasionally skipped History, Philosophy, English—without any explanation. Some boys skipped gym, but the girls attended Dima Dimych's class diligently and cheerfully. Adorable, gorgeous, sweet Dima did not torture anyone with backbreaking training; instead, he dedicated most of the time to games. He gave long lectures on the human body with the goal of making the training more effective. Naïvely, he demonstrated the location of tendons, the structure of muscles—first on an educational poster, then on a live model. The live models requested more details and explanations. Dima blushed and explained again and again: here is the knee joint, here is the ankle joint, and these here are very tender ligaments, which are frequently pulled and can even tear . . .

Sasha liked watching the young teacher from a distance, somewhere atop a stack of gym mats. The boldness of her classmates, their audacity and cheekiness surprised and embarrassed her, but also made her a bit envious.

Truancy was fine in the other classes, but Specialty was always meticulously attended by all nineteen students of Group A. And every one of them studied the textual sections diligently. Portnov was a master of coercing. In fact, coercing seemed to be his sole teaching skill.

"Why do we need these lectures? To learn how to read?" bristled Laura Onishenko, a tall busty girl who carried a plastic bag with her knitting everywhere.

"It's not education," Kostya said. "It's obedience training, in the best-case scenario. In the worst-possible-case scenario, it is brainwashing. How's your head—does it feel normal after one-on-one sessions?"

Kostya wasn't wrong. To a certain degree, one-on-one sessions were even worse than the lectures. Fifteen minutes twice a week. According to Portnov, he controlled their knowledge, although from Sasha's point of view, they learned nothing, and his method of control smacked of shamanism: Portnov's ring blinded her, made her thoughts scramble, time made a dizzying leap, and meanwhile Portnov managed to find out everything she had learned, did not quite learn, or did not learn well.

"You did not finish Section 5. Tomorrow you will do Section 6, and again Section 5."

"That's not enough time!"

"I am not interested."

It appeared as if Group B was experiencing the same: rosy-cheeked Oksana looked pale and drawn, and spent all her free time at her desk. Lisa continued to smoke in the room, one cigarette after another. Sasha thought she was doing it on purpose; she seemed to enjoy watching Sasha cough and squint from the tobacco smoke.

Two weeks of classes passed by. Once, during lunch break, when everyone went to the dining hall, Sasha returned to the dorm, found a stash of cigarettes (several packs) among Lisa's belongings, and flushed them down the toilet.

Lisa said nothing. But the next day the entire contents of Sasha's makeup bag—powder, eye shadow, lip gloss, and an expensive lipstick, a birthday gift used rarely, only on important holidays—all of it ended up in the trash, broken, crushed, and smeared over the rusty metal sides of the garbage can.

Sasha discovered the debacle later in the morning, when Lisa had already left the room. Blind with rage, Sasha dashed to the lecture hall, intending to rip the witch's hair out. She was too late: the first block, Specialty, had started, and a new dose of the sickening gibberish cooled down Sasha's wrath faster than a bucket of icy water.

After all, she'd started it. She threw out Lisa's cigarettes. But what else could she do if that witch ignored all her requests! Nothing: as far as Sasha knew, Lisa was supposed to find a rental apartment and move relatively soon. And then Sasha could breathe easier. Oksana would never be a problem.

It couldn't come soon enough.

Five minutes remained until the end of the class. Sasha finished reading the section and wiped her moist forehead with a wet, weak palm.

"Samokhina, come over here."

Sasha jumped. Portnov stared at her directly over his glasses.

"I said, come over here."

Kostya threw her a worried glance. Awkwardly, Sasha climbed from behind her desk, stepping over her bag.

"Everyone, look at Samokhina."

Eighteen pairs of eyes—indifferent, sympathetic, some even gloating—stared at her in anticipation. Sasha couldn't stand it: she looked down.

"At this point, this girl has achieved the highest academic success. Not because of her talent—her abilities are fairly average. Some of you are significantly more talented. Yes, Pavlenko, that goes for you as well. Samokhina is ahead of your entire group because she works hard, while the rest of you are wearing out the seats of your pants."

Sasha was silent, her face burning. Some people's faces reddened as well. Lisa Pavlenko was the color of a ripe tomato. Kostya went pale.

Portnov held a long, weighty pause.

"Having demonstrated an excellent result, Samokhina gets a personal hands-on assignment. Speech is silver . . . all of your words are trash, garbage, not worth the air spent in speaking. Silence . . . Silence is what, Samokhina?"

"Golden," Sasha squeezed out.

"Golden. From this point on, Samokhina, you are to be silent. This exercise is intended to speed up certain processes, which are beginning to emerge, but are way too slow at this moment. You are not to speak a single word, neither here, nor outside. Nowhere at all. I forbid you."

Sasha looked up in astonishment. The bell rang in the hall.

"Class dismissed," Portnov said. "For tomorrow, Section 12, close reading, red text is to be memorized. Samokhina, that goes for you too. Study. Work hard."

That day Sasha missed her first gym class. She simply could not re-main among the crowds, even at the gym, even with such a lovely teacher as Dima Dimych.

Besides, Group A needed some time without her. They needed to discuss her in her absence. She understood perfectly well.

She went back to the dorm. Halfway there, she turned around. An empty smoke-filled room, the remains of her favorite makeup in the garbage can—chances are, all this would hardly cheer her up, so she left. Walked down the hall, and down the stairs.

Walked out of the school.

Sasha followed Sacco and Vanzetti toward the town center; she passed the post office and thought of Mom. How was she supposed to call her now?

Oddly, she never considered violating Portnov's taboo. But she wasn't sure she could have, anyway: her lips, tongue, and larynx ceased to obey. Forty minutes after the end of the last block she could not open her tightly clenched teeth.

It frightened her, especially when she suddenly felt incredibly thirsty. She purchased a bottle of mineral water at a grocery store, having to resort to gestures to explain to the salesperson what exactly she wanted. Only then her teeth unclenched and chattered on the glass lip of the bottle. Sasha drank the entire bottle greedily. Her stomach rumbled; she had to sit down in front of the post office.

She'd called Mom last Sunday. Mom had said that Valentin was back from Moscow, but their wedding had been postponed again. Despite everything, Mom sounded cheerful and unconcerned. *They are happy without me,* Sasha thought.

With that in mind, she went into the post office, gestured for one of the telegram slips, and wrote the following: "Everything fine will not be calling telephone broken." She gave the slip to the surprised woman behind the counter, paid for the telegram, and walked out again. Relieved, a thought hit her:

So now I'm the top student.

It's not surprising that Pavlenko blushed like that. But Sasha would give up her favorite lipstick—not just the lipstick, she'd give *anything*—for Pavlenko to be shown off, for her to be called the best student, despite her average talent, and forbidden to talk. And she, Sasha, would go to the gym with everybody else, and would chat about this curious episode, and tell Dima Dimych about it, and play ball, and sprawl on the stack of mats . . .

Why does she have to be silent? What can she possibly learn that way? What sort of "emerging processes"?

At first she planned on skipping Philosophy as well, but did not want to miss anything important. Her notes were becoming so logical, so harmonious, that she did not want to leave a gap in Plato's place. She went to class.

General lectures were attended by both Groups A and B. As usual, Kostya sat on one side of Sasha. Oksana settled on the other side.

"Congratulations," she whispered into Sasha's ear.

Sasha raised an eyebrow.

"'*The world of ideas (eidos) exists outside of time and space. This world has a certain hierarchy, on top of which is the idea of Good . . .*'"

"Portnov was heaping praises on you," Oksana babbled. "He says no one in our group even comes close to you . . ."

Sasha sighed.

"'*In the allegory of the cave, Good is portrayed as the Sun, and ideas symbolize the creatures and objects that pass in front of the Cave, and the Cave itself is a symbol of the material world with its illusions . . .*'"

"And the objects themselves—are they shadows of ideas?" Kostya asked out loud. "Projections?"

The professor began explaining. Sasha turned away—and caught Lisa staring at her from the opposite corner of the lecture hall.

"To a certain degree, this solves the problem. If Samokhina shuts up, living here is actually a possibility."

Sasha was silent. Lisa couldn't relax; she wandered between the beds in her underwear, picked something up from the floor and dropped it again, opened the wardrobe, and went through her suitcase.

"You were going to rent a place." Oksana scowled. "And get the hell out of here."

"I *am* getting out. I just don't have the time to deal with it. I'm leaving at some point, don't you worry."

"I am not worried."

"Well, you shouldn't!"

Oksana was the type who gets excited about other people's exclusivity, even the most minor kind, and who looks to befriend such a person. Lisa was one of those people who long for their own exclusivity and are offended to find themselves overshadowed.

Sasha could have said: there is no reason to envy, and no reason to be angry. Lisa herself said that this was not education and not any kind of science, but instead a clear case of shamanism, hypnosis, psychosis, and whatever else. So what should I be proud of—my accomplishments in psychosis?

But Sasha was silent. Her only attempt at speaking—last night, with Kostya, when she completely forgot about her ordeal—ended in grunting and spitting. Thinking of it made her feel ashamed.

Lisa opened the window wider. The cold September night smelled of dead grass and moisture. Lisa lit up demonstratively.

"We asked you not to smoke," said Oksana.

"Go to hell."

Sasha closed her eyes.

Meaningless sentences rotated in her brain like tank treads. Sasha was reading Section 20. It was the second week of her muteness, and it seemed as if the world around her was slowly descending into silence.

She felt like a blimp filled with soap bubbles. The bubbles—her unspoken words—rose up in her throat and crawled out, hung on her tongue, like clumsy acrobats on a trampoline. Then they popped, leaving a bitter aftertaste. Not a single word was strong enough to conquer the barrier, escape, and fly away.

"Your words are trash, garbage . . ." *Portnov was right,* Sasha thought. Words did not matter. Glance, inflection, voice—all these thin threads, the antennae pointing into space, informed people of indifference or empathy, calmness, anxiety, love . . . Words did not. And yet, without the words it was much harder.

She read *words,* though. Or, rather, she read gibberish, she memorized complete nonsense. All in vain: it was a Sisyphean task, the desperate efforts of the Danaides. An Indian summer followed the cold September days. Lisa Pavlenko never found an apartment. She continued smoking just as much, but by now Sasha was used to the constant smell of smoke. She had to write a paper for Philosophy class. Sasha chose Plato and went to the library, for some reason bringing her copy of the *Textual Module.* It was forbidden to talk in the tiny, confined reading room cramped with bookcases. Sasha was happy about it: nowhere else had she felt as mute as she did in a noisy crowd.

She strolled along the bookcases, then chose a seat by the window and opened the *Module,* purely automatically, unaware of her own intentions.

Only a few pages of the book remained unread. Sasha started the familiar process of scraping through the nonsensical combinations of letters. She kept reading until, suddenly, the words broke through the rasping in her brain:

"*. . . as enthralling as daylight; she perceived thoughts as a ray of sun . . .*"*

---

* Marina and Sergey Dyachenko, *Pandem*

Sasha jerked her head.

She was the only person in the reading room. The day outside the window approached nighttime. Through an open window she could smell a distant fire.

She tried to reread the paragraph, but nothing worked. She returned to the beginning—having forgotten about Plato and his eidos, about her paper, and the closing time of the reading room, she pored over *Textual Module* 1. Her headache grew. She felt as if a hundred metal spoons banged on iron pans behind a thin wall, but she kept reading and she could not stop, like a barrel tumbling down a hill.

"*. . . that makes its way down the corridor and then everything in the world gains the gift of speech; and the sunlight speaks to you . . .*"

The librarian who showed up to lock the room found Sasha prostrate over the open book.

She went to the post office and bought three graphed notebooks. A picture was on the back of the cover—a rippled mass of dots and squiggles. If one did not stare directly at the ripples, but instead unfocused and looked through the paper as if through glass, eventually the ripples gave way to a seemingly three-dimensional image: one notebook had an Egyptian pyramid, the other, a horse, and the third one, a fir tree. Some time ago, her physics teacher explained the principle of creating pictures like that, but Sasha had forgotten.

She walked down the street, notebooks under her arm. Something niggled at her—something about the very nature of her time at the institute. What it came down to, Sasha thought, was this: That which we are forced to learn has meaning. We do not comprehend it. But it is not just brainwashing, not just cramming: meaning seeps in through this sluggish mess just like a three-dimensional image rises out of dots and squiggles; it is not a "horse," and definitely not a "fir tree." Chances are this science cannot be described by a single word. Or even two words. Perhaps words that describe this science, this process, do not even exist. Not a single second year, not to mention the third years, had ever deemed it possible to even hint at what we are being taught here. Maybe Portnov—or some other teacher—made them silent? Maybe. Or, perhaps, they don't know that either.

Victor, the one-eyed third year, told her that after the winter finals his entire group would be going to "another location," where the fourth years and the graduates reside. Sasha thought of the third year of school, especially the winter finals, as something unbelievably distant, and she did not even feel any curiosity regarding where this "other location" was, or why the older students had to be separated . . .

Darkness came early now. The tops of the linden trees on Sacco and Vanzetti, just yesterday so thick and opaque, now let through the glow of the distant streetlights. Yet the unseasonable warmth did not allow one to believe in the yellow leaves underfoot or the upcoming winter. Sasha stood for a while, taking deep breaths and watching the stars over the tiled roofs of the town of Torpa. Eventually, though, she had to go inside. She had two choices: walk through the school building or through the narrow alleyway that led directly to the dorm. Having considered both options, Sasha decided to take the shortcut.

"Why are you playing hard to get?"

The whisper eventually grew into a low male voice.

"Why are you acting like a virgin? On Friday . . . in Vlad's room . . . that wasn't you, was it, huh?"

"Leave me alone." Sasha recognized Lisa Pavlenko's voice.

"C'mon, kitten . . ."

"Go to hell, you moron!"

Sasha stumbled on an empty bottle. The bottle clinked on the pavement; the voices ceased.

"Who's there?" the man asked.

Sasha could not answer. She turned around and, staggering on the rocks, exited the alley.

The key for room 21 hung on the board downstairs. Sasha grabbed it, jogged up to the second floor, made a short visit to the bathroom, and quickly brushed her teeth before climbing into bed.

Oksana was the first to return. She rustled her plastic bags (*where did she get all that crackling plastic?*), then settled in with great big sighs, turned a few pages of her textbook, clicked off the lamp, and went to sleep. Sasha lay in the dark, listening to anonymous laughing, shrieking, singing in the kitchen, the banging of dishes; Oksana slept undisturbed, but Sasha could not close her eyes.

"Sunlight speaks to you . . ."

Why did Sasha feel so happy when a meaningful sentence swam, all of its own accord, out of a sequence of letters? These words were familiar and grammatically correct, but an actual meaning was still missing—sunlight does not speak. Sunlight is a stream of photons characterized by a wave-particle duality . . .

One cannot imagine it anyway. It's the same thing as seeing a closed door from both sides simultaneously. By being both on the inside and the outside.

It's so incredibly stuffy in this room . . .

She tossed and turned, and then finally got up, opened the window, and gulped some fresh air. A streetlight burned outside, and its bright artificial rays poured over the windowsill with its many layers of white paint. A makeshift ashtray—a mayonnaise jar—stood in the corner of the window, and somebody's philosophy textbook lay forgotten.

Almost without thinking, Sasha opened the book in the middle. The first page she came across stated:

"According to Nominalism, universals are names of names, but not of absolute reality or notion . . ."

This phrase, too, has no meaning, Sasha thought in disappointment. And really, if one repeats the same word over and over again—"meaning, meaning, meaning"—it disintegrates into sounds, and becomes just as informative as the tinkling of water in a fountain, and . . .

She held her head. *Something is happening to me,* she admitted. Perhaps I am losing my mind. After all, second and third years look pretty much insane. All their idiosyncrasies. The occasional physical deformities. The way they come to a standstill, staring at some invisible point in space, or the way they overshoot for the door when they enter the kitchen, or how they "get stuck" in the middle of a simple movement, like rusty old machines . . .

Sometimes, of course, they seem fairly intelligent; they demonstrate a sharp sense of humor, occasionally they even sing fairly well . . .

"Nominalism dates back to antiquity. Its first representatives in early antiquity are Antisthenes of Athens and Diogenes of Sinope, both of whom opposed Plato's theory of 'the world of ideas . . .'"

Heavy steps sounded in the hall; before Sasha had a chance to jump into her bed, the door opened.

The light was on in the corridor, and their room was dark, so Sasha saw only a black cutout silhouette of a disheveled, ruffled girl. And Lisa—Sasha knew—saw a ghost in a flannel nightgown, awkwardly frozen in the middle of the room on the way to her bed.

"You are not asleep," Lisa stated.

Sasha could not speak, but neither did she want to. She got into bed and put a wall of blankets between herself and Lisa. She heard the door shut. Oksana sniffled in her sleep, but did not wake up.

The key turned in the lock. Taking tentative steps, Lisa walked over to the window. Sasha heard the click of a lighter.

"You know," said Lisa thoughtfully, "I don't really care what you think of me. What sort of thoughts swim in that tiny head of yours. I was in a dance troupe. Then *he* came . . . showed me a coin. Said: 'Remember this sign, not the zero, the other one.'" A drag from the cigarette. "'When a stranger approaches you and shows you a coin like that, you must go with him without any questions, and do everything he asks—also without any questions.' He said, 'I never ask for the impossible.' And the next day my boyfriend, Lyosha, was arrested for an alleged homicide. He didn't know the victim, he'd never even seen him, but they did a ballistics evidence test, and they had witnesses . . . Lyosha bought that gun illegally. He always said, a girl like me had to be protected. And then this random guy comes to me, forty years old, and pokes that coin at me. And I went with him, like a sheep. Next morning I threw up money. And two days after that, Lyosha was released. I don't know if his parents bribed someone, or maybe something else happened, but the witnesses and the gun—they all disappeared. Must have been a nice bribe. I know he never used that gun for shooting, maybe only shot a few bottles in the woods for practice. But those guys . . . they came to me every month. They stuck their coins under my nose. I spread my legs for all of them, and every morning I threw up money, and Lyosha was there, and he could feel something . . ." Another puff. "I quit dancing; there was no way I could still dance. Lyosha left me. And *he* . . . he says: I never ask for the impossible."

For a long time now Sasha's nose had been above the blanket. The room was filled with the smells of hangover breath and cigarettes. Oksana slept (or pretended to sleep), a sharp ray of light still lay on the windowsill, highlighting half of the pale face of the girl sitting on its edge.

The red end of a cigarette darted in the dark. It made loops in the air.

"Are you still mute? Whatever . . . is it written on my forehead? Why do they stick to me, and leave you alone?"

Sasha was silent. She couldn't think of anything to say even if she could.

"I suppose I loved him," Lisa's voice was unexpectedly sober, harsh. "I suppose I did, if I did it for his sake. Well, it does not matter anymore. I have a little brother. I have a grandma, she's old. There is a hook I can be caught with. Everyone has a hook . . . But why did he say: I don't ask for the impossible? I see this sign in my sleep now." The cigarette twitched, making circles in the air. "I began avoiding men, all of them. Lyosha went away, and did not leave me his number. And he says: 'I don't ask for the impossible!' Ah, to hell with all of this!"

And suddenly, jerking the window open, Lisa tumbled over the windowsill and disappeared.

A wet and sticky pile of leaves lay along the front garden, reaching about five feet at its peak. Shaking the leaves off her jeans, Lisa emerged out of the rustling pile and inspected her palms. She massaged her lower back.

Sasha was silent. She had run outside in her nightgown, barely getting a chance to stick her feet into sneakers.

Half the windows were lit, half were dark. Two stereo systems were blaring at the same time. Someone was dancing on a table, and shadows streaked behind closed curtains. Girls flying out of windows or running around the dark streets in their nightgowns did not shock or interest anyone.

Lisa swore through her teeth, her words pitiful and dirty. Nobody was there to laugh, be surprised or help out, and only Sasha stood there, wondering whether she should offer her classmate a hand or whether it would be considered an insult. At that moment, a sharp gust of wind flew through the unmoving linden trees, leaves fell like raindrops, and the stars vanished for a second and then lit up again.

Sasha could have sworn that a gigantic dark shadow flew over the dorm roof. More so, the shadow descended upon the antenna and stayed there, covering Cassiopeia. Sasha's mouth fell open . . .

The sensation was very quick, almost instantaneous. Stars blinked and lit up once again. Lisa, staring ahead, was already limping toward the entrance to the dorm, and Sasha, looking back cautiously, ran after her.

Lisa passed their room. She proceeded farther down the hall, where a door was opened, and where a battery of empty beer bottles stood by the entrance. Autumn leaves kept falling off Lisa's jeans; Sasha caught her war cry—"Party on, boys and girls!"—and, waiting for nothing else, ducked back into her own room, into the darkness.

Wind danced around the room; shaking and chattering her teeth, Sasha shut the rattling window. She shivered, longing for warmth, but the hot water was turned off, and making tea in the kitchen filled with all those people having so much fun simply was not an option.

Oksana stayed immobile, blanket thrown over her head. You are awake, Sasha wanted to tell her. You are simply hiding, waiting for the finale. Good for you—tomorrow you can say with an honest look on your face that you had no idea what was happening, you can admit to sleeping soundly the entire time . . .

Words bubbled up to her throat and, suddenly, without warning, flooded out. Bent over, Sasha fell onto the dirty linoleum and, with a fit of coughing, vomited the remains of her supper . . .

Along with a handful of dull gold coins.

That night the Indian summer ended as if finished off with a single hammer blow, and cold windy autumn took its place. Windows were now shut tightly, but the ceiling lamp swung in the cold, drafty air, and wind howled under the door as if traveling through a chimney.

The next day, Oksana begged the superintendent for two reams of paper for winterizing the windows and a roll of foam that resembled an octopus with its weak yellowish tentacles. While Sasha untangled the octopus and pushed the foam into cracks and crevices in the window frames, clever Oksana managed to score some flour and prepared a thick paste that looked like gray snot with a starchy smell. They did not have any brushes, but Sasha thought of using a piece of the foam to smear the flour paste onto paper ribbons. The paper lost its cheerful white color and starchy density, becoming limp, sticky, and pliable. *The paper becomes just like us,* thought Sasha, taping up the windows.

"Don't tape over the side pane," Oksana ordered. "We need it to air out the room."

Sasha touched the cold radiator. The heating season was nowhere in sight, and it reminded her of just how cold it could be, like when she stood here, last night, shivering. She had spent a long time collecting the coins, which had rolled all over the room. She'd wiped up the floor, then washed it. She'd then wrapped the coins in the first plastic bag she found and buried them in the suitcase under her bed before finally falling asleep. When they'd woken up to go to class, Lisa was in her bed, and she had stayed there for the first two blocks, recuperating, getting up only to attend Specialty.

It was a very difficult day: two blocks of Specialty, third and fourth. The class was reading sections of *Textual Module* 1. Somehow Portnov always knew whether a student was reading or studying a bug crawling over the page. The silence in the auditorium was occasionally broken by a sharp bark:

"Korotkov, work. Kovtun, pay attention!"

Sasha worked hard, waiting for the words—the other ones, the meaningful ones—to materialize out of the white noise, as they did in the library. But nothing happened. She was exhausted, developed a headache, and was now convinced that her experience in the reading room was just a figment of her imagination.

"Samokhina, how's the thumb twiddling going?"

She did not even notice how her attention had wandered, how she concentrated on a corner of the page. She thought she noticed a faint mark of a nail. Who'd read this book before her? One-eyed Victor? Or Zakhar, Kostya's roommate? Who entered any door only on the third try? Who'd put the note into the storage unit at the train station? What good could the note do?

"Samokhina." Portnov was standing next to her. "I am not pleased with your reading. You are goofing off—I did not expect it from you. Have you thought of a word worth saying out loud yet?"

Sasha was silent.

"Samokhina, you will remain silent until you realize why you need a secondary signaling system. Simians manage with having only the primary system, don't they?"

Sasha was silent.

"For tomorrow's one-on-one session"—Portnov took a few steps in front of the class—"repeat all the underlined paragraphs. Memorize them. Tag, you are it." He smirked. "Prefect, schedule Samokhina for the last time slot."

Sasha kept asking herself over and over again: What if Kozhennikov had given the same assignment to her as he had given to Lisa? Considering that for Sasha even skinny-dipping in the wee hours of the morning—when no one was watching—was a colossal ordeal . . .

"I don't ask for the impossible."

Lisa's hatred, then, toward Kostya was not surprising. Even though it had nothing to do with Kostya. The very name of Kozhennikov made Sasha's own skin crawl.

Sasha's classmates took turns entering auditorium 38. Upon exiting, their faces were different: some angry, some anxious, some girls were clearly crying. That was Portnov for you, yes. He knew how to make your blood boil.

Sasha was the last one to enter. The fourth block had ended, the fifth just begun. In the third-floor gym a table tennis class was about to start.

"You are losing steam," Portnov stated drily. "You are not working as hard as before. Look at me."

The ring he wore only for the one-on-one sessions approached Sasha's face. She blinked at the sharp flash of blue light.

"Keep looking, don't turn your face . . . I see. Sit down."

Only a few chairs fit in the small auditorium. Sasha lowered herself gingerly onto the wooden chair nearest her, which had a dangerously twisted leg.

"Do you feel yourself changing on the inside?" Portnov asked softly.

Sasha nodded.

"Good. That is what should be happening. Any change—vision, hearing, memory—should not alarm you. I'm going to give you one more book, a set of exercises. You'll have to work harder"—at that, she started, but he quickly continued—"don't worry, your back will not break. You will do five exercises for me each week. They must be done mentally, only mentally, one after another, without any mistakes. I will be checking, Samokhina, checking every one of them very carefully. And if you twiddle your thumbs like you did yesterday—well, you are taking the risk of remaining an invalid for the rest of your life. *Your* life, not mine. Is that clear?"

Someone knocked on the door. Sasha still had five minutes left, and she was surprised at the interruption.

It was Kostya. He was anxious to the point of losing all his instincts for self-preservation.

"Oleg Borisovich . . . There . . . Phone at the front desk . . . Samokhina got a phone call. It's a long-distance call, her mother is calling . . ."

Sasha froze. She looked at Portnov. He shifted his glasses farther down his nose and glanced at Kostya, who hunched over under his stare.

"It's her mother. I thought . . . Something may have happened . . ."

"You are dismissed," Portnov's voice was full of ice. "Samokhina, take the book."

Out of his desk drawer he pulled a fat volume, bright red, with the familiar pattern of blocks on its cover.

Blocking out every thought but the one about Mom, Sasha grabbed the book. She caught herself right before leaving the auditorium and nodded a curt good-bye to Portnov. She walked out; Kostya took long strides, almost running in front of her.

"Come on, hurry up, the attendant said she'd wait. It's a restricted office phone, actually . . ."

Sasha was not listening.

Here was the hallway with the gigantic equestrian statue. Here was the glass booth of the guard; here was a custodian in a blue robe, and here was the black plastic receiver next to the phone, and a spiral cable . . .

Sasha clutched the receiver, put it next to her ear, and listened to the silence. Mom was waiting; helpless, Sasha turned to Kostya. He seized the receiver from her and yelled, for some reason very loudly:

"She'll be right there! She's fine, she is a good student—yes, the dorm rooms are heated!"

Sasha heard Mom's voice changed by cables and distance. Mom was saying something to Kostya, her words fast, ringing, and anxious.

"No!" Kostya shouted. "She . . . she's lost her voice a little. You know, I don't think she can leave the class at the moment, we have one-on-ones right now . . . Did something happen? You can tell me, I'll pass it along . . ."

Mom began speaking again. She sounded high-strung and on edge; Sasha took a step forward, snatched the receiver from Kostya, and—amazingly, *finally*—spoke.

"Mom, what is going on? What happened?"

"Sasha, sweetheart, is that you? Why didn't you call? Those telegrams of yours . . . I haven't heard your voice in a month! Why didn't you call, you nasty creature?"

"So everything is good?" Sasha asked, bewildered.

"No, it's not good! Because you have not called! Valentin and I are going crazy! I had such a tough time reaching you . . . Are you healthy? What do you eat? What was this kid telling me about you losing your voice?"

Kostya stood in front of her. The attendant on duty kept throwing worried glances at Kostya and Sasha.

"I haven't lost my voice." Sasha tried not to cry. "Everything is fine."

Portnov stopped her near the back entrance. It was clearly against his rules, meeting his students in the hall; he usually did nothing more than nod curtly.

"Samokhina, come with me."

"I have table tennis."

"You just got your speech back, and your nose is already growing."

Sasha lowered her eyes. She hadn't had a chance to sign up for tennis.

"I thought you'd still be silent for a couple of months," Portnov murmured. "Although . . . Come on, I need someone to see you."

Sasha obeyed. They went to the basement, passed the dining hall—closed at this hour of the day—and then went even lower. Sasha had never been in this area of the school before.

"My colleague's name is Nikolay Valerievich Sterkh," Portnov said. "He'll be working with you later in the process . . . I hope."

They walked down a wide corridor, following a row of doors upholstered in brown imitation leather. Portnov stopped in front of one such door, one with a plaque that said RECEPTION. Without knocking, he peeked in, nodded to someone on the other side of the door, and gestured for Sasha to enter.

Indeed, it was a reception area, just the way Sasha imagined it. A large desk, several bookcases, a switchboard, a selection of office supplies. A young woman—secretary?—in a revolving chair.

Sasha was still breathing heavily, and her eyelashes were stuck together like arrows. On one hand, she experienced tremendous relief. On the other, she had an acute sense of guilt about her mother. On the third hand—and there was a third hand—she was aggravated and deeply offended by Portnov.

"Is Nikolay Valerievich available?" he asked.

The secretary nodded, pushed a button, and whispered:

"Nikolay Valerievich, Oleg Borisovich is here to see you." She motioned to the door covered with black leather.

Portnov moved to enter, leading Sasha in front of him, like a miner pushing a coal wagon. Sasha walked to the middle of a spacious, windowless office—and stopped.

A man with a gray, ashy face was sitting behind a large desk, opposite a lit table lamp. Long silver hair fell onto his shoulders. His smoothly shaven chin looked sharp enough to cut its owner's chest at any sudden movement. In addition to all this, he had a hump, and his black suit jacket folded into ridges on his curved back.

"Nikolay, I want you to take a look at her," Portnov said without any preamble. "Just in case."

The man rose from behind the desk. He threw back his shoulders, stretching out his numb back. He took a few steps toward Sasha: she went still, like a frog in front of a heron.

Like everything else about the man, the hunchback's eyes were gray, almost without pupils. Only tiny black dots, like poppy seeds, in the middle of enormous, storm cloud irises.

"Alexandra Samokhina." The hunchback had a low, dullish voice. "Seventeen years old. Ah, to be seventeen again . . ."

Hitching up his left sleeve, the hunchback uncovered a bracelet on his wrist. It was not a watch, as Sasha thought at first. It was a convex metal badge on a leather band. Its instantaneous burst of light flashed into Sasha's eyes and made her squint.

"Samokhina," the hunchback repeated; for a second, Sasha thought his voice quivered. "My dear, please wait in the reception room for a few minutes."

Sasha left. The secretary was openly busy with her knitting, something pink and fluffy. Silently, Sasha sat down on the leather sofa near the window.

Even a short while ago she'd probably have said something to the secretary. She'd want to signify her presence with some simple words, common interaction between humans: I am here because of this, and need that, and will be leaving at this time . . .

Yet the prolonged silence that ended only half an hour ago made her personality more somber than could be expected. Or, perhaps, it was not only about the silence?

Portnov came out in fifteen minutes, not five. He nodded to the secretary and escorted Sasha along the corridor back up the staircase, and one more staircase, into the hall; Kostya was sitting in the shadow of the enormous equestrian. There was absolutely no one else in the huge empty space. Even the guard's glass booth was empty.

"Go and work hard," Portnov said, addressing Sasha, but looking at Kostya. "You have a great deal of outstanding work to do, mountains of work, an entire ocean. If I were you, I wouldn't waste precious time on any nonsense."

"Good-bye," Sasha said.

Portnov glanced at her sharply over his glasses. He smirked and departed. Only then Sasha realized how exhausted she was. And how heavy the bag on her shoulder was. And how all she wanted to do was to lie down, close her eyes, and think about nothing at all.

She sat down on a granite pedestal next to Kostya and leaned back into the bronze hoof.

"You know what I don't get?" Kostya mused. "This thing, this horse, I mean, it wouldn't fit through any door. Which means that first they made the statue, and then they built the school around it. How is that possible?"

Sasha shrugged silently.

"What did he want from you?" Kostya asked softly.

Sasha took her new textbook out of her bag. It looked worse for the wear, faded red, worn out.

"What is it?" Kostya asked.

Sasha opened the book. There was no introduction, no author's name, no explanations. Just "Exercises, Stage One."

"That's better," Kostya noted. "At least, the words are familiar."

"'Number One. Imagine a sphere, in which the exterior surface is red and the interior surface is white. Maintaining the continuity of the sphere, mentally distort the sphere so that the external surface is on the inside, and the internal on the outside—'"

"How?" Sasha asked helplessly.

Kostya took the book out of her hands, glanced at the page, and gave the book back to her.

"How is your head?"

This question, with its precision and its double meaning, made her laugh despite her exhaustion.

"My head does not hurt. Yeah. If that's what you meant."

It was cold. And it was raining. Water sputtered in the drainpipes. Sasha went through her entire suitcase, realizing that she arrived at school in the summer, wearing jeans and a T-shirt. The pile of clothes that Mom stuffed into her suitcase despite her loud protests—the pile that seemed so bulky and so unnecessary—was now not only essential, but almost too flimsy in the face of the approaching winter: a jacket; one thick woolen sweater, and one a bit lighter; a pair of woolen socks; a pair of tights to go over pantyhose.

Despite the winterized windows, it was chilly and raw at the dorm: the hot water was turned off again. They washed themselves using basins and water heated up in a large pot in the kitchen. Laundry hung over cold radiators remained wet overnight and even longer.

And yet none of that misery compared to Sasha's exercises.

"Imagine two spheres, one with a larger diameter, the other smaller. Mentally place the first sphere inside the second ensuring that the diameters of both spheres do not change . . ."

Doing these was even worse than reading nonsensical paragraphs and memorizing gibberish. Portnov distributed the exercise books to Group A, then, a day later, to Group B. Besides that, each first year received a new *Textual Module* with a number 2 on its cover, and every day they *also* had to read and memorize paragraphs. English, History, Philosophy—everything went down the tubes, and students were constantly running out of time. Only the gym class—where sweet Dima Dimych offered the first years basketball, volleyball, and elements of dance aerobics instead of long-distance races and qualifying standards—served as a ray of light shining through the granite wall of never-ending cramming.

Sasha's deadline, Saturday, was approaching without pity, and out of five exercises, she'd barely managed two. Closing her eyes in the dark at night, she watched all those spheres, spirals, and tubes that refused to slip through the other ones, the ones with smaller diameters. The exercises made her eyes itchy and her throat sore.

"Sasha, we're sending the boys on a vodka run," Oksana informed her on her way back from the kitchen. "Give me some money, and you can join us. You're growing mossy here."

"I don't drink vodka."

"Mix it with Pepsi then."

"Listen, I have five exercises due tomorrow, and I—"

"All work and no play! You can pull an all-nighter. Come with us—at least you'll get warm!"

Sasha wavered.

"Can I bring Kozhennikov?"

"Sure! Just tell him to bring something to eat or drink. We're going to be in the second-floor kitchen. Come on over!"

Lisa sat at the desk in front of an open textbook, staring at a point in space without blinking. Perhaps at this very moment she was turning imaginary spheres inside out as well.

Or perhaps she was remembering something from the past. Sasha did not have the guts to speak with her since she'd regained her gift of speech. She got up and quietly left the room.

Kostya, exhausted and slightly under the weather, did not resist. His roommates, second years, had left for a party of their own. In one of their side tables Kostya found a cheap can of anchovies in tomato sauce.

"I'll pay Zakhar back later," Kostya promised, either to Sasha or to himself. "Let's go."

The kitchen was hot and filled with smoke.

"Group A has arrived!" Oksana shrieked, handing them two clean plastic cups. "Here's to the eternal friendship between our groups, the first two letters of the alphabet!"

Kostya drank half a glass of vodka and got so smashed that he requested more right away. The can of anchovies was immediately dissected with a rusty can opener and passed around: with an aluminum cafeteria spoon, students grabbed hold of the tiny, lifeless fish in the depth of bloodred tomato sauce and plopped them onto thick slices of rye bread. The sauce spread in a bloody puddle; the can was passed further. Sasha and Kostya made themselves a couple of sandwiches and perched on a lukewarm radiator. Sasha found a bottle of Pepsi on the counter and added it to the vodka in her cup; the result was sweet and reasonably alcoholic.

"I'm not sorry for my chance encounters, I just know that on one of these perfect days . . ." A guy from Group B was singing, his voice beautiful and poignant. Sasha remembered only his first name, Anton.

She was tipsy.

In the warm kitchen, with an anchovy in her teeth, in a cloud of cigarette smoke, she felt free. And, therefore, happy.

Kostya's hand landed on her shoulder.

"And all will return!" A tuneless choir of female voices filled the room. *"Everything will certainly return! And this world, and fine weather, and the circle of my friends!"*

Sasha hugged Kostya with all her might. Right now he was the most precious person in the world to her. More so than Mom. Because she was too old to hug Mom like that, and Kostya had strong arms and large hands, and his ribs could be felt through his sweater. Sasha thought of how only a year ago she'd dreamed of sitting like this, with a group of friends, next to a boy, and hugging him, and drinking out of a plastic cup, and singing, and laughing . . .

"Guys!" somebody yelled, bursting into the kitchen. "Hot water is back on in the showers!"

The "guys" roared happily in response, like a crowd of fans at the stadium. Kostya leaned toward Sasha and kissed her on the lips. Sasha tried to elude him—at first, she thought it was unpleasant—but then gave in.

And a minute later, she realized that she liked it.

"Haven't you ever kissed anyone before?"

Sasha wanted to say that she was an ogre among normal girls, that she spent the golden years of her youth behind a writing desk, but couldn't quite manage. Kostya knew how to kiss, he was perfectly normal, and even good-looking, not a loser like her . . .

But she just shrugged, smiling shyly.

They stepped out of the kitchen. Kostya had the foresight to pour some vodka into the half-empty bottle of Pepsi, and now they could drink the sweet liquid straight out of the bottle.

"And the crimson chimes of sunrise . . ." The song continued in the kitchen.

Sasha had not noticed how they'd ended up in Kostya's room. Zakhar and Lenya, the third roommate, were still out. Kostya lowered Sasha onto his bed, took a gulp from the bottle, sat down next to her, and pulled off his sweater.

"Let's . . . I'll lock the door from the outside. I mean, the inside. Come on!"

They fell on the bed in a tight embrace. The bedsprings groaned piteously.

"Have you ever . . . ?"

Kostya was trying to undo Sasha's bra, but the rotten little hooks clung to their loops.

"What the . . ."

Giving up, Kostya slid his hand underneath the elastic. Sasha arched her back, instinctively following a well-known scheme. Back in high school, her girlfriends convinced one another that in bed a woman was supposed to be passionate, and that meant to arch your back just like this . . .

Kostya was unzipping Sasha's jeans. It was terrifying and spellbinding. It was beautiful and appalling. A cold wind flew into the half-opened window. Kostya tugged on Sasha's panties; abruptly, she twisted away and sat up.

"Come on . . . Sasha . . ."

She slid from under his skinny, sweaty body. The enchantment of the evening was melting fast, the light-headedness was now replaced with nausea. Kostya's hands, suddenly very aggressive, pulled the white cotton panties off her, and at that moment Sasha leaned over the side of the bed and vomited a handful of gold coins.

"Did I tell you how important this was? Did I warn you?"

"I tried," Sasha said, staring at a half-circle scratch on the desk. "I tried. But I . . ."

"You owed me five exercises. You barely managed two. That's less than half!"

"I tried my best . . ."

"You tried your best? You drank like a sailor, and you spread your legs in bed!"

Sasha raised her eyes. Her cheeks, pale just a second ago, now became burning hot, the skin about to burst.

"That's not true. Why are you speaking like that to me?"

"Because you deserve it, Samokhina. Because you are a little bitch who has a great talent and is flushing it down the toilet. I refuse to deal with you. Now you're Farit Kozhennikov's responsibility—you're his charge, and his responsibility."

Sasha closed her eyes for a second. She thought of Lisa. "I don't ask for the impossible."

"Wait," she said, trying to stay calm. "I will do seven exercises by next Saturday."

"Ten. As well as the first two. Numbers one through twelve."

Sasha stared at him. Portnov stared back, over his glasses as usual.

"Ten . . ." she whispered. "Ten . . ."

"And you will polish the first two. Numbers one through twelve. And every day—a paragraph from the basic textbook."

Sasha was silent. She no longer cared.

▪ ▪ ▪

The first thing she did after leaving the school building was call Mom. She didn't really know why. She just needed to make sure everything was all right at home, and she needed to hear Mom's voice. Immediately.

Darkness fell, the rain stopped, then started again. The wind twisted her umbrella inside out. Sasha fixed the warped spokes, shook the water off her boots and her umbrella, and stepped into the warmth of the post office, filled with yellow light and the smell of sealing wax. A couple of people stood in line for long-distance calls. Sasha sat down in a corner to wait.

Today she missed three blocks—Philosophy, History and PE—the entire schedule, with the exception of Specialty. Everywhere she looked, she saw derisive sneers and meaningful glances, as if everyone knew in minute detail about all the pathetic and hilarious things that had happened last night in Kostya's room.

And she simply could not face Kostya. She felt humiliated and ashamed, and she had absolutely no idea how her life was supposed to go on. How was she going to deal with him on a daily basis?

The line stalled; a woman in the long-distance booth kept talking, nodding, agreeing, and laughing into the receiver. Sasha watched her through the dark glass; the woman seemed happy, the illusory telephone connection—the wires and cables—did not seem to bother her, and only the person on the other end of the line, the one she listened to and probably loved, was real to her.

A week remained until Saturday, her deadline for the one-on-one session. Ten exercises . . . Unfeasible. "I will not ask for the impossible," Kozhennikov had said.

He'd lied.

She took her textbook out of her bag, opened to the same first page and began exercise number three:

"Without using projection and hidden mirrors, envision a non-transparent rectangular parallelepiped so that four of its panes are clearly visible. Mentally distort the parallelepiped so that . . ."

The woman finally left the long-distance booth, her place taken by an old man with a gray mustache. The connection was lousy, and the old man must have been slightly deaf; he kept yelling something about the two hundred rubles that somebody's nephew owed somebody else . . . and Sasha could not picture any parallelepiped: not a parcel post, not a package of pasta, not even an ordinary brick.

"Exercise number five: in succession, repeat exercises one through four, avoiding pauses or any interruptions. Exercise number six . . ."

Sasha saw Kostya's face, with its lower lip sticking out like the rim of a pitcher. How revolting that whole thing was, how stupid and disgusting . . . And those anchovies in tomato sauce—the gold coins were smeared in red, as if covered in blood. Sasha had crawled on the floor in her underwear, picking up the coins, overcome by nausea because of that stupid vodka and Pepsi mixture . . .

A general assembly was scheduled for tomorrow in the assembly hall after the fourth block. There would be no way out of this, she'd have to go with everyone else, and bear the suggestive looks, the laughter, and deal with Kostya's presence . . .

"Miss, are you asleep? Are you planning on making that phone call?"

Snapping out of her trance, Sasha bolted to the phone booth and picked up the still warm receiver. Beep . . . another beep . . . one beep after another.

"The person you are trying to reach is not responding."

Sasha checked the time. Half past seven. Mom should be home by now.

She sat back down. The hour hand on the round clock above the door very slowly approached eight. Sasha read a section from the second textbook. Steel axles and chipped gears rotated inside her head, grinding together. The person she was trying to reach was not responding; somewhere, in an empty flat, the telephone kept on ringing.

"Miss, the post office closes at eight."

"Please try dialing again."

"There is no answer. Perhaps they went to the theater?"

Sasha walked out into the rain and darkness. Two rows of buildings on Sacco and Vanzetti Street hovered over her: empty balconies, peeling plaster, glistening cobblestones. Naked linden trees. Of course, Mom and Valentin could be at the theater. Or at a party. And it was absolutely normal that Mom was not home when, out of the blue, Sasha felt like calling her . . .

She walked along the edge of the sidewalk, umbrella hanging by her side. Raindrops beat on her hood. Fallen leaves turned slimy and musty, losing all their poetic beauty. Water flowed between the stones in the pavement.

A car drove by toward the center of town, a Zhiguli stained by moist dirt. The yellow hands of the headlights snatched the tree trunks and walls for a split second, reflected like flames in each cobblestone, drowned in the darkness, and disappeared. Darkness fell again, and only occasional lit windows and distant streetlights illuminated the road for Sasha.

A gust of wind made the nearest linden tree shake and toss raindrops and its last few leaves on the ground. Sasha shivered and pulled her hood farther down on her head. For some reason, she thought of that warm starry night when Lisa fell out the window. Why did she think of that? Maybe the sensation was similar . . . The same gust of wind, as if something dark flew over the sky. Sasha thought that, in its despair and helplessness, Lisa's "suicide" was analogous to her and Kostya's "love" . . .

"Good evening, Sasha."

She turned her head. A second ago she was alone in the street.

"Why aren't you using an umbrella? Is it some sort of a new fad with young people—soaking down to their bones?"

It took Sasha a few seconds to recognize the very tall man with a hump and long gray hair tumbling from under his hat now standing next to her, wearing a dark coat and carrying a large black umbrella. Nikolay Valerievich.

"Hello," she said, more nervous than polite.

"You must be freezing. Would you like a cup of coffee?"

She'd never been in this restaurant before, even though she'd noticed the sign the few times she'd passed it before. The restaurant was definitely not geared toward students; Sasha's wet jacket was removed by a cloakroom attendant in a black sports coat. A fire burned in the room separated from the common area with heavy drapes, and Sasha immediately held out her hands, red from the cold.

"Will you have anything to eat?"

"Just coffee . . ."

"Perhaps a sandwich?"

"Well . . ."

"Caviar, salmon, ham?"

"Ham," Sasha chose, thinking ham might be cheaper.

Nikolay Valerievich moved his shoulders. The gesture seemed

habitual for him; Sasha couldn't stop thinking that his hump must make him uncomfortable, as if something were folded awkwardly, rolled up, and crumpled on his back, under his jacket.

"Sasha, tell me about your parents."

She did not expect that question. Actually, she had no idea what to expect.

"Mom's a designer. I have no father."

"Is he dead?"

"No. They divorced, and . . . we haven't communicated in many years."

"Who sent you to the institute? Farit?"

Sasha swallowed. "Yes."

The waiter placed a cup of coffee in front of Sasha and a large snifter of cognac in front of her companion. A few inches from Sasha's nose appeared a platter filled with tiny sandwiches: caviar, ham, salami, cheese, and smoked salmon crowned by leafy greens leading an intricate dance under the yellow sails of lemon slices.

Sasha realized that she was ravenous. And had been for a while. She'd missed lunch, and she hadn't even tried to eat breakfast. Everywhere she looked, she saw those stupid anchovies in tomato sauce.

"Lean college years," Nikolay Valerievich murmured to himself. "How about a main course? Cutlets? Pork chop? Soup?"

"Pork chop . . . Thank you."

"Don't mention it. Sasha, do you have any idea what sort of institute you have been accepted to, and what you are being taught?"

Sasha swallowed once more, but this time said, "No."

Her companion nodded.

"No one even asked me!" Sasha said bitterly. "No one wondered whether I even want to study here or not. I was forced. We're not being taught, we are being trained, or brainwashed, humiliated, and . . ."

She stopped short. Nikolay Valerievich was smiling, as if she'd said something amusing.

"That's a perfectly ordinary situation, Sasha. You don't want to learn? But what *do* you want? Look into your soul, and you will realize: all you really want is fun and pleasure. Any instance of learning is coercion. Any form of culture must be enforced, alas. You are immature internally, and you must be forced, and forced cruelly. All of you hate Farit . . . and without a good reason."

Sasha was no longer hungry. She sat at the table, her head hanging low.

"Well now," the hunchback said softly. "Don't be upset. You're one of the best, Sasha. And you have a bright, interesting future ahead of you. A really big future. Now take another bite, will you?"

Sasha forced down a sandwich. She chewed half of her pork chop, leaving the sides untouched. She drank the cooling cup of coffee and then one more cup, fresh and hot, and then a large cup of tea with lemon. The whole time Nikolay Valerievich sipped his cognac and watched her across the table. His pupils looked unnaturally narrow, like poppy seeds, both in the light and in the semidarkness.

"I will be teaching you next year," said the hunchback. "And then during third year as well. I am really counting on you, Sasha. It will be very interesting to work with you. Does Oleg Borisovich give you a lot of homework?"

Sasha gave him a sardonic smile.

"You see, it is really necessary," Nikolay Valerievich said seriously. "It is difficult, but you must try hard, Sasha. Try not to pay any attention to this way of life, the disorder, the unsettled state of everyday affairs. Work hard. And you and I shall meet again. In a while . . ."

Leaving the restaurant, Sasha strolled along the streets. The rain ended, the wind died down, and stars peeked through the shredded clouds; this blazing magnificence was worth taking a little time before going back to the stuffy room. She returned late. To her enormous joy, both Oksana and Lisa were already in bed.

Sasha turned on her desk lamp, sat down, folding her legs under her, wrapped herself in a blanket, and opened the exercise book.

On Monday, after classes ended, the entire first-year body congregated in the assembly hall. Portnov paced up and down the stage; an irate-looking superintendent occupied one of the corners.

"What is this?" Portnov asked, holding up a book with a soft gray cover.

No one knew the answer. The audience fidgeted on squeaky chairs, chewed gum, and spoke softly to one another.

"This is a set of additional exercises for first years. In this case, it is a set of penalty exercises."

The audience ceased fussing.

"In the last few weeks I have received too many complaints about the first-year students, who behave abominably in their dormitory with their drinking binges and debauchery. Why did you come here? To get drunk on vodka? Or maybe you're here to smash windows, break doors, and dismantle faucets? Copulate with whoever is available?"

"Tell them to turn on the heat," said a grim voice from the back row.

"You'll have your heat, Komarov. After the meeting, take this textbook and do exercises one through three. Your deadline is your individual session on Saturday."

The auditorium was absolutely still.

"Starting today," Portnov informed them wearily, "consumption of alcoholic beverages is strictly forbidden in this dormitory. Any type of alcoholic beverages. Raids will be conducted regularly. If I find half a bottle of beer in anyone's room, I will be assigning ten exercises, and don't even think of not completing them."

Sasha was sitting at the end of the first row. Kostya sat behind her, in the third row, diagonally. She sensed his presence. Portnov's every word resonated in her head like the growl of a low-flying airplane.

"Is everybody clear on this?"

Silence.

"Return to the dormitory and check your rooms. All the alcoholic beverages are to be emptied into the sink and the bottles returned to the recycling center. If anyone gets drunk tonight, I guarantee he or she will not have a free minute up until New Year's Eve. Even more so, he or she will not have any time for sleep. That's all, you are dismissed."

The hall filled with the slapping sounds of emptying seats. Sasha picked up her bag from the armrest and moved toward the exit, avoiding eye contact.

This time there was no line at the post office. Sasha listened to one or two beeps, and then Mom picked up the phone—apparently Sasha's unexpected phone call really surprised her. Of course, they were just fine. Yesterday they went to Irina's birthday party and took a cab back home; it was late, after midnight. Was anything wrong?

Sasha listened to her unconcerned voice, thinking that Mom must look younger these days. She and Valentin were happy together. As strange as it was, Farit Kozhennikov was right: three's a crowd, and Sasha would have been in the way. Nothing had happened, no accidents, no catastrophes, no illnesses; all of it existed only in Sasha's feverish mind . . .

She hung up and left the post office, relieved.

She walked and ran through her exercises at the same time. Her feet tripped upon each other. An old woman glanced at Sasha suspiciously: she must have thought the girl was plastered. Sasha stopped to rest and leaned on a wrought-iron bench. The sun was setting; orange flames burned in the windows in the building across the street.

"Take the mental formation you accomplished as a result of exercise seven and reconfigure it so that its projection on any imagined surface is shaped as a circle . . ."

And take this text, underlined in red, impossible to commit to memory, which must be memorized.

Darkness came early. A desk lamp was lit in the room smelling of stale cigarette smoke. A book was open in front of Sasha. The dormitory was unusually quiet. Oksana busied herself with transferring moonshine from its container to a hot water bottle purchased at a nearby drugstore. Lisa ran out of cigarettes, took a trip around the dorm, and came back with half a pack. None of what they did mattered to Sasha. Pulling a second (or third?) all-nighter in a row, she was cranking the sequence of exercises in her head. In a cloudy broth of insomnia she was beginning to feel that she was thinking somebody else's thoughts. The thoughts felt so foreign to her that they didn't even fit in her head. Sasha imagined that processing these thoughts was just as difficult as picking up a pen with a horse's hoof.

She was afraid of falling asleep over the book, but the exercises kept her awake, like bright lights or loud music. Swollen eyelids itched, and every now and then she had to stretch her aching back. Tomorrow (actually, today already) was Tuesday—Portnov was going to check her knowledge of the paragraphs. So at four in the morning, Sasha put aside *Exercises* and opened *Textual Module* 2. In this one, the paragraphs were longer than in *Textual Module* 1, and each one of them ended in almost a full page underlined in red.

I can't read this, Sasha thought, staring at the page scattered with the discordant nonsensical words. *I cannot commit this to memory. Let Farit do what he must.*

Many hours of studying did something to her head. She felt like a crystal: transparent, fragile, and perfectly calm. Like a dangling icicle. Like an apathetic chunk of glass. She tried to cry, as a child tries riding a scooter after a long winter break. She eventually managed. Large tears rolled down her cheeks, but Sasha felt neither sadness nor despair, nor any emotions whatsoever—as if her tears came out of an open faucet.

She stopped crying—again, simply by willing herself to stop. Wiped her cheeks. She harnessed herself into the text and pulled it; she felt as if she were untangling a knot of barbed wire with her eyes.

". . . fear of death and did not find it . . . There was no fear because there was no death . . ."*

She kept going. That first time, in the library, the erupted meaning was bright blue. This time, it was gray, with a dull shine—steely, almost. Very disconnected. Sasha understood almost nothing aside from "fear of death." She continued reading anyway, hoping for another eruption, but the lines stretched like rusty centipedes, leaving footprints in her brain, and their meaning eluded her.

At seven in the morning an alarm clock went off under Oksana's bed.

In the bathroom mirror, a monster with a wrinkled pale countenance and red inflamed eyes stared back at Sasha. Her pupils contracted oddly and seemed very small; she blinked several times, trying to figure out what was wrong with her own reflection. Her pupils went back to normal about ten minutes later.

She skipped Math and English. Put some makeup on to look a bit more normal. She walked the school corridors, head low to the ground, avoiding her classmates. Today's schedule of individual sessions was posted on the bulletin board: Sasha had the three thirty slot. She hid in a far corner, hopped onto the windowsill, and stretched her tired legs.

Seventy-two hours without sleep. She'd never thought she was capable of that. But she did not even feel sleepy. Forty-five minutes remained until her time with Portnov; she leaned on the wall to run through the underlined text one more time and lowered her lids for just a moment.

When she opened her eyes, the window was dark. And the hallway was dark. Around the corner only a day lamp was on.

Sasha jumped, covered in cold sweat. She looked at her watch—ten minutes before six; the individual sessions had ended an hour ago.

---

* Leo Tolstoy, *The Death of Ivan Ilyich,* translated by Leo Wiener

She ran. Her steps resonated in the empty corridor. The door of auditorium 38 was locked; Sasha tugged it a few times, hoping for a miracle. She looked around. Alexandra Samokhina was the only human being in the entire long dimly lit corridor. Silence prevailed within the institute, and only somewhere above her, laughter and screaming could be heard as table tennis players congregated at the door of the gym.

Sasha adjusted the bag on her shoulder and went down the hall. She did not know why. She probably should be going to the dorm. She probably could not change anything at this point. Perhaps as early as tomorrow she would have to explain to Portnov . . . At the very thought of explaining anything to Portnov, Sasha started crying, this time for real, out of pity for herself.

"Where have you been?"

Kostya leapt at her out of the shadows, from underneath the bronze belly of the horse.

"Where the hell have you been? I tried . . . I went everywhere, chased everyone down, changed the schedule, made sure somebody took your slot, and then more people . . . more changes . . . I kept thinking you'd show up . . . I waited until the last possible moment! Where *were* you?"

"I fell asleep," Sasha said, letting her tears flow. "I memorized everything. Last night. I fell asleep."

"Damn," Kostya said after a pause. "You should have seen . . . He totally lost it. He yelled at me, at everyone else. All because you did not show up."

Sasha sat down on the granite pedestal and wrapped her arms around herself. Kostya sat next to her. The way he was sitting there, silently, his side touching her side, the way he was sniffling and staring directly in front of them, made Sasha catch her breath and momentarily hate herself. She hated herself for staying away from him. For the anchovies in tomato sauce. For avoiding eye contact and missing classes. For everything.

"I wanted to go twice," Kostya said. "For myself and then for you."

She broke down sobbing. Going to the individual session with Portnov twice was equivalent to dying twice; Kostya was ready to do that for her, and she had run out of his bed, thrown up all over his room, and thumbed her nose at him for nearly a week!

"Is he gone yet?" she asked through her tears.

Kostya shrugged. "He's still at school. I've been here for a while, since the one-on-ones finished up. He hasn't left yet. Listen, what if I go tell him that I found you, tell him you are sick? Passed out . . . Why not?"

Because Sasha was shaking her head. Lying to Portnov equaled suicide. Kostya's volunteering to be the messenger equaled self-sacrifice.

"I'll go see him myself." She was conscious of her tears causing her mascara to cover her face in black streaks; but it was all that damn snot that made her nose swell up and redden. "Before he leaves. Let him do what he wants."

"He's livid! Don't go now—let him cool down a little bit."

"Cool down? *Portnov?*"

Sasha got up. The concierge in the glass booth gaped at her with bewilderment and sympathy.

"Just wait for me," Sasha said feebly. "It'll be easier for me if I know you're waiting."

Kostya nodded.

Sasha went downstairs, toward the dining hall door, closed by now. Across from the entrance was a full-size mirror. Sasha did not pay much attention to her overall reflection, but she cleaned up the black streaks around her eyes as well as she could. She took a deep breath and went farther down, to the corridor with brown imitation leather doors. The first one, wide, double-paned, bore a sign:

TEACHERS' LOUNGE.

Sasha knocked softly, and the sound was drowned in the leathery thickness. She knocked on the doorknob.

"What's the matter?"

The voice was harsh. It was Portnov's voice.

Sasha tugged on the door handle.

She saw a long, softly lit room, furnished with several couches along the walls, a coat hanger with a few raincoats, and a completely naked plastic mannequin. Farther away from the door, Portnov sat behind an old writing desk. He stared at Sasha over his glasses, his eyes ice-cold and immobile.

Kostya is waiting for me, she reminded herself and swallowed.

"What do you need, Samokhina?"

"I learned it," Sasha said, trying not to show her fear. "I learned everything. I'm ready for the one-on-one."

"What time is it?"

"Six thirty."

"What time was your individual session scheduled for?"

"For three thirty . . . But I am ready! You can check . . ."

"Why do I need to spend my own personal time on you?"

Sasha was taken aback.

"You missed your session, Samokhina. The ship has sailed."

"But I had a legitimate reason!"

"No, you did not. No reason is legitimate when missing an individual session. I'm writing a report to Kozhennikov, and will let him take disciplinary action."

"But I have memorized everything!"

"I am no longer interested. Our next meeting is in class this Thursday. Good night." Portnov pointed at the door.

Sasha left. Then she came back, unable to believe the injustice of the situation.

"But I memorized everything! It's only fifteen minutes! Just check . . ."

"Close the door, Samokhina. From the other side."

Dragging her bag behind her, she went up the stairs. She stopped in front of the dining hall entrance. The tears had dried up, and her face now seemed white and long, like a bandage.

"What happened?" Kostya flew to meet her.

For an entire minute Sasha could not speak. She remembered that conversation in the summer, almost a year and a half ago:

"My alarm did not go off . . ."

"It's very bad, but not terrible . . . it's even good for you—it'll teach you some discipline. The second such blunder will cost you a lot more, and don't say I didn't warn you."

"Just tell me what happened!"

"Do you have . . . do you know how to reach your . . . your father?"

Kostya recoiled.

"What for?"

"I need to speak to him," Sasha said hopelessly.

Kostya was silent.

"Do you?" she asked again.

"He gave me his number, but I threw away the piece of paper." Kostya took a deep breath. "Listen . . . You didn't do anything horrible, right?

"Sasha?"

▪ ▪ ▪

Sasha managed to get hold of Mom the next day. The voice in the receiver sounded dull and tired. At first Mom made excuses, and only then admitted that the previous night on her way home from the office, she'd fallen awkwardly and broken her right thumb. It was not anything terrible. Just annoying because it was her right hand. But it could have been much worse. If she hadn't slipped, she would have fallen into a manhole—somebody had stolen its cover, and it was dark, and the streetlights were out . . . The open manhole was only two steps in front of her! On the sidewalk, at night! So it was a blessing in disguise. We're fighting with the regional administration, Mom said, might even go to court. But the thumb will heal. Don't worry. Everything will heal.

After her conversation with Mom, Sasha took a long walk around Torpa. The first snow fell and melted immediately.

On Thursday the heat was turned on. Almost immediately a pipe burst in the room next to Sasha's, and the heat was turned off. Plumbers stomped in the corridor, swearing and clanging metal tools.

By nighttime, the windows turned sweaty in their room. It became warm; the radiator was decorated with freshly washed socks, tights, and underwear. Sasha went to the kitchen, poured some boiling water over a bouillon cube in an enamel mug, and, sipping the hot liquid, started the exercises.

She felt as if she had just avoided an enormous tragedy. Actually, it was the same feeling she'd experienced two summers ago, when she saw her dazed Mom next to the stretcher where then-still-a-stranger Valentin lay. It was almost joyful—instead of a big tragedy, she faced a relatively small, easy to survive trouble.

"Why is he doing this?" Kostya asked, dunking a moist cracker into his cup of tea.

"You didn't ask *how* he is doing this."

They fell silent. Sasha was almost happy, because the torrent of events completely washed that night, those anchovies, that wrinkled sheet, and those coins on the floor out of their relationship.

"Kostya," Sasha asked softly. "What if you . . . What if you wanted to drop out of school? Just get up and leave. Would he let you go?"

Kostya's face darkened.

"He and I had a discussion about that," he said, attempting to fish out wet pieces of his cracker with an aluminum teaspoon, "and frankly, I'm not even going to try. My mom is not the healthiest woman, and my grandma's old . . . I will stay at school."

"Right." Sasha sighed.

Nighttime came. Lisa roamed around somewhere. Oksana fidgeted at her desk for quite a while, trying to memorize a paragraph, then threw the book aside, gulped some moonshine from the rubber hot water bottle all by herself, and went to bed. Sasha just hunched over her textbook, honing one exercise after another, climbing up a precipitous icy wall:

Read exercise nine, fall into utter despair for a couple of minutes—*no one can accomplish this, it is simply impossible*—rub your eyes, go back to exercise eight, force yourself to repeat it, reread exercise nine. Try it. Squeeze your temples with both hands. Repeat exercise eight a couple more times; again, attempt exercise nine and realize that an outline exists—it's palpable, you just need to be very careful. Concentrate very, very hard . . . get as far as half of the exercise and lose it. And again—lose it right at the beginning. And again—almost get to the end. And again—finish it, but recognize that you will not be able to repeat it. Go back to number eight, run through it, repeat number nine, wincing from the tension. Repeat again. And again. Catch your breath, wipe your tearing eyes, allow yourself a minute of rest, take a sip of cold tea. Read exercise ten . . .

And again fall into despair.

Friday passed this way. And Friday night through Saturday morning went the same way. At eleven ten, right on schedule, Sasha walked into auditorium 38. She carried no fear, no anger. The world around her was dark, and Sasha's vision narrowed down to a round window the size of an automotive tire.

Instead of Portnov's face, she saw only his hand with a ring.

"I'm waiting, Samokhina. Full set of exercises, one through twelve. If you make a mistake, start again from the very beginning."

She placed a chair in the middle of the auditorium, steadied herself against its high back, and began.

"Imagine a sphere . . . mentally distort the sphere so that the external surface is on the inside, and the internal on the outside . . ."

Twice she lost her place. Once, while transitioning from number seven to number eight, and then on twelve, the trickiest one. Both times she stopped and started all over again. On her third try she finished the entire series without a single pause—like a song, or a dance. Like a tongue twister. Like a long balance beam exercise sequence. . . .

The bright window in front of her eyes narrowed even further. She couldn't make out Portnov's face. She saw his desk, the edge of his notebook, and his hand with the ring, clenched into a tight fist.

"Good." His voice sounded hollow. "For this Tuesday: paragraphs eighteen and nineteen. For next Saturday: exercises thirteen through seventeen."

"Good-bye," Sasha said.

She stepped out of the auditorium, nodded to Kostya, blindly found her way to the dorm. She lay down on her bed and switched off her consciousness.

"Samokhina, get up. First block is Specialty. Get up, do you hear me?"

Lisa was wearing expensive and very exotic but harsh perfume. Sasha opened her eyes.

"What?"

"It's Monday morning! Get up, class starts in half an hour! If you miss one more class, Portnov will burst!"

"Isn't it Saturday?" Sasha inquired.

"Not anymore! You snored through the entire weekend!"

Mom, Sasha thought. I promised to call her every weekend. I never called . . . And what about Kostya?

Lisa thrashed about the room half-dressed, pulling on a pair of tights for extra warmth, then stepping into her jeans.

"Oksana! Did you take my pads?"

"I did, the package is in your desk."

"Idiot, what the hell are you doing, stealing my stuff?"

"Stop screeching, there are some left. I'll buy you some more."

"Yeah, sure, you'll buy me more. If I see you stealing them again, I'll stick those pads where the sun don't shine!"

Sasha slipped on her bathrobe and shuffled into the bathroom. In the mirror, a pale, haggard—but calm, and even handsome—face looked back at her. Sasha blinked: her pupils unfolded and snapped shut again, like a camera lens, then went back to normal.

She took a shower and washed her hair; only then did she discover that her hair dryer had burned out.

"Who broke my hair dryer?"

"Wasn't me." Lisa was ready to leave. "The bell is in ten minutes, and I'm not going to listen to Portnov's hysterics because of you!"

"You'll have to deal with it, thanks to whoever broke it! Oksana, let me borrow yours."

"I lent it to Luba from room 19, and she hasn't returned it yet. Just wrap your hair in a towel—you'll be fine!"

Sasha dried her hair with a towel as well as she could. She pulled on a knit cap, scrambled into her jacket, threw some books and notepads into her bag, and ran across the yard toward the main building. She burst into auditorium 1 and plopped into her seat next to Kostya the same second the bell rang.

A minute passed. Portnov was not there. First years exchanged glances and began to talk softly.

"Think he might be sick?" someone asked hopefully.

"Yeah, right . . ."

"Keep dreaming . . ."

The door flew open. Conversations stopped mid-sentence. Portnov walked in, tossed a quick hello, and sat behind his desk. He inclined his head and gazed at the students over his glasses. The silence in the auditorium felt sterilized.

"Half of this semester has come and gone," Portnov stated. "Winter finals are fast approaching. You will have two graded exams: Philosophy and History. And pass-fail exams in all other subjects. Obviously, one of them is Specialty; those who do not pass the first time will have an unpleasant conversation with your advisors."

A pencil rolled off Zhenya Toporko's desk and fell on the floor with a thump, but she did not dare pick it up.

"I told some of you today during your one-on-one sessions, and now I will tell all of you," Portnov continued. "The exercises that you are working on, overcoming your tunnel vision and your laziness, change you from the inside. Perhaps you have already noticed. If you have not, you will notice it later."

He paused. Sasha longed to look at Kostya, but she restrained herself.

"We stand at the very beginning of the road," Portnov spoke in dry, precise sentences. "Preliminary work is being done. Considering the rate we're going at, I can swear: in many years, I have never had to teach a more undisciplined, indolent group of students. The only group worse than you is Group B, but they are way below any expectations, and I highly doubt half of those students will be attending the graduation ceremony."

Silence.

"Samokhina," Portnov barked.

Sasha got up.

"Come here."

Sasha went to where Portnov was and faced the auditorium.

"How many exercises have you completed?"

"Twelve."

Portnov faced the audience.

"Have any of you wunderkinder accomplished twelve exercises by now? Pavlenko, how many have you done?"

"Six," Lisa breathed.

"Toporko, you?"

"Eight . . ."

"And you, Kozhennikov?"

"Three," Kostya said. Despite bright red blotches, his face appeared very pale.

"This girl gets an automatic pass." Portnov did not look at Sasha. "She knows how to study. She became a leader after the very first class. Now she has gone far ahead of all of you and can face the winter finals with confidence. You—the rest of you—remember: there are only two graded Specialty exams, a midterm in your third year, and a placement exam in your fifth year. However, the pass-fail test at the end of each semester will be a significant life-defining event for all of you, I promise you that much. Samokhina, you may sit down."

Sasha went back to her seat. Behind her back, Group A was hushed. *Everyone will hate me,* Sasha thought almost cheerfully. *Although, you'd think . . . what is there to envy?*

At that moment she felt as if a low ceiling had spread open within her. Massive concrete walls drifted apart, hit by a ray of light. All that was hairy and dark, all that frightened her, trampled her . . . in this light, it all looked comical and pathetic. As if the underside of a low-budget horror movie was suddenly revealed: used and worn-out monsters, Death in a shroud bearing a dry-cleaner's stamp, a diminutive, overweight director . . .

"Hey, what's with you?"

Sasha willed herself to close her eyes—and then open them again.

Her classmates scurried around, noisily moving chairs around, somebody laughed out loud. Something had happened.

Portnov was no longer in the auditorium. The door was wide open.

"What happened?" Sasha squinted.

"The class is over," Kostya explained drily. "Gym's next. Did you bring your uniform?"

Things were now happening very fast. Left to her own devices, Sasha reached the third floor after the bell; she joined the line still wearing her jeans and a sweater.

"Look who's here!" the young gym teacher exclaimed. "Alexandra! How come you never come to class? And when you do show up, you're not wearing your uniform."

"She has no time. She's on a special advanced program," Lisa volunteered. Somebody sniggered.

"You must remember that Physical Education is a major subject, along with Specialty," Dima said. "And that a winter exam awaits all of you, without pity or consideration!"

The line giggled.

"I'll go change," Sasha said.

"Go, but hurry up! We're starting the warm-up! Turn . . . Right! And go! Korotkov, hold the tempo!"

Sasha trotted to the locker room. She shook her wrinkled jogging suit and sneakers out of her bag. The narrow, stuffy locker room was overflowing with shoes, foppish boots with fashionable platform soles, and stylish stilettos. Jeans and skirts hung on metal hooks like beef carcasses at the butcher's, a bunch of sweaters lay crumpled on the bench. Somebody's sweater had fallen on the floor. Automatically, Sasha bent down to pick it up.

She felt no fear. No courage, either. She felt detached, like a fish in slow motion. One-two-three-four, counted Dima Dimych. Sneakers *thump-thump*ed on the gym floor. Warm-up was in progress.

"She didn't take it."

"How do you know that?"

"I know! You're trying to get even with her for something . . ."

"Shut up, stop yelling . . ."

First years from Group A surrounded a bench in the yard. Lisa perched on the back of the bench, stiletto heels propped on the dirty seat.

"Samokhina! I had a hundred bucks in my jacket pocket. Give it back, or you'll be really sorry."

Sasha stopped.

The fourth block was over. During Philosophy and History, lists of sample exam questions were distributed. Sixty questions each, one hundred and twenty altogether; obviously, she wouldn't have time to learn it. She owed Portnov exercises thirteen through seventeen by Saturday, and tomorrow was Tuesday, so that meant individual session, paragraphs . . .

"Samokhina, are you deaf?"

After her experience during the first block, Sasha's brain indeed was moving a bit slowly.

Students crowded around the bench: Lisa in the company of guys, her friends and minions. Kostya, his face red and pathetic. Andrey Korotkov, massive and grim. Zhenya . . . Igor . . . Denis . . .

"What did you say?" Sasha asked.

Lisa jumped off the bench and approached Sasha face-to-face, lipsticked mouth pulled into a thin line.

"You were alone in the locker room. My jacket was hanging there. A hundred dollars in the pocket."

"In the right pocket?" Sasha asked.

Kostya's eyes widened. The other boys exchanged glances.

"In the right one," Lisa agreed softly. "A bunch of thieves around here. Give it back."

Sasha closed her eyes. She was sleepy. And simultaneously she was hungry for more exercises. Just like she would normally get hungry for food.

"Your money is behind the lining. Just check."

The bench stood under a linden tree; the leaves had fallen off and had been collected by the janitor. One or two remaining leaves still twitched, clawing to the illusion of life, the branches beat upon one another, scratching and rustling. Aside from that sound, the silence was absolute. It was quickly getting dark. The windows in the main building were lit. A streetlight went on in front of the dorm.

"Go ahead," Kostya said nervously. "Check."

Lisa stuck her hand into her pocket. She took a long time. Then her delicate face reddened in the dusk, darkened like a ripe fruit.

"And how did you know that?" She twisted toward Sasha. "How did you know? You checked my pockets, didn't you?"

Sasha shrugged. "No. I just guessed. And now you need to apologize. Say: 'I'm sorry, Sasha.'"

"*What?*"

Again, Sasha lowered her eyelids for a second. The feeling she'd experienced during the first block was about to make a comeback.

"Apologize. Now, in front of everyone. You accused me of theft."

"Buzz off," Lisa suggested.

Sasha took a step forward. A streetlight illuminated her face.

"You heard me, Pavlenko. Don't push it."

Lisa stared into Sasha's eyes. Very quickly, like a slide show, emotions alternated on her face: anger, surprise, embarrassment, and, finally, a flash of fear.

"What do you want?" Lisa mumbled.

"Apologize."

"Fine, I apologize . . ."

In total silence, Sasha's classmates let her pass. She walked through their formation toward the entrance of the dormitory.

Snow fell in November. Early mornings, before sunrise, Sasha would leave the dorm and jog around the yard, leaving a chain of footsteps. Around and around. Stepping into her own footsteps. Just like a year ago.

No one forced her. She simply realized that without those running sessions, without the silence of the deaf and mute morning, without snow under her feet and a cloud of her breath, she would never survive the pressure. Neither physical nor psychological.

At first Kostya ran with her, but then he begged off. He hated getting up that early; he usually slept through the first block (unless the first block happened to be Specialty). Sasha did not mind, though—she needed to be absolutely alone. Complete silence and the sound of snow under her feet, crunchy or squishy, whatever her luck happened to be.

Mom still wore a cast. She assured Sasha over the phone that everything was just fine, that she'd gotten used to the cast, and that her thumb did not hurt anymore. She and Valentin sent Sasha a care package: winter boots, tights, socks, and even a new jacket with a fur-lined hood. The jacket was a bit small.

A wintry atmosphere also reigned in room 21: Lisa ignored Sasha,

Sasha took no notice of Lisa. At first Oksana attempted to make them reconcile, but then gave up and got busy with her own life: she had frequent guests, girls from Group B and sometimes even second-year boys.

"Open house," Lisa murmured through gritted teeth, but no one was listening. Something had fallen through with that rented apartment of hers. Either she could not afford it, could not find a decent place, or perhaps—Sasha could believe it—Portnov forbade her.

On the way to the post office one Sunday, the day Sasha always called home, she saw Farit Kozhennikov and Lisa walking ahead of her along Sacco and Vanzetti. They walked side by side; Kozhennikov was talking, Lisa was listening, and glancing at her face, Sasha felt a great deal of pity for her.

She slowed down. Snow melted during the November thaw, streams of water ran between the cobblestones just like in the spring, and bright yellow leaves swam on the bottom.

Kozhennikov and Lisa separated at the intersection in front of the post office. Kozhennikov nodded and turned left, crossed the street, and disappeared around the corner. Lisa leaned on a naked linden tree.

Sasha longed to go over and say something to her. She took a step; a large puddle made a squelching sound. Sasha leapt aside and went back to reality.

Lisa would not be pleased. Sasha had no power to change anything, at least right now.

She slid behind Lisa's back and entered the stuffy post office filled with amber warmth. The whole time she waited for her turn in the long-distance booth, she envisioned how some day she would spit in Kozhennikov's face. How she would gather a mouthful of saliva and spit; the old man in front of her was already finishing up his conversation when Sasha realized—feeling bewildered and discontented—that a fraction of her hatred for Farit Kozhennikov fell on Kostya.

"The son is not responsible for the sins of the father," she reminded herself. Kostya was just as much a victim of Farit's as Sasha herself. He had ripped and thrown away the paper with his father's phone number. Farit wasn't his real father—just a biological one.

"Are you going to make the call or not?" asked the girl behind the counter.

Sasha went into the booth. But even while speaking to Mom, she could not get Kozhennikov and Kostya out of her mind.

▪ ▪ ▪

"Haven't you slept with him yet?" Oksana sounded worried.

She was washing the dishes. No matter who made the mess in the kitchen, Oksana ended up doing the dishes. Sometimes she threw pots and pans against the wall and shrieked: "What a pigsty!" but then did the dishes anyway. Greasy plates piled in the sink drove her insane.

"They are all hypersexual at this age." Oksana must have been repeating somebody else's words. "You are going to lose him, you know."

Sasha bent over a paragraph. Room 21 overflowed with Lisa and Lisa's friends and acquaintances. They parked themselves all over the place, even on Sasha's bed. Sasha did not feel like arguing, so she took her books and went to the kitchen, which at that time of night was empty—not counting Oksana and her dishes.

In the past few months of dorm life Sasha had gotten used to sleeping despite loud noises and studying in the middle of an earthquake. But Oksana's words unsettled her, and she found herself constantly returning to the beginning of the paragraph.

"You are a strange creature," Oksana mused. Her back was turned to Sasha; Oksana was soaping up a plate and could hear nothing except for the sounds of running water and her own voice. "Are you eighteen yet? In the spring? You're a peanut. Portnov gave you an automatic pass, the only one out of thirty-nine people. And you are still cramming, like a wound-up toy, morning to night. Kostya is a good-looking guy, and we have tons of pretty girls around here; somebody will steal him away, you know. Even the local chicks are not bad here, the schoolgirls . . ."

The door swung open. One-eyed Victor, the third year, came limping in, still lopsided and strange. His sweatpants formed bubbles on his knees; his plaid shirt had seen better days. Huge leather gloves covered his hands, and his face was hidden behind enormous dark glasses. Sasha shuddered.

"Hey, girls," Victor croaked. "Will you pour me some tea?"

Oksana turned her face to him. "Don't you have any of your own tea?"

"I'll get it," Sasha put aside her book. She couldn't concentrate anyway.

The electric teakettle began to hiss; the smell of burned duct tape filled the kitchen.

"Victor, what happened to your hands?" Sasha asked in passing.

Victor looked down at his hands, which were hidden by the gloves. He wiggled his fingers. "Ah, you know . . . The winter finals are coming, girls, the winter finals. Must survive the winter finals, that's the thing."

"Must survive the finals," Sasha echoed.

Victor's dark glasses turned to her. "What are you worried about? You are only first years—have fun and play games. Celebrate New Year's Eve. For third years there is a placement exam this winter, ladies."

Oksana turned off the teakettle. She turned to him, wiping her hands on an already wet dish towel. "Is it difficult?"

Victor inclined his head. "I guess you could put it that way. . . . *difficult*. After this exam we are moving to another location. Whoever passes it, obviously."

"It might be easier at the other location," Sasha suggested without a hint of conviction.

None of the first years had any clue about where the "other location" actually was, or what exactly it entailed. Some people said it was a very advanced institute, equipped with extremely sophisticated technology, with a dormitory recently renovated according to the contemporary European standards, with a computer on each desk. Others said the place was hidden underground, in deep catacombs. It was also said that the other location was in another city.

Some students—Sasha had heard it herself—believed that the other location happened to be on another planet.

Once Sasha suggested to Kostya that the "other location" for the upperclassmen was a mysterious region beyond the grave that no one knew anything about, because no one ever returned from that place. Kostya had had a strange reaction to her joke: he went pale and asked her not to make that kind of a joke ever again.

"It *might* be easier," Victor agreed melancholicly. "What can I say, girls. I really meant to be a merchant marine . . ."

Sasha plopped a tea bag into an enamel mug and poured steaming boiling water over it.

"Sugar?"

"Two teaspoons. No, three."

Sasha placed the mug on the edge of the table. Victor picked it up with both hands—awkwardly because of the leather gloves—and poured the boiling tea into his mouth, like water.

Sasha stopped breathing. Victor put his empty cup on the table, smiled, and licked his lips.

"Thanks."

"Wasn't it too hot?" Sasha asked softly.

He shook his head.

"Nah . . . Well, girls, I should go study. Thanks. And remember me kindly!"

He left the kitchen.

Sasha stepped into her room, a textbook stuck under her arm. The room was dimly lit by a desk lamp and a few burning cigarette ends. Faces were hard to distinguish in the thick smoky air. Lisa sat on the desk next to a stereo system, and about ten people, first and second years, perched wherever they could find a place. Two people sat on Sasha's bed—a sturdy girl whom Sasha had seen around and her boyfriend. Her name was Natasha; his, Slava. They were making out.

"Lights out," Sasha said. "Eleven o'clock. Everybody out."

No one heard or listened to her. She approached the desk and threw the stereo system onto the floor. The top broke off. Conversation died.

"Are you *nuts,* Samokhina?" Olga, from room 32, asked in complete silence.

Sasha switched on the light. Everyone squinted; Sasha's eyes were wide open, even slightly bulging.

Maybe she *was* nuts. But standing in this room, no one could possibly matter because, just a few minutes ago, accompanied by laughter and voices, she had finished exercise twenty-five (even though Portnov gave her only numbers thirteen through seventeen). It just so happened that after she had completed number seventeen, Sasha had read the next one, out of curiosity—and had understood absolutely nothing. But instead of simply closing the book, she had read it one more time. This time, the words were familiar. The images were relatively clear. However, she could not imagine what she was supposed to do with them, and *how* it was meant to be done.

And that is when the bee in Sasha's bonnet resurfaced. Perhaps it had something to do with her personality as a straight-A student. Perhaps her investigative instincts had kicked in. Whatever the reason, she had begun pulling a thread from number seventeen to number eighteen, followed it into utter darkness, and a few minutes later she had stumbled upon what she thought of as a "contour" of the new exercise.

And then she was *sure*.

Truly happy, she had started gently kneading number eighteen. From that one, she had sensed threads stretching to number nineteen, and then to number twenty. And then Sasha had felt an epiphanous illumination of truth, and she had thrown herself into the exercises, one after another, and the light had become brighter, until finally, on exercise number twenty-five, she went blind.

The inner light had flashed brilliantly and then faded. Sasha had rubbed her eyes; she hadn't been able to see the kitchen or her textbook. For a second she had thought she was *inside* the exercise. She was a dark contour in a space without upper or lower limits; she did not have a chance to get scared. What had finally snapped her back—at least a bit—was when she heard the door slam, felt a cold draft, and then heard the refrigerator door open.

"Bitches! Who ate my herring?"

"Idiot, did you leave it in the common fridge?"

"I can't keep it in my room! It stinks!"

"Should have eaten it right away."

"Morons . . . Whose sausage is this? I'm going to eat the whole bloody thing."

"Don't—the sausage is Elena's, it's spoiled. It was already going bad when she got it."

Sasha had heard the voices very near her. She had sensed the draft on her face, perceived smells.

But had seen nothing.

She had felt the textbook sliding off her lap. She had managed to catch it. There had been no fear: Hadn't Portnov said something about this, that vision may change?

What if her vision was lost forever?

Sasha had swallowed her terrified howl. She had rubbed her eyes, as if trying to gouge them out, and a few seconds later she could discern the white blur of the fridge. And one more minute later she had detected the head of a herring on the tiled floor, somebody's feet in slippers, fragments of a broken cup . . .

Her vision had returned.

Reeling, Sasha had shuffled off to her room. Something was happening to her. Something serious. She could not—and did not wish to—stop it. So when she had flung open the door, had become aware of the burning ends of cigarettes and a necking couple sitting on her bed, she had not thought about anything and acted on pure instinct.

"Everybody out. Are you deaf?"

"Too much studying, sweetheart?" the guy on her bed asked her softly.

He looked into her eyes.

It seemed to her that only a few seconds had passed. In reality, when she came to, the clock showed half past eleven, and she was alone in the room. Cigarette butts lay on the floor. The tobacco smoke made her nauseated: she moved to the window, ripped off the paper she and Oksana had taped on the frame, plucked out the foam, and threw open a panel, gulping the icy November air.

"You know, I am getting to be quite scared of you," Kostya said. "Sometimes you have this look on your face . . ."

They sat on the windowsill in the corridor near auditorium 38. Kostya had come out of his individual session ten minutes ago; Sasha had five minutes to wait before hers.

"Sasha . . . what exactly did happen in the kitchen? Something happened, and none of them would admit it, as if they were ashamed."

"Nothing." Sasha waved her hand without much enthusiasm. "They can all go to hell."

"You have changed," Kostya said.

"We're all changing."

"Yes, but you . . . Maybe you are a genius. Or something worse than that?" Kostya attempted a joke.

"I gotta go," Sasha said.

Actually, she still had a couple of minutes—she just was eager for her one-on-one. That feeling was definitely a first.

She stopped in front of the auditorium. Portnov's voice was sharp and loud behind the door. It sounded as if he were flogging someone, or hammering in nails. Sasha thought that today he would definitely not yell at her. Today she brought not five, but *thirteen* exercises. Twenty-three . . . She felt anxious and happy, like when she was a little girl riding a Ferris wheel.

Zhenya Toporko left the auditorium, strangely hunched over, holding back tears. *Probably deserved it,* Sasha thought without pity. She entered the auditorium.

"Good morning, Samokhina. Have you finished?"

Sasha nodded. She leaned over the straight-backed chair and began the mental process starting from exercise number thirteen.

She lost it on number fourteen and began again. Made a mistake on number fifteen and went back to the beginning. Portnov watched her, his lips pursed skeptically. Ready to panic, Sasha started again and lost it on number thirteen. Portnov was silent.

"Give me a minute, I just need to concentrate."

"Then concentrate."

"I . . ."

Sasha stumbled. She remembered last night. Oksana and her dishes. Victor and his gloves. "Haven't you slept with him yet?" Scalding tea . . . Flashes of cigarettes in the dark.

She started number thirteen—and felt the exercises *glide*. One after another. Like the links of a chain. Like familiar thoughts. Insane. Alien.

She passed number sixteen. Seventeen. Immediately merged into number eighteen. Nineteen. Her heart seized; Sasha felt like a tightrope walker, dancing on a wire over a screaming crowd, she could almost hear their ecstatic shrieks—although in reality the auditorium was quiet, somewhere in the hallway students spoke to one another, and she stood grasping the back of the chair, staring into space, and across from her Portnov sat and watched her, and somehow—how?—he knew and saw her dance on the wire, and he was her only spectator. Or listener? Accomplice? What was happening to her, and how could he sense it? And what exactly about her thoughts and exercises did he see?

Right after the twenty-fifth exercise, she went blind. Just like last night in the kitchen. A flash of light—then darkness, like a closed container. Obscurity.

And stillness. Portnov did not move.

"Sit down."

Holding on to the chair, she walked around it and sat down. The seat squeaked.

"Which numbers were you supposed to study?"

"Thirteen through eighteen."

"Then why the hell did you touch the twenty-fifth?"

Sasha swallowed.

"Answer me!"

"I wanted to."

"*What?*"

"I wanted to!" Sasha was ready to snap and talk back at him. Had she still had her eyes, she would get up and leave, and slam the door behind her. However, she was blind and afraid to appear ridiculous by running into the door frame on her way out.

"What can you see?" Portnov asked an octave lower.

"Nothing."

"Nothing at all?"

Sasha blinked a few times.

"Nothing," she said finally, her voice barely audible. "The same thing happened last night. But it went away almost immediately."

"How many times did you do number twenty-five?"

"Twice. Last night and this morning."

She heard Portnov get up and approach her. She rose; Portnov took hold of her chin and sharply, almost cruelly, jerked her face up. There was a flash of light; Sasha blinked.

Right in front of her eyes was Portnov's ring. Its green light dimmed little by little.

Portnov removed his glasses. He looked at Sasha—perhaps for the first time in her life, he looked not above his lenses, but straight at her. His pupils were tiny, like poppy seeds. They reminded Sasha of the eyes of the hunchback, Nikolay Valerievich, who once treated Sasha to a restaurant dinner of sandwiches and pork chops.

"Listen to me, girl. If I say something, that means you have to do it *exactly* as I say. You may not do less. You may not, *should not,* do more. If you *want* to do more, come to me first and ask. And here is something else: You have two exams coming up. You are missing a lot of classes. I checked attendance—you've missed almost as many classes as Pavlenko. Have you made peace with her yet?"

Sasha was silent for a moment. The last question caught her off guard.

"I didn't . . . didn't fight with her."

"If you kill someone, you will go to prison. Have you turned eighteen yet?"

"No . . . what do you mean, if I *kill* someone?"

Someone knocked on the door. Sasha's individual session should have ended two minutes ago.

"Wait!" Portnov yelled with irritation—he had never made anyone wait before. He turned to Sasha again.

"Your aggression levels are over the limit. It's just a stage. But in your particular case, it's close to out of control."

"In *my* case?"

"Yes. Think about it. That's it, you are dismissed."

Sasha departed, making way for Andrey Korotkov. Almost right away she bumped into Kostya.

"I thought he killed you."

"Listen, am I aggressive?"

Kostya did not say anything for so long that Sasha got really worried. "But I never . . . Just the opposite, I . . ."

"You are strange," Kostya said after a long pause. Before she could respond, though, he said, "Tell me, what are you doing tomorrow?"

They spent Sunday strolling around town and doing absolutely nothing. Kostya took Sasha to a café; they had ice cream and watched sparrows huddling near the kitchen's air vent for warmth. Sasha kept thinking that Kostya expected something of her. It was in the way he gazed at her, and in the way a minute pause accompanied each of his words, as if he wanted Sasha to interrupt him.

His expectant manner made her feel uncomfortable.

"Do you want to go to the post office with me? I have to call my mother."

Mom insisted on knowing every detail about Sasha's studies. Sasha told her how she was praised for her work, and how she was now the best student in her class; Mom promised her a "nice little gift" to celebrate after the finals. Then Kostya talked to his family, his mother and grandmother. By the time they paid for the phone calls and left the post office, dusk had turned to darkness, and it started to snow.

"Well, don't you think it's beastly to smoke in the room when you have been repeatedly asked not to smoke? What does it have to do with her personal issues? I've always been nice to her. I understand she has issues, and Kozhennikov drives her insane . . ."

Sasha faltered. Kostya walked by her side, hunched over, hands stuck in his pockets.

"Maybe I should change my last name," he commented bitterly. "Take my mother's."

Sasha did not know what to say. Snow continued to fall, draping over the black twigs of the linden trees, the wrought-iron benches, stucco corners, and tin awnings. Here and there steam rose over the roofs, white steam on the black sky. It was beautiful.

They continued to walk in silence. Sasha felt Kostya's tension, as if he were a member of the audience in the dress circle, and Sasha had just appeared in the limelight and was holding a theatrical pause. But if Kostya bought his ticket, then wasn't she obligated to say or do something?

"Let's walk back to the dorm," Sasha said. And added, after hesitating for a second, "Don't you need to work on the exercises?"

Kostya turned sharply to face her:

"Is that all you talk about? The exercises?"

"Not all the time . . . I . . ."

She faltered. Then stopped walking. Kostya faced her with so much disappointment and reproach that Sasha felt utterly lost.

"Do you really think that I . . ."

And again she could not find the right words.

"Don't you understand that I . . ."

Then she felt deeply offended. Her throat felt tight.

"And in any case, that's my business!" she screamed and walked away very quickly, slipping and stumbling on the wet pavement.

Kostya caught up and held her in his arms.

They kissed in foyers. The town of Torpa had plenty of dim, echoing, empty foyers. The foyers of some buildings smelled of cats, some of perfume or wet plaster. Some smelled of nothing. Old mailboxes, ficus trees in planters painted so many times that they looked monumental, a child's sled, perambulators, a disassembled kid's bike—the annals of the town were opening up to them, lobby after lobby, and Sasha learned to kiss properly on the brink of her eighteenth birthday.

Before, she'd considered kissing a useless ceremony. Now, with Kostya, she finally understood the hidden meaning of this ritual; Sasha longed for one of these locked apartments to be theirs. She wanted to enter now—and remain inside for a long time. To live like that, forever holding hands.

It was snowing outside, and they ran in the snow, from one building to another. They drank coffee to warm up, and looked for another secluded nook. Once somebody, probably a street cleaner, caught them off guard and yelled into their faces: "What do you think you're doing here?" And they threw themselves out of the foyer like frightened children, into the snow. They ran and laughed, and knocked the snowflakes off their faces.

It must have been the happiest night of Sasha's life.

November flew by like a commuter train. It was now December; the dormitory was cold once again. The radiators felt as if they were barely working, and wind howled through the cracks.

"Verification: using empirical data or experiment to confirm the truth of theoretical scientific hypothesis by 'returning' to the visual level of knowledge, when the ideal nature of abstract entities is ignored, and they are 'identified' with the objects observed. For example, the ideal geometric objects—points, lines—are identified with their empirical images . . ."

Sasha thought of the lengthy definitions as baby dragons curled into a ball. All she had to do was find its tail, and then carefully unwind the entire thing: the question led her, like a thread, along the creature's spine. From tail to the heads, and there may be several of those.

Sometimes Sasha enjoyed simply understanding the text. Sometimes she'd feel disillusioned, and think of the Philosophy textbook as a brick of premasticated food. Other times she learned definitions that were the result of somebody else's inner life, but could not imagine the process that led to that result. She went to the library and requested books no one had wanted for the past few decades; she studied.

During those chilly days, the joy of learning, this heightened experience, had to compete with another newly found pleasure: kissing in dark hallways, behind the curtains in the assembly hall, in the empty classrooms. The closer the winter finals were, the more insistent Kostya became. His roommates, the second years, spent very little time in the dorm, and all they needed to do was to skip a block and lock the door from the inside, but Sasha stalled, trying to buy herself some time; her memory of their first try was still too awkward. And also—she liked that tightly stretched thread that now connected the two of them. She wanted her "kissing affair" to last forever.

New Year's Eve was coming and while the town of Torpa draped itself with snow and now resembled a half-developed photograph, the second years were preparing a celebratory roast. Black trees under the white sky, gray buildings in white muzzles of balconies, diffused contours, everything rippled and very clean. Sasha completed the book of exercises given to her by Portnov, while Kostya had barely made it to number thirty-five.

The schedule of winter finals had been posted. The amount of noise and number of late-night parties decreased to a minimum. With all this going on, Sasha continued to run in the snow that fell overnight, beat her new footsteps into her own, and call home every Sunday. Mom asked when she was coming home for the winter break. Sasha did not know what to tell her.

English was their first pass-fail exam. Sasha passed easily. The gym teacher, Dima Dimych, gave everyone a passing grade, and for the rest of the block they played volleyball. The Math exam required a serious effort, and so Sasha had a sense of accomplishment when she passed. The Math professor had a long intricate signature: Sasha studied her report card like a work of art.

Their last exam was Specialty, scheduled for January 2. "They did it on purpose," Oksana stated gloomily. An excellent homemaker, she managed to dig up some pine branches, put them into a glass jar wrapped in aluminum foil, and decorate them with tinsel. Now, in Oksana's opinion, the room looked properly adorned.

Kostya either pranced around with sparklers and fireworks or turned catatonic over a textbook.

"I don't understand it, and I never will. The human brain is just not cut out for this! It cannot be imagined!"

Sasha made many attempts to help him, but every time she realized that her experience wasn't worth a dime to Kostya. She failed to demonstrate how to move from number thirty-five to thirty-six. "Verification" proved to be of no use: Sasha gesticulated; drew pictures; talked about a bicycle chain, a spiderweb; referenced Escher's drawings of bees, fish, and lizards. Desperate in his failure, Kostya concentrated on kissing.

"Will you just do him already," Lisa suggested one winter evening, when Oksana lay in bed with a book, and Sasha sipped tea, about to start her new book of exercises. "It's painful to watch how you string him along."

Sasha took hold of Lisa's blond mane and gave it a sharp pull. Lisa howled. Oksana, who tended to stay neutral, hid deeper under her blanket and watched Sasha and Lisa trying to gouge each other's eyes out.

Finally, Lisa withdrew and disappeared for the rest of the night.

▪▪▪

At the end of December, a tree was erected in the assembly hall—the institute was getting ready to celebrate New Year's Eve. On the thirtieth, the school filled with holiday hustle and bustle. Second years ran last-minute rehearsals; the dining hall staff moved tables, getting ready for the evening buffet. By six o'clock the assembly hall was packed; Sasha was surprised to see some of the teachers in the first rows—some she had seen before, some she'd never met. Hunchback Nikolay Valerievich was there as well—he sat next to Portnov, telling him what must have been a very amusing story. Strangely enough, Portnov was not wearing his usual glasses.

The dusty velvet curtain opened and Zakhar, Kostya's roommate, came out wearing narrow glasses nearly identical to Portnov's. His coordination was a little off, and he got tangled up in the curtain, but once establishing himself in the proscenium, he stared adamantly at the audience and, looking over his glasses in a very recognizable manner, informed them that everyone who did not pass the New Year's Eve's celebration on the first try would have an unpleasant conversation with their advisors. Sasha was stunned; the joke seemed way too audacious to her, but the second year managed such a sharp and precise caricature of Portnov that only a minute later she laughed, and her laughter merged with the delight of the entire room.

Only when Zakhar was stepping off the stage, throwing ferocious looks and gestures at the audience (here he was going overboard, but the compliant crowd forgave him easily), Sasha realized that the glasses on Zakhar's nose were real, actually belonging to and borrowed from Portnov. Shocked, she was about to mention it to Kostya, but at that moment second-year girls in very short skirts burst onto the stage accompanied by a deafening soundtrack.

She was still focused on Zakhar's act, though: never in her entire life would Sasha have imagined someone like Portnov lending his glasses to an impersonator for a better effect. But it was much harder to imagine that somewhere in this school was a person capable of actually submitting such a *request* to Portnov. Shaking her head, she tried to relax.

Sasha had never been to a real holiday roast, and this one was really well done: with a great sense of humor, reasonably loud, and very colorful. The audience squealed with laughter; music roared and colored lights danced everywhere. Sasha laughed alongside Kostya, holding his hand.

"Do you think Zakhar will have to pay for this one?" she asked during a short and somewhat disorganized change of sets onstage.

Kostya shrugged. "I don't know. Honestly. But I wouldn't risk that much, if I were in Zakhar's place."

Sasha nodded.

And then the concert was over.

The cheerful crowd pushed their way out into the corridor. Kostya dragged Sasha behind the curtains and kissed her, pressing his entire weight onto her body.

A sharp corner of the windowsill cut into Sasha's back.

"Wait," she said with a note of irritation. "You are so . . . clingy."

She could not see his face in the dark.

They emerged from behind the curtain, holding hands. Downstairs in the dining hall the celebration continued in full swing. A hired band played songs from children's cartoons as a warm-up. At some point Sasha and Kostya had separated—she went to the bathroom, he pushed through the crowd to congratulate the courageous Zakhar. In all her almost eighteen years, Sasha had never encountered such a celebration, so much noise, delight, and commotion; she felt intoxicated without drinking wine.

Not that it wasn't available—alcohol was quietly being distributed in both the boys' and girls' bathrooms. Sasha took a swig of champagne from a plastic cup, stunned by her own courage. The band took requests, the music never stopped, and cheese and salami sandwiches, bread, cookies, and orange slices disappeared quickly from the dining hall tables.

Sasha looked for Kostya in the crowd, taking bites out of her sandwich and smiling.

In the middle of the room a dance floor was set up. It looked as if Dima Dimych danced with three partners at the same time. The gym teacher wore a formfitting sweater; watching him dance, Sasha realized how much she wanted to touch those bulging muscles. A while back Dima had hoisted Sasha onto the balance beam; she still remembered the sensation.

Thankfully, none of the other teachers were present—Sasha could not imagine anyone having any fun in Portnov's presence. However, there was no sign of Kostya either. Zakhar was reaping the fruits of his glory amid a large group of people. Cameras flashed here and there. Sasha swiveled her head—in this crowd, it was very easy to miss a person, especially if he was sitting on the floor, his back to the wall, like those kids in the corner . . .

By then the gym teacher requested swing music and commenced to perform different stunts with all the eager girls. Some girls shrieked, with fear or delight; Dima threw his partners from arm to arm like a coat, easily tossed them behind his back and pulled them out again, and they glided on the hardwood floor between his wide open feet. The girls somersaulted, mouths open in surprise, Dima tossed them up and caught them again; the crowd cheered. A line of potential partners waited for Dima. Those who tried to take another turn were angrily pushed aside.

Sasha fought with herself for one long minute. She really wanted to dance with Dima, but was too timid.

The swing number had no end—one variation merged with another, like the exercises from her textbook. Sasha stepped out of the room, which was getting too stuffy, and saw the burning ends of cigarettes in the dimly lit corridor. Somebody was speaking softly in the dark. When she came out, the conversation stopped.

"Looking for someone?" Lisa asked.

Sasha was unpleasantly surprised. In the last few days they had demonstratively ignored each other. "Not for you."

Lisa did not respond, but the cheerful mood flew off Sasha like the last leaf off an already naked tree.

No idea where to go, she moved down the corridor. In every window, behind every curtain, somebody was making out, breathing heavily and giggling. It seemed to Sasha that she was strolling along a dimly lit museum, where all the statues had gone mad and started necking.

She went down to the coatroom to get her jacket. Of course, she probably could have gotten back to the dorm without it . . .

They were sitting under the counter.

Zhenya Toporko, with her schoolgirl braids and her blouse unbuttoned, and a completely drunk, red-faced Kostya. He was kissing Zhenya, who giggled hysterically, and his shaking hand slid over her chest.

Sasha walked out, leaving her jacket on the hanger.

▪▪▪

She spent the remaining New Year's Eve walking around the town of Torpa. She had to get out of the institute; the dorm shook and bellowed, every room blasted its own stereo system, and every kitchen's table groaned under a smorgasbord of cheap fare. Eventually too cold, Sasha went back and talked the concierge into unlocking the coat check room where, amid empty hooks, Sasha's jacket was still on its hanger . . . and Zhenya and Kostya were nowhere to be seen.

She gave the concierge a chocolate bar to thank her.

The town of Torpa was celebrating, the festivities muffled by the snow. Colorful lights blinked in the windows of buildings and shops. Cabs lingered in intersections. Sasha strolled toward downtown, walked back along Sacco and Vanzetti, then continued toward the river.

The river was frozen, and ice was covered by the snow. Somewhere clocks chimed and happy people shouted; Sasha stared in front of her and involuntarily—almost automatically—ran through the exercises from Portnov's book.

The exercises flowed, one after another. Smoothly. Sasha did not go blind after the twenty-fifth, and her arm did not grow numb after the forty-third, as it had initially. She remembered them all, from number one to number one hundred twenty-five, the last one in the book. She sat down on a fallen tree trunk, smiled, closed her eyes . . .

And opened them on a bright sunny morning.

Snow was piled on her head, on her shoulders, in her lap; it sparkled like Portnov's ring. Even brighter. Sasha squinted. A total silence spread over the frozen river and the cattails, over the entire town.

Sasha swallowed, then jumped up. A huge pile of snow fell off her lap. Had she stayed here the whole night? She must have frozen—perhaps she'd frozen to death. Something was most certainly frostbitten!

She raised her gloveless hands to her face. Her fingers felt warm and moved easily. She touched her nose: it was almost hot. Her feet in their thin boots were warm. Her ears were definitely not frostbitten. Sasha looked around: she stood in the middle of a field, covered by fresh snow. Snow hid her footsteps from last night, and it was easy to believe that Sasha had flown down from the sky.

She found it difficult to disturb such magnificence. But she discovered that she was very hungry.

▪▪▪

She showed up at the Specialty exam, along with the entire class, on January 2, at ten in the morning. Portnov required everyone to be present in the classroom for the duration of the test.

"Good morning, Group A." Portnov slid his glasses to the tip of his nose and glanced at the rows of students. "Samokhina, hand me your grade book."

She approached his desk and watched him write "A" in the row marked "Specialty."

"This is a graded test—everyone remembers that, correct? Prefect, please collect the grade books and place them on my desk."

Head hanging low, Kostya started down the aisle. Sasha stepped from one foot to the other.

"Samokhina, you are dismissed, free to go. Thank you, Kozhennikov. Who's going first, do we have any volunteers? Samokhina, did you hear me?"

Avoiding eye contact, Sasha collected her bag and left the classroom, shutting the door behind her.

"You are dismissed, free to go."

Go where? She has not been free for many months now, as a man at gunpoint is never free. Crossing the yard on her way to the dorm, she asked herself whether she would ever, perhaps in her old age, be able to escape Farit Kozhennikov's power.

In a trance, Oksana hunched over her books. Group B had the exam scheduled for noon. Even knowing that she could not make up for lost time, Oksana still tried desperately to squeeze in numbers 106 to number 115. Sasha knew it was impossible, but hoped that Oksana's honest efforts on 105 exercises would earn her at least a C.

She lay down on her bed and stared at the ceiling. Two exams remained, History and Philosophy, on January 8 and 12. That meant she could get a ticket for the evening of the twelfth and go home for winter vacation.

She'd never thought of that before. She hadn't allowed herself—she was scared to entertain the idea. And now she had no more classes. No Specialty. She could go home. Home.

Oksana froze over the book, staring into space. Perhaps she was beginning to understand the exercises. Sasha counted what money she still had and left the dorm without looking back.

▪▪▪

She returned by lunchtime, a train ticket in her side pocket. The train stopped at the Torpa station for two minutes, from zero twenty-three to zero twenty-five in the morning. On her way home from the station, Sasha stopped at the post office, got hold of Mom, and told her she would arrive on the thirteenth, just in time for the Old New Year's Eve.* The burst of joy on the other end of the line served as her reward for the long queue.

When Sasha got back to her room, Oksana was sitting under the improvised tree engrossed in her knitting; her permanent smile told Sasha that at least in this case she had nothing to worry about.

"What did you get?"

"A B!" Oksana could not stifle a giggle. "It was my hangover, Sasha, I swear, it caused enlightenment. There are no As in our group at all, half got Bs, half Cs. And three people failed."

"You're kidding!"

"Nope. And three people failed in your group, too. That moron Lisa is one." Oksana sighed. "I'm worried about her. Plus Denis Myaskovsky and Kozhennikov . . . Zhenya got a C. I am telling you, Kozhennikov's hanky-panky cost him . . . Are you feeling sorry for him? *You?*"

"What's going to happen now?" Sasha asked after a pause.

"All six people have a makeup test on the thirteenth."

"And . . ." But Sasha faltered. Finally she asked, "And where is Pavlenko?"

"I don't know. She came back after the test, looked like hell, and then she left right away. You know, she should have studied more, instead of running around with all those guys. She asked for it."

Sasha woke up in the middle of the night to complete silence. It was never that quiet in the dorm.

She got up and put on her bathrobe. Oksana was asleep, but Lisa's bed remained empty. Sasha went out into the corridor; the clock showed half past two. Under the ceiling lights the linoleum floor had a morbid sheen.

Without any reason, Sasha went downstairs to the first floor. Someone was there, in the kitchen at the end of the hall.

---

* Based on the Julian calendar, Russians still celebrate on January 14 as well, the *Old* New Year's.

She stopped at the door.

Kostya was weeping noiselessly, kneeling on the floor, stuffing the hem of his blue T-shirt into his mouth. On the table, among dirty dishes, lay a crumpled piece of yellow paper—a telegram.

Sasha already knew what had happened. She just could not believe it.

"Grandma," Kostya managed through the tears. "I won't forgive . . . never . . . Grandma!"

He doubled up and touched his forehead to the floor.

Several times during the last eighteen months Sasha had heard the crackling sound with which the threads that held together the familiar world ripped apart. She thought she was used to it.

The catastrophe that happened to Kostya once again reminded Sasha that all these months she'd walked along the edge of a precipice. All her cramming, the dusty textbooks, the endless little everyday things—they all added up and formed a razor's edge, upon which Sasha was balancing . . . and keeping that balance. So far.

Others clearly weren't, though.

On January 3 Kostya departed for the funeral. Half of Group A went to the train station to say good-bye. Sasha did not go.

Lisa did not go either.

Denis Myaskovsky, with whom Sasha had never been friendly, sat on a bench in the middle of the yard, blindly doodling in the snow with a twig. In response to Sasha's questioning glance, he shook his head and said, "Nothing terrible. Could be worse."

Denis's advisor was Liliya Popova; that night Sasha thought that Denis was lucky.

In the evening Lisa went somewhere. Before she left, Sasha asked timidly whether she could be of any help, and Lisa gave her such a look that Sasha's lips froze in mid-sentence. Lisa had her own relationship with Farit Kozhennikov, and fainthearted Sasha preferred not to know how exactly Lisa was going to pay for the failed exam. Meanwhile, the winter finals continued; Sasha overheard one second year telling another: "Did you hear, the little 'uns had a lot of casualties . . ."

"It's not like they weren't forewarned," his companion reasoned.

Sasha was having trouble sleeping again. She went to bed, stared at the ceiling, tossed and turned, then rose and went to the kitchen to make tea. Oksana slept soundly; Lisa sat over the exercise book. Sasha could imagine her fear. Portnov was capable of failing her again; he wasn't likely to show mercy. This institution of higher education had no such concept as mercy.

"Vita nostra brevis est . . ."

Sasha thought of her mother. There, far away, existed a normal world and a normal life. People worked, laughed, watched television. Soon Sasha would appear there—but not for long. Only for a month. And then she would have to return to the institute, work on the exercises and read the paragraphs, and feel the iron choker tighten around her neck, spikes on the inside. It was a harsh collar, very cruel. She went where she was led. She was changing, fading internally, thinking somebody else's thoughts. And she could not escape.

The entire first-year class, both Groups A and B, sank into their studies. Kostya came back on the seventh, on Orthodox Christmas Day, before the Philosophy exam.

Sasha volunteered to be the first and waived her right to prepare her answers. She rattled off her facts about Aristotle and Kant. Smiling genially, the professor gave her an A.

"Please," Sasha said softly, "don't fail Kozhennikov. There is a tragedy in his family. His grandmother just died."

The Philosophy professor gazed at her in surprise. She did not say anything, just gave Sasha back her grade book.

Kostya got a C, even though, according to eyewitnesses, he never uttered a single word.

January 12 was approaching, the day of the last exam and everyone's departure. The frightened hush that reigned among the first years after the Specialty exam was slowly disintegrating. Already people laughed, kissed, already they furtively—under their jackets—carried vodka and red wine into the kitchen; people seemed happy about their Philosophy grades and hoped that the History professor would be just as lenient.

Kostya did not talk to anyone, though. He did not seem to notice Zhenya Toporko, who followed him everywhere. He also—Sasha understood that, and her terror rose higher and higher—stopped studying, stopped working on the exercises. He moved—no, rolled—down a sharp slope, toward his second failure.

"Don't feel sorry for him," Oksana advised. "I heard he and Zhenya broke a bed in room 19, with all their humping. They ended up propping it up with a brick."

Sasha did not respond.

"He's your advisor's son, after all. Family matters."

"Yeah, I've noticed."

"Well," Oksana hesitated. "How old was his grandmother? Seventy-six? Not exactly a spring chicken, was she?"

Under Sasha's glare, Oksana stopped talking and pretended to be very interested in the contents of her cooking pot. It seemed that out of the entire population of the dorm, Oksana was the only one who knew how to cook; from time to time she spoiled herself and her neighbors with some delicious homemade ragout or cabbage dumplings.

Sasha left the kitchen, went downstairs, and knocked on the door numbered 7. Zakhar's voice answered:

"Come in!"

Sasha walked in. The room was indescribably messy. Items of clothing from underwear to winter jackets were strewn on the chairs and the floor. A thick layer of textbooks, glossy nudie magazines, crumpled sheets of paper, socks, and dirty plastic plates covered the desks. The miasma of old cigarette smoke was far heavier than in Sasha's room.

Zakhar leaned over a book. Lenya, the third roommate, stood in the corner, holding up his hands and staring at some point in the distance. He did not blink. Had Sasha seen this earlier, in September, she would have been scared to the point of getting sick to her stomach. Now she was pretty sure that Lenya was simply going through his mental exercises.

Kostya lay on his bed, facing the wall.

"Eh." Zakhar caught Sasha's eyes. "I keep telling him, study, you moron, it'll just get worse. But he's had it, he's done. We had a guy like that last year . . . The winter finals broke him."

"Was he expelled?" Sasha asked idiotically.

Zakhar gave her a gloomy sneer.

"Expelled? Yeah, they expelled him—all over the place. He went kind of crazy, and . . . Did you want something?"

Sasha looked at Kostya.

"Zakhar, how did you get Portnov's glasses?"

"I went over to him and asked."

"And he agreed?"

"Of course. He said it'd be cool."

"Is that what he said?"

"Well, more or less. Why?"

"No reason . . . What will happen to us?"

Zakhar clicked the switch of his desk lamp. "You and I will graduate. Lenya as well. That one . . . I don't know."

"What will happen to us when we graduate?"

Zakhar hesitated. Then said, "We will change. Everything will change. Our vision, hearing, our entire organisms will transform themselves. Then, during the winter finals, there will be this crucial placement test that qualifies you for moving to another level. And then . . ."

"And then what?"

"I don't know. Do you think they tell the second years everything? But I think we'll stop being human altogether."

"Then what are we going to become? Robots?"

"I think it's different for everyone. Specialization begins during the third year, after the placement exam. I guess that's what happens."

"But what's the point? What is it for? *Who* is it for?"

Lenya did not blink. Whatever was happening in the room held no interest for him. Zakhar rubbed the tip of his nose and smiled uneasily, as if Sasha and her questions embarrassed him.

But she wouldn't give up. "Are the teachers human?"

"The gym teacher is definitely human . . ."

"I am not talking about the gym teacher! You know who I mean!"

Zakhar licked his lips.

"I know as much as you do. What color is your hair?"

"Black," Sasha said, puzzled. "Dark brown. Why . . . ?"

"I keep thinking it's purple." Zakhar closed his tired eyes. "Everyone has yellow hair, and yours is purple. Colored spots. Portnov says it's normal, it's supposed to go away."

Sasha looked at Kostya again. He was not asleep. Sasha knew he was simply pretending.

"Be careful on vacation," Zakhar said. "One girl in my group went home after the winter finals, enjoyed her vacation, freedom got into her head, and she said to her parents: 'I got into a totalitarian cult, I am being poisoned with psychedelic drugs, I'm losing my mind, save me.' Her parents had money, so they put her into some prestigious clinic for treatment . . ."

"What happened?"

"When Farit brought her back a week later, she was already an orphan. She lasted one semester, failed the summer finals, and that's when she went really mad. She's at some nuthouse now."

"No way!"

Zakhar closed his eyes. "Listen, I passed Specialty, but I still have my English exam. Did you want to tell Kostya something?"

Sasha took a deep breath. She picked up a mug with leftover tea and upended it over Kostya's head.

He leapt up. Of course, he was awake; he stared at Sasha as if at an executioner.

"What do you want? What? Just let me die! All of you, let me die!"

"Control yourself," Sasha said.

She was surprised to hear Portnov's notes in her own voice.

Kostya's makeup test loomed in three days.

"You must do this. Everything else we'll deal with later."

"I can't. I—"

"Shut up! You're a weakling, you're not a man, you're slime, impotent! You don't know how to fight!"

His shoulders slumped in response.

"Listen," Sasha said. "If we learn all this, if we get to the end of the course, we shall become *just like them.* And we shall speak their language. Then we'll take revenge upon your father. I promise."

Kostya slowly looked up. For the first time Sasha noticed something besides grief and despair in his eyes. She pressed on.

"And if they crush us, we won't be able to avenge ourselves. Right now we are weak. But we'll become different. We'll find a way to pay them back."

"I just can't," Kostya said. "Ten exercises in three days—it's not possible."

"It's possible. I did twenty once."

"What?"

"Pick up your book! Read the exercise out loud!"

Hour followed hour. Often Sasha wanted to hit Kostya, punch him to make him focus, to make him concentrate and finish up what he'd already half completed. She could not peer inside his imagination, but managed to distinguish success from failure by his eyes and his breathing.

When he missed a cue at the end of a long sequence of five complex exercises, she lost her patience and slapped him on the cheek. He recoiled, clutching his face.

"What the hell?"

"Concentrate!" Sasha screamed in his face. "Focus and do it from the beginning, or I swear, I'll do it again!"

Belatedly, she felt her palm burning. She was surprised at her own reaction: never in her life had she actually hit anyone. Even as a joke. And now she was ready to grab a broom with a long handle that happened to be standing in the corner of the room and beat him with that handle, thrash him, cause him pain . . .

In the evening Kostya wanted to go to sleep, but Sasha wouldn't allow him to. She sat up with him the entire night, and at daylight, around nine o'clock, he suddenly became aware—and understood *how* these exercises were to be done.

They sat on chairs they brought into the hallway from his room. Around them things were happening—people stomped by, yelled, laughed, complained about lack of sleep, asked for snacks—and it was at that moment that Kostya accepted as reality that in two days he would pass the exam.

And only then did Sasha understand what agony he'd carried around inside him all these days.

"Sasha! I'm so glad you called! We are getting ready to meet you to-morrow, and we have such a huge surprise for you!"

"Mom . . . I am sorry, I won't be able to come tomorrow."

Pause.

"Sasha . . . How? What happened?"

"This boy here is taking a makeup test. I'm helping him."

Another pause.

"Who is this boy?"

"My classmate."

"Oh. But we are so anxious to see you . . . It's the Old New Year . . ."

"I will do my best to arrive on the fourteenth," Sasha said. "I honestly . . . I just can't get home earlier."

Strangely enough, she got another A in History, considering that she did not study at all. She got very lucky: she knew the question really well, having attended the lectures and taken notes (and apparently her notes were really good), and now she could remember everything to the minutest detail.

"I wish I had more students like you," the History professor beamed at her. Lowering her eyes in false modesty, Sasha asked:

"Please . . . Kozhennikov just had a death in the family . . . he's devastated. Please give him a C, I'll make sure he catches up."

The History professor tortured Kostya for nearly a full hour, got absolutely nothing out of him, wavered, and pursed her lips, but at the end gave him a C.

That night almost all the first years departed. Only a few people stayed behind, people whose trains arrived in the morning, and those with makeup tests scheduled for the thirteenth.

Sasha stayed.

The third years' placement exam—that very important one, the one that was crucial for the next level—was scheduled for the thirteenth as well. No jokes were made about the unlucky number. The dorm was half empty and oddly quiet.

In the morning the third years congregated in the assembly hall. Lisa, Denis, and Kostya waited in auditorium 1 (the misfits from Group B were scheduled one hour later). Sasha roamed the halls; not a sound could be heard from the assembly hall. As if it were completely empty.

Then Portnov emerged. Sasha thought he looked aggravated. She managed to hide behind the bronze stallion's leg just in time. Portnov entered auditorium 1. Sasha heard his dry voice: "Get ready. Pavlenko, you're first."

Sasha bit her lip.

Five minutes passed. Ten. Fifteen.

Then Lisa popped out of the auditorium. She was pale as plaster. Sasha felt scared.

Lisa spotted her. She swallowed.

"What happened?" Sasha couldn't help asking.

"I passed," whispered Lisa.

And, hugging Sasha's neck, she burst into sobs.

It was unexpected, and it actually hurt: Lisa's watch snagged on a lock of Sasha's hair and pulled it quite painfully. It also felt weird: no one had ever sobbed on Sasha's shoulder. She'd encountered this only in novels. Her sweater became soggy with Lisa's snot and tears; shyly, hesitantly, Sasha stroked her back.

"You see . . . you've done well. Everything is good now."

Lisa detached herself and, wiping her face with her sleeve, ran toward the girls' bathroom; on the way she stumbled, then tried to perform some swing dance moves. *She did it all on her own,* Sasha thought. *I don't know what Farit did to her, but it did not look like any sort of leniency.*

Denis was the second one to emerge. Unlike Lisa, he was red rather that white.

"How did you do?"

"A C." Denis could not believe it himself. "Holy cow . . . It's just . . ."

"How's Kostya?"

"He's up right now." Denis was already thinking of something else. "Sasha, I'm going to get wasted. I'll go into town. I'll drink myself to the point of oblivion, like a pig in the mud!"

He smiled beatifically, like Cinderella before the royal ball.

Denis left.

The third years' exam was still going on, and silence reigned in the assembly hall and in the entire school. Losing her composure, Sasha measured the hall with her footsteps.

The sun came out. The glass dome over the statue was set ablaze. The humongous equestrian swam out of darkness as if lit up by limelight. Who was he? Why was he placed there? Sasha walked and walked, listening to the sound of her footsteps. Time passed. Kostya did not come out.

Finally, the door opened; Sasha flew toward it and almost ran over Portnov. It was him, not Kostya, who exited the auditorium: glasses on the tip of his nose, blond ponytail thrown over his shoulder.

"Samokhina."

Sasha stepped back. Portnov gave her a once-over; they hadn't seen each other since he recorded an A on her grade sheet.

"I passed him . . ." Portnov gave a casual nod toward the auditorium. "I passed him, although . . . Come with me."

He turned to the concierge's glass booth. Sasha peeked into the auditorium and saw Kostya, sweaty, exhausted, but not brought to his knees.

"Did you pass?" she called out.

He nodded curtly, as if not believing it himself. Portnov got the keys from the concierge and signed her journal.

"Samokhina, auditorium 38."

He walked along the corridor, jingling the keys in his hand. Sasha followed him as if on a leash.

"Did you hit him?" Portnov asked her.

The key turned in the lock.

"No. Well, yes. It just sort of happened . . ."

"I understand. Come in."

She entered. The chairs were stacked feet up to the ceiling, seats down on the only table in the auditorium. Portnov flipped the chairs upright.

"Come over here."

A bright-green light, refracted in the pink stone of Portnov's ring, shot into Sasha's eyes. She staggered. Portnov grabbed her elbow.

"When is your train?"

"I don't know . . . I returned my ticket for today . . ."

"I see. There are no tickets for tomorrow; you may not be able to leave."

Sasha swallowed hard. Portnov took out a pack of cigarettes and a lighter. He lit up, but immediately put his cigarette out. "Sorry. I forgot you don't smoke."

That surprised Sasha. Portnov would be the first person in the school to notice such a minor detail, and it was obvious that he really wanted a cigarette.

"I don't care," she said. "I'm used to it. Please smoke."

He put away the cigarettes anyway, then sat down and motioned for her to do the same. Sasha gingerly lowered herself onto the edge of the chair.

"Kostya's . . . Kozhennikov's grandmother died because of you," she blurted out.

"Because of *me*?" He almost seemed amused.

"Because you wouldn't pass him the first time."

"I didn't pass him because he was not ready. The rest is Farit's business."

"And Farit is what? A machine that executes the sentence? A guillotine?"

"Ask him yourself." Portnov gave her a weak smile. "Why did you hit that lazy bum?"

Sasha looked down.

"He didn't want to . . . could not concentrate."

"Farit does the same thing. On his level."

Sasha clenched her fists in her lap.

"Why do you do this to us? What for? Are we somehow different, did we do something wrong?"

Portnov clicked his lighter.

"No. You did not do anything wrong. But you must study, must work hard, and you do not want to."

"Because you never explained to us what we are being taught, let alone why!"

"You would not be able to understand it. It's too early." Sasha watched his lighter release a tongue of fire and pull it back in. "When a child is taught to draw circles, does he understand what fine motor skills are? When a village boy is accepted to an academy—does he understand a lot about what's going on?"

"A lot? He understands the main idea! A good teacher can elicit interest . . . can explain . . ."

Portnov nodded.

"What is verification, Samokhina?"

"Verification: using empirical data or experiment to confirm the truth of theoretical scientific hypothesis by 'returning' to the visual level of knowledge, when the ideal nature of abstract entities is ignored, and they are 'identified' with the objects observed," Sasha said, caught off guard.

Portnov nodded.

"Your learning process is an object of observation. More precisely, it is a process happening under observation. What is happening to you in reality—you are not yet capable of comprehending in your current state of development. It is as if we caught a bunch of young chimpanzees in the jungle, collected them in one place, and, using a certain process, kicked off their transformation into . . . no, not into humans. Into models of worldwide systems and actions of all levels. Inflation, globalization, xenophobia.

"Do you know how to turn a chimpanzee into a model of stock market crisis?"

Sasha was silent.

"And there's your verification." Portnov smirked. "You are a good girl, Sasha, and you are balancing right on the edge. On the very border. I don't want to lose you."

Sasha stared into his immobile eyes with narrow pupils.

"Listen to me carefully. Tomorrow you are going home. I don't know how the ticket situation is going to work out, but let's hope you will get lucky. During your vacation—until February fourteenth—I forbid you to touch any books on Specialty. Do you understand?"

Sasha nodded, still staring at him.

"Watch yourself very carefully. Stifle your aggravation. Keep your aggression in check. I know, you are not used to it, but you are very dangerous to others right now. Especially to those who knew you before and who remember you as a calm, compliant girl."

"I cannot be dangerous to others," Sasha said.

"Close your mouth when I am talking. Avoid large crowds. Stay away from stressful situations. Make sure to get your return ticket in advance. I want to see you here on the fourteenth—do not be late. And here's something else: no heart-to-heart talks with your mother. I am telling you this because I wish you well."

"I noticed," Sasha said hoarsely.

Portnov smiled.

"You are dismissed. Free to go."

Kostya met her in the dark hallway and hugged her, nearly breaking her ribs.

She waited politely for a minute, then detached herself.

"Sasha . . ."

"Congratulations," she said officially. "I wish you further success in your studies. Sorry, I have to pack, I'm going home."

Leaving him behind, she went back to the dorm. Oddly enough, her heart felt light and calm.

Oksana had left the day before. Lisa was not in the room. Sasha threw all her stuff in her suitcase, could not close the lid, and put half of her things back in the dresser. It was quickly getting dark. Sasha glanced at the clock: half past six. The train was coming at 11:23, but she had no ticket and no idea what she should do.

Should she go to the train station? Or try the ticket office first?

Breathing heavily, she hauled the suitcase out of the room and managed to drag it down the stairs. A memory flashed in her mind: she and Kostya, new kids stepping over the threshold of the dormitory for the first time, the stairs, the suitcase . . .

As usual, the concierge's desk was deserted. Sasha put the room key on the hook for number 21.

It was snowing again. Sasha walked along the narrow alley to Sacco and Vanzetti and looked for a cab.

There were no cabs. There never were when she needed one. Sasha would have to walk along the snowy streets, hauling the suitcase behind her, until she reached the town's center, and then she'd have to wait for the bus. Oh well, she had enough time.

"Alexandra!"

She recognized the voice and froze on the spot.

"Sasha, I've been waiting for you."

She refused to turn around. She simply stood clutching the handle of her suitcase. Then the suitcase was taken out of her hands.

"I'm waiting to give you a ride to the train station in my car. Shall we?"

"I won't get in your car," Sasha said, feeling how her eyes, which had been dry for so long, filled with tears. "Please go away."

Snow fell slowly. The streetlight glowed.

"You and I need to settle a bit of a debt," Kozhennikov said, his voice completely different, businesslike. "Coins."

Sasha remembered leaving the bag of coins in the dorm, in her room, under the mattress.

"They are in my room."

"Go get them."

She finally looked at him. Snowflakes reflected in his dark glasses.

"One minute."

She ran back to the dorm, tore the key off the hook, went upstairs, found the bag of coins, and locked the room. She went back outside; Kozhennikov was waiting for her, her suitcase placed on the ground.

"Here."

He weighted the bag in his hand:

"Thirty-seven . . . Your inner life is in quite a turmoil, Alexandra."

She held her tongue and did not respond.

"Sasha, I can get you a ticket, even if there are none at the ticket office. And I will bring you right to the train station."

"I don't need your help. Good-bye."

She walked down the street, not looking back, pulling the suitcase behind her. It was getting heavier and heavier, struggling to turn over, its wheels catching on the pavement. A car followed Sasha, not falling behind and not getting ahead; she did not look to see if it was

Farit's. She only heard the soft sound of an automobile crawling over the snow.

Breathing heavily, she finally detected the lights of the central square ahead of her. The bus was coming in half an hour, and a pretty large crowd was assembled at the stop. Kozhennikov's car, a milky-white Nissan, stopped nearby.

Sasha purchased a bus ticket and took her place in the queue. The snow stopped. The wind chased away the clouds and pulled the remaining heat from under Sasha's jacket.

The bus was running late. When it finally arrived, small and slow, it became obvious that not everyone was going to get on. Bickering followed. The driver promised to return quickly and do one more round-trip.

Sasha was chilled to the bone. It was the Old New Year's Eve. Stars broke out in the sky. Kozhennikov stood next to his car. He did not leave. He waited, his hands stuck in his pockets, and stared up into the sky.

The second time the bus arrived shortly after ten. Gasping for breath, Sasha managed to drag her suitcase into the narrow entrance and placed it next to someone's bundle; this time, she got yelled at—apparently, she'd stepped on someone's foot. Trying not to pay any attention, she folded herself into the space next to her suitcase and sighed with relief once the lights of Torpa started creeping backward. She had more than an hour until the arrival of the train, she was going to be fine. It was unthinkable that the ticket office would not have one single lousy ticket . . .

The bus skidded and got stuck in the snow. All the passengers, except for the frailest old ladies, had to come get out and push it; the engine roared, dense smoke poured out of the exhaust pipe, snow flew from under the wheels. Sasha's toes felt frostbitten; at first she was anxious, then angry, then she stopped caring.

The bus reached the station four minutes before the train was scheduled to arrive. Those with tickets sprinted to the platform. Sasha dashed to the ticket office; the window was closed and a sign indicated NO TICKETS.

Sasha sat down on a wooden bench. Again she thought of the morning she'd spent there with Kostya, the sandwiches, the note that read "Leave now . . ."

Kozhennikov walked into the station. He stopped at the locked ticket window. Sasha did not look up.

She heard the train arrive, but did not even attempt to get up.

People scurried around. The breaks screeched; then screeched again, the train started gaining speed, whistled—and was gone.

Kozhennikov came over and sat down next to her.

"Listen, I respect your choice . . . but in half an hour, the train stops at Galcy, fifteen minutes away by car. May I take you there?"

Sasha turned her head.

"What do you want from me?"

"I want to help you. I am responsible for you."

"And are you responsible for Kostya? For . . . all this? Who do you answer to?"

"I surely will answer to someone," he said seriously. "Let's go."

He picked up her suitcase.

She was too tired and too chilly to resist. He put her suitcase in the back of the white car and opened the door. Sasha walked into the warmth; the door shut with a smacking sound.

Kozhennikov sat next to her, removed his gloves, and took out a thermos.

"Here, drink this. It's tea with cognac."

A freight train roared by. Sasha took a sip and burned her lips. She caught her breath and took another sip.

"Take my business card. Just in case."

He placed a business card in her lap, a white rectangle with a telephone number, but no name.

"Use your seat belt."

The car got onto the highway and immediately gained speed: Sasha threw a sideways glance and saw the speedometer arrow vacillate at eighty miles per hour. Kozhennikov stared at the road; forest trees sped along both sides of the highway. The long rays of his headlights jumped, dove, and flew up on uneven road.

She pocketed his business card.

"Are you human?"

"Let's agree on the terminology. What is a human? A two-legged creature without feathers . . ."

"I'm serious."

"I'm not joking."

Sasha fell silent.

"Listen, Sasha. I'm very thankful to you for what you have done for my son. You pulled him out by his ears—*saved* him—from some very unpleasant things. You are a brave soul, my girl."

"You are telling me this? *You?*"

He kept his eyes on the road. Ten minutes later they reached a tiny station, flanked by woods on all three sides. Fifteen minutes later, the train arrived; Kozhennikov had a short exchange with the train attendant, slipped something into her palm, and nodded to Sasha.

"Have a good trip."

He lifted her suitcase onto the train.

The train carriage turned out to be split into compartments. Silently, the attendant showed Sasha the top berth in the staff compartment. Sasha hopped in there as she was, in jeans and a sweater, and when she woke up, snow sparkled outside in the sun, and it was almost eleven in the morning.

The train arrived on time. On the platform Sasha saw Mom and Valentin, who searched for her, looking nervous. A few moments later, Mom clutched her, held her tight, then stepped back a little:

"Wow! What happened to you?"

"What?" Sasha was startled.

"You seem taller . . . You've grown, a couple of inches at least!"

They grabbed a cab and took their student home in style. Mom chatted and laughed, and everyone around her was told that Sasha got straight A's on all her winter finals. The cabdriver learned about it, and the neighbors they saw in the elevator learned about it, and all Mom's girlfriends who called that day were given that information immediately. Sasha thought that Mom had changed as well: she seemed more cheerful, more relaxed, happier . . . less intelligent? She chased away that thought.

Mom's hand had healed, and the cast had been removed. The apartment smelled different—the smell of Valentin, who'd settled in a while ago, was mixed with the familiar atmosphere. *Now it was his apartment, too,* thought Sasha with a hint of sadness.

Her room had not changed. Same rugs, same books on the shelves. A new calendar on the wall, its pictures showing snow falling on forest trees, January . . . Sasha had a tough time convincing herself that it was actually her room, her apartment, her bathroom, and there was no need to wait in line for the shower, and no need to bring toilet paper: there was plenty of it in the bathroom, lemon-colored, the embodiment of comfort.

Was it truly just yesterday that they had stood in the empty hall under the belly of a bronze stallion—she, Kostya, Lisa, Denis?

Was it truly Farit who gave her a ride to the train last night? "I am very thankful to you . . ."

Was all that happened to her . . . for real?

Sasha lay down on her bed. That sensation—of a familiar hard bed rather than an orphanage-style steel-mesh bed—assured her that she was truly home.

That night they had a big party. A custom-made cake was delivered from a bakery. Mom's friends congratulated her; Valentin, who had gained a bit of weight in six months of his new family life, labored in the kitchen, eliciting praises from the gathered women.

Sasha smiled, nodded, and spoke occasionally. Even so, the guests glanced at her, at first curious, then surprised, and finally uneasy. For some reason, Mom looked nervous. Sasha apologized and went into her room, lay down, fell asleep, and did not hear the guests depart.

"Sasha, do you feel well?" Mom asked the next morning.

"Sure. Why?"

"You've got this stupid new habit—you freeze mid-word and stare into space. What's all this about?"

"I don't know," Sasha said sincerely. "Maybe I just pause to think of something before I speak?"

Mom sighed.

Sasha really had grown two inches in the last four months. The notches on the door frame did not allow for mistake: Sasha had stopped growing in ninth grade at a normal human height: five feet five inches. And now she was five feet seven inches. Mom was surprised and happy about it.

"Do you have some special physical education classes there?"

"Oh yes, we have such a cool gym teacher!"

Mom wanted to know everything about the institute: living conditions in the dorm, what she was eating, about all the teachers. Sasha mostly stuck to the truth, carefully filtering everything Mom was better off not knowing, though. Dima Dimych presented some excellent topics for discussion: his kindness, his youth, and his dancing skills.

"I suppose all the girls have a crush on him?"

"Yeah, pretty much." Sasha blushed, remaining perfectly calm inside. Her intuition suggested that at this moment blushing would be appropriate.

Another excellent conversation topic was provided by the History and Philosophy professors. Sasha boasted about the homemaking skills of her roommate, talked about winterizing the windows and making their room nice and warm. Central heat? There were some interruptions, but only short ones. Alcohol? Are you kidding, Mom, they watch us like crazy in that dorm, the superintendent checks all the rooms all the time . . .

"So what about the transfer?" Valentin interrupted her at some point.

"What transfer?"

"You wanted to transfer out of Torpa. Remember?"

"Yeah." Sasha was caught off guard. "But frankly speaking, it's a good school, the teachers are excellent, and the kids are great. Maybe I should stay put."

Mom and Valentin exchanged glances.

"Sasha, just think for a minute," Mom said carefully. "Imagine you are trying to get a job. You will immediately be asked: What school did you graduate from? And you will have to tell them that you have a diploma from a completely unknown provincial school in a teeny town no one has ever heard of . . ."

"I'll think about it," Sasha said quickly. "But if I transfer, I shouldn't do it right after the first semester, don't you think?"

"But we should start planning in advance," Valentin stated with a great deal of authority.

Sasha nodded, trying to wrap up that conversation as soon as possible.

A few days later she realized she missed the institute.

It was impossible, but nevertheless it was true. Sasha missed the dorm and her classmates. Individual sessions on Specialty, paragraphs and exercises, the familiar strain and tiny achievements, the ordinary labor of anyone who desires to learn—all this turned out to be the point of Sasha's existence. Here, at home, in warm comfort, life had no meaning. Whether you woke up at ten in the morning or at noon, whether you watched television, went for a walk in the park, or went to the theater or attended a concert—none of it mattered; there was no point, a day was lived in vain, then one more day, and then a week. Sasha felt blue, stared at the ceiling, slowly but surely sinking into a real depression.

"Sasha, what are you doing stuck at home? Go for a walk. Call somebody. What are your former classmates doing? Who is studying where? Don't you *care?*"

But she really didn't.

A week before the end of her vacation Sasha went to the park. The very same park she'd measured with her steps so many times, dotted with familiar overgrown bushes. This winter the park had undergone a metamorphosis: a skating rink was built, the trees were decorated with lights and garlands, and skates could now be rented at a shack that stood nearby, unused, for many years.

Sasha hadn't skated since seventh grade, but now something drew her to the rink. She stepped on the ice and moved forward, spreading her arms, ready to be clumsy and slow. Not even close: only a second later, she accepted the dull blades of rented skates as a continuation of her own body, and the uneven, dented ice seemed familiar and comfortable.

She went around in a full circle. Ceased to think and simply moved. She flew, imagining the surface of the ice as the snowed-in ground far below. Lights flickered in naked branches, multihued snow shimmered. Sasha skated, oblivious to her surroundings, a little surprised, but joyful; a couple of hours passed before she got tired and looked around for a bench.

They were sitting at the edge of the ice. A rather large cluster: four guys and as many girls, and in its epicenter reigned Ivan Konev, a law student now, owner of a soft curly beard.

"Hey, Kon."

"Hey, Sasha. Decent skating. Guys, move over."

Sasha joined the group.

All of them went to the most prestigious schools, except maybe one girl, somebody's sister, who was still a high-school student. But even she, of course, was looking forward to something economics-internationalish with a concentration in law. They had plenty of questions for Sasha, all with a hint of sympathy: What's there to do in Torpa? Do they sell pickles at the stores there? Are there bedbugs in the dorm?

"Only cockroaches," Sasha assured them.

"Ivan! It sounds fabulous! Maybe you should transfer to Torpa."

The girl who asked the question was a daddy's girl in an expensive-looking pale pink sheepskin coat. She had trouble understanding why they were wasting time at some stupid ice-skating rink, when normal people were enjoying themselves in decent clubs. Sasha seemed to aggravate her to no end: the girl must have some interest in Ivan Konev. Her cell phone kept ringing ostentatiously.

"I just might transfer there," Konev said. "Why not?"

Sasha changed her shoes and returned the skates to the rental office.

"You've grown," Ivan said, giving her a once-over. "I wasn't imagining it."

All of them went to a café, had a few beers, and Sasha felt unexpectedly relaxed. She even managed to crack two or three jokes that made everyone laugh uproariously, even the girl with the cell phone. It was already almost midnight when the group dissipated; most people got into cabs, and Ivan Konev walked Sasha home by himself.

"Listen, Samokhina, you have changed so much."

"How? I'd like to know myself, really."

"Well." Ivan spread his arms. "I look at you, and it seems as if we've never met. And I've known you since first grade . . ."

"Yes," Sasha said. "But they say it does happen. People mature, you know."

"Maybe I really should transfer to Torpa . . ."

Sasha bit back her response.

"Your face has changed," Konev continued. "Your eyes are strange. Your pupils . . . Listen, do you—are you on drugs?"

"No," Sasha said with surprise. "Of course not."

"What is your profession called?"

"That will be decided during the third year," Sasha said after a pause. "Transferring to the next level . . . Specialization."

"I see," Konev said, and it was abundantly clear that he saw nothing. "Just one more thing. When you stare at something in the distance, what do you see?"

"Me?"

"Yeah, like right now. I thought you'd forgotten about me . . ."

"I did?"

"Listen, are you seeing anyone in Torpa?"

Sasha slowed down. "No. There was this one guy, but . . . anyway, not anymore."

"I see," Konev repeated. "But seriously, you are going to transfer, right? To a normal school, and closer to home?"

"Seriously? No."

They stopped in the dark yard of Sasha's building. The windows were lit, a lone streetlight emitted a dull shine, and a man in a fur hat strode down the path from the underground walkway, a briefcase under his arm. Probably working late.

"I am leaving in a week," Sasha whispered.

"It's a shame. At least give me your address."

"Town of Torpa, Sacco and Vanzetti Street, 12, room 21, Alexandra Samokhina. Write, if you . . ."

Three figures emerged out of the darkness behind the passerby. The man with a briefcase didn't have a chance to even look back: he received a blow on the head and fell down. His hat rolled away and was immediately snatched up.

Ivan grabbed Sasha's hand. Three people, having brought down the fourth, did not rush to scurry away with their loot: they just kicked the fallen man, punched him in the stomach, in the face, stomped over him . . .

She felt as if a glass had cracked and burst into shards. As if the shards flew into her face. Sasha tore away from Konev's spasmodic embrace.

"Hold it! Freeze, you bastards!"

She remembered Portnov's caution, but could do absolutely nothing about it. Her hatred toward the thugs beating up a helpless victim was far stronger than any warning.

They dropped their victim and turned to face her. They seemed surprised to see a girl running toward them; one even stretched his lips in a smirk . . .

A thin rivulet of blood spattered onto the white snow that sparkled blue under the glow of distant streetlights. And immediately—a stream, a fountain. Stars were smeared before her eyes in the ripped fabric of storm clouds; a sudden chill cut her like sandpaper. Sasha found herself sitting in a snow pile, three people lying unmoving near her, the fourth crawling away, wheezing, toward the main road.

Her hands hurt. Her palms. Sasha looked down: both index fingers were covered in a sticky film of blood, like a dark latex glove.

She glanced around, looking for someone, but all around her was stillness, darkness. A car drove by without stopping.

Sasha dipped her hands into the snow.

There was a telephone booth in the underground walkway. A call for an ambulance was free. Just dial 003.

▪ ▪ ▪

In the morning, getting ready for work, Mom was slicing bread and singing softly. Sasha came out of her room, and words fought to get out of her, rising up her throat.

"Mom," she wanted to say, "don't let me go back to Torpa. I can't go back. They are doing something with me, I don't know what. I can't go back, I am scared!" But she said nothing.

"Good morning, Sasha." Mom smiled and tucked a loose curl behind her ear. "Would you like an omelet? With sausage?"

Sasha saw her face, tenderly lit by the morning sun. Mom was alive, healthy, and happy. Sasha could hear the sound of water—Valentin was in the shower.

"Mm-hmm." Sasha nodded, her lips squeezed tightly together.

She went back to her room and closed the door. She fell on her knees and threw up: unspoken words rolled around the room, gold coins smeared in slime.

"Miss! Get up!"

"What?"

Darkness. The train rocked softly.

"Miss, we will be in Torpa in fifteen minutes! Get up, you have a ticket to Torpa!"

Passengers slept under dusty, railroad-issued blankets. Windows were sweaty and frosted over in some places. Snow, nothing but snow, swam along both sides of the train. Somewhere a spoon jingled in an empty glass.

"I want it to be a dream," Sasha murmured.

But nothing happened.

PART TWO

At the end of April the prolonged chilly spring suddenly gave way to almost summery warmth. One morning at half past four Sasha woke up with an unyielding need to wash the windows.

Birds were waking up and night clouds parted. Sasha sat up in her bed. Since the third years had passed their placement exam and moved to a different location, the dorm had become more spacious. Lisa had finally found an apartment and now lived in town, in an alley between Sacco and Vanzetti and Labor Streets. Oksana now shared a room with a friend of hers from Group B, and Sasha—what an unexpected luxury—now had the entire room 21 at her disposal.

She felt about for her slippers. She registered: "These are slippers. They protect me from cold floors." She got up, then stood for a while, establishing the ever-changing gravitational vector. Approached the window.

For the past few weeks she'd felt like painting her image on the glass. She painted at night when the light was on inside, and it was dark outside. Sasha traced her reflection with gouache paints. Every day the painting looked different. The morning light tried to get through in vain: the gouache was opaque and lay in a thick, dense layer.

Must get water, Sasha thought. *Windows are washed with water.*

She moved to the door. The door frames had a lousy habit of slithering out of her reach like a marinated mushroom escaping the fork. That's why Sasha first felt for the door with her hands, found the obstacles on the right and left sides, and only then exited the room.

The linoleum floor shone dully. A distant window was reflected on the painted wall. *So beautiful,* Sasha thought.

She walked along the corridor, trailing her hand on the wall just in case.

The tin bucket stood in its usual spot under the sink. Sasha filled a one-gallon jar with water and transferred it to the bucket. One more jar. And one more. *Three gallons of water.* She picked up the bucket by its narrow handle and carried it to her room.

In her absence the door had managed to shift a couple of feet. Sasha bumped into the door frame and splashed a little bit of water. *It is fine. Now I will be able to enter.*

She found strips of old pillowcases that served as cleaning rags behind the radiator. The heat had been turned off two weeks ago. Sasha tore off the paper strips, pulled out the yellow foam, wet one of the rags, and, dripping water on the floor, guided it over the painted image: up and down and left to right. For some reason, her painted reflection had blue eyes.

Eyes. Must see. Lately she could think only of things that could be seen through her eyes. Lines in textbooks could be viewed: Sasha read, trying not to move her lips, and the pages changed colors under her glance. Redness inched slowly from the book's spine, filling the page with cranberry juice, and then the page faded, became yellow, and then an emerald color. When she read, Sasha stopped thinking altogether.

The paint was becoming blurry. Sasha moved her hand from side to side, every now and then dipping the rag into the bucket, but she did not squeeze it dry; her body felt relaxed, blurry like the picture on the window. As if she, Sasha, were but a puddle of hot wax. The space around her contracted and stretched, time broke off the hands on her watch and got tangled up in the bowels of the electronic alarm clock. Time served no master and answered no one. It was just half past four—and then here it was, eight o'clock, time to get ready for school.

Sasha dropped the rag into the bucket. She glanced at the sky through the still cloudy glass. She opened the window: outside the air was cool and smelled of lilacs.

"Get ready for school."

She moved her eyes to the slightly ajar door of her wardrobe. *Wardrobe is for clothes.* Put on clothes. Get books. Notepads. Time for classes. First block is Philosophy.

She would move in a crowd of first years, greeting them, nodding, occasionally even smiling. *These are people. Must speak with them.* She would take her usual seat and open her notes. She would listen to a succession of unfamiliar words, her face static, unmoving; she would laugh when everyone else laughed. She would take notes, write down word after word.

She would always try to be the last one to exit the room—in order to let others hold the door open. Slowly. Gradually. The second block was free—no class. It was time to read the textbook.

Holding on to the wall, she would go to the library. Greeting the librarian's chair, she would sit by the window and open the *Textual Module* in the spot where, instead of a bookmark, lay a birthday card from Mom. The card depicted a sheep with a bouquet of bluebells.

She'd picked this card on purpose. Common sense told her that her birthday was important for her mother. She'd called home and, while speaking, held the card in front of her eyes. Only Mom's voice remained now: Sasha could not see her and could not imagine her, so she'd spoken to the sheep. The sheep had smiled; Sasha knew she was supposed to feel happy, and she'd smiled back.

Since that day, the card reminded her of something she could not imagine. This is a sheep; the sheep is happy. It was my birthday. I am eighteen years old. I must read paragraphs seventeen and eighteen.

*"He did not sleep all night. He had plucked the flower because he saw in this action a deed he was in duty bound to perform."**

Nonsensical combinations of letters stretched like caterpillars, grabbing onto one another with tin hooks. The process resembled swimming in muddy waters: Sasha would see nothing and hear only the screeching of her own ground-up thoughts. Then suddenly she would swim up to the surface, and in front of her—just for a moment—opened distant flashes of meaning.

"At the very first glance through the glass door the bloodred petals had attracted his attention, and it seemed to him that from this moment it was perfectly clear what in particular he was called upon to perform on earth."

"Samokhina, go eat something. The dining hall closes in fifteen minutes."

---

* Vsevolod Garshin, *The Signal and Other Stories*. Translated by Captain Rowland Smith of the British Embassy, Petrograd.

"In this brilliant red flower was collected all the evil existent on earth . . . all evil. It flourished on all innocent bloodshed (which was why it was so red), on all tears, and all human venom."

The flashes of meaning ceased, and only muddy waters remained. Sasha would finish the paragraph. She placed the bookmark on the page: the sheep's smile reminded her of something, but she had a tough time figuring out what it was exactly. Sasha would close the textbook, put it into her bag, locate the door frame (the library doors were especially nimble and slippery). She would walk out; the corridor would seem very dark, then, filled with extremely bright lights that made visible every parquet plank, every crack, every cigarette butt on the bottom of a tin urn.

I am walking along the corridor. Dining hall is over there. I must eat. Here is my lunch ticket.

". . . what in particular he was called upon to perform on earth . . ."

Every second the world around her altered. Some connections strained and grew, others broke. The process resembled convulsions. Every now and then Sasha would stand still, listening to herself: inside, an invisible thread would tauten, cutting and rehashing, weakening and twitching again. Occasionally, she saw herself from the outside: a small lake of melted ice cream, and in the coffee-colored slush swam a tiny acrid nubbin—Sasha's fear. Sasha did not like looking at her fear. It looked like a half-digested chunk of meat.

But she was not afraid, because she could not see anything that would frighten her, and she could think only of things she was able to see. Time stretched and tightened, until it was time for summer finals.

"Samokhina, what are you thinking regarding the summer internship?"

Brilliant rays of sun beat on the window of auditorium 38. They seemed nearly as dazzling as the reflected beam of the pink stone of Portnov's ring.

"Nothing."

It was true. The fragile thread of Sasha's thoughts was gradually turning into a dotted line. She observed things—the dust particles in the sunbeam, that desk with a deep scratch, and those green tops of the linden trees outside the window. Yet she did not *think* about them.

"Listen carefully, here's what needs to be done. The summer finals will be over on June twenty-fifth. Internship starts on the twenty-sixth. Don't forget to notify your parents."

Sasha was silent.

"In August you can spend two weeks at home before school starts again."

"Fine," Sasha said, watching the sunbeam.

"Good for you," Portnov said. "And now show me exercises fifty-two through fifty-four. Simultaneously, don't forget. Three branches of the process must be led in parallel, with a half-measure step between them. Concentrate."

In the middle of July, on the anniversary of her meeting with Farit Kozhennikov, Sasha balanced on a branch of a large cherry tree. Her summer internship responsibilities included going up a ladder into the thickness of tree branches, locating red berries amid the light and shade, taking hold of them with her palm, carefully picking them off, and placing them in the basket that hung on her chest.

The orchard was enormous. The cherry branches intertwined; the berries hung in clusters and could be picked from the ground, but the real magnificence started on top of the trees.

Sasha swallowed so many cherries that her mouth was sore. Cherry juice covered her white T-shirt. Her lips seemed huge, as if blown up. Cherry juice collected under her fingernails. Sasha was happy. The only thing that upset her was having to return all her textbooks to the library. Sasha told Portnov that she'd lost the *Exercise* book, but he'd simply gone into her room and pulled the textbook from the crack behind the radiator—apparently, she wasn't the first student to try this. Since then Sasha had stopped studying. Neither did she think. She just watched. And felt: warmth, light wind, her palms touching the tree bark, cherries caressing her face.

It was a summer day—very warm and bright; leaves protected Sasha from the blazing sun. In the morning, trucks brought the first years—no, second years already—to the garden. At midday they would be given food. Yet time stretched, lacquered cherries reflected the sun—and Sasha's face. Lunch hadn't arrived yet, but the day had already passed. And here was a whole week, even though this day hadn't yet ended. Time resembled a neat bow.

Then the weather changed. Clouds crept all over the sky, predicting a thunderstorm. Sasha spread the branches over her head and watched the sky, as if trying to commit it to memory: the edge of a cloud moving over the sun and the resulting color of mercury. A brim of a cloud, reddish like a jellyfish. A flat whirlwind in the sky, resembling a thumbprint. *Thunderstorm,* Sasha thought, *the rain is going to be heavy, I need to hide under an awning . . .*

She was still thinking of what she could see. Yet she was beginning to feel anxious: it seemed she was starting to look into the future. Predicting what was going to happen in a few minutes.

"It is going to rain," she said out loud.

No one answered. The orchard was too big. The interns had lost track of one another a long time ago.

Sasha slid down her tree. Carefully transferred the cherries from her basket to a box. To be on the safe side, she covered the berries with a piece of plastic that lay nearby on the grass.

Then she lay on her back and stared upward. Stillness descended upon the orchard, like during Portnov's lectures; the leaves froze. Sasha stared straight ahead.

A thin layer of hot air surrounded her face. Above she detected another layer, filled with whirling flies. Higher still was the thick top of the cherry tree; to Sasha it seemed transparent. Above that—frozen masses of air, and beyond—a thick layer of clouds. Higher, still higher, the stratosphere . . .

The clouds swirled into a funnel, and simultaneously Sasha fell into the sky. This used to frighten her. In her childhood, at a summer retreat, she had lain on a field just like that, stared up, and had been afraid of tumbling into the sky.

And now it was happening, but she wasn't scared.

Wind tore the plastic sheet off the box, and the cherries stared out of it in a multitude of dark eyes. Sasha saw herself from their point of view: the picture would splinter, then collect into a whole, and that would cause a stereo effect.

She was caught and pulled up like a kite, while her body on the grass remained inert. A thread that connected her to this anchor helped her soar, yet also kept her close. She felt the trees as her arms, and the grass as her hair. Lightning struck, torn leaves flew by, and Sasha laughed with pure joy.

She knew herself to be a word spoken by the sunlight. She laughed at the fear of death. She understood what she was born for and what she was destined to carry out. All this happened while the lightning remained in the sky, a white flash.

And then it began to rain, and she came to her senses—soaking wet, her T-shirt stuck to her body, a lacy bra, coquettish and pitiful, peeking through the wet fabric.

"Greetings, second years."

Specialty lectures were still held in the same auditorium 1. Second-year students of Group A sat behind the same tables that looked like high-school desks.

Sasha looked around, surprised to see many familiar but entirely forgotten details. Here was a blackboard, just like in high school. Here was a dent on a painted wall. Here were the people who had stayed close to her almost the entire summer . . .

At some point, all of these things had ceased to mean anything, had become transparent like soap bubbles. But now the second year was starting—and everything was gaining new meaning.

Sasha herself had changed. It felt as if she had been taken apart—and then put back together again, but at first glance she seemed exactly the same. Sometimes even she herself thought that she was exactly the same as last fall, when they had listened to "*Gaudeamus*" in the assembly hall.

Portnov opened the thin paperbound attendance journal.

"Biryukov, Dmitry."

"Here." Dmitry covered his face with his hand, as if the sunlight blinded him.

"Bochkova, Anna."

"Here." Anna blinked, too often and too fretfully.

"Goldman, Yulia."

"Here." Yulia sat lopsided, doodling in her notepad. Every now and then her head twitched.

"Korotkov, Andrey."

"Here." For some reason, during the summer Andrey had shaved his head and now resembled a very young suntanned army recruit.

"Have you decided to save money on hairbrushes?" Portnov squinted at him. "Not bad, not bad, it suits you. Kovtun, Igor."

"Here."

"Kozhennikov, Konstantin."

"Here." Kostya raised his head. His hair was bleached by the sun and stood on end. He sat next to Zhenya Toporko, but not right beside her—an empty chair remained between them.

"Myaskovsky, Denis."

"Here."

It was abundantly clear that the entire group was present, but the roll call continued, a solemn ritual. Sasha breathed deeply. The very smell of the institute, the smell of fresh paint, plaster, dust, and linden trees outside reminded her and stressed the point: she was alive, her life was rich and colorful, and everything was back to its normal state—September, learning, auditorium 1, sunlight.

"Pavlenko, Lisa."

"Here," said Lisa.

She was wearing exaggeratedly wide jeans with decorative suspenders falling along the pant legs. Unexpectedly, the baggy jeans only emphasized Lisa's thin, fragile figure; she had a tan that made her blond hair seem even lighter.

"Samokhina, Alexandra."

"Here."

Portnov measured her with his eyes, but did not comment.

"Toporko, Zhenya."

"Here."

"I can see you enjoyed your vacation." Portnov squinted. "You look like you spent it at an expensive resort."

Zhenya seemed unperturbed. She'd visibly matured since last year; out of a frumpy teenager emerged a sexy, shapely young woman. Her schoolgirl braids remained in the past; this summer Zhenya had cut her hair fashionably short. Her tanned face boasted a gentle blush; sitting near Kostya, she looked at Portnov almost without fear: beautiful, yes, I am fully aware, now what?

Roll call completed, Portnov gave the group one more glance over his glasses.

"We all had a good rest and are now ready for new accomplishments. This semester, as usual, we prepare for hard work. You will have another Specialty subject: Introduction to Applied Science. Your professor is Nikolay Valerievich Sterkh. He is an excellent teacher—try not to disappoint him. With that addition, you will have fewer subjects on general education. Physical Education remains a mandatory subject, though. Has anyone yet spoken with the first years who just moved into the dorms?"

A light whisper ran through the rows.

"I have," Sasha said. "I got two new first-year roommates this morning. Am I not allowed to?"

"You are allowed. However: if anyone here has a discussion with a first-year student regarding the profile of our institute, its specialization, education program, or educational style—that person will answer to his or her advisor. Therefore I suggest you restrain yourselves."

The murmur of voices in the auditorium became louder.

"But what should we tell them?" Korotkov asked. "In case they ask?"

Portnov smiled unexpectedly.

"Give them good advice. Convince them to study hard and attend all their classes. Comfort them in case of hysterics. You are mature people—come up with something. Remember how last year the former third years gave you moral support."

"We'll support them," Denis said.

Sasha glanced back. The entirety of Group A was watching their professor; some people sat leaning to one side. Some had a tough time focusing their eyes. Some twitched, some giggled uncontrollably. A gathering of freaks.

"Some of you are still going through the deconstructive stage," Portnov said, as if addressing her thoughts. "Which is not surprising, considering your laziness and lack of energy. I want to remind you: only those who study hard have a short and easy path to normality . . . to the state that you deem normal at this point, that is. Reminder: alcohol is forbidden on the premises. The first years are going to drink, and at first they will not be punished. But if I see even a trace of alcohol in your blood—and I am not even talking about drugs, because those of you who attempt to smoke pot at this point in the process are doomed. If I find alcohol in anyone's room, I will make sure that you will vomit every time vodka is even mentioned. Is this clear? Any questions?"

His glasses reflected the windowpanes. No one had questions.

"That's it for the administrative issues," Portnov said. "Prefect, the textbooks are on the table. Please distribute them to the class: *Textual Module,* Level Four, and the *Problem Set,* Level Three."

"Am I prefect again this year?" Kostya ventured.

Portnov raised an eyebrow.

"Group A, are there any other candidates?"

"Let Samokhina be the prefect," Lisa said. "She's our star student and a community leader."

Someone giggled, but the sound died down immediately.

"Samokhina"—Portnov wasn't looking at Sasha—"has enough work this semester. Kozhennikov, you've already taken up two minutes. Just do your job, I beg of you."

The textbooks were old and smelled of dust. Sasha couldn't help herself and peeked at the first page of the book of exercises.

"Samokhina!" Portnov's voice lashed at her like a whip. "I did not give permission to open the book!"

Reluctantly, she closed the book. But the first lines of the very first exercise had already caused her to sink into delicious ecstasy.

Back in Torpa, she no longer felt the enormous pressure of living at home. The two weeks that she'd spent with Mom and Valentin had turned out to be harder than she'd thought: she had been constantly forced to check herself, listen, hear, give appropriate answers, and smile at regular intervals. Sasha had done her best, but Mom had kept getting more and more worried.

"Sasha," she had said one morning when they were alone in the apartment. "You know what . . . Show me your arms."

At first Sasha had had no idea why she was asking this. It had turned out Mom was looking for needle marks, but, not finding any, had not completely relaxed.

"Mom, that's just silly. What made you think that?"

"You are acting so strange. You answer out of turn. You look . . . detached. What is happening to you, can you tell me? What's going on? Do you smoke? Sniff? Are you taking pills?"

"I swear to you," Sasha had said tiredly. "I've never tried anything like that in my life. I don't even drink vodka."

Yet Mom had not seemed convinced. She had seemed anxious herself, at first high-strung, then cheerful, she would look preoccupied, then forget about her worries, and finally Sasha had ended up asking her:

"Is something going on with *you*? What happened?"

"Can you tell?" Mom said after a pause, and she blushed.

"Tell what?" Sasha blinked.

"I am expecting," Mom had said simply. "We are—Valentin and I."

"How?"

"The usual way," Mom had said, trying to be unflappable, even sarcastic. "I am not as old as you may think."

"I don't think that," Sasha had mumbled. "I meant something different. But . . ."

"But when a man and a woman love each other, it is perfectly natural that they want to have a child. Valentin wants a baby."

"And you?"

"And so do I!" Mom's laugh had sounded a bit tense. "Don't you want a baby brother? Or a baby sister?"

"I don't know," Sasha had admitted, having considered the possibility. "It's all sort of transcendental."

At that moment she'd understood Mom's state of mind, and she also had known why the subject of drugs and Sasha's unusual reactions had not developed any further. Sasha had no idea what she would have done had Mom pressed her against the wall with questions like: What do you do in Torpa? But Mom was too busy. She was growing a baby, and that unborn baby, and not grown-up Sasha, was getting all her attention.

Sasha thought about it, realizing her own unfairness. Mom was not indifferent to her fate. Mom was torn between her new family and Sasha, and Sasha felt torn in half herself: she desperately wanted to return *and* for her mother to release her from Torpa. She knew perfectly well that her latter wish was unattainable and criminal. She was terrified that one day Mom would learn the truth and would attempt to free Sasha—and would perish in the struggle, because she had absolutely no chance in the fight against Farit Kozhennikov.

"If only you went to a normal school close to home," Mom had said the night before Sasha's departure. "You would have enough time . . . and you would want to . . . and you would see the baby grow up, you would help me . . . It would be good for you; someday you will have children of your own. Have you thought any more about transferring?"

"It would be too crowded for the four of us," Sasha had said. "The apartment is too small."

"But this is the only apartment we have! Perhaps a bit later we'll find a bigger apartment, but for now . . ."

"For now I will stay at Torpa," Sasha had said. "They have a really nice dorm."

Mom had sighed. At that moment she had desperately wanted to believe that the dorm was indeed very nice.

"I'm going to pack." Sasha had gotten up. "The train's tomorrow and I haven't even started packing."

She had gone into her room, sat down on the couch, dropped her shoulders, and imagined that soon nothing familiar, kind, or old, would exist. The next time she came home, everything would be different. A new life, a new childhood would begin. Sasha's room would change, and the cold draft would blow the memories that lay on dusty bookshelves out the window. Yes, Sasha was selfish, she was used to having Mom all to herself. But now there was Valentin, and soon there would be somebody else who would own the informational space of this home. And Sasha, back on the periphery, would be slowly transforming into a new creature herself. Into an unknown entity. Perhaps into something life-threatening. She would transform silently. And it was a good thing that Mom had Valentin and that she would have that baby, because the girl who had been born and grown up in this home no longer existed . . .

Sasha had felt sorry for herself. Then she had discovered—and had not been surprised by her discovery—that she no longer knew how to cry.

"Introduction to Applied Science will be taught for two semesters. We shall have a test in the winter, then in the summer there will be another one. During the third year you should expect a full semester of hands-on projects, followed by a placement exam. This is serious stuff, my dear children. Experience shows that students who excel equally in Specialty and in the Introduction to Applied Science pass the placement exam easily. This means that from now on you must share your efforts between two major subjects: mine and Oleg Borisovich Portnov's. While you have worked with Oleg Borisovich for a year, you do not yet know me . . ."

The hunchback smiled.

He stood in front of the class, almost hitting the ceiling with his head. If he stood up straight, he'd definitely reach it. Nikolay Valerievich wore a black old-fashioned suit. Every now and then he moved his shoulders as if his curved back bothered him.

"We shall study on an individual basis. Perhaps later we will break into smaller subgroups, three, four people in each, but first I have to figure out the professional abilities of each student. At this point there is only one person here whose future is more or less obvious . . ."

"And that person is Samokhina," Lisa suggested.

Nikolay Valerievich raised his eyebrows. "My dear girl, didn't Oleg Borisovich teach you to be quiet when a professor is speaking?"

Lisa reddened, but did not look away.

"Yes," Valerievich said, "this person is Alexandra Samokhina. She has very vivid professional abilities that became evident during the first year, and Alexandra will have a customized program. That does not, however, mean that any of you will be left unattended." He smiled genially at the class.

Apparently, unlike Portnov, not all of the professors here had manners worthy of the Spanish Inquisition. The hunchback seemed kind enough. Second years exchanged hopeful looks; some even seemed to think that they might be able to goof off just a little bit.

Sasha had no such illusions.

The hunchback made his own schedule of the individual sessions, not trusting this task to anyone else. Sasha was the last one on his list; she had time to go to the library and experiment with the new set of exercises.

The first glance did not deceive her: the new exercises were similar to the old ones, but were substantially more complex. Multilevel transformation of entities, infinitely abstract, that sometimes formed a circle, sometimes compressed to a single point, but always seemed ready at any moment to break through and rip apart the fabric of visualized reality; if these were somebody else's thoughts, they were so decidedly inhuman that Sasha was simply scared to imagine a brain naturally capable of producing these chimeras. At the same time—Sasha already knew enough to see this—these exercises were astonishingly beautiful in their harmony.

She remembered her session with the hunchback a minute before her scheduled time slot.

Auditorium 14 was located on the fourth floor; it was squeaky and echoed. Sasha ran down the corridor, made an effort to calm her breathing, and knocked on the door.

"Hello, Sasha. Sit down, let's chat."

The auditorium was furnished with desks, just like a classroom. Sasha chose the one near the window. Below her—all she had to do was to reach out her hand—a green sea of linden trees rustled softly.

"The first year has gone by." The hunchback sat across from her at the teacher's table. His ash-blond hair, long and straight, framed his face in two falling curtains. A sharp chin lay on a high white collar. *He is so antiquated,* Sasha thought.

"Sasha," the hunchback said pensively. "Has anyone ever told you that you are a very different, a very special person? Someone who has an extraordinary and very important mission?"

"No," Sasha said quickly.

The hunchback smiled.

"And it's for the best. We don't need any superiority complexes. However, Alexandra Samokhina, this is your time. You are not only our best student, you are also a rare talent and, let's admit it, a rare gift. You have a magnificent future ahead of you. And what does that mean?"

Confused, Sasha did not respond.

"First and foremost, that means that your present is one of daily hard labor, like that of a slave, without idleness, fear, or doubt. The preparatory work that you have done during your first year is nothing compared to what you—we—will have to learn, grasp, and master. Today, right now, we begin to prepare for the placement exam that awaits you in the winter of your third year."

She listened, leaning over a small desk. The hunchback spoke with a slight smile on his face, but he was not joking, oh no, Sasha knew perfectly well that he was serious.

Linden trees swayed outside. Sasha's left cheek felt the warm wind tasting vaguely of autumn.

"Sasha, do you consider yourself a corporeal entity?"

The question was posed in such an indulgent, casual manner that Sasha involuntarily blinked.

"Aren't I?"

The hunchback smiled. In front of him on the teacher's desk lay a thin attendance journal and a portable CD player.

"Yes." Nikolay Valerievich nodded. "At this stage you are quite a bit more physical than I would have liked. We have three semesters to fight this, three semesters during which you will continue destroying your material constituent and building up your informational element. Your conceptual aspect. Your ideal, if you prefer, although in this case this definition is not precise. And we will fight for precise definitions, Sasha, this is going to be very important to us—the accuracy of our definitions. Did you have a question?"

Portnov never allowed the luxury of questions. Sasha looked away for a moment and watched the linden trees outside the window. On the first day of September they looked green, like in the middle of the summer.

She could ask what they should expect at the placement exam in a year and a half. Or, what sort of professional abilities she has demonstrated, and what she would be doing for a living. She could have asked a hundred questions that Portnov refused to answer and that puzzled all her classmates. But all she asked was:

"Do you happen to know—back then, during winter break—if I killed anyone?"

The hunchback did not seem surprised.

"No. And by the way, this episode is quite typical. That was the first time in your life when your informational constituent jeopardized the material aspect. Unfortunately, the manner in which it happened was impossible to control, spontaneous and very dangerous. Did you suffer?"

Sasha looked away.

"I see. If you think that you're being trained to become a monstrous killer, you are mistaken."

"What am I being trained to become?" The words escaped, surprising her.

The hunchback moved his shoulders, as if stretching his aching back.

"Too early, my girl. It's too soon for you to know. Right now you are still a slave of a framework, a plaster mold with a hint of imagination. With memory, with a personality . . . Yes. I am going to lend you this thing." His hand, with very long, pale fingers, touched the CD player. "If you wish, you can also use it to listen to music. You are allowed. But this disc"—a paper envelope was placed on the table—"this disc I'm giving you to work on. Please take care of it. You are a second-year student—you know how important certain objects are.

"And one more thing: before we begin working together, I want to discuss a rather delicate matter. Sasha, it is highly desirable for you to part with your virginity. It is becoming a serious impediment in your development."

Sasha blushed so fiercely that her cheeks ached.

"What . . . What difference does it make?"

"*Everything* makes a difference. You will be changing not only from inside, but . . . you will undergo all sorts of changes. Your sensual experience makes a difference, your hormonal status . . . as well as physiological aspects. Informational balance of your organism. I appreciate your serious attitude toward life, your restraint. Your virtue.

But work is work. I'm not saying today or tomorrow. You have time. But start thinking in this direction. Agreed? Good.

"Let's begin."

The swallows hadn't left yet. They circled over the yard, perhaps for the last time. Their young flew around in small clusters.

Sasha estimated the distance to the dorm—across the yard. Every day it was different. Occasionally she managed it in only two steps (a sensation of falling and wind in her ears). And sometimes it took her a few hours, as if she had to cross a desert. Her bag pulled on her shoulder, and Sasha kept walking toward the entrance, which kept moving away, becoming more and more distant.

She fixed the strap on her shoulder and balanced on her spot, catching her equilibrium. She took the first step; the swallows swept past her face, nearly trimming her eyebrows with the sharp points of their wings.

Here's a tree. And here's the bench. And the porch. Sasha placed her foot on the lower step, held it there to make sure that the porch did not slide out of reach. That's it. She'd made it. Every time it got easier; perhaps Portnov was right, and soon she would again be normal . . . or, rather, return "to the state that is deemed normal at this point."

The key from room 21, which Sasha had had at her complete disposal the entire spring and summer, was missing from the board. As usual, Sasha fumbled for the door frame leading to the staircase. She turned her head—and met the eyes of a new first-year student.

Short hair, very pale skin. Blond, dark eyes. He stared at her with a terrified expression on his face. Sasha smiled, trying to comfort him.

"Hey. Welcome!"

"Hey. What happened to you?"

"Nothing. Why?"

The boy licked his lips.

"Nothing. So, I'm gonna go, all right?"

"My name is Sasha," Sasha said, surprising herself.

"I'm Yegor."

"Good luck, Yegor," Sasha wished him.

Carefully probing each step, she traveled up the stairs.

Her roommates had already returned from their classes. Sasha entered without knocking; suitcases stood open on the floor. One roommate, Vika, her hair dark and curly, was hanging up her clothes. The other one, Lena, plump and white like a cinnamon bun, sat on her bed with an expression of utter despair on her round, blue-eyed, almost doll-like face. Next to her on the bed lay the *Textual Module* with the number "1" on its cover.

Sasha sniffed the air.

"Were you smoking? Fair warning, girls: if I catch you smoking in this room, I'll throw you out the window, along with the cigarette. We have bathrooms—smoke there."

Vika did not reply. Lena hunched over on her bed, hugging her shoulders with plump arms. Sasha stepped over to her desk and lifted the bag, meaning to take out the CD player. But the pattern of scratches on the desktop reminded her of something. Immediately, involuntarily, one of last year's mental exercises rotated in her head; when Sasha finally placed the player on the desk, it was much darker outside, and something in the room had changed.

She turned her head. Her new roommates stood side by side and stared at her with terror.

"It happens," Sasha said. "I was just thinking of something. Don't mind me."

"Sasha," Lena murmured through her tears. "Tell us, please, what will happen to us? Are we going to be just like you?"

Sasha smirked.

"It's not that scary. Just survive the first semester. Work as hard as you can. It's for your own benefit."

She used the first years as a mirror. She saw her own reflection in their eyes: broken, twisted, and fully submerged into herself. Occasionally freezing mid-action. With an intense, terrifying stare. They watched her, unable to hide their fear—and sometimes their revulsion.

Sasha did not feel offended. These kids were going through tough times: threats and blackmail drove them to Torpa, where they were handed a backbreaking academic load. Finally, they were surrounded by freaks: sick, crippled, and even insane.

Of course, they tried to handle the situation and pretended nothing strange was happening. Somebody brought a guitar, somebody had a stereo system. The dorm hummed, and the students drank and had fun; strangely enough, some of the third years joined the parties. Leaving her room with a towel thrown over her shoulder, Sasha saw Zakhar, Kostya's roommate, making out with one of the new girls. The lightbulb went out, or perhaps somebody broke it on purpose; laughter, whispering, the sound of footsteps—the girl escaped to the kitchen, Zakhar followed her, and Sasha shuffled to the showers.

The water was really hot, just like at home, and Sasha felt partly recuperated. She rubbed herself with a towel and wrapped it around her hair in a turban. The first day of classes had passed: she had tons of homework, and tomorrow she had an individual session with Nikolay Valerievich Sterkh, and she had to show him what she'd learned for the first time.

The very thought of the player with the CD inserted into it gave Sasha the chills even in the hot steamy shower room. She put on her bathrobe, secured the towel on her head, and shuffled back into her room—it was getting late, and her work was not going to get done all by itself.

Her roommates had disappeared somewhere, probably to cry into someone else's beer, thought Sasha. She dried her hair, lay down on top of the comforter, placed the CD player on her stomach, and thought back.

During today's lesson Nikolay Valerievich had put headphones on her head and switched on the player. And Sasha—for the first time—heard *that*.

The CD contained silence. Deep, dense, devouring everything in its sight. Trying to devour Sasha as well; Sasha had panicked and struggled, like a fly on a strip of flypaper, using all her strength to stay on the edge, terrified to fall into this soft all-encompassing nothing, resisting this grave alien silence.

Nikolay Valerievich had been talking—she'd seen his lips move. She hadn't been able to hear the birds outside the window, the rustling of the trees, the distant steps in the corridor—everything had been flooded over by a cement-like silence.

The first track on the CD had lasted ten and a half minutes. Sasha had been bathed in sweat as if after a long run. Her blouse had stuck to her skin.

"Sasha, that is not the right way to do it," the hunchback had said gently, removing her headphones. "You should not resist. You must let it in and let it flow through you. Slowly, not all at once. Without that first step we cannot take another one, nor the third. And we have thousands of steps ahead of us. Here we just lost an entire session, the exam became one day closer, and who knows, perhaps that very day is what you will lack to be fully prepared?"

"What should I do?" Sasha had asked.

"Work on the first track. Play it on repeat. Your goal is to make peace with what you are listening to, and for this you will need to cross a certain line within yourself. A line of commonness. It may be difficult. But you must try. You cannot learn how to swim without getting into the water. Tomorrow I shall wait for your first results. I have a great deal of trust in you, Sasha. I'm waiting."

Thus spoke Nikolay Valerievich and he had let Sasha go. She had left with the CD player in her bag and a feeling of anxiety in her heart, and here it was, time to work on the first track, but Sasha could not force herself—she could hardly switch on the player.

The dormitory was full of noise. Guitars strummed, stereo systems roared, people laughed, shouted, broke dishes. Sasha held her breath—and pressed the round Play button.

Silence came and stuffed Sasha's ears. It came very close, and was deafening, all-encompassing, ready to pull Sasha inside itself, to envelop and digest. It was revolting and terrifying. Twisting out of its grasp, Sasha tore the headphones off; the drunken voices singing heart-wrenchingly and off-key behind the wall now sounded to her like a choir of angels.

She made another effort—right before her individual session, when she had no way out. Sitting in the half-empty reading room, she turned on the player and became almost physically aware of the transition from silence—into Silence. Into the sucking Silentium.

She probably could have entered an autopsy room. She could pick up any revolting critter. She may have been able to stroll along the school corridors naked if it had been required to pass an exam.

Yet she could not and did not wish to "let in" whatever was recorded on the disc. She used all the forces to resist it, to build a defensive wall between herself and the Silence. The track ended. Sasha dropped the player into her bag and shuffled up to the fourth floor, to the sunny auditorium 14.

"Good afternoon, Sasha, glad to see you . . . What happened? Did you listen to the first track?"

"Twice," Sasha mumbled.

"Twice? That's not quite enough . . . Let's check. Put on the headphones."

Sterkh hitched up his sleeve, extricating a small mirror on a leather strap. A sunbeam danced on the mother-of-pearl surface, disintegrating into a rainbow, and then reassembling, its white flashes biting into Sasha's eyes.

"We're listening to track number one, take a deep breath . . . No, Sasha, no, what are you doing? Let's start again from the very beginning, but this time you will absorb the new material rather than reject it, agree?"

Sasha stared down, at the dark-brown wooden floor, striped with gaps between the long, painted planks.

"Sasha." The hunchback hesitated, as if considering something. "Sit down, let's chat."

She sat behind a table that resembled the desks she'd had in high school.

"You have earned a terrific reputation in Oleg Borisovich's class. You have demonstrated an exceptional talent. But you struggled at first, didn't you?"

Sasha nodded, still looking down.

"The same principle can be applied to this class. You are struggling, I know. Because your efforts are connected to—or, rather, limited by—what is internally permissible. You have a very clear notion of what is acceptable and what is not. I'm not talking about everyday things, the so-called principles, I am talking about the inner configuration of your personality, and of your ability to overcome stereotypes. You are a stubborn girl: at this point, it is an obstacle, because we cannot proceed until you learn to work with the CD tracks to your full potential. Instinctively, you realize what is required of you, and just as instinctively you resist. I am not entertaining the possibility of your doing it on purpose. Right?"

Sasha swallowed, but nodded.

"There is no need to be this stressed out," the hunchback said gently. "You must focus, concentrate . . . And take that first step. Just one step, just that first track. Let's try it right now, and I will do my best to help you."

Sasha left the auditorium feeling completely drained, with a pounding headache. In half an hour of nonstop trying, the wall that she'd erected between herself and the recording on Sterkh's CD became stronger and thicker. Maintaining that wall required very little effort on Sasha's part. The silence now existed on its own, separately from Sasha.

Sterkh had been very upset. For a long time he had not said anything, shaking his head, looking at grim-faced Sasha, then staring out the window. Then he had sighed.

"Try track two. You seem to have fully blocked that first one. Such energy, such inner strength you have demonstrated, Sasha, but it's directed in a diametrically opposite direction! You work very hard at resisting it, instead of processing it!"

"I'm trying," Sasha had said.

"You are trying to achieve the antithesis. You are fighting for your own conventional image, two arms, two legs. You dream of a warm shower, maybe, or a soft bed. But, Sasha: nothing corporeal has any significant value now. Anything that is truly valuable is beyond material substance if you think about it. You will understand, you are an intelligent girl, I have a lot of faith in you."

Then he'd let her go, and she left. Yulia Goldman was waiting for her turn in the hallway; when door number 14 closed behind her, Sasha massaged her face with both hands, rubbed her temples, and squeezed her eyes.

She knew that track two would have the same effect. The very thought of having to listen to *it* again nearly drove her insane.

Sasha's class was offered very few liberal arts seminars this year. She did not like Constitutional Law and Fundamental Principles of Government. The professor was older and cantankerous, and the subject itself had nothing in common with the concept of learning: it was more of an excursion that skimmed the surface of criminal and civil code. The stream of bureaucratese disgorged by the professor made Sasha sleepy. At the end of the class she did fall asleep for a second and dreamed of Sterkh, who stood in the middle of the auditorium holding an enormous pair of scissors. The bell rang; Sasha woke up. The professor threw a contemptuous look at the students and said good-bye until the next lecture.

The next block was English, and Sasha found this class just as nonsensical and boring as the previous one. Endless grammatical constructions, exercises that she had to write down, topics she had to pass every month; Sasha felt time stand still. She remembered getting this desperate feeling in high school, albeit rarely, mostly in the spring, especially during a meeting or a homeroom assembly. But now it followed her everywhere.

Entering the hallway, she stopped at the bulletin board with the posted schedules. First years gathered around, and Sasha had to push aside some gaping girl in order to move a little closer. Physical Education three times a week, and then Specialty took almost all the rest of her time: Portnov, Sterkh, individual studies and group lectures. Plus homework: paragraphs, exercises, Sterkh's CD . . .

Sasha pushed her way out of the crowd and shuffled downstairs to the dining hall.

Denis Myaskovsky sat in front of an empty plate, studying some sort of illustrated magazine with several bright inserts depicting blurred colorful spots. In line for food, Sasha listened to his conversation with Korotkov:

"What do you have there?" Andrey asked.

"It's from Sterkh." Denis hesitated, as if holding back. "Didn't you get one?"

"He gave me a book," Korotkov seemed timid. "Just a regular book, though . . ."

"Andrey, it's our turn!" Oksana called to him from the buffet. "Give me your ticket and get your soup!"

A little later Sasha saw that Sterkh indeed had a very individualized approach to each student. Oksana, Lisa, and Andrey Korotkov studied Introduction to Applied Science using textbooks. Kostya had a printout rolled into a tube. Zhenya Toporko carried around a thick notepad. Three or four people had portable players, but unlike hers, those used cassette tapes. However, no one discussed their progress—individual sessions with the hunchback were a forbidden topic among second years from day one. It was taboo.

"Thus, meaning is a projection of will onto the surface of its application. Meaning is not absolute and depends on the choice of space and the method of projection. Last year the most gifted of you stumbled upon fragments of meaning while studying the *Textual Module*. However, the first year is over! Now you must apply conscious efforts to use the *Textual Module* as an intermediary between you and the archive of meanings available to you at this stage. Theoretically, you may encounter just about anything, including a fragment of your most feasible future. We have thirty seconds before the bell rings, does anybody have any questions?"

Sasha sighed. Now she saw Portnov's classes in a completely different light. Even though reading the *Textual Module* still resembled swimming in muddy waters, flashes of enlightenment waited for her on the surface. Even the sets of exercises, which flowed from one to another and formed a highly complex pattern in her mind, now made her happy.

"Toporko, do you have any questions?"

"N-no . . ."

"Good. Class is dismissed, individual sessions are tomorrow. Prefect, please compile a list. Samokhina, nice work."

Portnov praised her; she was pleased with her progress in his class. But the sessions with Sterkh were becoming more and more tortuous.

She managed neither track three nor track four. Sterkh ordered her to return to the first track; Sasha hated this process, and the more time passed, the harder it was for her to even climb up to the fourth floor and enter the sunlit and spacious auditorium 14.

Sterkh was getting gloomier with each session. Hints of aggravation were now discernible in his gentle voice.

"Sasha, I am very disappointed. Two weeks have passed since the beginning of this semester, and you . . . I am getting the impression that you are consciously sabotaging my class."

"No. I . . ."

"I am not threatening you. I'm just sorry . . . I'm worried about you. I never write reports to advisors, at least not during the semester itself. But in the winter we have an exam, and the result of this exam is a document. It's going to be recorded in your grade book, and your advisor will be forced to take action. I won't be able to do anything at that point."

Sasha bit her lip.

"Nikolay Valerievich," she said hoarsely, "maybe I just don't have any talent? Could it be that I'm unsuited for this work? Maybe I should"—she stumbled—"maybe I should be expelled, because there is just no point? You don't need useless students, do you? Because I am trying, honestly, I just can't . . ."

The hunchback stroked his chin with long, thin, white fingers.

"Sasha, just drop it. First, if you have been accepted, you are fully capable. Second, you must study hard instead of dreaming or twiddling your thumbs."

"But I *am* working hard," Sasha said. "I always have. I'm doing my best."

"No," Sterkh said sharply, steepling his fingers. "You are not making an internal effort. Your classmates have gone far ahead of you, new leaders have emerged in your group; Pavlenko is doing very well, Goldman, Kozhennikov . . . And you are way too restricted; you have gotten yourself into a corner. All your preparatory work—a whole year of extremely intense work!—is being wasted right now. I wonder—have you thought about solving our delicate issue?"

"What, right here and now?" Sasha could not help it.

"Not right this minute." Nikolay Valerievich smiled as if telling her: *I forgive this cheek, you silly girl, I understand you are stressed out.* "But the sooner, the better. Better for you, Sasha."

There were no more swallows. For a while Sasha stood in the middle of the yard, watching the clear September sky. A sparrow flew by, and above it, over the rare clouds, flew an airplane. Sasha imagined herself in an airplane seat, looking out the window, watching the quiltlike ground beneath her—fields, forests, lakes, and a tiny populated area, a town called Torpa. She wondered if one could even see it from an airplane.

Sasha dragged her feet to the post office. Rather, she simply started walking, but her feet dragged her to the post office; she ordered a long-distance call and a minute later stood in the stuffy booth with a plastic receiver in her hand.

"Hello," said a man's voice.

"Hello," said Sasha after a minute pause. "How are things? Can I talk to Mom?"

"Mom sends you her love," Valentin said readily and cheerfully, almost too cheerfully in Sasha's opinion. "She's at the hospital, on bed rest. She could have stayed home, but you know, it's just safer. She has a terrific doctor, a comfortable room, good conditions. And an excellent prognosis—it looks like you are going to have a baby brother!"

He spoke easily, without pauses, free of any noticeable tension. Sasha relaxed her shoulders.

"When is she coming home?"

"I'm not sure yet. It's much better to err on the conservative side, you know? I'm going to buy her a cell phone, and you will be able to call her directly!"

"Cool," Sasha said.

"What's new with you? How is everything going? How are your classes?"

"Everything is fine." Sasha rubbed the polished telephone shelf. "I have to go now. Tell Mom I said hello."

Kostya stood at the entrance of the post office. In the last few weeks they had not exactly avoided each other; rather, they'd behaved like distant acquaintances and limited their communication to simple greetings.

"Hello," Sasha said.

"Hello." Over the summer Kostya had changed; the skinny teenager had been replaced by the confident physique of an adult male. He had a tan, and his face looked windblown. Sasha remembered that on September 1 he still stuttered and limped on his right leg, but now all the consequences of Portnov's "stage" were gone entirely. Kostya had restored himself from the ruins and once again become himself.

Or nearly himself, Sasha thought sadly. *Just like the rest of us.*

"Did you call home?" Kostya inquired, suddenly violating the standing order of their current relationship.

"I did," Sasha said. "Why?"

"How are things at home?"

"Mom's having a baby," Sasha admitted, surprising herself. "With the new husband."

"That's what's going on," Kostya murmured.

"Yes, that's what it is." Sasha forced herself to straighten up. "See you."

"Wait," Kostya said to her back. "Do you have five minutes?"

"Five, but no more."

"But no less, either?" Kostya smiled tensely.

They moved toward a gray park bench covered with picturesque yellow leaves. Sasha blinked; for a moment she imagined that the bench was purple, and the leaves blue. In the last few days she'd learned to change the colors of the outside world—or rather her perception of those colors—on her own accord, and now during boring lectures on constitutional law she could entertain herself by mentally changing the color of her professor's face, the tint of her hair, the shades of her blouse and handkerchief.

"Sasha," Kostya said. "I need to talk to you."

"I noticed."

"I love you," Kostya said.

"*What?*"

"I love you." He shrugged, as if apologizing. "Forgive me, I was an idiot. I love you. Marry me."

The leaves turned green, the bench—bright orange. Sasha blinked.

"But I don't love you," Sasha said. "And I am not going to forgive you. If you crave regular sex, and you can't afford a prostitute, then marry Zhenya. She'd love to marry you."

Kostya paled. Sasha saw his Adam's apple twitch. His tan, bronze just a minute ago, was now yellow, like a lemon.

"Good luck," Sasha said, and her voice broke. She did not know why she'd said what she said, and why she had used those particular words. However, a word spoken was past recalling. Sasha turned and, with increasing speed, followed Sacco and Vanzetti toward the institute.

Where did he come from? Why did he come to her right now, when winter exams hung over her like a guillotine? While Mom was on bed rest, and Valentin was discussing their bright and happy future in a forced, cheerful voice? During the summer she'd never thought of Kostya . . . Actually, she thought of him only when she saw him, just as detached and indifferent as she was herself. Back then she had not cared about Kostya; she'd turned into a puddle of warm wax, she'd seen through the sky, but she couldn't walk through an ordinary door. And on September 1 he'd sat next to Zhenya, and Sasha had taken it as a sign of fate, and she never wanted to think in this direction again.

But why had she brought up prostitutes?

On the other hand, why had he slept with Zhenya on New Year's Eve, when he and Sasha had not even had a fight? If they had quarreled, screamed at each other, slammed doors . . . then she would understand. Of course, Sasha would not have forgiven him then either. Or maybe she would have, because a fight is one thing, it's another thing entirely to just get drunk and jump into somebody else's bed . . .

A group of third years stood by the school entrance. Zakhar turned and waved to Sasha. "Greetings to the young nubile generation! How's it hangin'?"

"A little to the left," Sasha responded and wondered where she could have picked up that vulgar turn of phrase.

The third years laughed heartily, as if it were the funniest joke they'd ever heard.

▪▪▪

October came.

Sasha sat in auditorium 14, and across from her sat Sterkh, and they had been quiet for the last fifteen minutes. Sasha's lips were dry; all the words she could say—"I'm trying," "I'm working hard," "It's not working for me," "I cannot"—all these words had already been said multiple times. Sterkh, sad and haggard, moved his shoulders more than usual.

Rain fell outside. The water rustled in the pipes. Tiny drops flew into the open window.

"How are you doing in Specialty? Oleg Borisovich seems pleased with your progress . . ."

Strangely enough, in the last few weeks Portnov's exercises had become Sasha's safe haven. Mind-bending, occasionally almost crippling, they "worked"—they gave in to her efforts. And Sterkh's assignments did not; for almost a week now Sasha had not even tried to play the CD. She felt disgust; no, even worse—she felt repulsion.

"Did you work on it yesterday?"

"No."

"And the day before yesterday?"

"Nikolay Valerievich, I can't!"

The hunchback shook his head heavily.

"This is not good, Alexandra. I hate threatening someone, reprimanding people—punishing them . . . But right now you are your own worst enemy. Only you, no one else. Go and think about your fate. About the winter test. About the exam, which is a little more than a year away. And think about what your advisor is going to say regarding your 'I can't.' As soon as you feel ready to work, let me know. I am prepared to give you additional time. I will help you as much as I can. But you, yourself, have to step over the threshold.

"*You* must make that decision."

Denis Myaskovsky was waiting for his individual session with Portnov, eating chips out of a plastic bag. Sasha hopped on the windowsill next to him.

"Denis, I have a serious question for you."

"Shoot."

"Liliya Popova—who is she?"

Denis choked. Potato chips first got stuck in his throat, then flew out of his mouth in a fan of crumbs.

"Ugh." Myaskovsky coughed.

Sasha knocked him on the back. Myaskovsky fought to control his breathing.

"Did you put a lot of thought into this?" he sounded offended.

"I need to know," Sasha said. "I am failing Introduction to Applied Science."

Denis gaped at her. "*You?*"

"Yes. I am going to fail for sure. I need to know, I want . . . Maybe it's possible to change advisors? What do you think?"

"You have Kozhennikov," Denis said slowly.

"Yes." Sasha rubbed her palms together nervously.

"I don't envy you. Lisa, for instance—if anybody mentions Kozhennikov's name in front of her, she goes white and starts shaking before she starts punching them. And then, their face beaten into a bloody pulp, they take a long time explaining to her that they actually meant Kostya, who is a perfectly normal guy and is himself suffering in the clutches of his father . . ."

"And Popova?" Sasha asked. She didn't care about Kozhennikov or Lisa. "Have you tried negotiating with her?"

Denis looked grim.

"Actually, you know . . . she wears velvet gloves. But there is definitely an iron fist. And really, I was just talking to some guys here, and all the advisors are the same. It's just that some drop F-bombs, and some don't."

Denis smirked, pleased with his own joke, and was about to say something else, but at that moment the door of auditorium 38 opened, and out came Zhenya Toporko, looking very pale and solemn.

She met Sasha's eyes. Zhenya suddenly went red, raised her chin up in the air, and walked by without a single word.

"What is up with her?" Denis murmured, grabbing his bag. "Well, wish me luck."

At that point Portnov himself appeared in the doorway, an unlit cigarette stuck behind his ear.

"Come in, Myaskovsky, and open the window. Samokhina, is this your time slot? What are you doing here?"

"She is wondering whether it's allowed to change advisors," reported guileless Denis. Sasha froze.

Portnov gave her a sharp glance.

"It is not allowed," he said curtly. "Myaskovsky, open the window, I am going to smoke. Samokhina, good-bye."

■ ■ ■

The next day the sun came up, clear and even warm, surrounded by an insubstantial escort of diminutive transparent clouds. Sasha skipped the first block, gym class. When her roommates finally left for their Specialty lecture, she opened the dresser and there, in the crowded jumble of her own and someone else's clothes, she found her old winter jacket.

She stuck her hand into the right pocket. Empty.

She tried the left pocket. Also empty, aside from some loose change.

For some reason she thought of the day when, out of the blue, Lisa Pavlenko accused her of stealing a hundred dollars. She remembered figuring out that the bill had fallen behind the pocket lining. Sasha remembered *seeing* the bill for a split second. She'd never experienced anything like that afterward. Almost never.

Almost without hope she put her hand back into the right pocket and there, behind the thin synthetic lining, she found a paper rectangle.

Impatiently, she made the hole in the pocket bigger and pulled out a business card, along with some crumbs and pieces of thread—a single phone number, no name. A cell phone number, even though here in Torpa cell phones were still a rare commodity.

The alley that led to Sacco and Vanzetti smelled of leaves and decay. Yesterday's rainwater stood in deep puddles—the brown mass of leaves filled up the drains. Sasha stood for a while near the corner phone booth, lifting her head to the warm sun.

The she picked up the receiver and dialed the number listed on the business card.

"Hello," said a very distant male voice.

"Hello," Sasha croaked. "It's me, Samokhina."

"Hello, Sasha. Is anything wrong?"

"Not yet. But it soon will be."

"You're scaring me," said Farit Kozhennikov.

"Did Sterkh . . . Has he said anything to you about me?"

He was silent. Then he said, "Sterkh wouldn't say anything, Sasha. At least before the test. What happened?"

Sasha paused, not knowing how to explain.

"Sasha? Can you hear me?"

"I am going to fail his test," Sasha said. "I won't pass this exam, not the first time, and not the second. This is it, this is the end."

One more pause.

"Where are you calling from?"

"I'm on the street corner. In the phone booth. The thing is, my mom is having a baby . . ."

"I understand. Meet me in half an hour, in front of the institute."

"She's due right around the winter exams."

"And?"

They walked slowly along Sacco and Vanzetti. Past a street sweeper gathering leaves, past a girl with a dachshund. The stucco moldings of an old building dampened with rainwater, the pale faces of caryatids staring blindly and dispassionately.

Sasha avoided Kozhennikov's eyes. She gazed up and ahead, where blue sky peeked through the balding treetops.

"I want . . . I want her to be healthy, and the baby, too."

"That's a perfectly natural wish. So?"

Sasha stopped in her tracks and turned to face him. Saw her own reflection in the dark lenses.

"I want to make a deal with you. Pay whatever I can. I can do a hundred exercises in one night. I can . . ." She stumbled. "I can do anything. Except for those . . . those CD tracks. I physically cannot. And mentally, I cannot. You can chop off my hand if you want . . ."

"And what would I do with your hand?"

"What do you do with all of this?" Sasha whispered fiercely. "Why do you need this institute? Why force us to do these things? What have we done to deserve this? What—"

She forced herself to shut up. The town of Torpa continued to lead its unhurried, picturesque existence; steam rose out of several chimneys. Smoke-blue and black pigeons stomped about in a puddle and swallowed, throwing their heads back, allowing water to slide down their throats. Dewdrops sparkled on the withered grass of the boulevard.

Kozhennikov stood, leaning his head to one side. Sasha saw two reflections of herself in his dark mirrored glasses.

"There is absolutely no way of negotiating with you, is there?" she said, her voice as low as a whisper. Her lips felt numb.

"Sasha," he answered in the same manner, almost whispering and almost friendly. "The world is full of entities that people cannot negotiate with. But somehow people survive, don't they?"

"Some do." Sasha's toes froze inside her sneakers. "Some die."

"That has nothing to do with you," Kozhennikov said even more softly. "And nothing to do with your family. I know you can do it. There is no reason why you couldn't pass this test with excellent results. *No reason at all.*"

"I *can't.*" She shook her head. "I cannot do what he wants me to!"

Kozhennikov took off his glasses. He did this so rarely that Sasha had forgotten what his eyes looked like: brown, common, even ordinary. With normal pupils.

"I once said that I would never ask you to do anything impossible. That is still true. But think about it: everything you've ever done for me has been based on overcoming an obstacle—a small step over an internal limit. It was difficult. But it could be done, Sasha. It can be done now."

Sasha shook her head in despair.

"Think of Kostya, think about him passing the winter exams," Kozhennikov continued softly. "Do you remember—he had given up, washed his hands. He could have died and brought others to destruction. While it was absolutely feasible—possible!—to pass the exam and survive. There was an exit—and you proved it to him. I'm very sorry that Kostya is not able to pay you back for that act of grace. He can't help you now, he doesn't have enough . . . Although that is not important."

"Tell me," Sasha said with effort. "Kostya's grandmother . . . You were related to her—did you know her? And how did you kill her, tell me, please? By yourself? Or did you have help?"

Kozhennikov's eyes remained undisturbed.

"What makes you think I killed her? She was very sick and bedridden most of the time. Sasha, the average life span around here is sixty-seven years. Seventy-six is a stroke of luck."

"And if Kostya had passed the exam the first time?"

"People are mortal. All of them."

A cat slunk out of the doorway, pale-orange, almost pink. The pigeons simultaneously flapped their wings and flew up, circling Sacco and Vanzetti and disappearing over the tiled roofs.

"I am very sorry about the way things turned out between you and Kostya," Kozhennikov said.

Sasha looked away. The conversation was *definitely* over now. Kozhennikov could continue chatting, or he could be quiet, it did not make any difference. None whatsoever.

"Listen." Kozhennikov put his glasses back on and pushed them up with an index finger. "I believe I know how to help you."

"How?"

"Break through the impossible. Simply a mechanical gesture. Steal a wallet at the market. Break a window with a naked fist. Do something that you consider impossible. It will loosen your rock-hard stability and will help you to burst through to the next level. Do you understand?"

"Doubtful," Sasha said.

Kozhennikov got behind the wheel of his milky-white Nissan, waved to Sasha, and drove away. She remained standing in the middle of the street, watching the pink cat lapping up autumn water from a puddle. Blink—and the cat turned emerald green in her eyes, and the water became carmine red; Sasha rubbed her face with her fists.

The town market was only ten minutes away, if she walked slowly. Steal a wallet?

The window of the bakery was conveniently located at the level of Sasha's chest. Slam her fist into it? What could she possibly do to "cross the threshold," to stop being herself?

Maybe buy a ticket and leave Torpa. Forever.

Nothing felt more impossible than that.

She walked without purpose, not toward the market, but away from the center of town. She passed the institute; two first-year girls teetered out of a ground-level café. Both were absolutely smashed; holding on to each other, they crossed the street and disappeared into the alley. What are their parents thinking? Sasha wondered. Doesn't anyone care about the fate of the children who left the family home to study in an unfamiliar town?

What is my mother thinking?

Mom is thinking of her new, yet unborn baby. Of a creature, whose right to live has not yet been officially authorized. Of course, medical science has been developed and all that, and women over forty are giving birth all the time . . .

Sasha stumbled into a puddle. She stomped her foot, shaking off the water, and remembered that under her bed was a box with a pair of fall shoes. She'd brought them to school after vacation—she'd bought them with Mom at a store sale, a good, sturdy pair of shoes.

She missed Mom. She missed her so much that her eyes filled with tears. She had been thrown out, banished, forcefully ejected from the normal world, where Mom was always near, where she could hug her any time she wanted to, where the door could be open when Mom came home from the office. A normal, *human* world.

It was entirely possible that the parents of all the students in the institute were dealing with the most crucial life problems right now. Some might be going through a divorce. Some fighting a grave illness. Somebody might be in the middle of a custody battle, somebody else expecting a child. And all of them would prefer to think that their grown children were getting an education at a decent, albeit provincial, institution of higher learning. And no one would suspect that the success of their endeavors, their health, and even their very lives depended on the academic performance of their forgotten children, abandoned in Torpa.

Sasha had not noticed reaching the end of Sacco and Vanzetti; following what looked like a country road, she arrived at the riverbank. Yellow and brown leaves floated down the river; some flattened themselves upon the surface, trying to merge with their own reflections. Others bowed like sails, as if trying to fly away. Some chickens puttered around. And the log, on which Sasha and Kostya had sat a long time ago, and on which Sasha had spent her New Year's Eve—that very log was still there.

Sasha sat down and stretched her legs.

Five minutes passed, then ten, then half an hour. Sasha was now missing the second block, English; leaves continued to float in the river, an endless, solemn, unhurried caravan. Gazing at the black mirrored water, Sasha thought for the first time in two years—for the first time in her life, if she were absolutely honest—that perhaps it would make some sense to jump into that blackness from the wooden bridge that crossed the river a few hundred feet away from her. Jump, splash, break that mirror along with the sky reflected in the water.

She rose, still considering. Was it deep enough? Or would it only reach up to her waist? On the other hand, people drown in bathtubs that are certainly not made with suicide in mind . . .

Leaving footprints on the wet sand, she approached the water. The grass on the southern tip of the hill was still summery green and dotted here and there with wild asters. Sasha moved along the bank, circling the swampy parts, looking at the water and flowers on the hill. A yellow curtain of willow branches hung in front of her; yesterday, when she was working on one of Portnov's paragraphs, something about the willow tangle sounded in her head, and she was trying to recollect that sentence when she heard a splash, immediately followed by a scream, and then another splash.

Apparently Sasha was not the first one to think of jumping off the bridge. Somebody more courageous—or less intelligent—had just jumped, and now two people were being carried off by the river.

Sasha's mouth dropped open.

Both were fighting the current, one was shouting. The other one was trying to reach him, taking large wide strokes. The water carried both of them past Sasha, and she finally came to her senses and dashed after them along the riverbank. She tore through the willow branches and burst into a sandy horseshoe-shaped beach. Here the river changed direction slightly; the opposite bank was pretty high, with easily discernible swift nests. Under the steep bank whirlpools were visible, and there, into the vortex, the current now carried the two people. One was still shouting, choking, coughing, and shouting again.

Sasha looked around in panic—the beach was deserted. A hundred feet away stood a concrete wall covered by graffiti.

"Help!" Sasha yelled, even though it was abundantly clear that help was nowhere to be found.

In a state of sheer panic, she took off her sneakers. The wet sand was cold as ice, and just as hard. Sasha dashed to the water, staring at the drowning people in terror and realizing that she could not possibly save either of them; she had no chance—they would take her along with them.

The screaming was cut short. One of the drowning people had done something to the other one: Choke him? Held him underwater? The convulsive splashing was replaced by measured strokes: one of them swam to the shore, dragging the other one along.

Sasha thought he swam for a really long time. The current carried both of them lower down, where the ground was swampy and marshy, where it would be impossible to climb out. The swimmer turned onto his back and worked his free arm; the person he pulled along resembled a pile of wet rags.

Reaching the shallow water, the swimmer got up, and Sasha recognized him. It was the first year named Yegor: his blond hair was plastered over his head, his eyes were red, and his lips blue. The drowned guy was also a first year Sasha had seen around the institute, but she did not know his name. He looked much worse: face swollen and bluish, lips nearly black.

Yegor took a wondering look around the area and saw Sasha. "Got a cell phone?"

She shook her head.

"Go find a phone booth. Call an ambulance, hurry."

Sasha ran. She stepped on a shell with her bare foot, gasping with pain. She came back and pulled on her sneakers, hopping on one foot, not bothering with the socks. She had enough time to watch Yegor place the other boy on his stomach, and, muttering something, press braced palms on his back; after that she had no more time left.

She found a phone booth not far from the bridge, across from the last house on a quiet, almost rural road. Sasha tore off the receiver and was relieved to hear a distant beep; she had a fleeting memory of last winter, of pushing tiny buttons with her bloody fingers, and the bodies lying behind her in the snow, the bastards she'd mutilated herself . . . People.

A chill settled over Sasha, but at that moment a voice came on the line.

"Someone just tried to kill himself!" Sasha shouted. "He drowned! He was pulled out, but now he's not breathing!"

"Address?"

"It's by the river!"

"The river is long. What's the address? Where are we supposed to go?"

Sasha looked around. A few squiggles were painted on the fence across from the phone booth, vaguely resembling letters and numbers.

"Lugovaya, seven dash one!"

"Got it. Sending a car over."

The ambulance arrived thirty minutes later. By then, thanks to Yegor's resuscitation skills, the nearly drowned first year had not only started breathing, but had opened his blurry eyes and started writhing and struggling. He screamed, spewed profanities, and seemed to be completely deranged.

"Did he drown, or is it delirium tremens?" asked a grim nurse in a gray uniform, when the student was finally stuffed into the van.

"He jumped off the bridge—he was drunk," Yegor explained. "He's really a normal kid."

"Normal," muttered the doctor, exhausted, with black circles around his eyes. "We have two ambulances in the entire town. Right now someone's child might be dying, or there could be a heart attack somewhere, and here we are, messing with these drug addicts. Bloody students . . ."

The doctor spat on the ground.

"Where do you see . . . What drug addicts?" Sasha cried.

Indignation enveloped her, like a wave covering a sand castle. Strangers, alien indifferent faces. Yegor saved someone's life, and no one expressed even a word of thanks!

An icy-cold hand grabbed her elbow; Yegor stopped her and pulled half a step back.

"He drowned." He looked into the doctor's eyes. "He had water in his lungs, and there is sand and mud . . ."

"Any other learned advice?" scowled the doctor. "Is that all? Let's go."

The ambulance tore off and disappeared, leaving behind a cloud of malodorous exhaust fumes. Yegor and Sasha watched it for a few seconds. Then Yegor let go of Sasha's hand; he was beginning to tremble.

"Thank you," Sasha said.

"What for?"

"I can't get angry. When I get mad . . ." Sasha hesitated. "You know what—you need to have some vodka."

"Let's run," Yegor said, trying to stop his teeth from chattering.

He jogged up the street away from the river, Sasha following him.

Her body still remembered the once-regular daily jogging sessions; she ran steadily, keeping up with Yegor. He stomped his feet, dripping water, and the cadenced squelching of his wet sneakers in turn merged with Sasha's steps, and then formed a dissonance. Neither of them spoke; as always, running helped Sasha think.

First years. Hysterical fits, depression. Bouts of drinking. What was that kid's name? What if he really did drown? No, that couldn't happen: it was too ineffective, too ostentatious . . . He knew Yegor was nearby. Perhaps he didn't stop to think, but was simply really drunk to the point of delirium tremens, weak in the head from Portnov's exercises?

She fell behind somewhere along Sacco and Vanzetti. Yegor did not turn around, and when Sasha ran up the dorm steps, breathing heavily, he was nowhere in sight.

She went to her room. Both roommates were out. The room was an unholy mess: clothes piled up on the beds, shoes lying underneath in disarray, crumbs covering the papers on the table, a dirty jam jar and used plastic dishes all over the place. Sasha felt nauseated: she was certainly not a clean freak, but the excessive disorder created by her roommates aggravated her more and more.

She opened the window and tossed someone's right shoe, right sneaker, and a left stiletto down on the lawn. Perhaps that would make them think twice next time.

She changed into sweats and pulled on a pair of warm socks. She did not want to eat lunch, had absolutely no appetite. Individual sessions with Portnov were scheduled for the third and fourth blocks, but Sasha's time slot was for four fifteen, so she had plenty of time.

She sat down at her desk. Opened the textbook drawer and saw the CD player; immediately, memories flooded her brain. The conversation with Kozhennikov: *Steal a wallet . . . I am very sorry about the way things turned out between you and Kostya . . .*

She buried the player in the depths of the drawer and picked up *Textual Module* 4. Paragraph thirty-six: she had read the text three times from the beginning to the end when she heard a knock on the door.

"Come in," Sasha said without turning around.

The door creaked.

"I'm sorry . . . Are you studying?"

Yegor stood in the doorway. He'd changed into a thick warm sweater and a pair of dark blue sweatpants. In his hands were a left stiletto and a right shoe.

"Sorry . . . these were lying under your window. Were they supposed to be there?"

"Yes," Sasha said. She got up, took the shoes from Yegor, and tossed them back out the window. She wiped her hands. "I am working on some pedagogical character building with your classmates," she explained to the surprised Yegor. "See what they have done to my room?"

She pointed to the mess in the room with a wide sweep of her arm. Yegor's embarrassment over a display of women's panties on the beds was obvious.

"Don't be angry with them. You see, the first years . . ."

"You don't think I was a first year once?" Sasha narrowed her eyes.

"Was it the same thing with you?"

"Of course. And as you can see, we're still alive."

Yegor sighed.

"I wanted to talk to you . . . Sasha."

"Sure." Sasha smiled. "Do you want me to make some tea? Let's go to the kitchen, at least there is no loose underwear kicking about . . ."

She followed Yegor out of the room, locked the door, and put the key in her pocket. Let the silly goats scamper around looking for the key.

"I gathered some linden blossoms on Sacco and Vanzetti this summer," Sasha said. "Have you ever seen linden trees in bloom? Bees go crazy for them . . . they get so loud. And the smell of them . . . All over the street, and your room smells of linden blossoms when you leave the windows open . . ."

"Didn't you go home for the summer vacation?"

"I did for two weeks. The rest of the time we had summer internships. Nothing really special, we harvested cherries." Sasha spoke easily; at this moment it seemed to her that last summer, with its linden blossoms and the cherries, had been simple and carefree, a true summer vacation for a college student. "I couldn't even look at cherries afterward. And I have an entire tin of dried linden blossoms. It's just what you need after the cold water."

She put the teakettle on.

"What were you doing by the river?" Yegor asked, wiping the oilcloth-covered table with a dishrag.

"Just walking," Sasha said curtly. She lifted the top of a large tin can and inhaled the scent of blossoms. "I saw you two flopping about in the water. How did that blind drunk goofball manage to get up on the bridge, anyway?"

"He wasn't all that drunk," Yegor said. "It's just . . . Well, you understand."

"Shame," Sasha said sharply, thinking that only a few minutes before the incident on the river she was considering that bridge herself. Hot water bubbled in the teacups, the linden blossoms began to expand, and a lovely smell drifted over the kitchen.

"That's awesome." Yegor sniffed, his nostrils twitching. "Sasha . . . Why did you take off your sneakers? There, by the river?"

Sasha put the teakettle back on the stove and took a sugar bowl with a broken handle off the shelf.

"To tell you the truth . . . I don't know. But what else was I supposed to do? I think I was going to dive in after you. To rescue you." She twisted her face into a smile, avoiding Yegor's eyes.

"Thanks," Yegor said after a pause.

"What for?"

Yegor moved the teacup closer and held its warmth between his palms.

"It's Stepan. He is killing me with his hysterics. Every day he packs his suitcase and says he's going home. And then every morning he unpacks it again. He sent a telegram once to his mother . . . She must have been nervous, thinking about him, probably got distracted crossing the street, got run over by a car, and now she's at the hospital with a concussion. Stepan has an older brother—I spoke with him on the phone. He says that Stepan has been throwing fits since childhood, scaring his mother. When he was at a summer camp, he sent a letter telling her they got rat meat for dinner . . . He's like that. His brother thinks that Stepan is playing games again, making things up, that he just does not want to be independent, wants to crawl back under Mommy's skirts. And I, you see, Sasha, I was listening to Stepan's brother . . . and I was playing along! I told him, yeah, we have this great institute, terrific living conditions . . . Obviously, living in a dorm is not the same as living at home . . . And then I said to Stepan, 'What are you doing, you idiot? Don't you at least feel sorry for your mother?' And he . . . see what he did then?"

"I see," Sasha said. "Is he doing his work?"

"Are you kidding? Our Specialty professor, Irina Anatolievna, yells at him every single class, threatens to send a report to his advisor."

"She threatens him . . . ," Sasha repeated bitterly. "I missed one class, by mistake, and Portnov wrote a report right away. And then . . ." Sasha sighed. "Tell this moron that if he does not pass the winter exams . . ." She hesitated, not wanting to say out loud what was on the tip of her tongue. So instead she said, "I was really impressed with how you got him out." She smiled, changing the subject. "And your CPR skills are better than any ambulance technician. Where did you learn all that?"

They stayed in the kitchen for two and a half hours. Yegor skipped Philosophy and Math. People came in, left, smoked, laughed. The kitchen smelled of burned milk; Yegor assured her that only the linden blossoms could possibly save him from an imminent cold, so they had another cup, and then another, and then another.

Both his parents were emergency medical technicians. He was going to become a doctor himself. He even went to medical school for two years, but then Liliya Popova appeared and crossed out all his plans for the future.

Sasha listened and nodded. According to Yegor, it sounded as if Popova was not any better than Kozhennikov. Over the course of a single summer she'd managed to convince a mature, confident Yegor that the world is structured very differently from what he thought. And that he had no other choice but to drop out of medical school, where he had been a straight-A student for two years, and go to an unknown town and enroll as a freshman at an odd institute.

"My parents were in shock. But there was this one thing: my father has this project. If everything works out, he will have his own private clinic. He's in Germany right now—he left back in August—and they are trying to figure out the financing. It's almost settled. It's his dream, you know. And now it's like he's got other priorities, like I don't matter as much. Whatever has happened to me—he thinks of it as childish antics. Like I was just acting out."

"My mother got married," Sasha said. "She's having a baby."

"Seriously?"

"Uh-huh." She looked down. "You know what I think? Our families get some sort of an advance payment when we get here. Good luck . . . happiness. They stop caring as much."

Yegor did not respond for a long time.

"Well," he said finally. "I put so much effort into making sure they didn't figure it out, so I can't say that my parents don't care about me!"

"Of course," Sasha said in a reconciliatory tone. "Same thing with my mom."

Zhenya Toporko walked into the kitchen. She gave Sasha and Yegor a very distrustful look, took two glasses off a shelf, and left with a backward glance.

"What do they want from us?" Yegor asked softly. "What are they teaching us, do you know?"

"I don't," Sasha said. "Last year I also thought that second years must know that. But we don't. And third years don't know either. At least until the placement exam. And then they leave, and there is no one left to ask."

Yegor smiled suddenly. "You are not at all scary."

Sasha choked on her tea. "*Me?* Why would you think I was scary?"

"Do you know that our girls are terrified of you?"

"Of me?"

"Of course. Sometimes you just look at people, and if looks could kill . . ." He shrugged. "In the beginning Vika and Lena were afraid of sleeping in the same room with you."

Sasha giggled. "They *should* be afraid. They are probably walking around the lawn just about now, foraging for their shoes . . ."

They were laughing uproariously over their cups of cool tea when Kostya, grim-faced, walked into the kitchen.

He left immediately, without saying a word.

At four o'clock Sasha finally remembered her individual session with Portnov. She said a harried good-bye to Yegor, pulled on a pair of jeans and a sweater, grabbed her bag, and ran to the auditorium. Portnov listened to the gibberish memorized by Sasha, shone his ring into her eyes, and gave her a harsh dressing-down: he did not think that Sasha spent enough time reading the paragraph, she did not memorize it well enough, so for the next session she would have to complete three additional penalty exercises on top of the regular material.

Sasha agreed silently. The exercises did not frighten her any longer, and Portnov was right—in her excitement over the linden blossom tea she obviously had not studied enough. On the other hand, if she failed Sterkh's exam, what good would her success with Portnov be?

"By the way, Samokhina, what does Nikolay Valerievich think of your progress?"

The question caught her on the way out, as if he had read her mind. She turned back reluctantly: Portnov sat behind the teacher's desk, the daylight lamp reflected in his narrow glasses.

"It's all good," she said through gritted teeth.

It was nearly dark now. As soon as she left the room, the entire weight of the day pressed on Sasha's shoulders. Tomorrow she had another session with Sterkh: tomorrow she would have to make excuses, mumble, and listen to the revolting silence and struggle against it, knowing that fighting it was forbidden . . . and knowing she couldn't do anything *but* resist.

"Sasha, your roommates were looking for you." Oksana was carrying a pan with a hissing omelet down the corridor. "Vika and Lena. Did you hide the room key from them?"

"Sure did." Sasha unlocked the door.

"What are you doing, hazing them?" Oksana laughed. Sasha did not answer; she closed the door, but decided not to lock it. Gathering all her willpower, she took out the player. She set the first track on an automatic loop, gritted her teeth, put on the headphones, and fell on the bed.

Silence came.

Half an hour later the door flew open: Vika and Lena burst in, a shoe, a stiletto, and a sneaker in their arms like weapons. Sasha watched their lipsticked mouths open mid-scream, even saw fillings in their teeth. They were shouting, perhaps even threatening. Sasha looked through them and listened to the silence.

A few seconds later her roommates stepped back. They may have gotten frightened. They left the room. The room was now empty.

So was the silence. It was vast. It was devastating. It meant nonexistence. Sasha did not dare to blink: only the ceiling covered with tiny cracks, a spiderweb in the corner, and the iron headboard tied her to the existing world. "Nothing corporeal has any significant value. Anything that is truly valuable is beyond material substance . . ."

But what about a warm hand? And smell? And the linden tea?!

The silence went on and looped onto itself. Sasha lost track of time. Outside the windows the darkness was now absolute. Her roommates came back, turned on the light and turned it back off, somebody else came in and left; the silence bore down on her ears.

Midnight came—like the distant beat of a drum.

Sasha got up. She stuck the CD player in her pocket. The headphones now felt like an integral part of her head; the dormitory was wide awake, lights were on everywhere, people listened to music and sang, perhaps they laughed.

But Sasha heard nothing.

Yegor lived in room 12 on the first floor. Sasha knocked on the door with one crooked finger. Then she used her fist. Then she pulled the door open—it was unlocked.

Yegor was alone, hunched over the *Textual Module*.

"Listen," Sasha began, but she could not hear her own voice; she fell silent. Yegor pushed the textbook aside, rushed toward Sasha, asked her something: she could not hear him. Silence pressed into her soul, and all Sasha's energy went into preventing it from getting through.

Then Yegor turned off the light.

Sasha was caught off guard. Not being able to hear and see simultaneously—it was too much; she wanted to rip off her headphones, but they were now pressed so close to her ears that she could not say where the foam ended and her own ears began.

At that moment Yegor took her into his arms.

The world reduced itself to touch.

Sasha froze. Yegor breathed heavily; she felt his ribs move, go up and down. Perhaps he was sick, had a fever, or maybe that's just the way he was, hot, burning hot like a radiator. It didn't matter. They pressed against each other, stuck together like two figures made of Play-Doh. The player dangled between them, but somehow it continued to work, pouring silence over Sasha. Yegor embraced her, enveloped her, she felt his weight, his strength, and the silence ended abruptly—with a sigh, a moan, someone's off-key voice accompanied by a guitar, the distant chime of broken glass . . .

The batteries in the CD player had run out of juice.

The next morning, at seven o'clock, Sasha stood under the hot shower in the echoing second-floor bathroom. Heavy drops of condensed steam fell on the floor. Water flowed into the drain and carried away the soapy bubbles, whirling like a tornado. Sasha smiled, then scowled, then licked her tears off her chin.

Yegor and Sasha made their appearance at the first block clutching each other's hands. Sasha was wearing a man's green shirt that smelled of Yegor's cologne. In the hallway, watched by everyone around them, they hugged, kissed, and proceeded to their classrooms: Yegor to Irina Anatolievna's for a Specialty lecture, Sasha to Sterkh's, for her individual session.

The hunchback regarded her attentively. Sasha tensed up, expecting him to say something; Sterkh said his usual friendly hello and asked Sasha to put on the headphones.

The alien silence rose, drowning Sasha first up to her neck, and then completely over her head. Breathing became difficult. The hunchback moved his lips without a sound. Sasha watched him while a cold shiver ran down her spine and her hair stood on end.

The first track ended. Sasha quickly pressed the Stop button. Nikolay Valerievich strolled around the auditorium and stopped at the window where raindrops fell again.

"I can see you tried, Sasha. And I can see that you are truly having difficulties. Well, my girl. You have given me quite a problem."

He seemed uneasy and sad.

"Congratulations," said Lisa Pavlenko. She was having a cigarette in the women's bathroom, shaking the ashes into the sink.

"Thanks," Sasha replied automatically, thinking of the hunchback and his exam.

"Was it dictated by the heart? Or required for academic success?"

Sasha froze for a second, then slowly looked at Lisa over her shoulder.

"What do you mean?" she asked very slowly and very coldly.

Lisa blew a puff of smoke up to the ceiling, as if trying to reach the yellowing plaster, covered by water spots.

"No need to be embarrassed. You're not the only one with that sort of problem. Yulia Goldman has been looking for someone to deflower her for a while now. Of course, she's not the star student here, she has time . . ."

"Isn't it nice that *you* don't have that problem?" Sasha said, looking at Lisa in the mirror.

Their eyes met somewhere on the blurry edge between glass and reality. Lisa's eyes looked red and inflamed—probably because of the smoke.

"Group A, everyone close your books and look at me. 'Everyone' in-cludes you, Kovtun. Just so, thank you. Considering that half of this group has not been able to accomplish their goals with the *Textual Module,* additional individual sessions have been scheduled. Those students whose names I call will attend the individual sessions, and must come prepared, with memorized paragraphs. Tomorrow, Saturday, I am meeting with Biryukov, Onishhenko, Bochkova, Myaskovsky. Thirty seconds before the bell—does anybody have any questions?"

Kostya raised his hand. Zhenya Toporko, who was sitting next to him, blushed for some reason.

"Yes, Kozhennikov?"

Kostya got up, nervously clicking his pen. "I have an announcement."

"For me?" Portnov inquired. "Or for the entire group?"

"For you and for the group." Kostya was visibly nervous. "Zhenya and I've decided to get married. We applied for the marriage license at the local town hall. Anyway, we are going to have a wedding and I . . . we wanted to invite everyone."

Someone's whistle made the windowpane tremble. Somebody applauded. The auditorium filled with surprised and encouraging noise. Sasha caught a few openly curious glances.

Her back very straight, her face scarlet, Zhenya stared at Portnov; Sasha detected a hint of pride and audacity in her stare. Sasha herself looked at Portnov, thinking, *What if he forbids them to get married?*

The hum died down slowly. The bell rang, but no one moved. Portnov stood by the blackboard, his hands in his pockets, gazing at Kostya and Zhenya curiously, almost serenely.

A familiar silence descended upon the students.

"Thank you for making us aware of the situation," Portnov said benevolently. "May you live happily ever after, in sickness and in health, and all that. The only nuance I must warn you about is the following: any student who gets pregnant before graduation will end up having an abortion based on medical grounds, because any child conceived during the program will have grave birth defects and a life expectancy of zero. And I am not even going to explain all the problems a pregnant student would have with her advisor. Is this clear, newlyweds?"

Now Zhenya's face was beet red, and her eyes filled with tears. Sasha caught herself with a fleeting sense of satisfaction.

"Class dismissed," Portnov said unenthusiastically. "Samokhina, stay for a minute."

"But *why?*" Sasha shouted matter-of-factly, unexpectedly, very loudly, and almost hysterically.

Portnov's glance—and the surprised stares of her classmates—made her come to her senses and regain self-control as soon as possible.

"Because I need to tell you something," he informed her just as matter-of-factly. "Group A, hurry up, you'll be late for the gym."

The door was flung open. Outside in the hallway Sasha saw Yegor waiting for her. He'd be waiting even after the bell and the start of the next block; nervously gripping the handle of her bag, Sasha watched her classmates pile out of the auditorium.

Korotkov, the last one out, closed the door behind him.

"Come here," said Portnov.

She approached the teacher's desk, mentally shuffling through all the reasons and problems that could prompt Portnov to have a conversation with her.

"Listen, Samokhina . . . You do know how silly girls get in trouble?"

Sasha drew in air like a broken water spigot. "Why? What business is that of yours?"

"Who else would give you advice? Mommy? Daddy? Give me your hand."

His hard fingers found Sasha's wrist, hitched up her sleeve, and pressed a temporary tattoo on the back of her arm, just below her elbow, a cheap kind usually sold on the beach—a smiling face the size of a small coin.

Sasha jerked her hand away. She stared at the tattoo—it stuck to her skin like it was glued on. The little face, transparent just a few seconds ago, now filled with a carroty-orange color.

"It's a very simple test. On your safe days, it is green and yellow. When it turns red, you are absolutely not allowed to—and don't complain later that you weren't warned."

Sasha looked at Portnov. He leaned back on the chair and wiped his glasses with the hem of his shirt.

"You are dismissed, Samokhina. Go—your boy is waiting for you." Portnov bared his teeth in a smirk.

On her way out, Sasha allowed herself to slam the door. She lost her nerve at the very last moment, but the door did slam just a little bit.

In gym class, running laps, doing push-ups and sit-ups, throwing the ball into the hoop, Sasha managed to return to a certain mental equilibrium. Kostya is marrying Zhenya Toporko? That's terrific, and wasn't it she, Sasha, who gave him this wonderful advice? May you live happily ever after, as Portnov said.

Even in the gym class she continued wearing Yegor's green shirt. Under her sleeve, she barely felt the temporary tattoo on her right arm. Working on her passing skills under Dima Dimych's direction, Sasha admitted to herself that Portnov was right. Being eighteen years old, she was still inexcusably infantile when it came to "female business." Mom was too far away, and it's not like she would discuss it with Lisa!

On the other hand, Portnov . . .

How did he know? Why did he care about Sasha's personal life?

Yet maybe it wasn't too hard to figure out. Lisa knew. And Sasha and Yegor were not hiding anything. On the contrary—they had flaunted their love to everyone in plain sight.

All of a sudden she felt uncomfortable in Yegor's green shirt.

Kostya and Zhenya sat on the bench like two sparrows on a telegraph wire. Anna Bochkova sat down next to them, chatting, laughing. Sasha wondered if they were talking about her. About Yegor.

With a hollow sound, the ball hit the board, rolled over the rim of the hoop, and fell out. Kostya had chosen his fate, and she, Sasha, had also chosen hers.

And all this seemed utterly nonsensical considering that the winter exams were only three months away.

▪▪▪

Her next session with Sterkh turned into a nightmare. Sasha could not handle the tension; the alien silence crept into her soul, and the hunchback sided with that silent, clammy, heavy beast. Sasha no longer tried to let it in, neither did she try to force it out—she simply hung between the two chasms, as if writhing in a seizure. It seemed as if the session lasted many, many days.

Finally, Sterkh shook his head and removed her headphones.

"Sasha . . . It will be all right, don't get discouraged. Do not lose your heart."

It was her mind she was worried about, though.

For a long time he sat silently behind his desk. Sasha, sweaty and barely alive, stared out the window that faced Sacco and Vanzetti Street, but could see only her own reflection. It was already dark outside; Sterkh always put her name last in the schedule of individual sessions.

"Perhaps . . . No, I must consult someone. Let us go, Sasha."

One-on-ones with Portnov had not yet ended. When Sterkh opened the door of auditorium 38, Sasha saw Laura Onishhenko, who stood in the middle of the auditorium, staring fixedly at the opposite wall. Laura did not react to their emergence: tense, with her eyes nearly popping out of her head, she appeared both ridiculous and terrifying. Sasha looked away.

Sterkh nodded to Portnov. The latter motioned for them to wait. Laura inhaled with a hiss and coughed.

"We will do it one more time," Portnov promised coldly. "Get ready."

"I worked on it . . ."

"I am still hoping to see the result of that effort. You have one minute. Leave the room and try to concentrate."

Laura left, eyes lowered to the ground. Portnov looked from Sasha to Sterkh and back.

"I need a consultation," the hunchback said curtly.

Portnov cleaned his ring with the hem of his sweater and nodded to Sasha. She came closer. A sharp ray of light—harsher that usual—whipped across her eyes.

"Not happening," Portnov said. "I really don't think so."

Sterkh sighed.

"Fine . . . Let's assume you are right."

"You can play with it for another week or so," Portnov murmured as if considering different options. "But I would restructure right away."

"I see," the hunchback said. "Sasha, please wait for me in auditorium 14, I'll be right up."

The fourth-floor corridor was almost dark. Sasha located the light switch, entered the auditorium, sat down, and leaned her head against the wall. After what seemed like only a second, she jerked awake.

"Taking a nap? Of course, you must not be getting enough sleep. Never mind. Sasha, I made a mistake in your professional profile. You have a different nature, a different destiny, and I lied to myself and confused you. It is a shame. But let us not talk about that. Let's do this: put away the CD player, you will not need it anymore. We're going to try another approach, radically different."

The slightly open window let in the scent of rain and the rustle of the remaining leaves. In the space over the streetlight the leaves lived a little longer. Sasha had noticed it sometime last year.

Nikolay Valerievich rummaged through his black briefcase. "I am going to give you this study guide."

He pulled out a softcover album, the size of a glossy magazine, but completely black, and placed it on the desk.

"Shall we try right now? We still have a few minutes. Take it, Sasha, and open to the first page."

Obediently, she opened the album. Inside she saw nothing except for black pages that resembled an old kind of carbon copy paper. Sasha inhaled; she thought she could hear the smell of printing ink. "In a blackest-black city, on a blackest-black street stood a blackest-black house . . ."

Somebody might have smiled. But not Sasha.

"Page two," the hunchback said. "Fragment number one. You will see three white dots in the middle of the page. Can you see?"

Sasha nodded. The picture looked like the famous painting by Malevich, tainted by three drops of white oil paint.

"These three dots are the anchor for your sight, for the direction of your thoughts. You must look very carefully, holding your breath, slowly counting to ten . . . Do it right now, I will be watching."

The three dots looked like two eyes and a round mouth. Not thinking, just waiting for the session to be over, Sasha inhaled deeply and stopped breathing. "One, two, three—"

The three dots rushed toward her, turning into the train lights in a tunnel. For a moment she glimpsed a vivid, three-dimensional landscape. Sasha saw arched bridges penetrating one another, distant jagged mountains, tunnels that looked like interlaced tendons; she longed for oxygen, wanted to inhale, but for some reason she was forbidden to breathe. Darkness was absolute, and then the auditorium came into focus in front of her eyes, followed by the teacher's desk and the hunchback over the open briefcase.

Sasha gulped some air, like a diver who'd just nearly drowned. She breathed, swallowing bitter saliva, and the black album lay in front of her, black pages thrown open, as an invitation to repeat the experiment.

"Hmm," Nikolay Valerievich said uncertainly. "It's not exactly what I wanted, but this is a good working start, Sasha. It is a hint of future development, albeit a modest one. Please take this album and very carefully—as carefully as you can—work with fragment number one. Ideally, I would love for you to hold your breath up to two minutes. Count to one hundred and twenty."

"I must pass this test," Sasha chanted out loud. "I must pass this test!"

She opened the album given to her by the hunchback. The pages were numbered, and so were the black fields, the "fragments," which could be distinguished by these numbers only. Each one had three white dots in its center, like three stars or three holes in dark fabric.

"I must pass," Sasha murmured, held her breath, and concentrated on the three white dots. "One, two, three, four . . ."

Everything would amalgamate in front of her eyes, and then clear up again. Strange harsh outlines swam out of the darkness. Sasha saw a city, sharp roof peaks, intertwined ropes and wires; one-dimensional creatures, brown like coffee grounds, jumped over them like fleas on unwashed hair. Resembling check marks drawn with a thick brown marker on a list of groceries, they twitched their legs, wriggled, and made sudden jerky movements. Sasha would never be able to explain why she found these creatures so repulsive, but every time she shuddered at their appearance.

"Thirty-one. Thirty-two. Thirty-three . . ."

At "sixty," the brown check mark insects would notice that they were being watched. They saw or felt Sasha's presence and crawled closer, up to her very eyes, and moving her head was impossible.

Perfectly defined graphical landscapes unfolded in the background: mountains, arches, buildings, and towers, a gorgeous and sinister city. The oily pavement glistened, like a carbon-black ear of corn. From one fragment to another the distant landscape changed, filled with details, became three-dimensional; the amount of brown check marks grew with it. They threw themselves at Sasha like a cluster of starving bedbugs. Lacking arms, unable to breathe, she chased them away the only way she had at her disposal—by concentrating. By staring. Occasionally, she moaned over the album, frightening her roommates. But she didn't care about that.

"I must pass this test!"

"You don't even look like yourself anymore," Yegor would say softly.

Sasha memorized his schedule. Every day she showed up at the dining hall holding his hand. She had worn every single one of his shirts and sweaters. She made out with him in front of everyone, as if it were her last chance. Shamelessly, she kicked her roommates out and made love to Yegor, the door locked and secured with a broom handle.

Afterward, Yegor would pull on his sweatpants and go to his room, and Sasha would lay without sleep for the rest of the night.

She had to pass this test.

Or die.

At the end of November Kostya and Zhenya went through with their marital plans and had a "student" wedding at a small restaurant not far from the institute: vodka, mineral water, salami and cheese sandwiches, and endless jars of pickles. All the second years were invited; everyone was allowed to bring one guest. Sasha brought Yegor. Lisa did not show up at all.

At the wedding Sasha saw Kostya's mother for the first time—a prematurely aged, overweight woman, fidgety, with a shrill voice. She thought of Farit Kozhennikov, who had been married to this woman and then left her . . . Or had it been a mutual decision? She wouldn't be surprised by either.

That wasn't the pressing issue, though, because a more urgent thought kept bothering her: how could Kostya's mother not realize, not *see* that something was really wrong with her son's school? Or was a quick view from the outside not enough to notice the strangeness?

Sasha tried to imagine herself in this woman's shoes: her only son, about to be drafted, just started his second year at a provincial college, and now he was marrying his classmate. Everything was normal. Everything was perfectly natural. Next year her son would choose his profession, and his mother in her silk dress, too tight on her spreading body, hoped he would go for economics.

Sitting in Yegor's lap (there was plenty of space at the table, but it was important for Sasha to sit exactly like that at Kostya's wedding table), she was thinking that there, right in front of her, fifty young men and women were acting out an elaborate play for the sake of a single middle-aged woman. Everyone sitting at the table—second years, third years, even the first-year Yegor—knew that Kostya would never become an economist. Nevertheless, they all played out a well-known script. Toasts were proposed, music was played loudly, a pink-cheeked vociferous stand-up comedian hired as master of ceremonies told jokes (occasionally even funny ones) and sang karaoke and invited everyone else to sing along. Wine and shot glasses clinked, and Kostya's mother kissed her brand-new daughter-in-law, wiping her tears and wishing happiness to her "sonny."

Kostya looked awkward and pompous in his new black suit. It seemed as if he could not wait for the wedding to be over. The long tulle veil kept getting in Zhenya's way; behind the scenes, the girls discussed her wedding dress and declared it hopelessly low-class. Zhenya was upset.

In the midst of all the fun, when the floor trembled under the dancers' feet and tobacco smoke hung heavily in the air, Sasha and Yegor finally made their quiet exit. It was raining in the old park, the trees were now bare, and the fallen leaves lay under their feet like a rippled, glutinous rug.

Sasha and Yegor took a long silent walk under the same umbrella.

"I thought everyone would get really drunk," Yegor said.

"Portnov does not let us drink. Something to do with metabolism, I think."

They fell silent again. The rain thumped slyly over the membranes of their umbrella.

"Sasha . . . let's run away from the institute."

"What did you say?"

"Let's. Run away. Together. We'll earn some money, or steal it. Buy airplane tickets. They won't be able to get us."

Cold drops flew through the night, lit up by the ancient lanterns. Sasha walked, grasping Yegor's elbow, considering his proposal.

If she failed Sterkh's exam—and it looked like she would anyway, even if she killed herself studying . . .

What did she have to lose?

But then she shook her head, trying to get rid of excruciating thoughts. As far as she knew, Yegor was doing just fine in his Specialty sessions, there was no reason he should not pass his exam . . .

"Thank you for offering," she said.

They passed the alabaster arch and crossed from the park to Peace Street, a stone's throw away from Sacco and Vanzetti.

The next day, Monday, Portnov offered reserved congratulations to the newlyweds, immediately followed by the warning not to expect any leniency in their classes.

"The honeymoon has been rescheduled for your vacation, yes? Good. By the way, where are you planning to reside? Will you be renting an apartment?"

Kostya mumbled something incomprehensible about appealing to the dorm superintendent.

Portnov was shaking his head, though. "You will not be getting a family unit until after the winter exams, when some space will free up. Until then—deal with it as you wish, home is where the heart is. And with that the official part is over, so everyone open your books to page sixty-three. Samokhina, you don't look well."

"She was studying all night," Lisa offered under her breath. "Practicing new positions."

"Yeah, that's exactly what I was doing," Sasha snapped. "Jealous?"

Upon her return from the wedding, she *had* spent the rest of the night hunched over Sterkh's album. Yegor's words "Let's run away" rang in her ears, in turn loud and soft; they abated and came back, like an echo in an empty well. Yegor was only a first year; he had not lived through a single exam, he still did not understand anything. Even if his advisor was Liliya Popova, and she might be kinder than Farit Kozhennikov—if one could use the word "kinder" in this case—he simply did not grasp what exactly he was offering to Sasha, shuffling alongside her under the same umbrella.

It certainly wasn't freedom.

The brown check mark insects seemed to wait until Sasha opened the page and focused on fragment seventeen. Fidgeting and jerking their legs, they attacked her eyes. Sasha screamed; Vika and Lena woke up. Lena cried in fear, and Vika picked up her pillow and blanket and went to sleep in the kitchen, on chairs stacked next to each other.

■ ■ ■

"Sasha, what was your assignment for today? Fragment twenty-one? Did you work on it?"

It was yet another Monday. The day before, as usual, Sasha had called home and spoke with Valentin. Mom split her time between home and the hospital; her due date was January 12. The ultrasound showed a boy, a big one. Valentin sounded high-strung and happy; he informed Sasha that he would go shopping for a stroller, a crib, and all the other necessary things only after everything went well.

"That's superstition," Sasha told him.

"It's tradition!" Valentin's laughter sounded false. "How have you been? Will you come home for the winter break to see your brother?"

Sasha promised.

And this morning, the schedule for the winter exams had been posted. And Sasha found out that the Introduction to Applied Science exam for the second years in Group A was scheduled for the eleventh. January 11.

The day before her mother was to give birth.

It was snowing.

"I worked on it," Sasha said dully. "Nikolay Valerievich, I worked hard, honestly, I am doing everything the way you tell me to. I . . ."

Sasha stopped talking. Sterkh hitched up his sleeve: on his wrist, held by a leather band, instead of a watch, was a round metal reflector.

"Let us take a look at the condition of your, hmm, inner world . . ."

A sharp ray of light deflected by the metal made Sasha blink. The hunchback frowned, pulled his sleeve over the bracelet, and pushed his palm over his long gray hair. His face, usually pale, now seemed gray.

"Not very good. Not quite. Something is not right, Sasha. I am under the impression that you are using your uncommon willpower to resist my subject."

"No, I'm trying! Honestly! I'm doing everything I'm supposed to."

Snow fell gracefully on the naked branches of the linden trees. Below, a truck drove along Sacco and Vanzetti.

"Sasha, please have a seat."

She sat down at her desk by the window. Tremulous air rose above the radiator, and a cold draft curled around the cracks in the windows. Between the window frames, a large dead fly whiled away eternity.

"When I saw you for the first time, I was simply numb with happiness," the hunchback confessed. "I thought you had this gift . . . a rare, precious gift. The gift of an astounding clarity and strength. And now I don't know what to do with you. The test is only half the problem. The test you can retake, if worse comes to worst. But the placement exam!"

Sasha shook her head violently.

"I can't do any makeup tests! My . . ."

She stopped short. The hunchback held up his hand.

"I know you don't like makeup tests. None of you do. But the difficulty of the placement exam is that you may not retake it. You have to pass it on the first try. Only one try. And you have a little over a year before that exam, Sasha. Ah, what hopes I had for you . . ."

"If I'm that hopeless," Sasha whispered, "maybe you don't need me here in Torpa? Maybe I don't belong here? Maybe you made a mistake accepting me, and now you can . . ."

She fell silent, afraid to continue. Against her will, she saw herself being released from the institute, while Yegor stayed behind. She could forget Torpa, like a scary dream, and along with Torpa, she would forget Yegor . . .

Sterkh bent farther over the teacher's desk, making his hump seem even bigger. Sasha thought he now looked at her with certain interest. As if the idea, offered by the student, was not all that stupid.

"Listen, Sasha. At six o'clock tonight please meet me in the teachers' lounge. We have something to discuss."

"Let's get married," Yegor suggested.

They were sitting in the gym on a pile of wrestling mats. Yegor had just finished helping Dima Dimych fix the Ping-Pong tables; the first-year girls took over the paddles and the gym was filled with the cheerful sound of Ping-Pong balls flying from wall to wall.

Sasha went on as if she had not heard him. And only when he was about to feel really insulted—usually people have some reaction to this sort of suggestion—only then did she turn and look into Yegor's eyes very attentively.

"Why? Aren't we happy right now?"

Yegor was taken aback.

"Well, what do you mean, 'Why?' Why do people get married?"

The Ping-Pong balls knocked about, a celluloid rain.

"I am supposed to meet Sterkh at six o'clock in the teachers' lounge."

"So what?"

Sasha took a deep breath and exhaled again. Her hope wasn't based on anything serious. She simply desperately wanted to have this hope. *If I get out of here, I will certainly get Yegor out as well,* Sasha thought. *I just need to get out. Let them say we made a mistake; you have no talent for our profession, go home.*

In her mind Sasha pictured the hunchback sadly shaking his head and saying these words. She saw Portnov cleaning his glasses with the hem of his shirt. She saw herself pretending she was extremely upset, and then going and packing her things, and returning home . . .

"And after that?" Yegor asked.

Sasha flinched as if he had read her mind.

"What about after that?"

Yegor put his hand on her shoulder.

"Sasha. I love you. I . . . Will you be free after six?"

Automatically Sasha pulled up the sleeve of her jacket. The smiley face was bright red, as if ashamed. Sasha pulled the sleeve back over her wrist. She felt chilly.

"Yegor, I really don't know right now. Let's decide . . . later."

At six sharp she knocked on the faux-leather door with the TEACHERS' LOUNGE sign. She pulled the handle toward herself and peeked inside.

She'd been here only once before. Long couches were still placed along the walls, a coat hanger with several jackets still stood in the corner, but the nude mannequin was missing. Portnov and Sterkh were talking; Portnov was smoking what definitely was not his first cigarette: blue threads of smoke stretched up to the ceiling.

"Samokhina, wait," Portnov said curtly.

Sasha left. She hugged her shoulders.

She simply could not control her imagination. Sterkh was trying to talk Portnov into releasing Sasha. Into admitting that she was professionally inadequate and letting her go. She was going to walk in, and they would tell her to write a resignation letter.

On the first day of school Portnov had said that no one left the institute voluntarily. But there is no rule without exceptions. There is no such thing! They had had such expectations of Sasha, and here she was—a total blunder. Of course, it was not fun to admit one's own mistakes, but it wasn't fun *being* that mistake, either.

Time went on, and she still had not been called inside. The scene in which Portnov and Sterkh released her went through her head like a movie, five or six times—and then it became insipid, faded, lost its credibility. Were they stupid enough to lose control over her, give her freedom, when at least half of her had been changed? And if she did leave, could she even change back?

Yes—she *had* to.

She believed in the impossible. Like a child believes that on New Year's Eve he will be given a real pony. Chances were those two were arguing over what to do with Sasha, how to utilize this worthless material.

The underground corridor disappeared in the dark. Doors stretched to the right and the left, some covered with leatherette, some with real leather. Perhaps under the corridor there was another one, and one more; perhaps after the winter exams, third years—and fourth years, and the graduates—lived and studied underground?

And maybe, just maybe, she thought, *there is no such thing as the fourth and fifth year? Maybe the placement exam is a sacrificial offering? Appropriately primed victims enter the assembly hall—and never come out again . . .*

She imagined a conveyor, like a subway escalator that pulled third years onto the altar, one after another. Everyone held a grade book in his or her hand; rhythmically, a spiked wooden club rose and fell down again. Still alive, bones broken, students rolled from the altar down into a meat grinder, and the bloodstains on the pages of the grade books transformed into words: "Passed. C. Passed. A."

The door to the teachers' lounge flew open.

"Come in, Samokhina," Portnov said, stepping into the corridor, a cigarette in his hand. Adding no further information, he disappeared down the hallway, into the darkness.

Sasha stood by the door, motionless. They had made a decision; perhaps she, Sasha, would be asked to take the placement exam right now.

"Sasha," Sterkh said from inside the lounge, "come in, please. It's already a quarter past six."

Sasha entered.

The hunchback closed the door behind her. He seemed even more melancholy and paler than usual. His hump must have felt really uncomfortable; strolling around the long narrow auditorium, the hunchback kept moving his shoulders.

Sasha stood still by the door. The hunchback, taking one last stroll to the window and back, stopped as well.

"So, Sasha. I just spoke on the phone with Farit Kozhennikov . . . Don't be scared, we were only discussing how we can help you. You are not making the required progress, the exams are coming, and time is against you. So Farit will set you up with a loop, that's the only way to stimulate you. Encourage you, I suppose. But in reality, everything depends solely on your determination and perseverance. What's wrong?"

Sasha was silent. She found it hard to breathe.

"Sasha." The hunchback came closer, anxiously looking into her eyes. "What happened? Are you . . . scared?"

He was two heads taller than Sasha. A really tall man. His black suit set off his pale face. Sasha took a step back.

"You didn't understand what I meant! It's just a temporary loop, a perfectly ordinary thing, one may even say routine. Today is December sixteenth, and tomorrow for you will be December sixteenth, and the day after tomorrow . . . you will stay in this day as long as you need to complete the work. I spoke with Oleg Borisovich—you don't have to work on the module or the exercises that day. Only Applied Science. Only our session. What's so frightening about that?"

"But I don't want to," Sasha panicked. "I . . . what if I never . . . I don't even know what you want from me! What sort of result!"

"I want your most honest effort," the hunchback looked at her severely. "Just as any other teacher. And when you get the result—you will be the first to notice it."

Yegor was not in the corridor.

Sasha dragged her feet to the main entrance of the institute and stopped—no hat, jacket unbuttoned—inhaling frosty air and exhaling white steam.

A clean cotton strip of snow lay on the awning. Sasha gathered the snow into her hands and rubbed it on her face. Two older women walked by and gave her a strange look—residents of this town think we're drug addicts, Sasha recalled. She didn't blame them.

Her life had shrunk, turning into one difficult, absurd day. This had happened once before, except then she had retained the illusion that she, Sasha, controlled the passing of time. "I want it to be a dream!"

She wished she could say that now and wake up on a folding cot in the middle of the summer, two and half years ago. She wished to wake up.

"Sasha! Finally! I thought they must have killed you!"

Lit up by the white street lanterns, Yegor strode along the street, holding two pairs of skis under his arm—brand-new, narrow, without bindings.

"Check out what they had for sale at the sporting goods store! And the price was ridiculous! These are old—Soviet era, I think—but look how cool they are! Do you know how much these things normally cost? Tomorrow I'll buy bindings and wax . . ."

"Why not this morning?" Sasha whispered.

Yegor was taken aback.

"Morning? What do you mean?"

"It's a pity you did not buy the skis this morning."

And she looked up at the sky, at the only star in the slit of white clouds. It could have been a real day . . . She and Yegor would go skiing, and later he, flushed, would say: "Let's get married!" If one day must be chosen out of her entire life, why *not* a day like this?

Yegor took a closer look at her. "What did he want from you? Sterkh?"

"Can we ski today?" Sasha asked, paying no attention to his question.

"Today?" Yegor hesitated. "No. Tomorrow. Today . . . let's go to my place."

Sasha closed her eyes. She leaned into the collar of his jacket. Inhaled deeply the warm air, the steam of his breath.

"Let's go," she repeated sleepily. "Let's go, Yegor."

In the morning she woke up in her bed, barely alive, wiped out, and immediately asked Vika, who was busy setting her hair with a curling iron, what date it was.

"Monday the sixteenth," Vika answered grimly. "And if you feel like shrieking in your sleep, make your bed in the corridor!"

"Uh-huh," Sasha agreed.

Vika gaped at her over her shoulder. The room filled with the smell of singed hair.

The first block was Specialty. Sasha was the last one to enter the room, five seconds before Portnov's appearance.

"Good morning, Group A. Samokhina, you are free for today. Good-bye."

Her classmates' faces fell. Sasha gave Portnov an inquiring look: almost an entire day remained until his conversation with Sterkh. Did he already know that Sasha was "set up with a loop"?

Portnov nodded to her, answering the unasked question and simultaneously urging her to leave. When she still didn't move, he said, sternly, "Go, Samokhina, don't waste your group's study time!"

Sasha left. She went back to the dorm, took out Sterkh's black album, and focused her eyes on fragment twenty-one.

"Greetings, Sasha, how is your progress?"

"There is none."

"Please don't be so pessimistic. If I were an eighteen-year-old girl, I'd never lose heart, never despair. Did you work with the twenty-first fragment?"

"Nikolay Valerievich," Sasha said. "How do you do that? If today's the sixteenth, then you don't know yet what is going to happen tonight!"

Sterkh shook his head absentmindedly. "Sasha, you are a child who grew up in a beautiful cozy room, but you have no idea what is going on outside its walls. You think that the ticktock of the kitchen clock is an inherent attribute of time as a physical phenomenon. Open the album and let us work on fragment twenty-two together."

"Let's get married," said Yegor.

Celluloid balls noisily jumped on the tables, bouncing off the dense casing of the rackets. Larisa missed a shot, lost the game, and swore loudly. Dima Dimych, passing by, read her the riot act. Larisa threw the racket on the ground and went to the locker room.

"Lack of sportsmanship," the gym teacher stated grimly. "Sasha, do you want to play?"

Sasha shook her head.

"Didn't you hear me?" Yegor was insulted. "I said . . ."

"'Let's get married,'" Sasha continued with a heavy sigh. "Let's."

"One would think you get proposed to every day," said Yegor, deeply offended.

"I'm sorry," Sasha mumbled. "It's all Sterkh. You see . . ."

"What?"

"Nothing." Sasha pulled herself together.

"Come to my place tonight," Yegor said. "Stepan is out, and we'll ask Misha to take a walk . . ."

Sasha glanced at her arm. The temporary tattoo was bright red, but what was there to be afraid of since tomorrow was never going to come?

"I will."

■ ■ ■

She woke up in her bed, smelling burned hair. Vika had overheated the curling iron and was now cursing and trying to rid the metal shaft of the sticky melted hair.

"The bell is in twenty minutes! Are you going to Specialty?"

"No," Sasha said and closed her eyes again.

When she opened them for the second time, both Vika and Lisa were standing by her bed.

"What do you want?"

"Aren't you afraid?"

"I don't care," Sasha said and turned to the other side.

"Hello, Sasha. Did you work on the fragment? Let us take a look."

The sharp ray of light made Sasha squint.

"There is a bit of progress," Sterkh said soothingly. "Just a tiny bit, but still—it's a step forward. Work hard, Sasha, don't give up. And right now, here's what we are going to do. Let us go back to the first fragment and go through them again, slowly, one after another. Make yourself comfortable, focus, concentrate on the anchor. We have plenty of time. No reason to rush."

Plenty of time.

"Just don't tell me we should get married."

Yegor blinked.

"Sasha . . . what the heck?"

"Weren't you going to ask me to get married?"

"Yes, I was," Yegor admitted softly. "But why are you angry?"

"I am not angry," Sasha said. To herself she thought, *I'm not angry. I'm going mad.*

Kostya walked into the kitchen as she was pouring cold water on a freshly boiled egg. The kitchen was crowded—people were eating, having tea, washing dishes, or just hanging out—however, Sasha knew right away that Kostya had come looking for her. And now here he was.

"You didn't show up at Specialty today. What happened?"

"I am sick of explaining it to everyone." Sasha used a dessert spoon to lift the egg out of the pan. "Portnov let me skip today's class."

"*Portnov* did?"

"I don't see anything weird about that. I'm the best student in the whole class; I can take an occasional break. Why shouldn't I?"

She thumped the spoon violently on the top of the egg and peeled off the shell like an enemy's scalp.

"What do they want from you?" Kostya asked gently. "What have they done to you now?"

Sasha raised her eyes. The radio was on at full volume, a warm spell was expected tomorrow, then snow and gusty wind. Sasha thought how wonderful it must be to have "tomorrow." To listen to the weather forecast. Follow a schedule. Rip off pages of a calendar. Tons of people lived that way—and none of them realized their own happiness.

"I'm in a loop," she told Kostya, surprising herself. "This day keeps repeating. They did this . . . *he* did this to make me learn . . . to allow me to do this assignment for Sterkh. And I can't."

Kostya sat down as if his legs could no longer hold him.

"That's why Portnov let me miss today's class. Because for me it's always today."

Kostya was silent for a long time. "But then," he said finally, "if I go to class tomorrow . . . won't you be there? Tomorrow?"

"I don't know. It's not like you can jump a day ahead, then come back, and let me know what happens."

The egg on her plate was getting cold. Sasha lowered her chin onto her interlaced palms.

"I am telling you all this because tomorrow, I mean, this morning, you won't remember anything anyway."

Kostya shook his head, as if refusing to accept such a possibility, but she shook her head in response.

"I'm right. It all starts again. You will be surprised that I'm not in class. You might even ask me about it again. And I will think of some other explanation. I don't feel like explaining everything over and over again, to infinity . . ."

Kostya used both hands to ruffle his short hair, then rubbed his nose hard with his hand.

"What are you supposed to do for Sterkh?"

"It's a long story. At first, he gave me a CD with . . . tracks. That did not work. Then he gave me an album, with black pages. So now I'm fiddling with this album. It feels as if this *something* is knocking, knocking, trying to enter . . . and I'm not letting it in."

"And this *something* wants to break the door," Kostya added softly.

"This happened to you too?"

"Yes." Kostya looked around. The kitchen was noisy, filled with the smoke and laughter of the first years. There were no empty stools left. "Let's go someplace quiet."

They set off for the very end of the corridor, hid behind the wide-open door of the shower room, and hopped onto the windowsill side by side.

"Sterkh gave me a printout," Kostya said. "On this long roll of paper, like a parchment scroll. Told me to read vertically, by columns. I started to . . . and the same thing happened. As if something alien were trying to break in. I closed up. And this thing—bam!—broke my door. Or whatever is in there instead of a door. So that's what happened. Then the disgusting sensation went away. I heard music—it was even kind of nice. Sterkh is pleased with me . . ." Kostya trailed off. "It's all because I have weak willpower, though. And yours is strong. It cannot be broken easily."

"He told me I was special," Sasha murmured. "And later he said he made a mistake, and I was ordinary. Did he say anything like that to you?"

"No. You know his honey tongue. 'Very good, Kostya, for tomorrow please do this column, I marked it in red . . .'"

Kostya's impression of Sterkh was excellent. Sasha smiled sadly.

"How can I help you?" Kostya asked.

"Come over tomorrow, I mean, today, just like you did. And ask me again how come I missed the class."

Kostya turned to face her. By the expression on his face Sasha understood—he thought she was making fun of him.

"I am serious." She looked down. "I . . . I have no one to talk to."

"What about Yegor?"

Sasha was thoughtful for a while. She wasn't thinking about Yegor. Right now, on this cold windowsill in the drafty corridor, she realized for the first time that no one but she would remember this rough draft of a day . . . aside, perhaps, from Sterkh and Portnov, but they were not here right now, and they did not care about Sasha's personal life. This meant that she could tell Kostya anything she wanted. Everything would be erased. All would be deleted. Tomorrow morning Kostya would be surprised and anxious about Sasha's missing Specialty.

"If you had a day that would never count for you, that would never be recorded anywhere, what would you do?"

"I'd rob a bank," Kostya murmured. "There was this movie . . ."

"Yes, I remember . . . Mom rented it for us. And we watched it, just the two of us. Before Valentin. Back then I had no idea . . . would never have thought it would happen to me."

Anna Bochkova shuffled by and stopped at the entrance of the shower room. "Sasha, aren't you afraid of Portnov? Why didn't you come to Specialty?"

"They let me skip it, because I'm the best student." Sasha glanced at Kostya.

Anna clucked disapprovingly, proceeded into the shower room, and closed the door.

"She'll tell Zhenya," Sasha said.

Kostya bristled. "Tell her what?"

"She'll think of something. But it doesn't matter, because tomorrow everything will start anew, and all of this will play yet again. Listen, you say I have strong willpower. But I can't seem to take any action. Walk around the institute naked, scare the English professor with a live rat, or drown myself in an ice hole—those are the sort of stupid thoughts I've been having. And none of them can be realized. Because I must continually deliver new fragments to Sterkh. He says: 'There is a tiny bit of progress.' Three hundred sixty-five identical days, and a 'tiny bit of progress' will turn into a 'small progress.' Ten repeated years—and I might be allowed to take the first test."

"Sasha," Kostya said quietly. "I owe you. Let me help you."

"How?"

Water rustled in the shower room.

"Forgive me for saying all that stuff back then," Sasha said. "I was . . . I was wrong."

Kostya did not respond.

Sasha hopped off the windowsill clumsily.

"Anyway, thanks for your sympathy, but if I don't go back to work right now, tomorrow, I mean today . . ."

"Hold on," Kostya said. "Show me what you are doing for Sterkh."

At half past nine she remembered her promise to Yegor to stop by at nine. She thought about it and decided it was not worth worrying about. In the morning Yegor would not remember that she'd never shown up. They would perch on the pile of mats at the gym, and Yegor would say again: "Let's get married."

A sentence that seemed to bother her more and more every time, though she couldn't quite figure out why.

Sasha and Kostya sat in Sasha's room. Three white dots in the middle of a black page rushed at her like the headlights of a moving train, then shifted back like a constellation in the opaque sky. Sasha attempted to work on fragment twenty-four, but every time her concentration broke when she counted to seventy.

"I don't understand what is going on," Kostya admitted. "It's like a musical introduction that keeps repeating, but the song itself is not there. Maybe I should try it myself . . . Maybe if I look at this fragment, I'll have some thoughts? An idea, a hint on how to help you?"

"No," Sasha said quickly. "We shouldn't. It's not your exercise. Sterkh will kill both of us."

"I can talk to him," Kostya offered. "To Sterkh."

"Tomorrow."

"Yeah, but tomorrow may be too late." Kostya pulled lightly on his hair. "Have you thought of going back to those tracks on the CD, to the player?"

Sasha shuddered in revulsion.

"I think Sterkh was wrong when he gave you the album," Kostya said.

"You think so? Are you taking over his teaching position?"

"Don't laugh. He was wrong in the psychological sense. He decided the problem was the disc, and the problem is you! If he gives you a printout like mine or a notebook like Zhenya's . . . it won't work anyway, because you do not *want* it to."

"But you see how much I want it to! I'm climbing the walls here!"

Kostya shook his head stubbornly.

"You are resisting. You are fighting for yourself."

"Sterkh said the same thing," Sasha remembered. "You are fighting for your own conventional image, two arms, two legs . . ."

"Yes. And you are right—right to fight for it. I could not fight for it myself."

"Yes, but you have a normal life, and I . . ."

"I have a *normal* life?"

His words made them very quiet, and the silence continued for fifteen long minutes. Sasha did not dare to speak: Kostya, son of his father, grandson of his dead grandmother, husband of Zhenya Toporko (who refused to take his last name to avoid being Zhenya

Kozhennikov)—Kostya, second-year student of the Torpa Institute of Special Technologies . . .

"Forgive me," Sasha said.

"I'm sorry, too." Kostya slumped. "I want to help you, but I don't have enough anger in me. I'd beat you up"—he gave her a crooked smile—"but I can't hit you. I guess *he* is right."

"Who?" Sasha asked, already aware of the answer.

"He," Kostya repeated. "He has a very low opinion of me, you know. I tried to get my mother to open up. To talk about him. How did it even happen that he is my father?" Kostya slapped the windowsill in frustration. "How did I manage to be his son? Who is he, anyway?"

"What did your mom say?"

"Nothing. She does not want to talk about him at all. She starts crying hysterically—after all these years!"

"Then how did she allow you to go to Torpa?"

"How did *your* mother allow you to go? I am sure she had her reasons. My mother, as far back as I can remember, has always been paranoid about the army. I think a Gypsy told her that if I were drafted, I'd certainly be killed. Whenever she saw me playing with a wooden pistol, all hell would break loose!" Kostya sighed.

"He used her fear," Sasha said.

Kostya looked up at her. "Yeah. He uses everyone's fear. Yours. Mine."

Sasha did not answer. They sat next to each other, their heads hanging low and almost touching.

"Someday, Sasha, I would love to get up—and realize that I'm not afraid of anything. I am tired."

"Of being afraid?"

"Yes. Every second . . ."

"Even now?"

"I feel afraid even now."

"What are you afraid of now?"

"Of going to class tomorrow. What's the first block, English? And you won't be there. You won't exist at all, because you will have stayed . . ."

Kostya did not finish. With an almost maternal instinct, Sasha placed her hand on his shoulder.

"Don't be afraid. I will try. Tomorrow you will come to class, and I will thank you . . ."

Steps rang out in the corridor, and the door flew open. It was not

Vika, and not Lena—Zhenya stood at the threshold, red as a tomato, wearing a bathrobe, eyes white with hatred.

The town of Torpa was dusted with snow. Buildings were covered with light-colored hoods pulled down low onto the tin awnings; the air was moist and warm. Sasha remembered that a warm spell was expected tomorrow. Warm spell, then gusty winds.

She bought some batteries at a kiosk near the post office. All the batteries they had. A hundred of them; the salesperson had to run down to the storeroom to get more, and Sasha spent every single coin she had left after the last stipend.

She went back to her room. Put on the headphones. Placed the pack of batteries under her bed. Pulled out the dusty envelope with the golden disc, clicked the CD player shut, and started the first track.

Then the second track.

Eighteen tracks of different lengths. Eighteen fragments of unfamiliar silence. Oppressing. Indifferent. Detached. Eighteen varieties of quiet. A musical score of complete silence.

Dead batteries fell on the floor. Sasha replaced them with new ones; the silence was growing denser. Her ears popped. Sasha stared into the darkness.

In the middle of the night she was convinced she now had three arms. The third one grew somewhere around her sternum. Her body lost its outline; it distended and was barely contained by the bed; her body tried to escape its frame as rising dough escapes from a bowl. She endured it, grinding her teeth; the sequence of eighteen tracks repeated over and over, hours passed . . .

She was not aware of falling asleep. She slept deeply and serenely, still wearing her headphones.

Sunlight beat into the curtainless window and fell onto the dusty linoleum floor. The sheet looked like an old sail made out of tiny squares of intertwined threads. The blanket slipped; the square opening of the duvet made it look like an ace of diamonds. Sasha was surprised at how much she could observe at the same time.

She turned her head. Her neck felt stiff. The room twitched slightly like a reflection in the water caused by a light wind. Her roommates' beds were empty, blankets thrown over haphazardly. First block was English.

No, it was Specialty.

What time was it? What *day* was it?

Time, units of time, symbols. On her nightstand was an old notepad; it contained important information, binary code, time of day, four symbols, one after another . . . Individual session with Portnov in the evening . . .

Because today was Tuesday.

Sasha turned on her side, moved toward the nightstand—and saw her arm.

She screamed. She managed a croak rather than a scream. Something in her throat was making her wheeze. Sasha sat up in bed; something cracked audibly. Both her arms resembled mechanical prosthetic devices made out of ivory and semitransparent, dazzling-white skin. She lifted her right palm to her face and squeezed it into a fist: gears turned, ripped through the skin, and stuck out in jagged shards. There was no pain.

Sasha rose with difficulty. The floor did not shake under her feet, but her head felt enormous. Sasha was afraid to touch her head with her new white mechanical hands. What if she broke something?

She couldn't bend her knees. Her feet seemed to be made out of wood. Sasha hobbled over to the desk and found a mirror. She screamed—croaked—again.

Her eyes no longer had pupils or irises. Only the whites with red streaks. Sasha threw aside the mirror but continued seeing herself; now she realized that she saw with something other than her eyes. She saw with the skin of her face, her elbows, neck; shaking, she pulled off her T-shirt and saw the room through the skin of her back. She pulled off the sweatpants she'd forgotten to take off last night, along with her underwear. Now each spot on her body saw the entire picture, and combined, all these pictures constituted the world-without-Sasha. Her body—white, skinny, shaking in the middle of a messy dorm room—was the only entity outside this world.

Sparks ran along her skin. Shy little fires like rolling drops. Tiny flashes of lightning. Underneath the skin membrane, in nearly transparent places, she could see her veins, blood vessels, and tendons—a mysterious forest. Her back itched like crazy—something was going on with her spine—it crackled, it was nimble, alive, full of its own existence.

She heard steps in the corridor and realized it was really late. The two first blocks had ended, and lunch was almost over.

Two blocks and lunch of the new day! She broke out of the loop, she did something . . . and something was done to her.

Someone was approaching her door from the outside. She grabbed a broom with her white hands and stuck its handle into the door. At the same moment came a knock on the door—it was Yegor's knock, quick, confident: *knock. Knock-knock. Knock-knock.*

"Sasha?" Yegor's voice barely contained his anxiety and concern. "Are you at home?"

The broom lock twitched: he tried to open the door.

"Sasha? Hello?"

"I . . ."

Her voice sounded eerie. Sasha cleared her throat.

"Are you sick?"

"Yes," Sasha said. "I am sick. And I'm sleeping."

"Listen," said Yegor, and it sounded as if he was putting his lips right next to the keyhole. "We need to talk."

"I can't . . . I don't look well."

"Who cares," Yegor said impatiently. "I'll survive. Open up."

"I can't. Later."

Pause. Yegor was probably looking around, feeling like a complete idiot—standing there in the middle of the corridor, in front of a locked door.

"Let me in. Why am I standing here like a moron?"

"I can't . . ." Sasha croaked. "I'm sleeping."

"With whom?" Yegor asked after a minute pause.

She backed away from the door. She knew that right at this moment she should say something funny, make a joke in response. But she felt completely lost—and a little angry at the accusation—and couldn't come up with anything appropriate.

"I see," Yegor said softly.

She heard his steps moving away from the door.

She wore gloves to hide her hands. She put on her most opaque pair of black tights and her thickest pair of jeans. Two sweaters, one over another. Now she saw the world only through the skin of her face, and the picture was familiar, albeit incomplete.

Her dark glasses were not dark enough to conceal the whiteness of her eyes. She used markers to draw eyes on her eyelids. Walking around with her eyes closed was difficult and uncomfortable, but she could not come up with a better idea.

Hiding this way—primarily from herself, since no one else was in the room—Sasha sat at the desk and opened the *Textual Module*. It was simply a force of habit, because she wouldn't be able to read anyway.

Things were no longer at an impasse. The silence, or whatever it was on that disc, entered and acceded to the throne. Sasha's body continued to change; she felt her skin tauten up and then go limp, a gelatinous lump in her chest pulsate, and her spine twitch like a pipe pushing along masses of hot water.

Nothing would ever be the same again. Mom . . . Yegor . . . Kostya . . .

Petrified at her desk, Sasha thought that perhaps *yesterday* was better, and maybe she should have left things as they were *yesterday*?

Outside it was snowing. Warm spell, wet snow, wind! Everything they promised had come true . . . and tomorrow had come.

And Kostya went to class—and *did not see* Sasha!

She got up. Threw on her jacket. Sat back down. Kostya now remembered everything she had said . . . And everything that happened yesterday had already been entered into the history of their lives. The windowsill. And these batteries. They rolled all over the room, cheap Chinese batteries, but there were so many of them, she could not have gone through all of them in one night. Or maybe the night repeated itself as well—another loop, and one more, and one more?

Sasha darted from one corner to another. She opened the window. Closed it again. She should have gone to the first block! But how could she let herself be seen this way? How was she going to show herself to anyone?

She sat behind the desk and thought of Yegor. Was it love that led her to his bed, or the kind advice of the hunchback? "Your sensual experience makes a difference, your hormonal status . . ." She could lie to herself as much as she wanted, say that love snuck up on her and it was so timely, such a perfect coincidence . . .

Yesterday Yegor said: "Let's get married." No, no! Sasha held her head: yesterday, exactly yesterday, she cut him short in a bout of irritation: "Just don't tell me we should get married!" She never thought that this day, this angry reply, would remain in her life . . . and in his life. She'd lost control of her emotions. Then she did not go see him, even though she'd promised, and then this whole scandal with Zhenya, which was now written in history. Good for Kostya—he never apologized. But Yegor . . .

What was she thinking about while turning into a monster, perhaps dying?

Yegor was a first-year student. He had no idea what it was like to take winter exams. More important, he had no clue what really connected Sasha and Kostya. It was not a vulgar story about a boy who loved a girl, and the girl wouldn't put out, so he found himself another one, one who was willing. They were connected by Kostya's makeup exam last year, those slaps on the face that hurt Sasha's hands—she'd beaten him so that he would study, would pass, would survive.

They were connected by last night, when Kostya could not get up enough courage to hit her . . . but still paid her back what he owed. Because he wanted Sasha to survive. And goddamn those anchovies in tomato sauce, vodka and Pepsi, grimy sheets, and the door locked with a broom. Everything could have been different for them. Everything.

Yegor was possessive; his girlfriend had to open the door always and under any circumstances. And she *should* have opened it! Should have opened the door and taken off her clothes! So that he would understand.

But that's not what she'd done, and she couldn't relive this moment like she had yesterday for all those weeks.

Maybe Kostya would come. Ask her what happened. Or had Zhenya's actions last night made him wary of coming up to the second floor without a legitimate reason?

Sasha was alone. Absolutely alone in the cosmic sense of the word. And the reason happened to be not this terrifying metamorphosis, but someone's jealousy and someone's pride. The common things. One could even say ordinary.

The day outside was getting darker. It was time for her session with Portnov. Sasha got up with effort. Forgetting the open book on her desk, she put on her jacket. Coins jingled in her pockets.

She pulled down the hood, fixed the dark glasses on her nose. She left the room. The world swayed; Sasha watched it through the skin of her cheeks and it made her feel as if she were a few inches shorter.

Two first years were chatting at the end of the corridor. When they noticed Sasha, they stopped talking at once, their eyes nearly popping out of their sockets. She passed them with a clumsy nod, as if her head twitched. The first years stared in horror.

Let them tell Yegor, Sasha thought apathetically.

The snow outside was stamped with footsteps. Homeless dogs decorated the corners of the streets with yellow hieroglyphs. Sasha saw the eye of a raven perching on a naked linden tree. She saw each cigarette butt stomped into the mud in front of the institute. Turning her face, she saw air currents of different temperatures: warm streams rose out of the windows, moist haze trembled above the roof. A warm spell.

Answering a few random hellos, registering quizzical glances, she entered the institute. About to pull the door handle, she realized that she'd never even read the paragraph for Portnov.

She had no way out. So she walked in.

Zhenya Toporko was finishing her session. She was the very last person Sasha wanted to see at that moment—which was saying something, considering how many people she didn't want to see.

Sasha's black scarecrow image, complete with the hood and the dark glasses, made an impression on Zhenya. Shocked, she forgot to close her lipsticked mouth.

Portnov turned around, about to say something—and fell silent. For the first time in her life, Sasha saw his expression change.

"Toporko, you may go. Hurry up, you're taking up someone else's time."

Zhenya closed the book deliberately slowly, placed it into her bag, jerked the zipper—the zipper did not work. Zhenya glanced at Sasha and then back at her bag. She made a concerned face—how could she close that bag?

"Toporko! Out!"

Portnov's voice had a magical effect. Zhenya flew out of the auditorium like a crumpled piece of paper caught in the wind.

Sasha stood motionless.

"Come here."

"I did not read the paragraph."

"I see. Sit down." At the same time, Portnov took out a cell phone, pressed in a number, and barked, "She's here."

He stuck the phone back into his pocket.

"Is there coverage in Torpa?" Sasha asked quietly.

"There is now," Portnov said, shuffling his papers. "Progress is irrepressible. How do you feel?"

Sasha swallowed. Underneath two sweaters and a T-shirt tiny crackling sparkles rolled over her skin like drops of sweat.

"Take off the glasses. And get rid of this entire masquerade, Nikolay Valerievich should be here any minute."

Using her teeth, Sasha pulled off the woolen gloves. Her hands had evolved even further: her skin was now almost transparent; the white metal of the gears that replaced her joints shone brightly, and golden, viscous-looking liquid flowed in the pipes of her veins. Portnov leaned forward, looking almost as stunned as Zhenya. Sasha took off her glasses. Opened her eyes. Then closed them again, demonstrating the drawn pictures on her eyelids.

"Very funny," Portnov said in a hollow voice.

The door opened without a knock. Sterkh walked in and immediately locked the door. He was very pale, his ash-colored hair tangled as if he had taken a long stroll in windy weather. The hump on his back was more pronounced than usual.

Sasha unbuttoned her jacket and dropped it on the floor. Pulled her sweater over her head, then took off the other one, leaving only a dark blue T-shirt. She glanced at her forearms and shoulders; her skin had a bluish tint, was uneven, and in some places covered with purple feathers.

Portnov whistled and took off his glasses. His face had a different expression. If Sasha had not known Portnov so well, she would have thought it was fear.

"Are you pleased?" Sasha asked Sterkh. "Did I do a good job?"

"Yes, Sasha. I am very pleased."

Sterkh looked nothing like himself. Where was the delicate, slightly absentminded Nikolay Valerievich? The hunchback stood in a predatory stance, watching Sasha the same way a whale hunter watches his trophy prey. And Sasha had no eyes to respond to this stare with dignity.

"Thank you," Sasha said. "You have achieved your goal. You turned me into *this*."

The auditorium swam. Sasha watched it through her itchy skin, saw the wall behind her back, a key in the keyhole, a round tag with the number 38, a nick on the door handle. The Institute of Special Technologies reprocessed her, digested her as it desired.

"That's it," Sasha whispered. "I'm done. I can't do this anymore."

The hunchback caught her mid-fall. He held her close. It was so unexpected and so bizarre that she froze, afraid to struggle.

"I was right, Oleg. You see, I even underestimated her. You are a gift, Sasha. A talent. You broke out of your shell, you hatched. Have you ever seen baby chicks? They need time to get comfortable, to get acquainted with the new world and their place in that world. Stop, my dear. Everything is fine. You have broken through to the main road. Now you will walk along it, step-by-step, you will study and you will learn. And you will understand everything. But, oh, what a gift!"

And Sasha, who was watching the hunchback through the skin of her cheeks, saw tears in his eyes.

He escorted her down the corridor, and students parted to let them through. Sasha, in her jacket with the hood pulled down low, in dark sunglasses and woolen gloves, walked under escort, cringing, eyes low to the ground. Sterkh held her elbow—to prevent her from falling. Or maybe from escaping. It was quite possibly from both.

They reached the first steps of the staircase that led to the administration wing, when Kostya ran out from underneath the bronze hooves of the equestrian statue.

Sasha struggled to get free. Sterkh caught her by the hood.

"Kostya!" Sasha shouted. "I'm sorry. I couldn't come to English!"

Kostya stopped, looking from Sasha to the hunchback and back.

"What have you done to her?"

"Tomorrow," Sterkh suggested, smiling. "You will meet tomorrow and discuss everything you want. I apologize, Kostya, we are very pressed for time."

And he led, almost pulled, Sasha downstairs, into his office. She wanted to tell Kostya "Thanks."

But she couldn't say it.

By eleven thirty that night she was back at the dorm, barely alive, but at least she once again looked human. Sharp flashes still ran along her skin, and her spine was still sore, but her eyes once again had pupils and irises, and her arms, while still oddly white, had ceased to resemble prosthetic devices.

Sterkh had spent a long time with her; she thought it would never end. She'd sat at the table wearing headphones, a ream of paper in front of her, and a pencil in her gnarled hand. Sterkh drew symbols, one after another, complex and unfamiliar signs that at first sight appeared to be completely random, and Sasha was supposed to insert missing lines, and the silence pressed on her eardrums, and Sasha, giving in to the unavoidable, somehow knew what was missing, and pushed her pencil over the paper, and the stack of pages covered by her writing grew in front of her. Sterkh himself had replaced the CD in the player and changed the tracks.

During those hours Sasha had learned a lot about silence. The silence of a two-thousand-year-old tomb differed from the vacuum of an ice desert in a distant galaxy. Sasha had stopped feeling pain and time—she had been suspended like a fly in amber—and only a sharp ray of light from Sterkh's mother-of-pearl mirror had made her regain consciousness.

"All right, please look at me . . . Terrific. Now this is a completely different ball game. I am truly blown away by how much can be done here, and what kind of work lies ahead of us. You have a rare gift. An extraordinary one."

Behind the small door was a tiny bathroom with a full-length mirror. Sasha looked at herself and saw a haggard-looking girl, disheveled, with terror-filled eyes, but absolutely normal. She saw a human being.

"Are you chilly? Put on your sweater. Good. So here it is, Sasha—from now on, you will work according to a special schedule, you and I will meet every day except for Saturday and Sunday. You have a propensity for an indiscriminate metamorphosis, and we're going to deal with it first. Are you hungry? Would you care for some tea? Easy, Sasha, easy, this is your victory day, it is a cause for celebration. I know you must be tired."

Tired didn't even come close to describing how she had felt. She'd staggered back to her room holding on to walls. Of course, Lena and Vika were still awake over their textbooks.

"Where were you?"

"I had a one-on-one."

"They are really tough with you second years," Lena said with sympathy.

"Like they are so gentle with us," Vika grumbled. "And so much to look forward to . . ."

Both bent back over their *Textual Module*s; Sasha got into her bed and passed out.

She woke up early, around five in the morning, because it was time to get up and go for a run. She sat up in bed, utterly confused, shook her head, and only then realized that she was no longer required to run in the mornings, that she was a student at the Torpa Institute of Special Technologies, and that yesterday she had turned into a monster.

She remembered about offending Yegor. She had promised to stop by—and then never showed up. He'd asked her to let him in—she had not opened the door. And then there was the scene with Zhenya, which by now was surely part of the dorm's folklore.

Her roommates breathed heavily in their troubled sleep. Sasha got up, switched on the desk lamp, and only then noticed that her wrists were covered with scales, and so was her neck.

She found a mirror. Yes: pinkish, tinted mother-of-pearl, soft, but growing harder every minute—scales.

She took the CD player out of the bag. She hoped the batteries still worked; she inserted the disc given to her last night by the hunchback. She sat still for three minutes, absorbing the silence like a sponge absorbing water.

The scales morphed into skin, rough, windblown. Everything was going according to Sterkh's predictions. "Remember: relapses are possible, especially in the mornings. When you are sleeping, your body may get out of control in its unconscious state. Don't be alarmed. I am giving you this disc. It will not affect your development, and its only task is to stabilize you in your human body. When you get up in the morning, when you use the bathroom, brush your teeth—listen to the disc. Even if you feel perfectly well and everything seems normal, listen to the disc. And don't be afraid, Sasha—the worst is already behind you!"

Sasha rubbed her neck, massaged her wrists, lay on the bed, and stared at the ceiling.

Time to take stock. She had broken out of the time loop. She had her human appearance back. She felt normal, even well: she was wide awake, clearheaded, and able-bodied—she could easily go for a run right this minute. So . . . now what?

Yegor. Sasha felt obligated to atone for her involuntary crime. She had to explain what had happened. Although . . .

Sasha bit her tongue.

If Yegor found out that his marriage proposal had sounded to Sasha like a broken record, and that she'd never told him about the recurrent day . . .

But he'd never asked! Kostya had noticed that something was wrong, but Yegor . . .

Yegor had other priorities. He needed to concentrate, to focus before saying: "Let's get married." Or did he just blurt it out? After so many times, it was hard to remember.

Only one thing was crystal clear: if Yegor found out that yesterday was only a duplicate for Sasha, one of many identical days, he would feel like a complete idiot, and—due to his fragile male ego—there would be absolutely no chance of maintaining a decent relationship. That meant she had to keep quiet. She would have to ask Kostya not to say anything. It was in his interest as well as hers.

Sasha took a deep breath and lowered her eyelids. She listened to her body: everything seemed normal. She was a little hungry. Here were her arms, her toes—she could move the toes. Here was the bed . . .

Sasha's eyes popped open.

The bed was now part of her body. The sheets itched—they should have been washed a long time ago. The metal feet of the bed felt the linoleum; it turned out to be pliable, warm, even. Sasha swallowed; several feet of the floor under her bed were now also incorporated into her body. That part of her was a little rough, not particularly clean, but spacious and hard. And it was becoming more and more spacious.

Sasha gasped and pressed her fists to her chest. Here was her body. The bed existed separately from her. The room existed separately. And separate was Sasha herself.

A minute passed in total silence. A car drove along Sacco and Vanzetti.

I'm not going to try that again, Sasha said to herself. And was immediately surprised: Why not? Was it unpleasant? Was there any shame in it?

She relaxed a little and again possessed the bed. A little bit of the floor. The entire floor in the room. The walls. She became the room. She lightly shook the white dorm lamp shade and wrinkled her nose because of the dust. She banged the windowpane, as if slapping her knee with the palm of her hand.

A shard of glass fell on the floor. Sasha flinched with unexpected pain; the sensation was similar to breaking a nail. The sound of broken glass woke up Vika, who sat up in bed.

"Dammit . . . what is it? Did the wind break the glass? Damn, I remember shutting it last night!"

Sasha did not respond. Once again she returned into herself, two arms, two legs, sweat on her upper lip, and heart beating wildly. Silently, Lena helped Vika stuff a pillow into the empty window frame.

"Now what are we going to do? Use cardboard? It will be impossible to get them to replace the glass. And it's so windy . . . Oh well, it's only half past five, let's go back to sleep."

Again the room was silent. Sasha lay barely breathing and the bed under her was just a bed, nothing else.

What else could she do?

Perhaps even more pressing, what would she *be able to do* when she finished her education? The hunchback kept talking about brilliant prospects, wondrous discoveries. About Sasha having a phenomenal talent.

The alarm clock ticktocked gently. At the very edge of her desk, hidden under a stack of notepads, lay the hunchback's album. The one Sasha could not deal with before. Kostya was right. The problem was not in the disc or the album, the problem was in Sasha herself. *Had* been in her—she'd managed to conquer the disc.

She wondered whether she could now conquer the album.

Sterkh had not said anything about that. He had been too busy with other things . . .

No.

With determination, Sasha pulled the blanket over herself and turned over on the other side. She would return the album to the hunchback tomorrow. She would not open the fragments, and she would never ever again stare at the damned anchor.

She was so curious, though! It was like doing exercises for Portnov—unbearable at first, and then fascinating—so fascinating that she hadn't been able to stop. Now, having stepped over the invisible line, the pull of the black album was very tempting.

What exactly would she find?

The paroxysm of curiosity was similar to the sharp sensation of hunger. Sasha tossed and turned, wrinkling the sheets, and then got up. Unlike the feet of the bed, her own feet did not find the linoleum warm. She pushed her feet into slippers and approached the desk. She glanced at her English glossary, her notes for the Constitutional Law class, some other papers . . .

And then there was the album.

The black oily squares of the fragments glistened. An anchor of three dots gleamed in the middle of each square, like a white constellation.

She looked away.

She looked back.

Sasha opened the very last page. She focused her eyes on the white triangle in the middle and held her breath.

The three dots disappeared. For a few seconds Sasha was suspended in the blackness, as absolute as the silence in Sterkh's headphones. And then out of the blackness came—seeped through, developed—a city surrounded by an enormous wall that reached up to the sky.

Now Sasha saw the city in minute detail, all of it meticulous and very real. The city was the color of carbon. Bearing a slight resemblance to Torpa, it was truly perfect. Wearing slippers and standing on a linoleum floor, Sasha felt marble under her bare feet. She experienced wafts of air, both warm and cold, on her face. The smell of smoke rising from the burning pine in the fireplace. Cool stone and warm stone, smooth and rough, soaring walls, slender windows, spires rising into the sky . . .

Sasha felt happy. She threw her head back and looked around; she wanted to possess this city. She wanted to absorb it into herself, make it a part of her. She threw herself open and began to grow, rise, expand, and inhale outlines, smells, and the texture of the stone . . . In those places where Sasha stretched enough to reach the city, it ceased being carbon black and became softly gray, like an antique photograph.

Tiny check mark insects dashed around the edges of her vision. Now they seemed so insignificant that Sasha paid them no attention. She was capturing this life and this happiness; she inhaled the smoke, and the curve of a roof glistening in the rain, and the wisp of fog, and the majestic spire . . . The more she took, the more impatient she felt. She knew she would not stop until this city had become just as much a part of her as her hands, her chin, her hair . . .

But when she took in the city tower, it suddenly cracked, opened like a flower, and out of its depths a monster, the likes of which she had never seen before, not even in her nightmares, stared at Sasha.

Sasha drew back.

The monster slowly climbed out of the broken tower. It shifted, pulsated, spilled onto the ground, but Sasha saw only its eyes. Motionless. A bit cloudy. Staring at Sasha, and no one else.

And staring back into those eyes, Sasha realized with all her core being something that many understood before her: The creature did not care that Sasha was loved by someone. And that she loved someone herself. And that she had had a childhood, and she had splashed on the seashore; and that she had an old knit sweater with a reindeer embroidered on the front. There were plenty of people loved by someone, the ones who carried a seashell, a button, or a black-and-white photograph in their pockets. But no one had ever been saved by memories, no one had been protected by words and pledges, and those loved greatly by others died too.

Sasha was numb.

Expanded, with half of the city now fitting inside her, she watched the blurry penetrating gaze move closer. And when only a few steps—or seconds—separated her from the monster, she remembered that she was standing in the middle of her dorm room, that she was looking at a fragment, and that she still had a chance to escape.

She fell backward and hit the back of her head strongly enough to make her head spin. The chair that she apparently was holding on to crashed to the floor; a moment later, as if hesitating, the album slipped off the table and landed on the floor, spreading its black pages.

"Ah!"

"Goddamn!"

"What are you doing, you freak! Let us sleep!"

Waiting for the pain to subside, Sasha raised herself onto one elbow. She saw her own slippers in different corners of the room. A layer of dust on the molding. A shard of a teacup under the bed, the cup that broke a month ago. Both Lena and Vika shouted in harmony over her head; the neighbors thumped on the wall with something heavy.

The clock was ticking. If one was to believe the clock, exactly one minute had passed since the moment Sasha got up to look at the black album.

"You are a second-year student! Not a first-year novice! Your actions, Alexandra—your actions leave me absolutely speechless!"

She had never seen Sterkh so infuriated. He dashed around auditorium 14, and it seemed to Sasha that he barely stopped himself from kicking the chairs.

"But you gave me that album—"

"I gave it to you earlier! When you were still at a different stage! Do you understand? That album is not for you! It was my mistake; I should have taken it back immediately, but who knew you would go for the *hundredth* fragment?"

"I didn't know I couldn't. I'm . . . I'm sorry."

Sterkh stopped in front of her. He took a deep breath, getting himself under a semblance of control.

"Fine. Fine, we will just assume that you and I are both equally at fault for what happened. But no more amateur decisions, please! Work only on those projects assigned to you, and only at the appropriate time. No later and no earlier."

"Yes. I promise. But I just wanted to ask . . ."

"Go ahead." The hunchback seemed calmer. Or at least he was doing a better job of not showing his emotions.

"That thing that was there . . . What is it?"

The hunchback sat behind the teacher's desk.

"That, Alexandra, is too early for you to know. No need. I promise you, though—you will.

"You will find out during your exam."

She was late for the lecture on basics of law. She knocked on the door in the middle of the class and asked permission to come in.

"Alexandra, you've missed four lectures in a row. An entire month. I'm flattered that you've decided to honor me with your presence only half an hour late, but how are you going to pass the exam?"

The word "exam" echoed in Sasha's soul like an echo of a rock thrown into a well. It was just another euphemism for torture, along with "third-degree interrogation" or "civil law."

"Sit down, Alexandra. Or were you planning on staying in the doorway?"

Sasha sat down. Between her and Kostya was an aisle—and Zhenya Toporko. Waiting for the bell, Sasha pushed her pen idly over an empty sheet of paper; against her will, she kept producing three white circles on a shaded area. The circles watched Sasha like blurry motionless eyes.

The bell rang. The white sheet in front of Sasha was covered with patterns of thickly shaded triangles; she shut her notepad with distaste.

"Zhenya. I need to speak to your husband. Please give me permission. We are going to discuss only school-related matters, and nothing else." She made her voice loud and determined, making sure the entire class heard her.

Zhenya pursed her lips, threw her bag over her shoulder, and left the auditorium, head held high. The others—Yulia, Anya, Igor—did not seem to be in a rush, pretending to gather their textbooks. Sasha didn't care, though.

"Let's go," she said to Kostya.

Watched by several sets of eyes, they went out into the corridor, up to the fourth floor and higher, to the staircase that led to the attic. They stopped by the small round window.

"You saved me. But now I'm not sure; maybe it would have been better to remain trapped in the loop."

"What happened?"

The fourth-floor corridor was drafty, dust twirled in the column of sunshine that fell from the round window, and above them, at the end of the staircase that led to the attic, a door stared at them through a round keyhole.

"You know," she said, "this morning, for the first time ever, I thought that perhaps they are telling us the truth. We will finish our education and will comprehend something . . . incomprehensible. And then we'll tell them 'thank you.'"

"'Thank you,'" Kostya repeated with a strange intonation. "And what are you thinking now?"

Sasha sighed.

"I don't know. Then I was thinking, maybe they are training us to become fighting beasts. And this exam—maybe it's like a gladiators' arena. Someone we don't know will watch us and make bets. And we will fight and die in combat. But then I think that's ridiculous. This level of sophistication is not necessary to raise a fighting beast."

Kostya was silent.

"Look at them. At Portnov. Or look at Sterkh. When I showed up without eyes, without arms . . . he was crying with joy. Can you imagine that?"

"Think of what you told me," Kostya said.

"What?"

"'If we get to the end of the course . . . we shall become just like them. And we shall speak their language. Then we'll take revenge.'"

Sasha shook her head.

"If we get to the end of this course, we won't want to take revenge anymore. We'll become just like them . . . and we'll *want* to be like them."

Kostya bit his lip.

"Not me. I'll never forget any of this."

The bell rang.

Yegor was sitting on the bench cleared of snow. He smoked, looking up at the sky. Sasha came over.

"Hello."

"Hello," Yegor replied, still looking up.

"May I sit down?"

"Go ahead."

Sasha swiped her palm over the wet planks of the bench, thick with several layers of paint. She perched on the very edge.

"Did you get the bindings onto the skis?"

"What skis?" Yegor seemed surprised.

Sasha bit her tongue.

"Well, I heard at the sporting goods store they have these cross-country skis, the old-style ones, they are selling them at a ridiculous price. All you need to do is to attach the bindings . . ."

Yegor was silent.

This morning, getting ready for class, she had found his green shirt among her own things. The scent of his cologne lingered. She had wanted to put it on as a sign of reconciliation, but she had not had time to iron it, and the shirt was hopelessly wrinkled.

Obeying an impulse, she touched his sleeve.

It became a part of her skin—this thick fabric of his winter jacket with a layer of synthetic filling, the slippery lining made of rayon. Smooth and warm.

Warm.

Sasha reached for him. Embraced him. Not with her arms.

Yegor became a part of her. She took him, perhaps even stole him. On the bench in the middle of the yard in front of the dorm. In front of everyone.

For a short moment, she felt what it was like to be Yegor. She knew how prickly were his unshaven cheeks. How frozen were his feet in their thin shoes. How loudly his heart was beating—just when he was trying to appear indifferent. How insulted he felt, how he suffered . . . But why?

And right then, still being Yegor, having made Yegor a part of herself, she realized how deeply offended he was. Someone had told him about Sterkh's stipulation. He was made to believe that Sasha started seeing him because of purely physiological reasons—Sterkh had told her to get rid of her virginity, and she had . . .

Sasha perceived this insult as her own.

"But how could you ever believe this? You are such an idiot!"

She took the bench (cold, apathetic) and the linden tree (sleepy, unmoving blood), and the ground covered with dirty snow piles (melting snow tickled and itched like crust on a healing scratch). For a second she became a small country, and Yegor was her capital.

"It's a lie! What kind of a man are you, if you can be so easily fooled with sordid lies?"

He jerked and slipped away from her. Rather, she let him go, sensing his fear and feeling frightened herself. He fell off the bench, as she pushed him off, and immediately got up; his knees trembled.

"What are you doing?"

"Who told you? Pavlenko? You believed that bitch?"

He took a few steps back, staring at Sasha with terror that made her cringe.

"Why are you looking at me like that?"

He whispered something. Sasha thought she heard the word "witch."

And then Yegor turned and almost ran down to the alley that led to Sacco and Vanzetti Street.

In the morning Sasha's skin grew a chitin layer, and both her arms had three elbows each instead of one. She waited until her roommates left to take showers, took the player out of her bag, and played the disc she was now supposed to listen to every morning upon waking.

Three minutes of silence. Sasha swam within it like a fish.

Vika and Lena had spent the previous day desperately looking for a way to move out of the room and into another one. Sasha sincerely wished them luck, but suspected that until after the winter exams, neither one of them would have any other choices in the overcrowded dorm. "You may have to deal with it, girls," she had told them last night. "You should take notes—you've got the same thing coming next year."

The track was over. The silence departed, and Sasha snapped back to reality. She bent and straightened her arm. Touched her face: her cheek, cold and rough, was covered with human skin.

Sasha took a deep breath.

Strangely enough, she felt very well. A lot better than she had in the last few months. She wanted to get up, stretch, go for a run, jump into a hot shower, and then turn on the cold water and shout, making her scream echo between the walls of the shower room. And then go to Sterkh's lesson. Yes, astounded, Sasha suddenly realized that she *wanted* to study with Sterkh.

"All things are reflected in each other. Remember? Wind changes di-rection getting around a stone, the stone crumbles, reflecting the wind. The chameleon changes color, reflecting leaves. An ordinary hare turns white, reflecting winter. I am reflected in you when you listen to me. You are reflected in many people more or less deeply. The Sasha Samokhina whom you know is just a reflection of Sasha's true essence. And now this essence is changing—and its reflection is also trying to change, but this reflection is material, established, and that makes it difficult. Keep in mind that I'm speaking conditionally. The communication system that you and I are currently using allows only approximate explanations. That is why we do not bother explaining anything to the students—it would not clarify anything and would be a simple waste of time. Right now you and I are just chatting, enjoying a pleasant moment together."

"Nokolay Valerievich, I keep thinking that I'm disintegrating. Or growing."

"You *are* growing, Sasha. You are overgrowing your own borders, or, rather, those limits that you consider the boundary of your identity."

"Does this happen to everyone? I mean, to all students?"

"It does happen to everyone, but in different ways. You have an obvious inclination toward metamorphosis, Sasha, plus a very rich imagination. Did you paint when you were little? No? You could have . . . Imagine a chameleon that was placed, say, under a glass. Or, better, onto a stock market scroll."

"How?"

"Just like this. The chameleon is used to changing color according to conditions, but what if his new surroundings don't have a characteristic such as 'color'? No color at all? Or consider this. Imagine a newborn baby who suddenly, over the course of one minute, became a grown man with the appropriate constitution and physiological characteristics. His essence has been changed. Don't you think that his old shape would be an obstacle? A small body, swaddling, diapers—all that stuff would crack, letting out the new mature specimen. The same thing is happening to you, Sasha. Your essence is changing, and your shape is lagging behind and is not reacting adequately. That's the source of this minor annoyance, such as scales, feathers, and extra arms."

"Is it going to take a long time?"

"I don't think so. I would say a few days. Although regression is possible. Just don't be afraid, Sasha. Girls get scared of their first menstrual period, but to us, grown people, their fears seem ridiculous."

Sasha felt self-conscious.

"You will understand. Just a little bit of time, and things will get easier. You will realize that you are not being punished, but rather rewarded, and that you have a fascinating, exciting life and enormous possibilities ahead of you. Believe me, Sasha, you are going to be very happy very soon."

"I am scared of failing the exam . . ."

"But that is a perfectly normal fear! Every conscientious student gets nervous when facing an exam, even if the student knows everything. You must study as hard as you can, and then nothing in the exam will be insurmountable for you."

"And then what? I mean . . . after everything else? After the exam? After graduation? What will happen to me?"

The hunchback smiled.

"It shall be magnificent. Believe me. But at this stage I simply cannot explain it."

A few more days passed.

In those rare hours when Sasha managed to fall asleep, she dreamed of the monster from the black city. In her sleep she knew she had to fight, but felt no power, only terror and helplessness, and she would scream and wake up. Lena and Vika, who never managed to move, covered their heads with pillows.

Yegor was avoiding her. Sasha was very sorry that the most unpleasant day in their relationship was now written into her "life history." But despite all her losses and fears, despite the mind-boggling load of those days, Sasha now felt happier every day.

Her studies with Sterkh, the nightmare of her entire semester, now fascinated her. She did not exactly enjoy them, but was enthralled by the step-by-step progress of how a tiny success led to a bigger one. For the first time she realized the connection between her efforts and her growing internal power—and she no longer doubted her supreme powers.

Sasha used to ignore Sterkh's words regarding her "rare gift," but now she knew he was right, understood that she did indeed possess an *exceptional* talent in a still mysterious but infinitely compelling area, and now she, who always loved to learn, had these mesmerizing, not entirely clear, but alluring prospects open invitingly ahead of her.

She longed to speak with Kostya. Tell him everything, ask in secret—how was it for him? What did *he* feel when he followed the hunchback's instructions?

But Zhenya, ruddy-faced and menacing, always followed her husband like a shadow. Sasha did not dare to intrude.

"According to the tradition of our institute, second-year students are responsible for organizing the New Year's Eve party. Considering that our test is scheduled for January third, I'd prefer Samokhina to take care of the annual holiday roast. I will give you an automatic passing grade. And you too, Pavlenko, as long as you turn in all your work today. A bit of clemency on my part—to make sure Samokhina has some help."

"I can't do the roast," Sasha said.

Portnov put his hands behind his back.

"And why is that?"

"I'm very busy."

"You are busy." Portnov took off his glasses. "So you propose I interfere with the work of your classmates who at this point have equal chances of passing this exam and having a makeup date? Do you realize how many of your colleagues are hanging by a thread and at this last possible moment trying to accomplish a semester's worth of work?"

The silence in the auditorium was as absolute as in Sterkh's headphones.

"Don't look for trouble, Samokhina. Nikolay Valerievich is prepared to pass you right now and free up some of your precious time for the annual roast. Engage Group B, bring in the first years, but make it happen."

"I don't know how!" Sasha got up. "I've never in my life had anything to do with amateur performances! I am not going to do it—I don't want to!"

"Samokhina," Portnov said icily. "Your *responsibility* as a student is to study diligently and to meet your obligations regarding socially useful labor. And you *will* meet these obligations, otherwise you will have an unpleasant conversation with your advisor. Pavlenko, do you have any problems? Do you also have something against amateur performances?"

"No." Lisa put down her hand. "I will work on the roast, sure. But Nikolay Valerievich's test . . ."

"I will talk to him," Portnov promised magnanimously. "As far as I know, he is quite satisfied with your work this semester."

"I did not tell him anything, if you care to know. I wasn't the one who blabbed."

Lisa sat on the windowsill in her habitual pose, a cigarette smoking lightly in her hand.

It had been many months since she'd lived in, or even visited, the dorm. The sight of her old room seemed to cause her revulsion rather than nostalgia—she took a long time looking around, sneered, and even sniffed the air. Then she settled on the windowsill and clicked her lighter—only to hesitate.

"Alexandra, do you mind if I smoke?'

"Go ahead," Sasha said, pretending to ignore the sarcasm.

Her roommates, Lena and Vika, retreated to the kitchen. Sasha sat behind the desk and opened the *Textual Module*.

"Anyway, I did not say anything to Yegor. But I know for sure who did."

"I am not interested," Sasha said.

"At all?" Lisa took a drag.

"At all. Because it's a lie."

"Aren't you a cool customer?" Lisa waved her hand to disperse the smoke. "Fine. Do you have any ideas about this party?"

"Toporko should perform a striptease."

"Great idea."

"All we need to do is convince Toporko."

"All we need to do is to convince our guys to watch this massacre. Do you know any magic tricks?"

"Sure—as long as you agree to get into a box. And I can ask the superintendent for a saw."

"A chain saw?"

"A circular saw!"

"And we can put Kozhennikov into the box," Lisa said.

The room became very quiet.

"Farit Kozhennikov," Lisa clarified, avoiding Sasha's eyes. "But yeah, you're right. It was a stupid joke. So what are we going to do?"

A huge movie projector, a half-century-old technical wonder, stood in the projectionist's booth. There was also a primitive audio mixing console, and now Sasha, looking at the stage through a blurry window and listening to the actors' lines, cued different melodies through the speakers.

Lisa proved to be indispensable in preparing the traditional roast. Sasha was amazed—and kept mentally thanking Portnov for giving Pavlenko an automatic passing grade. Somehow Lisa managed to involve about ten first years, a couple of ladies from the dean's office, and Oksana from Group B (Oksana did not get to pass automatically, but she was a good student and was pretty sure of herself). In only a few days they planned, designed, and directed a half-hour show. Sasha's participation boiled down to sitting in the projectionist's booth and turning on the music.

The rehearsal went very smoothly, but when the hall filled with excited, noisy students, when the professorial staff walked in and settled in the third row, Sasha found herself to be exceptionally nervous. To add to her discomfort, the words spoken on the stage were not as audible as they were in the empty hall—Sasha was afraid to miss a cue and strained her ears by the booth's window.

The actors must have been nervous as well. The beginning was not particularly successful, one of the first years forgot a line, and the punch line of the joke was lost. Panicking, Sasha turned on the music way too loud; Lisa, forced to shout over the music, threw violent glances at the projectionist's booth, but Sasha, instead of lowering the volume, made it even louder. To Lisa's credit, she did not lose control; after the first few awkward minutes, the actors found their footing, the holiday roast started going smoothly, and the audience, anemic at first, was now laughing harder with each skit.

Listening intently to the actors' lines, Sasha heard the door behind her back open and close. She cued "The Dance of the Little Swans," and only then turned around.

"Sorry, do you mind if I sit here for a while?" Zakhar whispered.

Sasha was taken aback. They exchanged friendly hellos in the hallway, but were not exactly close friends.

"Sveta is looking for me everywhere," he said with a shrug. "And I'm not in the mood to talk to her."

"Sveta? First year from room 5?"

"The very same."

"Are you hiding from her?" Sasha asked with a hint of contempt.

Zakhar sat down gingerly on a three-legged stool. "It's not what you think. I . . . I am taking the exam on January thirteenth."

Suddenly remembering her job, Sasha dashed to the window and barely managed to turn off the music at the last second.

The audience laughter was continuous. It looked as if the holiday roast was a big success.

"So?"

Zakhar shrugged.

"For some reason . . . I don't know. I wanted to see my parents, my brother someday . . . my classmates. You . . . Sasha, I have this feeling like it's the end of the world. As if after this exam nothing at all will exist."

"Nonsense," Sasha said, recollecting her own nightmare in the administrative wing, when she imagined a conveyor belt, dragging third years onto the sacrificial stone. "You know it's baloney. We are not being educated only to be slaughtered later. We are simply going to be different."

"We are already different," Zakhar said. "This New Year's Eve . . . everyone is laughing . . . Sasha, you are a great girl. I want you to know that."

"What are you babbling about?"

"Me? Nothing. I just . . . Good-bye, Sasha. After all . . . Farewell."

Sasha gaped at him, her mouth wide open, and did not realize right away that the audience was suspiciously silent. The pause lingered . . .

The "Turkish March"! She was supposed to cue the "Turkish March"!

When, music booming in the assembly hall, meek as a mouse Sasha rose from the music stand, Zakhar had already left the booth.

The holiday roast was a big success. Only that triumph saved Sasha: if her mistake really had led to failure, as it seemed for a moment, Lisa would have murdered her with her own hands. Lisa did in fact admit to Sasha that very thought had crossed her mind—in very strong, undiplomatic language.

On January 2, the first years took their test. For a long hour and a half not a sound came from the auditorium.

Then it was as if a dam broke—two girls came out first, sweaty and happy, then a boy, then three boys at the same time. One after another, eighteen people came out; Yegor was not among them.

Hiding behind the bronze leg of the gigantic horse, Sasha bit her hand. If only Yegor passes . . . if only he passes . . . She would approach him first.

Just let him come out.

Minutes passed. Voices in the corridor died down. Yegor still did not appear.

I bring bad luck, Sasha thought in terror. *Those who love me—rather, those who* loved *me and left me . . .*

If Yegor has to take a makeup test, what am I going to do?

The door opened.

Yegor hesitated on the threshold—and walked out into the dark hall. Sasha jumped at him from underneath the statue's belly. Yegor staggered.

"Did you pass?"

"I passed." Yegor swallowed. "Yeah. I did."

Sasha embraced him, squeezed him with all her might. She pressed her face against his sweater, inhaling his familiar scent. She hadn't held anyone like that for so long. She wanted to freeze like this for an eternity, wanted Yegor's hand to lie on her shoulder, touch the back of her head, smooth down her hair . . .

But Yegor stood motionlessly.

Sasha heard the beating of his heart. Felt his breath.

She raised her head. Yegor looked down at her. He was not smiling.

"Yegor," Sasha said, still holding him tightly. "If I upset you, I am sorry. I love you, and don't you listen to anyone else. It's all a lie. I was in a very bad way, but now I'm better. Listen . . . let's go to my room."

Yegor was silent. She felt him tense up. Perhaps he was trying to control himself.

"Don't you believe me?"

Yegor did not respond. His arms hung limply along his body.

Sasha took a step back.

"I'm sorry," Yegor said. "I have to get ready for the English exam."

He left.

"Greetings, second years, Group A. The magical day has finally arrived, and our test is finally here . . ."

Portnov spoke, shuffling through the grade books stacked on the edge of the table. He pulled out two of them, took his time signing them, and moved them to the side.

"Samokhina, Pavlenko, congratulations. Samokhina, the leader of the class, keep up the good work. And Pavlenko who walked the path of glory from failure to a straight-A student. Both are dismissed. Take your grade books and get out of here."

"Such a bastard," Lisa said when they found themselves in the corridor.

Sasha nodded.

"I hope everyone in our group passes." Lisa moved her shoulders uneasily. "Listen . . . We should keep our fingers crossed for them."

Sasha nodded again.

The test lasted four hours, and no one left the auditorium during that time. Lisa couldn't handle the pressure; she went back into town. Sasha went with her, but came back halfway. She moved like a pendulum, back and forth, and listened to the sound of her own steps. She would sit down—and get up again; then repeat it all over. Everything was exactly the same as yesterday. Tinsel garlands still decorated the entrance to the assembly hall; Sasha couldn't banish the thought that garlands and wreaths were the traditional adornments of animals to be sacrificed.

Shortly after four, when darkness descended outside, the second years of Group A stumbled into the corridor. Some people remained standing, leaning on the wall. Some, eyes bulging, raced toward the bathrooms.

Sasha rushed over to Kostya. "How was it?"

"It was fine," replied Zhenya Toporko, coming out of nowhere.

"He passed everyone." Denis Myaskovsky was still breathing heavily. "He was brutal, that bastard. . . . Ugh."

Kostya squeezed Sasha's hand, silently and forcefully. Then he turned and walked down the corridor, Zhenya trotting behind him.

Exhausted, Sasha closed her eyes.

On January 12, exactly on the due date, Sasha's brother was born and named Valentin.

The day before, on the eleventh, she had taken Sterkh's test. The hunchback had called people in one by one. Sasha had walked in last. She had been shaking, but not with fear.

"Sasha, please don't worry so much, everything is fine. Take the headphones, I'm going to play a track that you have not heard before, and your task is to perceive it as fully as possible. It is not so much a test as it is an overview, a concluding lesson. Are you ready?"

Sasha had regained her senses once she left the auditorium. Her classmates, mad with joy, had been having a chicken fight: Zhenya on Kostya's back squared off against Lisa on Denis's back. The girls had slapped each other with rolled notepads, trying to get the other "chicken" off her partner's back; the boys had neighed, clucked, and kicked, and the entire corridor had brimmed with stomping and laughter. Sasha had thought that a medieval carnival—the momentary freedom from a hideous burden—in its hysterical glee, resembled the point when the Specialty test was definitely passed . . .

"What are the sparrows singing on this last day of chill? We live, we breathe, we made it, and we are living still!"

A few minutes before, Sterkh had written in her grade book the word "Outstanding." Specialty tests were always graded.

One more year remained until the placement exam.

On the morning of January 13 the first floor of the dorm was swamped with suitcases and bags. The rooms stood wide open. First years had left the day before, except for a few girls who stayed behind for some reason; Sasha suspected they wanted to say good-bye to someone.

"Good-bye, little'uns!" Zakhar saluted the first-year girls. "Until we meet again . . . on the other side!"

The third years walked into the assembly hall, one by one, and the door closed behind them.

On January 16, second years had a Constitutional Law exam. Sasha ended up with something about splitting assets after divorce. She couldn't remember how one was supposed to split property, and mumbled something inarticulate, burning with shame. The professor seemed displeased, but for some reason still gave her a B.

Kostya was sitting on the windowsill outside the auditorium. He was probably waiting for Zhenya.

"I left my grade book on the table," Sasha said. "Would you mind grabbing it?"

"Sure, no problem," he said. Then, lowering his voice, he asked: "When are you leaving?"

"I don't know yet," she replied. "I don't even have the tickets yet.

Mom's still in the hospital, I don't know when she'll be coming home, and I . . ."

Kostya stared at something behind Sasha's shoulder. She turned around. Ten steps away from them stood Sterkh; his ash-blond hair, this time brushed smoothly, framed his gray face, spilling onto his collar.

"Hello, Nikolay Valerievich," Kostya said.

"Good afternoon, Kostya. Sasha, have you taken the exam yet?"

"Yes," said Sasha.

"Then come with me, we have something to discuss." The hunchback motioned her over with a long finger, and she went as if pulled by an invisible rope.

She expected to be taken to his office. Instead, the hunchback grabbed his hat and coat, told Sasha to get dressed, and they went outside. The day was sunny. Clear sky encased Torpa in a blue dome.

"Have you eaten yet?"

"No . . ."

"Terrific. Sasha, congratulations on successfully completing your winter exams. To the left, please, toward the sign. There, on the second floor, is a fabulous restaurant."

"I have a new brother," she said, surprising herself.

"Then we have a perfect reason for celebration."

Restaurants, with tables draped with starched tablecloths, doormen, and cloakroom attendants, always made Sasha uncomfortable. The two of them were escorted to a private nook, and Sasha immediately tucked herself into a window corner—from there, she could see the street, pigeons on the molding, and a scrap of the sky.

"Here's the menu. Sasha, what will you have?"

"This." Sasha pointed her finger randomly. "And this. And mushrooms."

Their appetizers arrived.

"How do you feel?"

"More or less . . . not bad. I wanted to ask you—how are the third years? Are they doing well, did they pass? All of them?"

Sterkh shook his head.

"I cannot say anything until the final meeting of the examining board."

"But just a ballpark estimate?"

"After your vacation, Sasha, you will return and find out. The exam was somewhat tense, uneven, that I can tell you. But they did well, almost all of them. They are now facing a new life, new projects, new successes. It's remarkably fascinating, Sasha. It is so much more interesting than what you have right now. You will see—life begins after the placement exam. But anyway. Right now you're on vacation; you need to relax and get some rest. No Specialty textbooks, no studying of any kind. No emotional stress. And here's something else, Sasha. If I were you, I wouldn't go anywhere right now."

Sasha choked on a tomato slice.

"But I have to! I have a new brother! Mom's coming out of the hospital any day now, and she'll need help. Plus, she's waiting for me!"

"I understand. But, Sasha, remember what happened on your last winter vacation, a year ago?"

"I know how to control myself," Sasha said hotly. "A lot better than before. Besides, that was an accident. It was the first time in my life when somebody was attacked and robbed in front of me! It had never happened before, and I hope never happens again. I am responsible for my own actions."

"No, Sasha." Sterkh shook his head. "It's *me* who's responsible for you. You are older now, and your problems may be different. What is going on with your nails?"

Sasha hid her hands under the table. When she was stressed, her nails darkened and grew with mind-boggling speed. Having grown by three millimeters during the exam, they were now lengthening again—hard, shiny, like the chitin backs of brown beetles.

The hunchback rubbed his sharp chin.

"Sasha, I am not going to stop you. Frankly speaking, I couldn't—it's your business, you passed all your exams. But just think what your family is going to say if you enter a metamorphosis in front of them."

Sasha did not respond.

"Of course you've learned quite a bit. But just imagine: stress, extreme situation, a newborn baby . . . I'm afraid for you. You are too valuable to behave so irresponsibly."

"Nikolay Valerievich . . ."

"Yes?"

"Am I no longer human?"

"And why is it so important to you?"

Sasha looked up. Sterkh sat across the table from her, calm, benign. His ash-blond hair framed his pale triangular face in two parallel lines.

"I'm serious, Sasha: what is so important about being human? Is it because you simply haven't experienced anything else?"

"I'm used to it." Sasha looked down.

"*Precisely.* You have an unusually strong force of habit, and that is what made our breakthrough so difficult. But now things will move a lot faster. Ah, and here is our veal."

A huge valley-size plate was placed in front of Sasha. White steam rose above a lake of white sauce, above a thick tangle of dill.

"I have to go," Sasha swallowed fretfully. "They won't understand. Especially my mother. I haven't seen her in six months. And then I wasn't quite myself during the summer vacation. I miss her. Just for a few days . . ."

"A few days." Sterkh's shoulders slumped. "Oh, Sasha. I was hoping to talk you out of it."

Now he was the one who seemed troubled and despondent. Sasha was embarrassed.

"I am needed there, do you understand?"

"I do. It's your decision, Sasha. But I wouldn't recommend it."

She did not leave right away. She waited a few more days, but not be-cause, as usual, she could not get the tickets. And not because Mom was still at the hospital and Valentin was taking some time off work. Sasha wanted to make sure that she still looked human, at least on the outside. Without feathers or crust. Without extra joints. She understood Sterkh's point: after a very recent childbirth, Mom did not need a daughter covered by fish scales.

She left the dorm when it was beginning to get dark. She dragged her suitcase down Sacco and Vanzetti, and at the bus stop she spotted Yegor.

She stumbled and slowed down.

Yegor was looking away, as if he hadn't seen her. It was possible he *hadn't* seen her; next to him on the hard-pressed snow was a large gym bag.

Sasha stopped a few feet away from him. She did not know what she wanted—for Yegor to notice her, or for Yegor not to be there at all.

The bus arrived. Yegor with his bag entered through the front door,

Sasha and her suitcase through the back door. The driver checked the tickets, the punching device clicking. The bus started moving.

Sasha looked out the window. In front of her, among people's hats, bald spots, and hoods, she could glimpse Yegor's short light hair.

He never looked back.

The bus arrived at the station. Sasha got lucky: almost right away she purchased a really good ticket, a lower berth in the middle of the carriage. The train station café was still open. Sasha bought two pies and a plastic cup of warm tea. She went to the waiting room and through the window saw Yegor getting on the train without a backward glance.

She forced herself to finish the pies. Then she went to the station's bathroom, wet and foul-smelling, hiked up her sleeve, and tore off the temporary tattoo with a smiley face, by now slightly warped and green as grass.

She drowned it in the toilet.

That night on the train Sasha woke up feeling lousy. She was chilly and nauseated; holding on to the handrails, she stumbled into the bathroom, locked the door, and there, in the tiny smelly space amid the clang and rumble of the train, she grew wings.

It was cold. Chilly air rose from the toilet hole. Sasha saw her reflection in the mirror—and simultaneously in the dark window. She saw how her made-in-China turquoise jacket with white stripes tensed on her back, ballooned, pulsating as if a live creature were trembling between Sasha's shoulder blades. She did not feel much pain, she was no longer nauseated, but she had absolutely no idea what to do now.

She took off her jacket. Pulled off her T-shirt. On her goose bump-covered back two small pink wings twitched fitfully, covered with fluff. The train charged ahead as only night trains can charge through empty fields. Wheels rumbled under the thin metal floor—so very close. Sasha stood, naked from her waist up, slowly freezing, watching her wings settle down, stop shaking, and press against her back as if they were trying to find the most comfortable position.

Someone knocked on the door. Another knock came, this time more determined, and the voice of the train attendant asked loudly: "Are you alive in there? It is the health service time—I have to lock up the bathrooms!"

"Go ahead, lock it," Sasha said.

"What?"

"Hold on." She coughed. "I'm coming out."

She hurried to get dressed. A few tiny feathers, multihued and delicate, flew around the bathroom. One landed in the sink. Without thinking, Sasha rinsed it away.

She came out, hunched over, into the darkness of the corridor. The attendant gave her a sympathetic glance. "Are you sick? Is it your stomach?"

"Yes," Sasha said and went to her berth. The first thing she did was find scissors in her makeup bag and cut her nails, covertly, so that no one could see her. She pushed the clippings under the rug. The train rolled onto the night platform and stopped; somebody walked down the corridor, dragging suitcases; somebody rolled over on the upper berth. A workman shuffled along the train, knocking iron on iron, as if playing a huge xylophone.

Sasha found the player in her bag. She started the "rehabilitation disc" and dove into the absolute pacifying silence.

Valentin met her on the platform, thin and cheerful. He had a cellular phone, which he demonstrated to Sasha with a great deal of pride.

"We now have a twenty-four/seven communication line! After all, she is home alone with the baby, and you never know what she may need. Why are you so hunched over? Don't slouch, stand straight!"

"I'm tired," Sasha said, not exactly to the point. "The exams were difficult. And the train was too hot."

"Fair heat breaks no bones, as they say. I had a business trip back in November. That, I tell you, is when I was really cold . . ."

Valentin talked and talked, dragging Sasha's suitcase toward the metro. Sasha was no longer used to such crowds; standing on the escalator, she felt dizzy. Thankfully, she managed to regain control, and Valentin noticed nothing.

The wings did not disappear.

It does not mean anything, Sasha kept telling herself. It had happened before that the rehabilitation disc did not work right away. She remembered how once she grew spikes down the length of her spine—not particularly sharp, not long—made out of bone matter. They stuck out until that evening, and then drew back in by themselves. Chances are, this time the same thing will happen. There was only one problem: among the throngs of normal people that crowded the morning metro, Sasha, with her sweaty wings sticking to her back, felt awful.

The desperate shriek of a newborn baby greeted them at the

entrance of their apartment. Mom, wearing a bathrobe, stood in the doorway of her room, joyful and bewildered at the same time.

"He's not sleeping. I've been at it for two hours . . . Sasha, finally! Look, this is your brother!"

Sasha stretched her neck. A red-faced baby in a white diaper was writhing in Mom's arms, sobbing his heart out. He shrieked, moving around senseless blue eyes.

The "introduction" lasted about one second: Valentin mumbled something about drafts and germs, so Mom closed the bedroom door. Valentin stuck his feet into his slippers and ran to wash his hands, and Sasha remained in the entryway, leaning on the door.

The wings itched and ached. Sasha moved her shoulders as if her back hurt, and, pressing the toes of her right foot onto her left heel, began to take off her boots.

"Why are you slouching? Straighten your back!"

The three of them were sitting at the kitchen table. The baby had finally fallen asleep; Mom looked exhausted, Valentin, fatigued. Sasha kept on her thick knitted cardigan, even though the kitchen was warm, even hot.

"I caught a draft on the train. Something aches . . . probably pulled a muscle."

"We should rub it with ointment," Mom said. "I forgot what it's called . . . that one with the bee venom. Valentin, do we have any in the medicine chest?"

"There is no need," Sasha said. "It'll go away on its own."

"I don't like the way you look," Mom said. "Do you have a fever?"

She placed her hand on Sasha's forehead in a very familiar, natural gesture.

"Doesn't feel warm, but you're all sweaty. Take off your sweater—why are you wrapped up like that?"

The wings, stuck to her back, twitched. Sensing something, Mom reached for her shoulder—but at that moment Sasha's brother started bawling his head off, and Mom got distracted and hurried into the bedroom.

"The first month is the hardest," Valentin murmured, "but it's going to get better from now on. By the way, you should learn how to change diapers—you'll need it soon enough!"

He smiled, a friendly, sincere smile—but Sasha did not smile back.

▪▪▪

The pattern on the steamy tiles in the bathroom was familiar to her up to the tiniest detail; she remembered it from her childhood—since a gloomy mustached contractor installed the tiles. He did a great job—the tiles still looked good after almost eight years—and Sasha, again finding herself in the world of familiar things, felt lost for a second.

She stood in her own bathtub, in the stream of hot water—she, Sasha Samokhina, who had returned home. This bathroom remembered all her days; here she sleepily brushed her teeth, getting ready for school. Here she cried because of a chance C. Here she dreamed of Ivan Konev calling her . . .

She closed her eyes and directed the showerhead right on the top of her head. She thought of Konev, of their only run together in the park at five in the morning. Everything could have been different if, a year ago, she hadn't rushed to help a stranger . . . and had not mutilated three enormous men.

And if Konev had not run away, upon seeing that carnage.

Could she blame him, though? Would *any* guy stay with her? Who would maintain that friendship, or at least ask for an explanation?

One she wouldn't be able to give.

Warm water streamed down her face. Tiny feathers, black and gray, went down the drain. There were only a few, but Sasha was still worried of clogging the tub. She tried to catch them, but they slipped out of her fingers and down the drain, and Sasha was thinking apathetic thoughts of buying some unclogging chemical and cleaning the pipes in advance. That, at least, was easy enough.

But her wings . . . she did not know how to clean the wings. Underneath the thin feathers, tender pink skin collected into folds. The wings were totally useless. They could not be used for flying. White steam filled the bathroom, the mirror was sweaty. What truly bothered and tortured Sasha was not even the very presence of the wings, but this paradox: her bathtub, her home. Here, everything was ordinary. *She* was ordinary. But then—everything that had happened, and what still lay ahead. The placement exam next winter . . .

Mom knocked on the door.

"Sasha, are you going to be long? The baby just pooped, I need to wash him!"

"One minute," Sasha said.

Drying the wings with a towel was painful and uncomfortable.

Ideally, she should have dried them with a hair dryer, or simply spread them near a radiator, but Sasha no longer had her own room. She had no place where she could dry her trembling wet wings without interruption. She tried to imagine what would happen if Mom or Valentin found her in the process . . . and could not.

"Sasha, hurry up!"

"I'm coming."

She put on her robe and put a towel around her shoulders. She came out, hunching over. The baby cried in the bedroom. Mom was smiling.

"Come, I'll show you how to wash him. Your nails . . . what happened to your nails?"

Sasha stuck her hands under her arms.

"Are those artificial nails?" Mom asked horrified. "But it's so distasteful! Why black?"

"I'll wash it off," Sasha said. "It's nothing."

The next morning, her wings remained in place and even seemed to have grown a bit. Sasha used all her willpower to suppress panic.

Mom was not feeling well, and Sasha volunteered to take the baby for a walk. It was a warm, almost summery day, the sun was shining, and the baby was already ten days old. Half an hour, Valentin said. No more than that.

Wet poplar branches glistened in the sunlight, dripping with melted snow. Sasha walked, pushing the carriage in front of her and marveling at the unfamiliar sensation. Her brother was buried amid the mattresses and blankets, and only his tiny nose poked though—the pink nose of a deeply sleeping baby. The day was startlingly calm: deserted courtyard. Trees motionless in the still air. Sunshine.

Almost reaching the place where the slaughter took place last year, Sasha turned the carriage around. Of course, there was no sign of what had happened, and the new clean snow was melting slightly on the ground. Sasha took out her player and sank into the silence.

Anxious silence, as if in expectation of a verdict. It could last for hours, but by now Sasha knew: it was in her power to change the recording on that disc. The silence could become different. The observer influences the process of observation, as Portnov stated a while ago.

In order to manage that force, she had to let it into herself. Make it a part of her. Own it. And only then—on her own behalf—could she weave the pattern of the Silence.

The quiet before the storm. The hush of a cemetery. The silence that occurs when one runs out of words. The vacuum of a galaxy. Endless narrative; and the one who is listening is at once the narrator, the protagonist, the ear, the air, and the acoustic nerve . . .

A thousand people simultaneously held their breath. Something was bound to happen; Sasha walked slowly along the line of damp bushes, passing poplars and birches, an old willow, and a rowan tree with some leftover berries hanging on its branches. And to the right of Sasha walked her shadow, clutching the shadow of the carriage, her projection onto the world of packed water crystals, and it was long, tinted blue, and the color of the sky was an integral part of it.

Object and its projection had a reciprocated bond. That's what Portnov said some time ago. He spoke—"tossed at them," to use his own expression—words and sentences that sometimes lacked all meaning, and sometimes seemed like banal clichés, or were simply incomprehensible, and Sasha listened to and immediately forgot those words.

But now, for a split second, she sensed simultaneously—incorporated, made an integral part of herself—all her projections.

Her classmate still remembered words that, in the heat of an argument, Sasha threw at her at the end of the seventh grade.

The tree she planted four years ago had grown a little.

An impression of her shoe lingered in the hardened concrete near the new construction site.

She was reflected in Mom, in Valentin, in little Valentin Junior, in another hundred people: she was reflected—surprisingly sharp—in Kostya. She was Ivan Konev's nightmarish dream. She was reflected in the fate of a distant stranger—her father, who lived on the other side of town.

And she herself was a reflection. This realization made Sasha disintegrate into minute pieces, and then rebuild anew; when she opened her eyes, Valentin stood in front of her, his coat unbuttoned, and he looked bewildered and angry.

Sasha took off her headphones.

"It's been forty minutes! Do you expect me to run looking for you? He needs to eat!"

The baby was still sleeping soundly, pink nose peeking from the pile of blankets. Valentin took the carriage from Sasha and pushed it toward the entrance, so quickly that water splashed from underneath the wheels.

"Selfish bunch, all they want is to listen to their music," said an old woman who was sitting on the bench.

Sasha remained standing, breathing on her frozen fingers. Then she sighed, straightened her shoulders, and realized that her wings had disappeared.

Every day she went to the store with a grocery list. She ironed swad-dling blankets. Helped her mother with the baby's feedings: her brother was on formula, and Mom was heartbroken over it, while Sasha did not quite understand all the fuss about it. So her mother didn't have any milk, so what. All the hustle and bustle with the bottles and nipples was annoying, but then anyone could feed the baby. For example, Valentin. Or even she, Sasha.

Her brother elicited absolutely no feelings in Sasha. No tenderness, no aggravation. She learned to sleep through his crying, while Mom and Valentin took turns getting up—and the baby required them to get up every three to four hours. This was a world that revolved around one single heavenly body, it was completely subordinate to the baby. Mom, not entirely healthy, still noticeably weak, could think only of the baby. Valentin sank into household duties up to his chin, and was forgoing sleep and rest for the sake of the evening bath time. The neighbors said that a woman could only dream of a husband like Valentin.

Sasha felt like an asteroid in a temporary orbit. She still took walks with the baby in the carriage, catching curious glances from the passing women, old dames, and, rarely, men. She boiled the bottles, cooked and cleaned, occasionally changed diapers. Once or twice her brother smiled at her: it was a meaningless, albeit very sweet, almost human smile. Once, on a very sunny day, Sasha took the risk and brought the carriage into the familiar park. There, walking in circles over the clean paths sprinkled with salt, she thought, for the first time since the exams, of Farit Kozhennikov. And about what could have happened had she, Sasha, failed her Specialty test.

Her brother slept under his down blanket, swaddled like a tiny grain in a thick shell. He may not have happened at all. Everything alive was so fragile. "There is absolutely no way of negotiating with you, is there?" Sasha asked at the riverbank, watching autumn leaves swim by. And he answered: "Sasha, the world is full of entities that people *cannot* negotiate with. But somehow people survive, don't they?"

But how fragile was their chance of survival!

Snow was melting under her feet. Spring was coming. Grandmothers with grandchildren and mommies with carriages strolled around the park. A worn, scratched piece of ice remained in place on the ice rink, and three boys were playing hockey—only one of them wore skates, and he kept losing.

The baby stirred. Worried, Sasha rocked the carriage. It was time to go home. Too late, though: baby Valentin started crying during their walk, and shrieked nonstop all the way home—Sasha ran wild-eyed, scaring the passersby, cursing herself for going so far away from the apartment.

The baby smacked his lips and quieted down. Sasha took a deep breath, turned the carriage around, and almost immediately ran into Ivan Konev.

It was too late to pretend not to have seen or recognized each other. Sasha was the first one to regain self-control.

"Hey." She rocked the carriage nonchalantly.

"Hey," mumbled Konev and nodded at the carriage. "Yours?"

"Uh-huh," Sasha replied before she had a chance to think about it.

"Congratulations . . . A boy?"

"Yes." Sasha smiled beatifically. "And how are things with you?"

"Fine." Ivan licked his lips, not the smartest thing to do in the winter.

"Well, see you around," Sasha said indifferently. "Time to feed him."

"See you."

Sasha marched toward the entrance to the park without a backward glance.

The night before leaving for Torpa Sasha did not sleep at all. She lay in the dark listening to the ticking of the all the clocks in the apartment. The baby woke up, cried, then quieted down. He cried again. Sasha listened to her mother murmuring a lullaby in the next room. She suddenly recognized the song, or rather a singsongy recitative: it was a piece of her own babyhood. A small slice of information. A word blown away by the draft.

The baby fell asleep. Mom must have passed out right away; Valentin tossed and turned, then all was quiet again. The clock was ticking.

Sasha got up and stumbled over her half-packed suitcase. The glow of the streetlights peeked into the room through a gap between the curtains. A car drove by, its headlights passing over the ceiling.

Bare feet on the ice-cold floor, Sasha stepped into the next room.

The room was cramped. The baby's crib was pushed right against the big bed so that Mom could reach the baby without getting up. At that moment Mom slept, a hand under her cheek, her face pressed against the side of the crib.

Trying not to look at the sleeping Valentin, Sasha came closer to the crib. A ray of light from the outside crossed the blanket in a diagonal streak. The baby lay on his back. Miniature fists lay on the pillow above his head, eyelashes stuck together, tiny mouth half-opened.

He also was a word. A resonance. A material personification of someone's curt demand. Sasha had no idea how she knew this; she took another step and took the baby out of his crib.

His head dangled; Sasha managed to support it. The baby was a half-formed willpower, a mobile cluster of information; he was a part of Sasha. A part of her world. He was *hers*.

Two words merged into one sound.

The baby opened his sleepy blue eyes. He seemed to be getting ready to scream. The clock was ticking. Mom's breathing was shallow and uneven, tortured by the constant lack of sleep.

Sasha stared at herself. And again she stared at herself; it was similar to two mirrors facing each other. The baby, now integral to her essence, was quiet. His eyes darkened slowly. His stare was gaining comprehension.

Sasha barely contained her scream.

Just as silently, holding the baby to her chest, she went into the kitchen. Still not comprehending what had actually happened, she was already drenched in cold sweat from head to foot. She placed the baby on the kitchen table, then bent double, pressing her hand to her mouth. She vomited gold coins, for the first time in many months. The coins jingled, rolling on the floor, and every sound, every minuscule noise, could awaken light-sleeping Mom.

Unmoving, the boy lay on the table. His fists kept opening and closing. His eyes, now deep brown, stared intently, steadily. The meaning—a sum of meanings that this human being was comprised of—now dissolved inside Sasha as rapidly as soap in water. The lullaby linked them like shared skin.

Sasha struggled, trying the break the link. Trying to separate the baby into his own specific "informational packet." At some point she thought that she could understand and control everything: both their bodies as reflections of two similar meanings, two spoken words, one of which is a request, a demand, a clump of will . . .

That clump broke out of control. It absorbed the baby's absence of will as a large drop of mercury sucks up a small one.

The baby relaxed his limbs tiredly. He closed his eyes. At the same moment the bedsprings squeaked—Mom was stirring. In a second she would reach through the sides of the crib, and instead of her sleeping son she would find a cold sheet . . .

Keeping her eyes on the baby, Sasha moved to the door. She closed it; locked it. Thankfully, the kitchen door had a latch, in case of cold drafts.

Her hands shaking, she picked up the receiver. She dialed a cell phone number; this number was registered in her mind as something so extreme, something for an emergency only to be remembered in dire circumstances, as if it were written in scarlet letters on a concrete wall.

The clock showed half past three.

"The telephone subscriber you are trying to reach is currently out of range."

It cannot be! Sasha bit her lip and dialed the number again. Answer! Please!

Beeps.

"Hello," a calm voice answered. It did not sound sleepy. It was unlikely that this person was woken up in the middle of the night.

"Farit," Sasha murmured, using his first name for the first time. "I did something . . . something like . . . please help me reach Nikolay Valerievich!"

"What did you do?"

"I don't understand. Something with the baby. Please, help me!"

"Hold on," Kozhennikov said. A long pause followed. Sasha heard steps in the corridor and Mom's uncertain voice.

"Sasha? Did you take the baby?"

"Yes," Sasha said, watching the lifeless child on the kitchen table. "Go back to sleep. Don't worry. I'm rocking him to sleep."

The door gave a jolt.

"Sasha, did you lock the door? Open up!"

"Go to sleep," Sasha repeated, pressing the receiver to her ear. "Don't worry. I am watching him."

"What is going on? Open the door! Why did you lock it up?"

"I'll open it. Go back to sleep."

"Alexandra!"

Mom was fully awake. Now her voice contained anger—and fear. Something was going on, something was happening, there was trouble, she could feel it—but she could not recognize the nature of the danger.

"Sasha," Kozhennikov said very drily on the phone, "check whether the baby is alive."

"What?" Sasha babbled.

"Check his pulse."

"Open the door immediately!" Mom punched the door with her fist. "Valentin! Valentin!"

Sasha grabbed the baby's wrist. It was so tiny it was impossible to take his pulse; already sure the child was dead, Sasha suddenly remembered Dima Dimych's lessons ("Count the pulse in six seconds, multiply by ten") and pressed her fingers to the baby's small neck.

The neck was warm. The pulse was there.

"He's alive," Sasha rustled into the receiver.

"Open the door!" Valentin roared, trying to take the door off its hinges.

"Just wait!" Sasha shouted, tears in her voice. "What are you yelling about? Why are you screaming? I'll open in a minute!"

"Hang up the phone," Kozhennikov said. "Sterkh will call you back."

The screaming outside the door ceased for a second. Mom was crying, Valentin was trying to calm her down.

"No need for hysterics. What exactly happened, I don't understand . . . It'll be fine . . . just wait . . . Alexandra, open up immediately. I am counting to three. One . . ."

The phone rang.

"Hello!"

"Listen," Sterkh said without any introduction. "And work, work hard, focus, you have three minutes for the reverse transition. Go!"

And then silence drowned everything out.

The latch gave up first—little screws became loose, the wooden plank fell apart, and Mom and Valentin stormed into the kitchen.

By then their neighbors, awakened by all the noise, were already pounding on the walls and the radiators. Some genius had called the police. The yellow car with a blue stripe drove up to the building a full hour after the beginning of the incident.

Sasha sat in front of the kitchen table on which the sleeping child lay. He slept soundly, snoring, almost touching his face with tiny hands. Sasha was drenched in sweat, white-faced, disheveled, her hand clutching the phone.

The receiver emitted short beeps—Sterkh had rung off.

The rest of the night was spent in interrogations. Mom took valerian root, phenobarbital, Valium. In the heat of the moment, Valentin slapped Sasha in the face—and was then deeply uncomfortable. The baby was taken to his crib, and there he slept until seven in the morning; Sasha's heart faltered when she heard his hesitant whimper. Mom fed him, he ate, smiled, clearly in a very good mood, and again closed his blue eyes. Mom calmed down just a little.

"Can. You. Explain. To. Us. Why. Did. You. Do. This?"

"I didn't do anything." Sasha lied and looked away. "I thought, 'It's my last night, so who knows when I'll see him next time' . . ."

"What do you mean *who knows?*"

"I just held him," Sasha repeated stubbornly. "I just wanted to . . . sit with him. Why were you trying to break the door? What am I, a murderer?"

Mom and Valentin exchanged glances.

"You acted strangely," Valentin said curtly. "Why did you lock the door? Who were you talking to on the phone? At half past three in the morning?"

"It was a wrong number." Sasha was tired. She no longer cared, she just wanted to get away, stop this questioning, lie on the berth in the moving train and sleep until they got to Torpa.

They exchanged chilly good-byes. Sasha picked up her suitcase, rolled it onto the street all by herself, and walked—alone—to the metro station.

It must have been similar to childbirth: that night for the first time she recognized herself as a sum of information. She found something foreign within herself, and she pushed it out, delivered it, bloody and turned nearly inside out.

Until the last minute she hadn't known whether the baby would be restored as the original being in his original body. Mom had not noticed anything different in his looks or behavior—at least, not in the first few minutes. Sasha had no idea what would happen later.

She got to the station three hours before the train was scheduled to depart. They weren't yet seating passengers. Sasha found an empty seat in the waiting room and sat down, her suitcase placed in front of her.

She felt devastating pity for her mother. She shuddered at the thought of what could have happened to little Valentin. She knew Mom would never forgive her.

Human masses slowly shifted around the huge waiting hall. Socks and shirts, tubes of toothpaste, trousers, sweaters, books, chocolates, and toys swam around, locked inside the suitcases. All of this was material to the last thread. And all of this was only a shadow of something significant that hung overhead. Sasha was convinced that if she lifted her eyes to the ceiling, she would see an obstacle between her and the light, something enormous, throwing a complex system of shadows.

Last night, listening to the silence in the receiver, she'd made an internal effort compared to which all her school load seemed child's play. Again she had stepped over the line. One more step toward the world she knew nothing about. The world she was led and pushed to by force. And from where, it seemed, there was no way back.

They finally began seating the passengers. Sasha was the first one to approach the train attendant.

"Hold on." The attendant, a curvy blonde of about thirty, stepped in front of her. "I need my first passenger to be male—for good luck!"

Sasha did not reply. She stood by the carriage, staring up at the dark sky.

Streetlights burned in official white. No more snow could be seen neither on the platform nor on the rails—stomped on by many feet, cleared up by the workers. The ground twitched underfoot; a diesel shunter was moving parallel to their platform. A round-faced youth peeked out of the window, smiled, and waved to Sasha.

A middle-aged man with a suitcase approached the train. He presented his ticket and walked up the black open-work steps into the carriage.

"Now you can come in," the attendant said to Sasha.

The train was stuffy. Sasha found her place, pushed the suitcase under the berth, hung up her jacket, and lay down.

Why had she picked up a sleeping child in the middle of the night?

Why did she think that she and the child were one and the same? Why had she wanted to possess him, make him a part of herself? Why had it been so easy for her to accomplish?

And why hadn't she listened to Sterkh when he said "I don't recommend it"?

The carriage was slowly filling up with people: some of them looked dense, like wooden figurines. Others seemed vague, faded, and insignificant. Sasha closed her eyes to avoid seeing.

Tomorrow was February 14. Beginning of the second semester. Portnov was going to gather them in auditorium 1 and distribute the new books and exercise sets. Sterkh . . .

Sasha sat up in the berth at the thought of what Sterkh would say to her. Last night they had not said hello or good-bye: a second before Mom and Valentin stormed into the kitchen, Sasha had managed to whisper that the baby had regained consciousness, and Sterkh had simply hung up the phone. She was well aware of the fact that the hunchback's reaction to her crime had been immediate and professional, and if it weren't for him—and Farit's brilliant work as a dispatcher—things could have turned out differently.

Sasha tried not to imagine how differently.

The train began to move.

She would return to Torpa. Accept punishment from Sterkh. If he decided to punish her. And then she'd again bury herself in the books. In the exercises. With time she would completely cease to be human, and then she probably would no longer care . . .

But *why* should she return to Torpa?

She stopped breathing. In the last few years she'd gotten so used to the idea that she could never get out of Torpa, that she was doomed to study until she got her diploma, that she was facing the placement exam during her third year, and that her entire life depended on Portnov, on Sterkh, on Kozhennikov. Who for the past two and a half years had done whatever he wanted with her, all the time "not asking for the impossible."

But Sasha had changed!

Her neighbors, a married middle-aged couple, were getting ready for sleep. Sasha found a handful of coins in the pocket of her jacket; last night in the kitchen she'd gotten a chance to collect them . . . perhaps only some of them. Valentin had asked what they were, and Sasha had dispersed her habitual lie about game tokens. Mom had had other concerns. Mom had been scampering around with baby Valentin in her arms, and Sasha had crawled under the table, gathering gold coins with a sign of zero, a round symbol that seemed three-dimensional when one looked at it closely. Coins that nothing good ever came from.

The train rolled through the snow-capped forest. The light from the windows fell on the sinking, porous snow, here and there ripped by the thawing holes. Passengers ate and drank, smoked on the platform between the cars, laughed, slept. Anticipated reunion. Endured a separation. Played cards.

The train attendant brought in the sheets. Sasha sloppily set up the mattress and lay down again, covering herself with a sheet. The train would arrive at the station in Torpa at four thirty in the morning. She had plenty of time.

At two in the morning everyone was asleep.

Coals smoldered under a barrel of hot water.

On the table in the staff compartment lay a set of keys. The train attendant carelessly dozed off, leaving the door slightly ajar.

Sasha walked out on the platform between the carriages and closed the door behind her. Outside the windows, protected by the stripes of iron bars, pines rushed by.

She opened the door and choked on the wind. The warm spell did not reach that far from the city: sharp clumps of snowflakes fell from the sky, white and motionless, frozen-looking stars peeking through the ripped clouds.

She tiptoed back to the carriage and returned the keys to the table. After all, it was not the attendant's fault.

She stood in the doorway feeling the harsh wind on her face. Her skin burned and her eyes teared up—a normal, quite human sensation.

She stretched out her hand. Gold coins scattered and disappeared.

Sasha stood for a few moments, breathing with all her might, filling up her lungs. Then she unclenched her fingers, let go of the railing, and stepped forward. At least she imagined taking a step . . .

She imploded.

A gust of wind tore off her jacket, threw it over Sasha's head. Her sweater disintegrated into threads, the T-shirt ripped apart. To the right and left of her spine, a couple of inches above her bra clasp, two hot jet pipes burst open.

Sasha thought she saw the train from a distance, watching its long back with short pipes through which smoke rose in various stages of concentration. She saw all of it, realizing how dark it was outside; she sensed the air currents. She trailed along, shifted in space, or perhaps she glided as the shadow of an aircraft slides over the land.

Shadow knows no obstacles. Over water, land, snow; shadow easily falls into precipices and just as easily climbs back to the surface. Clouds hung in two lacy layers, one above the other. Above the clouds was a pearly-white layer of stars. And underneath was the dark forest, full of life. The unhurried snake of the train broke into the open space, into a field darkened by thawing patches. Water stood still under a tender coat of ice in a deep ditch. The ground was still sound asleep, still wintery, but already pregnant with spring.

Sasha wanted to sing.

She also wanted to own all of this. This pearly sky. This cold, helpless land. These seeds hidden deep under the melting snow. These hills . . .

She opened her arms. Every invisible seed in the frozen soil appealed to her as the shadow of a large, unbearably enormous word, "Life." Each root waiting for warmth. Each drop of moisture. Life, the center of all in the universe.

The only thing that had meaning.

"Mine!" Sasha shouted.

She was tossed like a wood chip in a whirlpool. Gray haze bore down on her. Sasha could no longer see the train, the sky, and the forest. She pushed upward, but the haze thickened. Then, hugging her knees with both arms, she fell downward, broke through into the light, saw half of the sun rising over the smooth horizon and did not recognize the landscape.

Then she disintegrated into letters. Into short, simple thoughts. A hundred years had passed, and a hundred more, and Sasha merged again—back into herself.

She lay facedown on the roof of a moving train.

She wore a sweater ripped into rags and an old pair of black jeans.

"Excuse me, which carriage is this?"

A short red-eyed man who was smoking on the platform between two carriages staggered back and almost fell. A girl hanging upside down looked at him through the slightly open window—on the outside.

"Which carriage?"

"Get thee gone!" shouted the little man, and Sasha realized that he'd drunk a lot last night. And perhaps the night before as well.

The carriage doors were closed. The railings were covered with frost. Sasha's palms flattened against the metal, stuck, and anchored her to the train, but it hurt to tear them off. She found carriage number 7; the door suddenly gave in and opened. For a second Sasha hovered over the entrance like a curtain, and then dove into the warmth—directly onto the wet, dirty floor.

The corridor was stuffy. A striped neutral carpet stretched along the carriage and looked long, like an airplane runway. The passengers were asleep.

Sasha slipped into the bathroom, looked at herself in the mirror—and started crying.

"Miss! Miss, we reach Torpa in fifteen minutes . . ."

Sasha only pretended to be asleep.

The night before she'd gutted her suitcase and put on everything she owned. All her sweaters and cardigans. A warm jacket. Hat and gloves. She'd wrapped a scarf around her face. Put on dark glasses.

It was dark when the train attendant let her out onto the Torpa platform—the train stopped for one minute.

When the train started moving again, Sasha sat down on her suitcase. She did not feel the cold. Her entire body was covered with a stiff crust, reddish-brown like polished wood. Chitin plates rubbed onto one another, cracked and squeaked with each movement.

The clock registered ten minutes to five. February snow drifted along the platform, and the next bus to Torpa was not coming for another two and a half hours.

Sasha took out the CD player. She put on her headphones, pressed a button—and closed her eyes.

"Samokhina, this class started ten minutes ago."

"I know."

"It's very bad that you know and still allow yourself to be tardy. I just informed your group that our first testing session is tomorrow at five thirty, according to a separate schedule. Sit down, please. Numbers one through eight on page five must be completed by tomorrow. Kozhennikov, hand her the textbooks."

Sasha shuffled over to her usual spot.

She'd almost decided not to go to Specialty. Almost. On the bus people had stared at her like at a leper, and no one was brave enough to sit next to her. She kept her headphones on the entire way, and by the time she turned the key in the lock of room 21, she'd regained her human likeness.

She'd had to throw away her tights—they had been cut up by the chitin plates. The jeans squeaked in her hands, covered with disgusting dust particles that resembled brown starch. Half naked, wrapped only in a towel, Sasha had proceeded into the shower room, shocking first years with her appearance. In the shower room she'd found someone's forgotten cake of soap and used it all up until it became a thin wafer. Still wrapped only in a towel, she'd returned to her room and pulled on her one intact outfit—a jogging suit.

Then she'd got into her bed, looked at the clock, and swore to herself that she would skip Specialty. Let them do what they want.

With a minute left before the class began, she'd cracked. She'd thought of Mom. She'd thought of baby Valentin—those minutes when he smiled at her. She got up, carelessly brushed her hair, and, as she was, in a stretchy jogging suit, she'd shuffled off to class.

"Now, second years, Group A, listen carefully."

Portnov's straight hair had grown even longer in the last few months. His blond ponytail now reached the middle of his back.

"What we call integral consciousness has done enough work for you during the previous semesters; now we require from you an intricate execution, but also a deep understanding of fairly complex concepts. Kozhennikov, am I supposed to wait for you?"

Kostya stood in front of Sasha's desk with a thin stack of books in his hands. It seemed as if he couldn't decide which books to hand to Sasha and which to keep for himself.

"Whatever you want to say to Samokhina, you can say after the class. Give her the *Textual Module,* the set of exercises, and the *Conceptual Activator,* that one, with the yellow cover."

Slightly turning her head, Sasha noticed that Zhenya Toporko had gained some weight. Not a lot, but enough to be noticeable. She shouldn't have worn that blouse, it was too tight. Lisa, on the other hand, had slimmed down; she wore a severe black sweater and wide-legged trousers, and a silver pendant sparkled on her chest—she looked stylish. Sasha suddenly realized that she was sitting in the auditorium in a wrinkled jogging suit, with her hair barely brushed, with no makeup on. And that everyone saw her looking like this, when she came in late. She shrugged it off.

"Meanings are manifold. They may estrange themselves from the willpower they originated from, they can encase themselves in a shell, decompress, and transform." Portnov strolled around the auditorium, chin held high. He lingered by the window behind the students' backs. He strode back, pressing his fists onto the teacher's desk; the winter light bleached his glasses for a split second.

"Considering that at this point of your development you are capable of perceiving only information presented in the traditional fashion, we will begin with the simplest concepts. In front of everyone here is a *Conceptual Activator.* Open to page three."

Paper rustled all through the auditorium. Indifferently, Sasha opened the thin textbook with the yellow cover. No author's name, no editor's credentials, no publisher's data: on the inside cover, on the clear white space, was a large phallus, in the state of arousal, and quite artfully depicted.

"What is the matter?"

Sasha wasn't planning on giggling like an idiot. Her lips stretched into a snigger all by themselves. The drawing was a challenge—rude and desperate, the escapade of someone who "encased" his "meaning" into the only accessible shell.

Portnov took the book out of her hands. He sniggered skeptically. "I see. Of course. You will stay after the class, Samokhina."

"What did I do?"

Without any response, Portnov strode over to his desk, slipped Sasha's textbook into the desk drawer and took out a similar book with a yellow cover, a slightly newer edition.

"Here you go, Samokhina. Now, page three. In front of you is a diagram that unfolds in four dimensions, which may present a certain difficulty for you. In general, the activator is one large interactive system that allows you to detect connections between informational fragments. By the end of this semester, assuming, of course, that you study rather than twiddle your thumbs, this book will seem to you a living being, a perpetuum mobile, a generator, and an absorber of great meanings. Then you may even stop drawing idiotic pictures on its margins. Now: in the horizontal row—line fifteen, depth one—you will see notational conventions. In the first diagonal column concepts are expressed verbally for your convenience. Open the notepads. In the next fifteen minutes, you must recognize the principle and write down as many verbal definitions for each symbol as you can.

"Starting now."

▪▪▪

The bell rang.

Sasha was bent over her notepad. The date, February 14, was scribbled in the corner margin. Below it a pattern of flowers and leaves—and, inexplicably, of bare human feet—curled around the page, fitting neatly into the graphed paper. Not a symbol, not a word.

"For tomorrow: paragraphs one and two from the *Textual Module. Conceptual Activator,* the diagram on page three. Class is dismissed, all but Samokhina."

The door shut behind the last student—Kostya. On his way out he threw a quick backward glance.

"I can see you've worked diligently on this," Portnov said benevolently, looking at Sasha's masterpiece over her shoulder.

Sasha did not bother lifting her head. Unhurriedly, Portnov picked up a chair, placed it in front of her, and straddled it, leaning onto the straight back.

"You do realize that Nikolay Valerievich had absolutely no obligation to pull you out of the mess you plunged yourself into?"

"I knew you were going to say that."

"Such acumen! I fail to understand where this rebellious temperament is suddenly coming from when, in my opinion, you should be meek as a lamb. But just in case, you should know: every wasted minute of the time that should be spent studying will cost you a whole lot more than last year. These cute little flowers"—he pointed toward Sasha's notepad—"have already been charged to your account. I will expect you tomorrow at the individual session, and you will report on the completed exercises, one through eight, in case you forgot."

"I haven't forgotten." Sasha got up.

Portnov narrowed his eyes. "You are way too eloquent lately."

"You can't make me shut up!"

"One through *ten,*" Portnov informed her evenly.

Kostya was waiting for her in the vestibule, in front of the concierge's glass booth. The recess was almost over: first years buzzed around the staircase and the hallway and Group B congregated in front of auditorium 1. Third years were no longer there, and as usual, after the winter exams the institute seemed empty.

"Hey," Kostya said.

"Hey," Sasha responded.

"Zakhar flunked."

"What?"

"Portnov told us before the lecture."

"He knew it," Sasha murmured. "He came to say good-bye to me . . ."

Kostya's Adam's apple twitched.

"Why . . . why him, do you know?"

Sasha stood motionlessly, her arms hanging by her sides. She was supposed to go up to the third floor and change into her gym uniform. The bell would ring in five minutes . . .

"Kostya, can you tell Dima Dimych I won't be there?"

"Portnov said he's instituting a penalty for missing gym classes."

"I don't care."

"Sasha . . ."

"Sorry, I have to go."

"Hello."

"Hello," Sasha said and coughed to clear her throat. "Hi, Mom."

"Hi," Mom responded after a short pause. Sasha could hear the baby crying on the other end of the line.

"How are you doing?" Sasha asked quickly. "How's . . . how's the baby?"

"He's fine," Mom said. "He's fidgety. Probably gas."

"Well," said Sasha and faltered. "I'm doing well, too."

"Sorry," Mom said. "He's crying, I can't talk right now."

Then she hung up.

Sasha entered auditorium 14 at three twenty sharp, according to schedule. Sterkh sat behind the teacher's desk; in front of him were stacks of books, thick notepads, and scattered sheets of paper. He did not lift his head when Sasha entered and did not acknowledge her greeting.

She closed the door behind her and remained standing on the threshold.

A fringe of icicles decorated the window. The sun shined through them, drops of water grew heavy on the sharp ends, fell off, and, sparkling, disappeared below. A minute passed. Then another. Sasha leaned on the door frame. Her knees felt weak.

Sterkh's sharp chin was almost touching the wide knot of his tie, gray-blue with a metallic sheen. Inclining his head, he was making notes in his notebook, as if Sasha were not standing there at all. Perhaps he wanted her to apologize. Or he was punishing her by this long silence. Or maybe he felt so much disdain toward her that he did not even want to acknowledge her presence.

Sasha stared at her hands. Her nails grew with each passing second. The skin on her cheeks was becoming tighter—something was changing there as well. The blood vessels pulsated, and each one of her heartbeats echoed with a dry click in her ears.

"You were lucky your brother is still very young. Had he been only one week older, the full rehabilitation would have been impossible. The child would have been an invalid with no chance of recovery."

Sterkh spoke without looking at her, still concentrating on the page of his notebook.

"Take the next disc. Work on the first track. Only the first one."

Sasha took a few steps toward the desk. She reached out with her hand; her nails, ugly, black, were curled into hooks. She squeezed the envelope with the disc between her palms and, pressing her hands together, stepped back.

"You are dismissed."

Sasha left without saying a word.

And yet she loved to learn. This almost unnatural passion saved her that night, when Portnov's ten exercises surrounded her like a pack of assassins, and not one of them would give up without a fight.

At first, she tried to convince herself: one more step, and I'll take a break. One more mental metamorphosis. One more. Vector, another vector, and here we have connecting threads, and now two mental streams have been associated, and now the first exercise is almost done . . .

A while ago she'd attempted to understand which part of her organism was responsible for completing these exercises. Brain? Yes, of course. Imagination? At top speed. Intuition? Yes, quite possibly. But all these things were parts of a larger mechanism, and not the most important ones; when this mechanism warmed up and started working at full force, it seemed to Sasha that she, Alexandra Samokhina herself, was only a fragment of the mechanism. A rear wheel.

It was a quiet February evening. A long crimped icicle hanging from a tin awning peeked into the window of room 21. A boom box was turned on somewhere—she could hear the rumble of the drums and a low sensual voice crooning something in English; then even the stereo got tired, the streetlights were switched off, the windows went dark, and the snow-covered lawn in front of the dorm was now pitch-black. Sasha cornered exercise number five and started number six.

Recognize associations. Compose a picture out of separate pieces. Take apart a mechanism, use the parts to compile a new one, then accidentally notice new possibilities, and, jumping over to a different orbit, discover an infinite field of operation. Sasha was carried away; at times she would come back, repeat first semester exercises from memory, reaching a dead end, bypassing everything in a roundabout way, and suddenly run into a simple solution—she sat over the book until six o'clock in the morning.

Exercise ten. Done.

Sasha stood still, feeling as if she, her body, were an old tower at the ocean shore, a heavy stone building, over which centuries flew. Inside, wind danced and sand rippled. Frightened by the authenticity of the sensation, Sasha moved—and came back to reality. Her arms felt numb. She was very thirsty and had to use the bathroom.

She drank half a bottle of mineral water. Shuffled to the bathroom and back. Got back into bed and reached for the CD player and headphones on her nightstand.

Numbers lit up on the tiny display. Track one . . .

"The child would have been an invalid with no chance of recovery."

Track one, one more time. Again. Then track two. Then three.

"The child would have been an invalid with no chance of recovery."

Track five, track eight. Sasha melted in the darkness like a sugar cube. She disintegrated. She stretched in long pliable threads from herself to Mom. She whispered something in her ear, and Mom tossed and turned in her uneasy slumber; the baby slept, his fists spread over the pillow. And Sasha stretched and stretched like telegraph wires, and she knew she could not hold out much longer, that she was about to break. It was too far . . .

And too late.

She made an effort and ripped off the headphones. The player rolled soundlessly down to the floor. No crunch, no thud. The round cover opened and fell off, the whirling disc caught the reflection of a streetlight and stopped. No wind, no squeak, no habitual fuss of the sleepy dormitory; the foreign silence continued.

She shouted—and could not hear herself.

Tangled in her blanket, she dropped off the bed, but even the pain in her bruised knees could not break the Silence. She jumped on her feet, realizing that she was about to choke on the Silence, but at that moment the alarm went off.

A simple electronic device played an old nursery rhyme melody. As soon as that sound broke into Sasha's consciousness, the Silence departed. She could now hear the wind, the distant radio, the shuffling of someone's slippers in the corridor, and someone's disgruntled voice: "Mikhail, any idea who's yelling?"

The first block was gym class.

It looked as if no one had slept that night: second years, Group A, sat and lay on the windowsills, on the mats, and on the naked floor—no one had any desire to look into anyone else's inflamed tortured eyes. Only Denis Myaskovsky was preternaturally cheerful; he ran around the gym and every now and then he jumped up and dangled from the basketball hoop.

Grim Lisa sat on the bench, looking from her sneaker-clad foot to a piece of broken shoelace in her hand. Dima Dimych forced everyone to line up and gave them a long lecture on how gym classes were as precious to second years as the air itself, because the study load would prove to be harmful unless they took care of their health.

"Dmitry Dmitrievich, I can't jump today," Sasha said. "My leg hurts."

"There is always something wrong with you, Sasha. And meanwhile your class is behind on the regulatory requirements!"

"I'll do the requirements later."

"You all keep promising. Short distance, long jump, triple jump . . ."

He fell silent, looking at Sasha with concern.

"Sasha . . . what's wrong?"

"Why?" She touched her cheeks. "Fish scales?"

Dima looked upset.

Sasha closed the auditorium door behind her. Said a barely audible hello, not hoping for an answer. She froze, staring at the cracks in the brown floor.

"Did you work on track one?"

Sterkh sat behind the teacher's desk; the curtain across from him was pushed aside, and in the stream of light from the outside all Sasha could see was his dark silhouette.

"Come closer."

Sasha approached. Sterkh rose, walked around his desk, and stopped in front of her: shockingly tall, hunched over, lightly smelling of expensive cologne. A flash—a reflection of the sun on the metal plate of his bracelet—slashed her eyes. At the same second Sterkh emitted a short sound—not quite a hiss, not quite the sigh of an asthmatic.

"Which track did I tell you to work on?"

"I started working on track one. It's not my fault that—"

"I said to work with *which track?*"

"It happened by itself! It's not my fault!"

The slap on the face startled the air like a shot from a starting pistol. Sasha flew off and hit her back on the desk.

"When you opened fragment number one hundred without permission 'it happened by itself.' When you decided to experiment with a baby, that also 'happened by itself.' Has your own academic program appeared to you? All 'by itself'?"

"I did not ask you to teach me!" Sasha screamed back. "I didn't ask to be accepted here! You decided to teach me! It's your fault! You . . ."

A release of energy. Transformation from one state to another. The insight was sudden, like a flash of light—Sasha sensed within herself the power to make things a part of herself, to absorb Sterkh, and Kozhennikov himself, and the entire institute. Moreover, she felt a pressing need to do it right this minute.

She detonated herself like a grenade, ran all over in a stream, and enveloped the entire auditorium in a thin fog. A split second, and the fog thickened and charged at Sterkh, storming into his nostrils, pouring into his throat, catching the foreign breath.

A scent of cologne flashed. It became dark.

One more second. Sasha lay crumpled like a wet rug. In heavy drops she poured onto the wooden floor, flowed into the wide cracks between the planks, collected into a puddle. A new second: Sasha lay limp, her clothes soaked through, gelatinous like a jellyfish, without a single muscle, without a single thought. The unseasonably warm February sun beat into the windows of the brightly lit auditorium 14.

"Finish me off."

Sterkh paced back and forth. Not quite controlling himself, he kicked a chair, which hit the wall and toppled over with a loud thud. Sterkh mumbled something, paced some more, then stopped.

"Aren't you ashamed of saying things like that?"

Sasha pulled her knees to her stomach and cried like a punished mutt.

"Sasha?" His voice contained no more ice. Only worry.

"Let's get up. It's the rule: when you fall down—get up. Hush. That's it."

Clutching his cold white hand, she managed to get up and immediately crouched, holding her head with both hands.

Sterkh lowered himself down next to Sasha and held her. He patted her gently on the head.

"You are growing. With dangerous speed. You're growing as a *concept*. Your potential power is ripping you apart. And since you have not yet matured enough, your own, still human, conflicts add more complexity to the problem. This shall pass. You need to be patient, Sasha, control yourself, and avoid making stupid mistakes."

"Why do I . . . why am I doing this?" Sasha sobbed.

"You cannot yet control yourself. When you feel like fighting—you throw yourself into a fight. As if you were three years old."

"No! What did I, why did I do that—with the baby? I can't live with it . . . I can't!"

"I see . . ."

Sterkh softly embraced her wet shoulders, pulling her to himself. Sasha did not resist.

"Get up. You shouldn't sit on the floor. You are at the stage of development, Sasha, when you desire a lot of external information. And not the crude, streaming information, but more sophisticated, organized, structured data. You want everything your eyes can see, and luckily they don't see all that much just yet. A newborn, a blood relative, a carrier of analogous information sequences—such a tasty treat. I should not have allowed you to leave, Sasha, but I could not imagine *how* strong you have become. Never, not once, have I seen anything like this. You are a phenomenal student. And a phenomenal idiot. Don't be upset with me."

"Mom won't forgive me."

"She will. You are her child, too. Don't exaggerate. The baby will be happy and healthy . . ."

"What if he grows up mentally retarded?"

"No. He will not. And do you know whom you should thank for that? Farit; he reacted instantly, and there was such a lucky chain of probabilities. But the details don't matter. What matters is that the child has been restored as an autonomous information system. As a personality. So enough torturing yourself, Sasha. Last night, for instance, you could have run into much bigger troubles. Get up, I want to take another look."

A flash of light slashed her eyes—the reflection from the metal bracelet. Sasha squinted.

"Sasha, open your eyes and look at me. Yes. I do apologize for hitting you. But you needed it. I would beat you up more if I could. Last night you nearly completed a transition from the basic biological state into an intermediary, unstable one. You have a colossal internal mobility. Right now you're ahead of the program by at least a whole semester. Stabilization is planned for the fourth year, before the summer exams. If I have to deal with your tricks for two and a half more years, I will not survive, Alexandra. I will retire."

He smiled, as if expecting Sasha to appreciate the joke.

"Have you turned nineteen yet?"

"No. In May."

"In May . . . you're a child. Your professional development is running ahead of your physiological abilities—with a terrifying tempo. And there is no way to slow down the process artificially. Yes, Sasha, as they say, you are a disaster and a gift in one little bottle."

"Will I pass the exam?"

"Don't make me laugh. You will pass with flying colors. If you don't stop studying, of course."

"Zakhar Ivanov"—Sasha's voice trembled—"did not pass."

"He did not." Sterkh stopped smiling. "Another thing that is bothering you, I see. No, he did not pass. I feel a great deal of pity for Zakhar, Sasha. It's a disaster. Why do you think Oleg Borisovich and I keep repeating like broken records: 'Study! Study, prepare for the exam!' Do you think we're kidding?" He patted her on the head like a little girl. "Study hard, Sasha. You have enough determination, but not enough restraint and discipline. Everything will be fine. And you really should thank Farit; all of you hate him, but without him you wouldn't have survived even the first semester. So, are we still friends?"

Sasha looked up. Sterkh watched her with a hint of a smile.

"Th-thank you," she said, stuttering. "You helped . . . with the baby. I would have died. There and then."

"There is no need to die. Admit it, Sasha—you enjoy learning, don't you?"

"I do," she took a deep breath. "Very much."

"Then do as I say. *Study.*"

She had no more decent clothes left. She stepped outside in her water-logged jogging suit and was surprised not to feel the freezing temperature.

She ran back to the dorm, took a shower, and sat in front of her open suitcase, baffled at the lack of clothing options. Forty minutes remained before her individual session with Portnov.

Wrapped in a towel like a Roman patrician, Sasha entered the kitchen; two first years sat by the window, along with her former roommate Lena and another girl, a very pale redhead with lots of freckles.

"Hey," said Sasha and took a good appraising look at both of them.

Lena was much heavier and wider in the shoulders than Sasha. But the redhead . . .

"What's your name?"

"Natasha."

"Stand up, please."

The girl stood up fearfully. Sasha swept her eyes over the girl: her height and general proportion satisfied Sasha completely.

"Please lend me your jeans and sweater. Right now."

The girl swallowed.

"These? The ones I'm wearing?"

"Those, or some other ones. But quickly."

"Uh-huh." Natasha breathed and swiftly left the kitchen. Petrified, Lena remained sitting over a cup of tea.

"It's temporary," Sasha said carelessly. "A friendly loan. And don't look at me like that."

She showed up at Portnov's door right on time, wearing black woolen slacks and a bright yellow, ornate, hand-knitted sweater. Frightened Natasha had sacrificed her best clothes for the menacing Samokhina.

"Pretty," said Portnov instead of a greeting. "I've seen these flowers somewhere before . . . nevermind. Are you ready for this class?"

"I'm ready."

"Go ahead. One through ten, but not in succession, rather in the order that I suggest. Start with number three."

Sasha felt lost for a second. She was used to doing the exercises based on the "snowball" method: the second came out of the first, third out of the second, et cetera.

Portnov sprawled over his chair. He stared at Sasha through the lenses of his glasses, his eyes utterly pitiless, fishlike. "Are you going to take a while? Will you need to warm up?"

Her hands grasping the back of a squeaky chair, Sasha took in a full chest of air and visualized a long chain of interdependent concepts that have never existed, but were now constructed by her imagination. Or by something else.

Concepts—immaterial entities, which Sasha envisioned as drops of grayish jelly—were measured by numbers and expressed by symbols. These numbers could not be written down, and the symbols could not be imagined; Sasha's consciousness operated in these substances, forced them to form chains, and the chains to interweave so that separate fragments would merge and form more and more new entities. And then she "unbraided" the chains imprinted upon one another, mentally, without moving her lips, feeling her right eyelid twitch from the tension.

"Seven! From this point on. Stop! Half a measure back! From that point—number seven, begin!"

Sasha's efforts made her queasy. The world re-created in several minutes leaned on its side. As if someone upended a beehive, an unhappy hum rose up; Sasha wove new chains of associations and meanings out of nowhere, made them into loops, and broke the circles, and her eyelid twitched stronger and stronger.

"Ten."

A new jump. Sasha had never performed the exercises out of sync, but her very being was part of an internal mechanism that had by now warmed up and started working in full force, fed by her stubbornness and hatred toward Portnov. Was he trying to humiliate her? Let's see who wins!

"Two!"

Sasha swayed. Regained her balance. She touched the tips of her fingers to her face, felt the surface of a rough fabric, as if someone had put a canvas sack over her head. Exercise two . . . almost from the very beginning, but where is the starting point? Which junction should she choose?

"Will you ever talk back again?"

The voice sounded from far away. Sasha saw Portnov's face as if through a multitude of interwoven fibers, shiny like silk.

"Stop, Samokhina. Stop. I am asking you: Will you ever give me lip again? Will you ever be late for my class?"

"I won't," Sasha muttered through her teeth.

"I'll believe you for the last time." Portnov smirked. "For tomorrow, work on the diagram on page three of the *Activator.* A little extra effort would be for your own benefit."

She stepped outside, but instead of walking out to the yard she went down Sacco and Vanzetti. The pavement glistened as if rubbed with oil. Sasha stopped under a large lantern stylized to look antique. Or perhaps it truly was antique. Its flame swayed behind the matte glass, the yellow dot of its reflection mirroring in each cobblestone.

The door of a café on the opposite side of the street opened. Out came a woman dressed inappropriately for the season, in a short, light-colored coat and a frivolous cap with a checkered visor. When she stepped onto the pavement, Sasha's eyes widened: How could one walk over the cobblestones in those extremely high, needle-thin stilettos?

Denis Myaskovsky came out of the café following the woman. Limping, he shuffled next to the woman, or rather slightly behind her—like a lapdog. Intrigued, Sasha observed the couple: something tense, dangerously explosive, was happening between these two entirely different, unsuitable people.

She retreated. Semidarkness reigned only a few steps away from the lantern. Sasha stood at the dark half-circle of the alley entrance.

"It could be worse, as you can understand," the woman said in a hoarse, almost boyish voice.

"It could not," said Denis.

He stood there in an unbuttoned coat, a white scarf hanging low to the ground like a twisted rope.

"It's just the beginning of this semester," Denis's voice trembled. "It's so far from the test . . . it's the very beginning of the semester!"

"The further it is, the harder it's going to be," the woman said.

Denis stepped forward. Sasha froze: he grabbed the woman by her collar and jerked her up, her thin stilettos dangling in the air; he was a head taller than the woman and twice as heavy, and the woman seemed completely helpless in his arms, but she did not even try to resist.

A second passed. Sasha did not get a chance to scream. With a strange sound, Denis put the woman back on the pavement. Regaining her balance, she managed to get her heel stuck between the cobblestones.

"Forgive me." Denis's voice was hollow. "I . . ."

And he suddenly sank before her, fell on his knees, and Sasha felt fear ten times stronger than a moment ago.

"You have been forgiven a lot," the woman said, trying to pull her heel out of the deep crack.

"Don't!"

"You can help them. You know how."

"I can't! I can't . . ."

"Yes, you *can.* Your classmates can. And you can. Look at Pavlenko's work. Look how Samokhina tears herself apart every day."

Sasha flinched.

"Do you remember the test after the first semester?" the woman spoke lightly, even cheerfully. "Do you remember what you promised me then?"

"I cannot memorize *that*!"

"You are not in kindergarten, Denis," the woman said with a hint of disappointment. "Everything depends on you. You must work hard."

And with the lighthearted *clickety-click* of her stilettos, she passed by Denis, frozen on the pavement, passed by the porch, passed by the entryway. As she moved past Sasha, she turned her head: she had a small white face shielded by a pair of dark glasses.

Sasha had never seen her before. But at this moment she recognized her.

Sasha made a cup of tea, dissolved a bouillon cube in a second mug of boiling water, carried everything back to room 21, sat at her dusty desk, and meditatively opened the yellow book—the *Conceptual Activator.* Page three, diagram number three. After the initial five minutes, Sasha could no longer tear her eyes away from the diagram.

The yellow book printed on lousy paper was a key that joined many jigsaw pieces into one picture. It stitched together—with rough, jagged sutures—the difficult experience Sasha had endured during her time at the institute, and her own perception of the world that became so unsteady in the last couple of years.

There are concepts that cannot be imagined but can be named. Having received a name, they change, flow into a different entity, and cease to correspond to the name, and then they can be given another, different name, and this process—the spellbinding process of creation—is infinite: this is the word that names it, and this is the word that signifies. A concept as an organism, and text as the universe.

The fourth dimension "sewn" into the diagram wholly eliminated the concept of time. The result was word, and word was the original cause of any process; circles swam in front of Sasha's eyes, the kind of slow bright dots that usually appeared if one bent down sharply or stood on one's head. Sasha's tea was now cold, the broth was covered with a film of fat, but none of that mattered.

The diagram on page three lay before her like a crystal model of a termite nest. Each fulfilling its individual task, concepts shifted, exchanged impulses, built a hierarchy and destroyed it to erect a new one. Sasha held herself by the hair; the word "harmony" disintegrated into hues like a ray of sunshine and restructured itself—to perfection.

"Holy cow!"

She pushed her thumb along the fore edge of the book. The *Activator* did not seem very thick; it was similar to the format of an old literary catalog Mom used to bring Sasha a long time ago. Each page had a new diagram, new but linked to the previous and to the subsequent ones, one more cell in the never-ending honeycomb of Sasha's *comprehension*. The colossal field that she saw for a second had no limit and no end.

"So beautiful," Sasha whispered.

The words slashed her with their inaccuracy, platitude, vulgarity. She blinked—chance tears fell off her eyelashes—and attempted to *say* the same thing without resorting to ordinary words.

A gust of wind shut the window. Sheets of paper covered with writing flew all over the room. Sasha shook her head as if falling out of nirvana. She wanted to close the book, but her hand trembled. Diagram number three, heart-wrenchingly perfect, pulled her back, demanded her attention—"it happened all by itself." It comes, it drowns you, and it becomes impossible to stop . . .

With a colossal effort she made herself close the *Activator*. Library dust flew up. Yet she wasn't relieved, because it was not yet time to relax. She still had the *Textual Module* to finish.

She finished her cold tea. Moved the *Textual Module* closer and opened to the first paragraph. She glanced at the page filled with nonsensical symbols. She closed her eyes in fear and anticipation.

The tickle of expectation. Now it will begin. Now.

And Sasha bit into the text.

She was used to focusing her attention, used to daily hard labor, and it made a difference. Sasha swam, the senseless text parting before her, and she had a lucid sensation that the illumination of truth, the breakthrough, was just around the corner. Just a little bit more . . .

Silently they passed a three-story building made out of pink bricks, and went up to the porch seated between two stone lions—their faces faded from frequent caresses, but the right one seemed melancholy, and the left one—ironic, even cheerful. The lions rigidly stared at Orion.

"Hello," said Kostya.

Sasha looked up. Kostya Kozhennikov stood at the threshold, a slice of pizza in his hand.

"Sorry," Sasha said. "I need to finish the paragraph."

Kostya nodded. The next time Sasha tore her eyes away from the book, he was sitting across from her at the table, his pizza eaten by then. Kostya moved crumbs on the tabletop with his fingers, making patterns.

"Sorry," Sasha said. "I lost track of time."

"Yeah . . . everybody is working today. They are all like mice, noses buried in their books. Portnov yelled at Myaskovsky today for the exercises . . . What happened to you, anyway?"

"I am growing as a concept."

"As a *what?*"

"I am a concept. I'm not human. You are probably a concept as well. All of us are structured fragments of information. And it turns out, I like it. I like being a concept. I am growing."

Kostya flicked the crumbs off the table.

"Yegor was asking about you."

"Who is that?"

"The first year you were sleeping with."

"And what was he asking you about me?"

"He wasn't asking me, he asked Lisa."

"Next time he asks, have Lisa tell him that I'm no longer human. And that is why I cannot sleep with anyone any longer. Have you ever seen statistical theory making out with Newton's first law of motion?"

"Sasha," Kostya said. "Listen. Just take care of yourself. You have it harder than all of us. I think . . ."

"Not at all." Sasha smiled and immediately became serious. "Myaskovsky, on the other hand . . . he needs our help."

"He's got Popova as his advisor. It's a little bit easier."

"It's *not* easier, Kostya."

He stared across the table at her in surprise. "You say it so confidently . . ."

"That's because I know. I'm sorry, I really have to study. I have tons of homework."

Kostya got up, but then paused. "Actually, the reason I stopped by: I was told at the dean's office that you are going to get an enhanced stipend. Since you are the best student, and all."

"Pavlenko will be overjoyed."

"Yeah." Kostya smiled. "Sasha."

"What?"

He looked at her for almost an entire minute, wanting to say something but never managing a single word. He shook his head as if asking for forgiveness, but only—finally—said, "No, nothing. I'm going, see you later."

He opened the door—and stood face-to-face with Farit Kozhennikov.

Kostya retreated, or, rather, flew back as if from a blow to his chest.

"Hello," offered Kozhennikov senior, looking at Kostya at the threshold and Sasha in the middle of the room with great interest. "Did you have a fight?"

Without saying a word or looking at his father, Kostya slipped past him into the corridor. Farit's eyes followed him. He then closed the door.

"I apologize for disturbing you."

The dark glasses, this time smoky opalescent, made Sasha's advisor look like a thrill-seeking skier. He came over, tested a rickety chair, and sat down, folding the hem of his dark raincoat.

"I don't have that money," Sasha said. "I threw it away. In the forest."

A stereo system was booming on the floor above them. A television set mumbled something behind the wall. A heavy-footed somebody ran along the corridor.

"I jumped off the train," Sasha said. "I wanted to run away. But I couldn't, and . . . anyway, I don't have the money."

"I'm not here for the money," Kozhennikov said. "I don't grow rich on you, as you can guess. The coins are only words that no one has said and no one ever will."

The light of the table lamp reflected in his glasses.

Sasha wiped her tears with the back of her hand. Tears of rage and relief.

"Forgive me," she managed through clenched teeth.

"No, I'm the one who needs forgiveness. I showed up and took your peace of mind."

"I haven't had any peace of mind in a real long time. Today I saw Liliya Popova, and here's what I know: there is no Liliya Popova. *You* are Liliya Popova."

Kozhennikov swayed on his chair—back and forth. The desiccated wood crackled.

"Am I right?"

"Of course you are." Kozhennikov smiled. "You are right. But please do not share your observations with anyone else. Who I am . . . what I am—we can discuss later. When you mature."

"In case you're wondering," Sasha said very softly, "I don't want to talk about you at all. I don't even want to know who—no, *what*—you are."

"Fine." Kozhennikov nodded and closed his eyes for a moment. "Agreed. Now get your things so we can go."

"Where?"

"The institute is renting you an apartment. Just for the time you are enrolled. Here, on Sacco and Vanzetti, across from the school building. It's an attic loft. Nice place."

"I don't want to," Sasha said rather awkwardly.

"Really. Aren't you sick of this cozy orphanage?"

He waved his hand around the room: three beds, two of them empty, bare under the striped yellow mattresses, and Sasha's bed, barely covered with a faded coverlet. A chair with peeling paint, and one more, with only three legs. An open suitcase. Littered tables. Crumpled papers in dusty corners. Sasha was struck with shame.

"Well . . ."

"Let's not waste any time. The landlady is expecting us at half past seven, and it's already seven o'clock. Do you have time after your classes to go back and forth with your suitcases? No? I didn't think so. Hurry up."

"You were wrong about Kostya."

The starry sky was suspended over the town of Torpa. Orion rose above the roofs. A thin film of ice stretched over the sidewalk and the pavement, and even the branches of naked linden trees gleamed under the streetlights. Sasha walked side by side with Farit Kozhennikov, carrying two plastic bags. Kozhennikov pulled her suitcase, and when the little wheels kept sticking between the cobblestones, he picked up the suitcase and carried it.

"Kostya was the only person who could help me. And you are making a mistake, thinking that he's a weakling. He's a very good, strong, honest person."

"Thank you for saying that." Kozhennikov glanced at her sideways.

"It's my fault things turned out this way," Sasha said. "It all happened because of a *word*. One single word."

"It happens. You and I better than anyone know the value of words, don't we?"

Sasha slipped on the ice. Kozhennikov supported her arm.

"Be careful. It's not far. We just need to cross the street."

It seemed to Sasha that the buildings on Sacco and Vanzetti had gotten closer, leaned over to her, almost touching the shingles on their roofs, leaving only a narrow path under her feet and a stripe of sky overhead.

"May I do some of Denis's work?"

"What?"

"If Denis does not make it, I'll do some of his load. And you . . . you just leave him alone, please."

They passed the institute. Almost all of the windows were now dark—it was late. A street lantern was lit in front of the dark alley; two empty beer bottles were stuck, frozen, in a deep puddle.

"Sasha, do you think I'm a sadist?"

"I don't think of you at all."

He laughed at that. "Yes, you do, I know that. Don't feel too bad for Denis. He's working hard—but only up to a certain limit. Sooner or later he needs to understand: if he doesn't jump 'above his head'—all is lost. The sooner he comes to that realization, the better."

"I . . ."

"And you cannot help him. You helped Kostya because you loved him. And you still do."

"That's not true!"

"It is true. Unfortunately, you silly puppies let your happiness slip through your fingers forever. And you shouldn't think it was your fault. His fault was primary—and the most crucial."

"I don't love him. I'm . . . we're friends."

"You are afraid for him. Love is not when you are aroused by someone, it's when you are afraid for that person. And you will never be able to forgive that kid, Yegor."

Sasha stopped. Kozhennikov walked a few steps farther and looked back.

"We're almost there. We need to go over there, to the lions. What?"

Sasha was silent. Kozhennikov came back.

"What happened?"

"He'll understand. When he gets to his second year, he'll understand everything," said Sasha with a catch in her voice.

"Of course, he'll understand. Shall we keep going?"

Silently they passed a three-story building made out of pink bricks, and went up to the porch seated between two stone lions—their faces faded from frequent caresses, but the right one seemed melancholy, and the left one, ironic, even cheerful. The lions rigidly stared at Orion.

Kozhennikov rang the door bell. A woman of about sixty opened the door, sinewy and swift. She took one of the bags out of Sasha's hands.

"Maria Fedorovna. And this is Alexandra Samokhina, Sasha. Here are your keys, take them."

Two gigantic keys—heavy heads, complicated shafts and grooves—lay in Sasha's hand. *How am I going to carry them around?* she wondered. *Around my neck, like a necklace?*

"The light key is for the entrance door. The dark key is for your room door. Let's go."

Inside, the building smelled of wet plaster and faintly of perfume. A small yellow lightbulb switched on automatically. The landlady disappeared; Sasha carried her bags up the spiral staircase, following Kozhennikov, who carried her suitcase. The staircase was so narrow that the suitcase kept getting stuck.

Sasha could not see much in the semidarkness. The thick railings curved like an antique musical instrument. The sound of their steps echoed in the dark. They passed the round window of the second floor, and there Sasha stopped as if her feet had been glued to the stairs.

Kozhennikov looked back onto the third-floor landing.

"Sasha?"

"I have a problem."

"Did your bags break?"

"No . . . I . . ."

"Come on up, the door is right here."

Sasha staggered up to the third floor. The corridor was dark, and Sasha stumbled onto her own suitcase.

"The switch is somewhere here," Kozhennikov murmured. "Ah, yes, right here."

The lightbulb was switched on. Sasha blinked. In front of her was a narrow door lined in blackened wood.

"Unlock it."

The key found its way in easily, without fuss. A soft click. The door opened. Sasha stepped in first and found the switch.

She stood on the threshold of a tiny, almost toylike apartment. The ceiling was very high near the door and tilted lower, reaching Sasha's height, near the window. Outside the window was a minuscule balcony encircled by naked grapevines, and farther out stretched Sacco and Vanzetti Street, mysteriously lit by the lanterns.

To the right was a simple white door, behind which a clean pink-tiled bathroom could be seen.

"Let's see. Here are some dishes, electric teakettle . . . Don't be shy, everything here is for you to use, so make yourself at home."

An antique writing desk, or rather a bureau—a multitude of shelves and drawers. The tabletop, made out of walnut, had at some point been stained with ink and then scrubbed almost flawlessly. A bookcase. An ironing board and a small iron. A wardrobe with plenty of hangers. A grandfather clock: the mechanism squeaked and softly, delicately, struck eight.

Still wearing her street clothes, Sasha sat down on the new, reasonably hard bed with an orthopedic mattress. Kozhennikov pulled her suitcase inside the room.

"So what is the problem?"

"I just had a strange thought."

"You don't have to tell me if you don't feel like it."

"I had this strange thought," Sasha repeated, "as if I read a piece from . . ." She faltered. "Portn . . . Oleg Borisovich said that one can read a fragment of a possible future in the *Textual Module*."

"Déjà vu." Kozhennikov smiled. "And what have you read?"

"About the lions. The ones at the front entrance. I'm absolutely certain."

"So what?"

"It's nothing." Sasha licked her dry lips. "I guess . . ." She spoke despite herself, quickly, excitedly. "You can direct time. You make time into loops. For you there is nothing strange happening when a person is reading something and in an hour it happens to her in reality."

"All the world's a text." Kozhennikov clicked the light switch in the bathroom. "And all the men and women merely words . . ."

"It's Shakespeare," Sasha said. "'All the world's a stage.'"

"Everybody makes their own definitions. Shakespeare expressed it that way. You may say it differently."

"Can I really read my future?"

"Easily. When you buy a train ticket, you are not only reading your future, you are forming it. Your ticket states the day of departure. The number of the carriage. Your seat. That means that in the most plausible future you will appear at the train station, approach the carriage that is mentioned on your ticket . . ."

"Do you like making fun of me?"

Sasha herself was shocked at the helplessness in her voice. Kozhennikov stopped smiling.

"Forgive me. I didn't mean to offend you. This question is too serious to discuss it without irony."

He placed his palm on the massive bronze door handle.

"Good night, Sasha. I'm leaving."

The door opened into the dim corridor.

"Farit . . ."

"Yes?"

"Thank you," Sasha mumbled, forcing herself. "You helped me. When I . . . did that thing to my brother."

"Don't mention it," he said tightly. "Anything else?"

Sasha shrank in discomfort.

"This apartment . . . I really like it."

"No need to thank me for that—you earned this place. Good-bye."

And he left.

In the morning, before the start of classes, Sasha approached Denis Myaskovsky. Silently holding his sleeve, she pulled him over to the side, by the window.

"What do you want?" Denis asked grimly.

"I had this happen to me," Sasha said. "I got stuck . . . but then I made it through. Myself."

"But you don't know what I have!" Denis was upset. "Why are you saying this? You don't know!"

"I *do* know." Sasha looked into his eyes. "I know, Denis. Kostya went through the same thing. Everybody has. Listen to my advice: don't get up from the table until you learn it."

"It's easy for you to dispense advice!"

"It isn't easy for me, Denis." Sasha smiled. "I know what I am saying."

The bell rang to signify the start of Portnov's lecture.

"'What's in a name? that which we call a rose/By any other name would smell as sweet.' In other words, the essence of an object does not change depending on its name. This is a common misconception, not unlike the 'world is flat' belief. By verbally identifying an object, by giving it a name, we alter it. And at the same time we prevent it from changing. A name is like a forked stick that we use to hold a snake on the ground." Portnov imitated using a forked branch to press down an imaginary viper. "By the way, consider this: the contradictory nature of a statement almost certainly proves its legitimacy . . . Come in."

Pressing his palms to his abdomen, Andrey Korotkov walked in; pale, bent over, he looked miserably ill.

"I am sorry," he mumbled, avoiding looking at Portnov. "I have food poisoning . . . Here's a note from the doctor." He tore his right hand away from his stomach and handed Portnov a piece of gray paper folded in half.

Portnov unfolded the paper and briefly looked at it—diagonally.

"Go, you are dismissed," he said brusquely.

A whisper flew around the auditorium. Korotkov jerked his head up. "But . . ."

"Go. We'll talk when you feel better." Portnov's voice sounded ominous.

"May I stay for a while?" Korotkov asked, nervously licking his dry lips.

Portnov handed the note back to him. "Then take *this* back, be so kind."

Andrey took the paper out of Portnov's hand and, still bent over, shuffled to his seat. Portnov waited until the auditorium was dead silent once again.

"May I continue? Thank you. However, there is also another misconception—by which a name automatically defines the properties of an object. Here is a pen." He tossed up and caught a dark-blue pen with a white top. "If I give it the name of . . . an earthworm, will it slither?"

Second years, Group A, maintained a tense silence. No one wanted to risk an answer.

"It will not." Portnov let the pen fall on his desk. "Because this given piece of plastic has nothing in common with the processes and events that we are talking about, that we spend time studying . . . between dance parties and dealing with gastrointestinal problems. Besides, when I say 'give a name,' I do not imply any of the languages that are commonly used by any of the living persons. I am talking about Speech, which you will begin to study during your third year. Some of you may start earlier. Samokhina, what time are you meeting with Nikolay Valerievich?"

"Six o'clock."

"Excellent. At four thirty I shall be expecting you in my office in the administration wing. Class, open your books to page four and five. Pavlenko, I would be eternally thankful to you if you would stop talking with Myaskovsky during my lecture. For tomorrow's class, please prepare the additional exercises eight A and eight B from the appendix in your textbook."

At four thirty-two Sasha was sitting at the table looking at a sheet of paper in front of her, on which Portnov had just drawn a straight horizontal line.

"What is it?"

"Haven't we done this before? Fine. Horizon. Sky and earth. Top and bottom."

"What else?"

"Space and surface. A field of application. A screen."

"A screen," Portnov repeated with a hint of pleasure in his voice. "Let's suppose . . . Here is a butterfly." Quickly, using only a few lines, Portnov drew a large butterfly on the top part of the sheet. "Here's its projection." Over the horizontal line he drew an approximation of a shadow with two wings. "How can we express an inverse correlation?"

"We cannot. There is no inverse correlation. I am reflected in the mirror. But the mirror cannot be reflected in me."

"Really?"

Sasha linked her fingers. She felt as if she were on the brink of understanding something very big, something simple and huge, but as sometimes one forgets a familiar name, that's how Sasha could not think of it . . . concentrate . . . recall.

"Do you remember the diagram on page three?" Portnov asked softly.

Sasha nodded.

"Reproduce it from memory. 'Creation.'"

Sasha flipped over the sheet of paper. She drew her pencil over the paper without picking it up. The result was a fully closed shape: it remained three-dimensional, while drawn on a one-dimensional surface.

Sasha swallowed. Her drawing existed *in time*—by itself. It had a beginning and an end. In a circle.

"I don't understand . . ."

"You will. Right now it's enough for you to reproduce it correctly. Write 'association' in this symbol."

Sasha closed her eyes. She drew her pencil over the paper; it became very hot in the room. A drop of sweat rolled down her back under her sweater.

"What do you get?"

Sasha gazed at the paper: it depicted the round symbol from the gold coins.

"It's 'Word.'" Sasha's answer surprised her.

"Yes," Portnov said. "'Word.' This is your first step into the world of Speech, and it shall also be your last . . . because 'Word' is tied and looped onto itself. 'Word' is at the beginning and at the end. You have learned to recognize it during your second year, that's pretty good, but when—if—you learn to *manifest* it, I will tell you that you have earned your diploma with honors."

Portnov stood up with the look of a man whose work was done well. His office was smaller than Sterkh's, and it fit only a table, a bookcase, and a strongbox in the corner. Portnov crouched in front of the strongbox, unlocked the steel door, and with a visible effort pulled out a very large book that resembled a gray brick. He placed it on the table in front of Sasha.

Sasha touched the cover.

"Hands off!"

She recoiled.

"How many times do I have to remind you—do not open books until I tell you? You don't know what is in there, you are not prepared for what you're about to see! How many times have you been burned because of your curiosity? A frog would have no trouble remembering that!"

Sasha demonstratively put her hands behind her back.

"This is a glossary," Portnov said, slightly less annoyed. "It is organized in layers. It has *five* dimensions. That means that you, with your measly experience, will be periodically thrown into the irrational 'pockets,' with the possibility of time loops. Should you be afraid of that? No. Is it dangerous? Yes! To avoid burning like a matchstick, you must take the greatest possible care in following the rules I am about to tell you. First . . . are you listening to me, or still pouting?"

"I am listening," Sasha said.

Portnov straddled a chair in front of Sasha. He wiped his glasses with the hem of his sweater.

"First, you may read only one informational layer per session. *One layer.* Second . . ."

He took a thin bright-blue stick out of his pocket, and Sasha was surprised to recognize a long birthday candle.

"Before you start working, you must cut off about three centimeters of the candle. It burns about a centimeter a minute, sometimes faster, but three centimeters should be enough. You place it between your fingers like this." Portnov stuck the candle between the pointer and third fingers of his right hand. "Secure it with Scotch tape. And then you light it."

Sasha swallowed. "Wouldn't it be easier to just burn myself with a cigarette?"

Portnov glanced at her over his lenses, and Sasha bit her tongue.

"When you are working with the glossary, Samokhina—if you manage to work with it, of course—you will not be distracted or taken out of your trance by an alarm clock, or a scream, or anything else. Only the sharp sensation of pain. A quick one! You will shake off the flame and be just fine. Would you like to try right now?"

"I would love to," Sasha said greedily.

The pain was like that of a mosquito bite. Sasha twitched, wishing to slap down the mosquito and return to studying, but the universe composed of a myriad of nuances was already sliding off her, like a hat carried away by the wind. This universe was set in constant motion, infused with associations, puzzling and inexplicit, and yet natural and harmonious. This universe that she had just begun to explore—she was already blown away by its wisdom and magnificence. This universe was ideally suited for exploring it deeper and deeper—from association to association, from leaf to root, and farther, and wider, analyzing, synthesizing, gasping with joy . . .

The world went dark. Sasha sat in Portnov's cabinet. A candlestick smoked between her burned, Scotch-taped fingers. Sasha raised her hand to her face: two blisters, one on her middle finger, one on her pointer finger.

"I didn't have enough time. I hadn't finished reading the layer. Let's do it again."

Portnov got up and slipped on his ring. Sasha tried to stand up, but he gestured for her to stay seated. He came closer to the table, grabbed her chin, pushed her head back, and slashed her eyes with a reflected ray of light.

Sasha squinted.

Without a word, Portnov picked up the glossary and put it away in the strongbox. Sasha stood up.

"You were going to give it to me!"

"It weighs ten kilos."

"So what! You were going to let me take it!"

Portnov glanced at her askance. He pulled out a pack of cigarettes and paused.

"You still don't smoke, do you?"

"No."

"Pity."

"Go ahead, smoke," Sasha allowed regally.

Portnov took a long drag.

Sasha watched him smoke. Never—very rarely—had Portnov even looked perplexed in her presence. And now he paced around his office, sending smoke rings up to the ceiling, occasionally tilting his head to the side, as if listening to a soundless remark.

Every now and then he would look at Sasha. These glances made her increasingly nervous.

"What have I done wrong now?"

"What is meaning, Samokhina?"

"Projection of will onto its field of application."

"And what are you? Ever pondered that question?"

"A human being."

"Try again."

"A student. An object of your sadistic experiments."

Portnov burst out laughing. He acted amused even less frequently than puzzled, and now Sasha felt sure—something was not right.

"You will be offered acceptance to graduate school. Think about it long and hard. If you are indeed what you appear to be, you should be very critical of any offer, even the most enticing ones."

"But I haven't even finished my second year yet," Sasha said confusedly.

"Precisely. Precisely, Samokhina." Portnov smiled triumphantly. "Fine, I'll give you a hint: you—the object that is sitting in front of me, a biological living creature with ineptly made-up eyes—is a projection. A projection of what?"

"You have nothing to do with my eyes!"

He waved that off. "I am asking you—a projection of what?"

"An idea?" Sasha suggested. "What do you call it . . . eidos?"

Portnov grinned triumphantly.

"Go. Enjoy yourself until six o'clock. For tomorrow, work with the diagram on page eight."

It was dark. Simultaneously with the darkness came a warm spell. The wind carried the scents of water and earth. Sasha stood in the middle of Sacco and Vanzetti, her face lifted up to the sky, and listened to the rustling of streams of water under the flattened layers of snow.

The last few days had been remarkably dense. She'd learned how to fly. Borrowed (stole?) clothes from a first-year student. Fought and made up with Sterkh. Saw a snippet of her own future. Spoke to Kozhennikov about Kostya. Burned her hand . . .

Actually, the burn, which she hadn't even noticed at first, was now growing increasingly painful. Sasha collected a handful of snow from the back of the iron bench and pressed it against her skin. For tonight, she planned a lot of work, but the thought of a salami sandwich had just appeared and now refused to depart.

A group of girls from Group B, Oksana's classmates, walked by. A door screeched loudly—the lights were on in the basement café across the street, somebody was laughing, and the radio was on.

Sasha crossed the street and went down five steps. She opened the door and entered the café.

"Hello. I'd like a salami sandwich and coffee. And tomato juice, please."

The wooden tables were occupied by students, mostly first years, smoking and chatting noisily. Sasha saw Natasha, the girl whose sweater and slacks she had been wearing for the last two days. Tipping her head to her shoulder, the girl was animatedly saying something, and next to her, with his head close to hers, sat Yegor.

Sasha approached, carrying a small tray in front of her. Natasha noticed Sasha first and fell silent, as if she were gagged.

Yegor turned around.

"Hello," Sasha said. "May I sit down?"

"Sure," Yegor said hoarsely. "But you see, we were just leaving."

"Don't rush." Sasha threw a meaningful glance at the barely touched pastries, at the full cups of hot tea. "Don't rush, I need to tell you something."

Natasha did not respond. With shock, Sasha realized that the girl was afraid—truly afraid, jokes aside.

"Look at me," Sasha said gently, addressing Yegor. "Why are you looking away?"

He looked up reluctantly. *It's a bit too dark in here,* Sasha thought. *If I could send reflected rays of light into people's eyes—just like Portnov and Sterkh—and in this light see the internal configuration of a person . . .*

Yegor recoiled.

"Why are you staring at me like that? Just like . . ."

"Like who?"

Yegor was silent.

"Listen to me, both of you," Sasha said, smiling beautifically. "Right now you are on your second semester. In a few weeks you will undergo the deconstructive stage. I think that's what they call it. You will disintegrate into parts . . . on the inside, and will only be able to think of what is in front of your eyes. You will feel no love, no fear, nothing that would distract you from learning. It is going to be not all that unpleasant, more like strange. And then, if you study hard, and you will, you have no choice . . . you will recompile. And then you'll be just a little different. And then, during your second year, when you begin Introduction to Applied Science, then you will remember my words, Yegor. And then you will understand. You will understand something, but chances are, I will never know about it."

Yegor and Natasha stared at her with open mouths. Sasha bit into her sandwich with gusto.

"You should eat. Your tea is getting cold. I wish you all the happiness in the world. Natasha, don't be mad at me, I'll return your pants and your sweater . . . at some point."

They silently watched her eat. Sasha drank her juice, finished her coffee, touched a napkin to her lips, and got up. They still hadn't touched their food. She shrugged.

"See you later, kids. Remember me kindly."

"But you don't understand . . . ," Yegor began.

"Did you ever buy those skis?"

Yegor did not reply.

"That's a shame," Sasha said. "Winter's almost over. All right, I'm off."

They may have continued watching her, even when the door closed behind her back.

Spring came.

Water flowed between Torpa's cobblestones in streams, and disintegrated paper boats rested in the deep puddles.

Sasha's life had drastically changed; the solitary existence in her own apartment, the ability to spend evenings at her writing bureau and read, reread, and simply think in the quiet atmosphere of her room, watching the lights of the lanterns on Sacco and Vanzetti—this was an expensive luxury, and Sasha valued her new status very highly.

She no longer attended lectures; she now had an individual schedule. She would sleep in until ten o'clock, then drink coffee she made on the tiny electric hot plate. Then she would open her notepad, in which Portnov wrote her assignments, and would begin working.

First, the *Textual Module*. No matter how hard she tried, none of the "meanings" incidentally appearing to her during her studies would qualify as a "fragment of a possible future." Still, though, she progressed through it. Then the *Conceptual Activator*. Portnov required her to work on it in writing, pulling all the available sequences and associations into one chain. By twelve o'clock the lines would merge in front of Sasha's eyes; sheets of paper covered with dense writing refused to fold, and when she leaned over, she could smell the gentle scent of the ink that filled her ballpoint pen. Sasha would inhale the scent and smile, thinking about the magnificent harmony of world order, about the beauty of logical constructs, and about the golden sparks of chances that appear without warning out of nowhere to highlight, set off, and emphasize the infinite precision and exactitude of the informational depiction of the universe.

Then she would go for a walk around the town of Torpa. Passersby stared at her, some with shock, some with fear, and some with curiosity; pretty soon Sasha got used to their stares and ceased to notice them.

The river spilled out of its banks and broke the wooden dock. Leaves popped out of buds. Sacco and Vanzetti was wrapped in green linden smoke.

First years ran into door frames trying to enter their rooms. To onlookers they looked preposterous and creepy.

Sasha wrote down her assignments in a separate notebook to avoid making mistakes. To avoid accidentally going further than necessary. Portnov still didn't let her work with the glossary on her own—the only time Sasha was allowed to fall greedily upon the glossary was during their sessions, under Portnov's supervision.

She had long ago returned the sweater and pants to Natasha. The special stipend allowed her to shop at the local store—not exactly haute couture, but there was no longer any need to wear hand-me-downs. At the hair salon she had her hair cut into a long bob; talking with the young hairdresser, Sasha recalled Valery, the third year she met when she first appeared at the institute. "You should get a haircut, a long bob. And a brighter lipstick." Where was Valery now, and what and with whom was he studying?

She painted her lips with a caramel-pink lipstick and remained fairly pleased with her looks. Dima Dimych, who normally expressed reserved sympathy toward Sasha, now acted as if he saw her for the first time: in turn demanding and even shrill, then confused and displeased with himself, the gym teacher now paid more attention to Sasha than to all the other girls in her group combined.

Sasha responded to his enthusiasm with amiable indifference.

The landlady had a telephone on the first floor, and for a small fee Sasha could now call home whenever she felt like it; no more going to the post office and no more sitting in line.

"Mom, hello! It's me!"

When Valentin picked up the phone, Sasha would hang up right away. After the first few times, Mom figured out her simple trick.

"Are you trying to avoid speaking to Valentin?"

"No, why?"

"Oh stop it. Don't talk to him if you don't want to. It's your business."

"I . . . it's just the connection is so lousy here."

"Right."

"How are things? How's the baby?"

"Fine."

"How is everyone doing?"

"Just fine. And you?"

"I'm fine. Well, I'll talk to you later."

"Sounds good."

In the beginning, Sasha felt depressed and cried after those conversations. The fact that the baby was healthy made the weight on her shoulders just a little bit lighter. But the tone that Mom used in speaking with her was utterly lethal. Detached, foreign.

With the coming of April, Mom mellowed out. She even called the landlady's number a few times and asked for Sasha. She called in the evenings, just when Sasha was bent over the *Activator.* Emerging out of her work was so difficult and so unpleasant that Sasha asked the landlady not to call her to the phone.

"Mom, I'll call myself. It's very inconvenient here, you understand."

"That's fine. I'll wait for you to call."

Every day the weather was becoming warmer. The sun was shining in the blue sky over Torpa from morning till night. Sasha took her walks, alone and happy, and one day, on her return home, she ran into Denis Myaskovsky.

Denis was hanging out by the entrance with the lions. He was clearly waiting for her, petting the face of the cheerful-looking stone guard.

"Hello. Are you waiting for me?"

"No. I have a window between two one-on-ones. I wanted to take a walk."

"Enjoy your stroll then." Sasha took out the light-colored key with a heavy shaft.

"Hold on. Just a couple of words."

Sasha turned to face him.

In the last few months Denis had grown a beard, not particularly thick, but curly. The beard concealed his soft chin and made Denis appear more masculine and a bit older.

"Kostya left Zhenya."

"What?"

"He left her, and now he lives with me. Three days already. And you haven't even noticed."

"Why would I notice?"

"You haven't been at the institute," Denis continued as if he hadn't heard her.

"Really? I don't hear anyone complaining. At least the teachers are not complaining."

Denis shook his head.

"You know what I'm talking about. Zhenya is really mad—she's managed to turn all our girls against Kostya. Lisa . . . for her, the name Kozhennikov is a verdict in itself. And you left, hid somewhere . . . as if you are not even one of us."

"What does it have to do with me?"

"Everyone knows it has a lot to do with you."

"Listen," Sasha said, immediately on the defensive, "Since I was a little girl I was raised not to meddle with other people's personal affairs. Tell Kostya that lovers' quarrels are easily mended."

She stepped up to the porch and recalled—it was right here, he stood right on this porch!—Farit Kozhennikov's words: "You and I better than anyone know the value of words, don't we."

"Denis, wait . . . I said something I shouldn't have said."

Denis, who by then had walked away, stopped again. "Do you really think it was him who sent me?" he asked.

"No."

"It's just that he's . . . he's miserable. Zhenya is feeding on her own anger like a spider. And Kostya found himself in such a mess. So you see how it is."

"I see." Sasha weighted the key on her palm. "But I cannot help him right now. You need to understand that."

Denis shifted his weight from one foot to the other.

"I see," he said bitterly, but she wasn't sure he did. "Are you coming to English tomorrow?"

"Probably not."

"Right. Well, I'm going."

"See you."

Sasha went upstairs to her room, and before making her usual tea, even before taking off her raincoat, she put on her headphones. She sat by the window and started Sterkh's latest disc. The player was plugged into a wall socket—Sasha had gotten tired of dealing with the batteries, and had invested in a charge cord.

In her assignment notebook, numbers seventeen and eighteen were written against today's date. Sasha steepled her fingers, leaned onto the back of her chair, and closed her eyes. And for the first time in many days, she realized that the silence—and whatever entered her consciousness along with the silence—was now beating at the glass wall.

Damn that Denis with his news! Even with her eyes tightly closed, Sasha still saw the flower box with the green sprouts, and Sacco and Vanzetti Street, and the streetlights newly emerging in the dusk.

If they hadn't been classmates, they would have forgotten about each other a long time ago. At least Sasha would try to forget about Kostya's existence as firmly as one can forget a man whose life one saved. It's not like she could dance all her life around the same vulgar story: a boy loved a girl, and the girl would not put out . . .

They'll kiss and make up, Sasha thought almost sympathetically. *And then they will continue carrying the yoke of their incidental marriage. There are so many couples who live like that.*

The seventeenth track ended and started again. And again. The streetlights burned brighter, the steps and muffled conversations outside abated, and the windows in the building across the street went dark. Sasha sat like a bump on a log wearing headphones, and grew consistently convinced that the next day she was going to show up in Sterkh's class unprepared for the first time in quite a while.

A boy loved a girl . . .

Sasha felt a long-forgotten nausea. She went to the bathroom and bent over the sink, but the nausea retracted as suddenly as it appeared. Did it mean that all unspoken words had not yet been turned into gold? Did it mean that Sasha still had a chance?

Stop.

She turned off the player, took off the headphones, and sat at the table. She placed a sheet of paper in front of her. From memory, without peeking at the *Activator,* she drew the symbol for "affection." Above, without taking her hand off the paper, she sketched "creation." Portnov was teaching her how to recognize and combine symbols; Sterkh had hinted that in the future, possibly during her fourth year, Sasha would learn how to *manifest* symbols, and that would bring her face-to-face with her professional pinnacle . . .

The symbol on the paper in front of her existed in three dimensions—while being drawn on a flat surface!—and this symbol was evolving in time. This was the second time in Sasha's life she'd managed to create this picture. But today's symbol was not enclosed in a circle, like "Word," which she produced a while ago by Portnov's request. This symbol lived and developed in a linear fashion, as far as Sasha could see.

She looked closer. The symbol was growing more complex. It doubled. Then doubled again. And there was something else: Sasha almost blacked out when she realized what it reminded her of. The division of embryonated cells?

The birth of the world?

She did not have a lighter, but a box of matches lay on the mantel. With shaking hands, Sasha crumpled the piece of paper with the depicted symbol, threw it into an empty pan, and lit it on fire.

The paper went up in flames. Yellow flashes danced on the walls. A black-orange flower blossomed, writhed, and went out. The drawing turned to ashes.

Sasha bit her lip. Let *them* never find out about it. Sterkh must never know about this; technically Sasha hadn't broken any rules, but assuming—assuming just for one second!—that she did in fact do this . . .

She imagined the entire universe burning, rolling into black petals. And she cried—for the first time in many days.

She woke up in the middle of the night. Or was it morning? The clock delicately chimed three. Sasha had been sleeping at her desk for four hours, her head buried in her arms.

She rubbed her eyes. Looked around: a burned piece of paper lay in the frying pan.

Nonsense, Sasha said to herself. It was just my imagination running wild, because I am tired . . . and because I had been thinking of Kostya. As Farit would say, let's consider it a dream. It was just a dream.

She threw the ashes into the trash. Yawning, she stretched and sat down at her desk. She was supposed to complete two tracks by ten, which left her five hours of solid work.

I know how to do this, Sasha said to herself, entering the number 17 on the display. *I have done it before many times. And I have been praised for it. I am talented. And that means that right now I will listen to the track, think it through.* Feel *it through.*

She pressed Play.

The clock struck five. By itself this sound could not attract Sasha's attention, but after the last stroke the clock wheezed and stopped. Sasha thought it was time to wind it up . . .

And in the next second she sat up sharply.

Something had changed. Something had happened. The number 56 blinked on the CD player's display, but Sasha could not comprehend its meaning.

She looked around. The room appeared to her a lot smaller than it really was. A box rather than a room. It was hard to breathe.

She moved toward the window and yanked it open. The glass rattled. Yellow strips of foam fell on the floor. Cold spring air burst into the room; only two hours remained until sunrise. Not thinking of anything, just wanting to breathe, move, live, Sasha climbed onto the windowsill. She squeezed through the narrow frame, stepped on the sprouts in the flower box, pushed off—and soared upward.

The stars, veiled with a thin layer of lacy clouds, opened up to her. Below lay the lights of Torpa. Straight as an arrow, Sasha flew over the tiled roofs. She brushed an old weather vane with her wing, looped-the-loop, descended a bit, and flew right above the pavement, easily steering clear of trees and streetlights.

She rose higher and hung there, spreading her wings like a heraldic eagle. Here she had plenty of air. Sasha observed and sensed the air as a gleaming soap bubble that embraced the semicircle of the horizon. She laughed; to her right and left, in her peripheral vision, two wings the color of burnished steel would come into view and disappear again. Not those chicken wings that were so difficult to towel dry. Two gigantic wings, the size of Sasha herself.

She folded them, unreflecting, like an umbrella, and dove down. She swept above the heads of two chatting street cleaners; they raised their anxious eyes up to the sky long after Sasha vanished into the thin air.

She made a circle over the central square and noticed a bus stop and a group of grim people waiting for the first trip. She rose higher and settled on the roof of a seven-story building—the town's tallest building.

The cold air sobered her up. Moving her wings slightly, Sasha attempted to figure out what she was going to do now, and where her adventure might actually lead. The speed she could reach in the air was quite impressive: Sasha recalled her longtime dream of leaving Torpa. Perhaps she could fly out of here?

The wind picked up. The clouds careened across the sky, flat and ragged. High above the clouds the trace of a jet stretched across the sky, but Sasha could see that it was actually an opening—a narrow crack that resembled a smile. The crack opened wide, then closed up again into a thin thread. Behind the opening, on the other side of the sky, warm lights sparkled festively.

Sasha jumped up, pushed off the shingles with her bare feet, and, moving her wings as fast as she could, charged upward. The smile of the crack became closer, and Sasha thought that behind it she could see a massive expanse lit by millions of lanterns. One more leap; the ragged clouds stayed far below. Sasha spread her wings, sizing up the best way to squeeze into the opening, and at that moment a blinding light flashed from the other side of the sky. Sasha shut her eyes. For a second she imagined standing in auditorium 14 in front of Sterkh, and him slashing her eyes with the white light reflected by the metal plate . . .

In this surgically bright light, a dark winged body rushed at Sasha from the opening.

Sasha turned upside down and lost her balance. Falling, she flew through the clouds, tumbled onto a sloped roof, rolled over—hurting her wing—and managed to break her fall at the very edge only by digging her toes into the drainpipe and flattening herself over the tiles. Directly in front of her—between her and the weather vane—a black shadow with ash-colored hair plummeted from the sky.

He stood a few feet away from her. In place of the hump, two colossal black wings spread behind his back. They blocked out the sky.

Sasha made a jerky movement trying to get up from the tiled roof. She slipped, turned over in the air, threw open her arms, legs, wings—and caught her balance right above the cobblestones. She folded her wings and, moving only the tips, streamed away—along the black precipice of the street: up, down, under the arch, smashing icicles. The black silhouette did not fall behind—just the opposite: with each sharp turn, Sasha saw it closer.

Thunder roared. Every now and then the sky lit up and crackled, ripped apart by the sudden storm. Flinching from the flashes, Sasha flew on, rushed by a narrow gateway like a pipe, made a sharp turn avoiding a theater poster board—

And then her entire body collided with an old chestnut tree.

She turned upside down and collapsed.

Thunder roared for the last time and hushed in the distance. The sky darkened, and the windows were unlit. An old lantern swayed on its chain, making a rasping sound. Once again, silence prevailed on Sacco and Vanzetti, and only somewhere around the corner a street cleaner's shovel made a hesitant scraping sound.

Sasha lay motionless on the cobblestones. She pretended to be dead, like a tiny insect.

"What did the symbol look like?"

"I can't repeat it. 'Creation' combined with 'affection.' I can't."

"Perhaps it was this?" Sterkh waved his hand. Right in front of Sasha's eyes the symbol in question—the symbol that existed in time and lived by its own commandments—wove itself in the air and immediately disintegrated into a multitude of sparks.

"Something like that."

"Something like that, or is that it?"

"That's it."

"How many times did it double before you burned it?"

"Three . . . or four."

"Was it three or was it four?"

Sasha sniffled.

"Four."

The sun was rising. Torpa's streetlights went off. Sasha sat on an iron bench, bent over, hugging her shoulders with both arms. Sterkh stood across from her, not bothering with the hunchback charade. His relaxed wings brushed against the moist pavement.

"What happened then?"

"I began listening to the track. Number seventeen. And eighteen."

"How many tracks did you listen to?"

"Nikolay Valerievich," Sasha said. "It was an accident. I short-circuited."

"Did it happen 'all by itself'?"

Sasha hid her face in her hands.

"I'm listening," he said gently. "But I need to know: how many tracks did you manage to work through?"

"Up to f-fifty-six . . . Forty altogether."

A long black feather caught in the wind, made a circle over the pavement, and got tangled in the thick shrubbery. Sterkh moved his shoulders; his wings unfolded to the full extent, tinted blue, shimmering and twitching slightly in the wind. They slowly folded over, pressing against his back, in the shape of a small hump.

"My office, today at noon."

She showed up to English class wearing a pantsuit, her hair meticulously coiffed and her face made-up. She was overall well-groomed, but also silent, as if she once again had lost her ability to speak. At the professor's request, she wrote down several sentences with irregular verbs on the blackboard, and did not make a single mistake.

The class ended at eleven. Kostya and Zhenya left the auditorium, avoiding each other's eyes and moving in different directions. Sasha went down to the dining hall, got a glass of apple juice, and sat at an unoccupied table. She opened the *Textual Module* and started reading from the beginning, from paragraph one. Repetition is the master of skill. No one had said she could not repeat things.

Slowly, meticulously, word by word—rumble, roar, meaningless noise. As if a million beautiful songs were being sung simultaneously, and their combination formed a cacophony. As if millions of declarations of love were being said one over the other, and the result was a din, babbling; not a single projection of a single will would fall onto the surface of application, and no meaning would be born . . .

> *In the middle of the town square, a tiny spot free of people, a throng of hands lifted and steadied a gigantic iron wheel. Inside the rim, a naked man was strung by his hands and feet. A sharp tip of the axle stuck out of his abdomen, and he was still breathing.*

The glass with the apple juice fell off the table and shattered, drops and shards flying all over the place.

> *The wheel started rolling, heavily at first, leaving behind a bloody trail, twitching on every stone on the pavement, nearly falling every second—but the throng of hands held it steady, keeping it from stopping or toppling over.*

The man in the wheel was dying. Perhaps his death would take a long time to come, and when, after a journey along the streets, the wheel would finally be pushed off the cliff—perhaps the man would find relief . . .

"Sasha? Sasha!"

She tore her eyes away from the book. Everyone in the dining hall was staring at her. Behind the counter, a young server's eyes seemed round with panic.

"Sasha, get ahold of yourself!"

Kostya stood next to her, broken glass crunching under the heels of his shoes. It appeared he had just let go of the lapel of Sasha's chic jacket.

"What happened?"

"Nothing, it's just that you were screaming and moaning out loud. Nothing special."

"Collateral damage . . . of the learning process." Sasha screwed her face into a smile. "Has it ever occurred to you that we live inside a text?"

"No," he replied without thinking. "Wait . . . *what did you say?*"

Sasha went down to the administrative wing pressing the *Textual Module* to her chest.

The receptionist was not there; her knitting was spread over the empty desk. The leather-upholstered door was slightly ajar.

"Come in, Samokhina."

She entered.

Sterkh was pacing around his office. Portnov was smoking, sitting on a low banquette in the corner of the room. And in front of the desk, one leg thrown over the other, sat Farit Kozhennikov.

Sasha stumbled over the threshold and nearly dropped her book.

Sterkh glanced at her over his shoulder. "Come in. Sit down."

Slowly, head held high, Sasha walked through the entire office. She sat down in a leather armchair across from Kozhennikov. She saw her own reflection in his mirrored lenses and noted for the first time that the underground office was very, very cold.

"How do you feel?" Sterkh asked mildly.

Sasha lifted her chin higher. "What?"

"How do you feel after everything that happened yesterday?"

"Fine."

Portnov coughed as if choking on the cigarette. Two wisps of smoke escaped out of his nostrils.

"Very well." Sterkh nodded. "Then you must learn something about yourself, Alexandra Samokhina. Oleg Borisovich, please go ahead."

Portnov put out his cigarette in the bottom of an ashtray, took off his glasses, and slipped them into the breast pocket of his checkered shirt. One of the temples got stuck on a button, and everyone waited about thirty seconds while Portnov struggled to free it.

Having wrestled down his glasses, Portnov pulled a new cigarette out of the pack and began to knead it with the tips of his fingers. It looked as if his hands were trembling.

"Without a doubt," he started, "you, Samokhina, are the strongest and most gifted student in this class. And based on that knowledge, you have clearly decided that you do not have to follow rules. That laws do not apply to you, that you can assign challenges to yourself, and that whatever your professors may say to you deserves at most a condescending smirk."

"But I've never . . . ," Sasha began.

"Be quiet!"

Portnov continued kneading his cigarette aggressively; crumbs of tobacco fell on the floor. "You are developing with an astounding speed, but your development is erratic, unmanageable, and wildly out of hand. At this point your abilities and the level of your responsibility have come to such a screaming contradiction that we, your professors, must make a decision regarding you. And we *will* make that decision. That is all I wanted to say."

Under Portnov's penetrating gaze Sasha pulled her head into her shoulders.

"Now listen to me, Alexandra," Sterkh began. "Yesterday, for lack of anything better to do, you manifested a highly intricate informational complex . . . it was—*ab ovo*—Love, as you understand it. You actualized it, transported it into the state of active projection, and then you burned it.

"But even that was not enough for you. You decided to *try* my track one after another, and in one hour you worked through the path of development designed for half a year! You are the first student in my experience who's managed something like that. However, if you had worked through fifty-eight tracks rather than fifty-six, you would have been turned inside out. Literally—it would have led to a mutiny of the matter. Intestines on the outside! Clothes, skin, hair—in a tiny clump. Have you ever turned a dirty sock inside out?"

"I did not know!" Sasha finally shouted. "You never explained it to me!"

"You were told enough!" Portnov barked back. "You had enough information to draw conclusions!"

"Don't yell at me," Sasha said softly.

Portnov narrowed furious eyes. Sterkh stopped for a minute, picked up a glass of water from the table, and shook it, watching a fly lifelessly floating on its surface. He put it back down in resignation.

"Alexandra, this morning you made yet another jump in your development. An impossible jump judging by my experience—*our* experience: mine and Oleg Borisovich's. You were extremely lucky not to perish. But now, now that you have survived, we have to deal with another issue . . ."

Sterkh halted. His usually pale cheeks flushed. The eyes with tiny pupils stared into Sasha's face until he blurted, "What the *hell* made you do this? What are we supposed to do with you now? What are we going to do, when you are completely unmanageable! You are a monkey with a grenade! It is impossible for a biological human being to have access to *manifestation* before the transformation, before the exam! And it is clear that you still *are* human, seeing how you behave like one! Like a silly girl! Like a stupid, infantile, irresponsible—"

He made a visible effort to cut himself off; he placed his hands behind his back and began pacing back and forth along his office. The silence was disturbed only by the sound of his steps, and a bell that rang in the distance, somewhere deep inside the institute building.

"Why am I unmanageable?" Sasha spoke, trying with all her might to control the trembling in her voice. "Explain to me, I will understand. Here you are insulting me, and you are not even trying to explain. You treat us like animals, like incompetent idiots . . ."

"Because that is what you are," Portnov said.

During all this Kozhennikov remained silent; he gazed at Sasha with a hint of interest.

"Regarding explanations," Sterkh began, his soft voice clearly spelling disaster. "Have I told you, Alexandra, that uncontrolled experiments are dangerous and forbidden?"

"But . . ."

"Have I, or have I not told you that?"

"You have!"

"I have. And you appeared to understand and gave me your word not to do anything above your given assignments. Is this true?"

"Nikolay Valerievich . . ."

"Did you give me your word? Or not?"

"Yes! But I did not understand . . ."

"You will understand now," Sterkh promised her ominously. "Oleg Borisovich, this is an exceptional situation. Your ideas?"

Portnov clicked his lighter, took a drag, exhaled a stream of smoke, and immediately squashed the cigarette into the ashtray. He fished his glasses out of his pocket, placed them on his nose, and gazed at Sasha over his lenses.

"I know one thing: this girl is not leaving this office until we find a method of controlling her."

"And unfortunately this method must be rather radical," Sterkh muttered. "Alexandra, we had no choice but to invite your advisor to join us."

Kozhennikov sat unmoving, and the direction of his gaze was concealed by his glasses. Sasha cringed.

"Farit Georgievich," Sterkh spoke with exaggerated decorum. "The student affairs office is requesting a guarantee that student Alexandra Samokhina abides by the academic rules and regulations of this institute."

Silence, long and sonorous, hung in the air. Sasha knew perfectly well that begging was out of the question. The only thing she could do at this point was maintain her dignity as much as was humanly possible. So she gathered her remaining strength and straightened her spine. She was wearing her best suit, and not a single tear spoiled her makeup. For a second she saw herself through their eyes and suddenly recalled the embryonic world writhing in the fire . . .

The world that she now knew was Love.

Dark glasses concealed Kozhennikov's eyes. His invisible—but easily sensed—gaze was directed at Sasha, just as it had been back in that July at a seaside town, on the Street That Led to the Sea. That time, the gaze had ended up leading her to the Institute of Special Technologies.

Now she wondered if that same gaze might lead her out.

Sasha looked down.

"Lessons completed without permission," Sterkh continued in a soft, colorless voice. "Intentional metamorphosis. Experiments with *manifestation* of entities. All this I would call a blatant violation of academic regulations."

The room was once again eerily quiet. And in this silent room Kozhennikov's voice was heard for the first time.

"Nikolay, there is one nuance."

"Yes?"

"I promised the girl not to ask anything impossible of her."

Sterkh raised his eyebrows. "What precisely on my list would you consider impossible?"

"Her development actualizes her identity." The lamps were reflected in Kozhennikov's lenses. "She cannot stop if the disc contains several tracks in a row. Give her one track per disc then—it's not complicated, is it?"

A pause lingered in the air. Sterkh's countenance changed; his wings twitched under his jacket, as if trying to unfold immediately.

Sasha shrank in her chair, wishing for the earth to swallow her up.

"It's not complicated, no," Sterkh's voice sounded hollow. "It's just . . . it lacks precedent. I have never had students who were capable of processing ten tracks one after the other. These are the standard learning materials—"

Kozhennikov cut in. "But shall we presume that we are dealing with a nonstandard case?" he inquired delicately.

"You are right," said Sterkh after a short pause.

"Then it's settled." Kozhennikov nodded. "As far as the manifestation of entities . . . Sasha, do you realize what you have done?"

"It was not on purpose. I didn't mean to."

Portnov choked on his smoke.

"So are you not aware?"

"Why not. Sure. I am aware," Sasha said quietly.

Sterkh raised his eyes up to the ceiling.

"Then why did you do it?" Kozhennikov continued his inquiry.

"By accident."

"That's not enough. What prompted you to do it? What were you thinking about before you picked up the pencil?"

Sasha swallowed.

"It is important." Kozhennikov nodded. "What were you thinking about? Or whom?"

"About Kostya," Sasha said. "About Konstantin Kozhennikov."

And she bravely met her own reflection in his dark lenses.

"And feeling emotional, you decided to play with meanings?" Portnov cut in.

Sasha turned to face him. "Not to play, Oleg Borisovich. I believe it was you who taught me to add symbols. It was you who praised me when everything came together. Have you ever warned me that it was forbidden?"

"I'd have forbidden you to run over the ceiling if I had known you were capable of that!"

"I didn't know either. I simply lived—existed, positioned myself in space, functioned, acted, continued, lasted . . ."

She caught herself monotonously listing words—each one of them had a fraction of the meaning she needed so desperately, but not a single one of them fit her purpose.

"I thought so," Kozhennikov said softly.

"So then, you are telling me," Portnov spoke sharply, almost aggressively, "that we cannot expect this girl to cease her games with the informational universe? Just because it means we're asking for the impossible?"

"No." A slight smile touched Kozhennikov's lips. "We've been able to specify a few things, and now our problem has become a bit clearer, and that means it can be solved. Don't worry."

He turned to Sasha.

"Sasha, I would like to speak to you today. What time will you be done with your classes?"

She came to her senses at the long table in the large auditorium where general educational lectures were usually held. In front of her was a sheet of paper torn out of a notebook, and Sasha was writing down the following: "At this time aesthetic experience is considered as an experience in value, and is treated within the limits of the philosophy of value." The auditorium was not full, and the professor kept giving Sasha strange looks.

Sasha leaned back in her chair. She loved to learn; lectures, even the most boring ones, and formulaic definitions, no matter how confusing, returned her to reality . . .

To reality in the sense that Sasha understood it.

The bell rang.

Not looking at anyone, not speaking with anyone, she returned to her loft. The ashes from the burned paper still lay in the wastebasket.

She tidied up the room, gathered the yellow strips of foam off the floor, and took out the trash. She sat by the window; for a long time she watched the green linden trees on Sacco and Vanzetti.

Whose love was it that she so stupidly, accidentally *manifested*? Once it became tangible, this love gained a carrier and an object of application—an object and a subject. When Sasha burned it, what happened to these people?

Her hands fidgeted, searching for something to do. She picked up a pencil, found a pencil sharpener in the desk drawer, and pulled a clean sheet of paper closer to avoid making a mess. She inserted the dull pencil snout into the sharpener, turned it once and then again. The wood shavings fell onto the paper, making a pattern.

Sasha gathered the shavings into her hand and shook them off into the wastebasket. She wasn't going to draw anything—she had been forbidden to manifest entities. She was not going to, no, no, no, she was only going to open the *Conceptual Activator* for just a minute . . .

Yellow paper, diagrams, columns, numbers: Sasha closed her eyes. A magnificent anthill of meanings with all their levels and associations, vectors, derivatives of multiple degrees, loops, figure eights, lines leading into infinity . . . No, no. Just watch. Just be amazed. Harmony.

The pencil slid out of the sharpener by itself, pointed as a needle. "Will." "Creation." "Word." *What am I doing?* Sasha thought in panic, while her entire being, commanding and supple, strengthened and developed by assignments and exercises, loved—existed, positioned itself in space, functioned, acted, continued, lasted . . .

And then her thoughts ended as well. A jump was completed to the next level, impossible to express in familiar terms. The pencil glided without a break, depicting symbols with an enclosed fourth dimension. Patches of sunlight on water, a small oar—yellow, bright yellow, plastic. It is not yet "Love"; it is a premonition, a forewarning . . .

The doorbell clanged like a fire alarm.

Sasha had never had visitors in her loft, and she'd never even heard that deafening ringing; her hand jerked. The pencil broke. In terror Sasha stared at the sheet of paper with a glimmering, nearly completed symbol.

The doorbell insisted on ringing. Sasha looked out the window and saw downstairs, at the lion-guarded entrance, Kozhennikov.

But not Farit, no. It was Kostya.

▪▪▪

"Your ringing scared me."

"Why should you be scared?" Kostya was upstairs now, looking around with suspicion and inhaling. "Did you burn something?"

"Ah, stuff . . . old papers. Have a seat."

Kostya sat down on the edge of a stool. He took another look around, this time more attentively.

"Nice place. Very different from our rathole."

"Are you fighting with your wife?" Sasha blurted out.

"You've been told?" Kostya avoided her eyes.

"It's not hard to figure out." Sasha sighed. "I'd offer you tea, but I'm out of tea leaves. Sorry about that." He shrugged. After a moment, she asked, "What did you want to tell me?"

Kostya swayed back and forth, suddenly looking so much like Farit Kozhennikov that Sasha cringed inside.

"What did they want from you? Why did they want to see you? I saw *him—he* was there, too."

Sasha sighed. Actually, Kostya was the only person with whom she could share everything; well, almost everything. Aside from a few details. So she told him. Kostya listened, anxiously leaning forward, unconsciously playing with a broken pencil.

"Are you telling me *he* stood up for you?"

"I don't know. That's what it looked like, though."

"'I'm not asking for the impossible.' When he sent Lisa out on the street corner, he also was not asking for the impossible."

"You know about that?"

"Everyone does. When he killed my grandmother . . . he also was not asking for the impossible, was he?"

"He was not. You could have passed the test on the first try. You passed it on the second."

Kostya's eyes turned into glass.

"But you did pass it," Sasha mumbled apologetically.

"You've changed a lot," Kostya said. "Sometimes I think you've become very much like *him*."

"But you *could* have passed on the first try." Sasha felt his growing antagonism, and it made her speak fast and commandingly, as if pressing her chest against a hurricane-force wind. "It's true, Kostya, it is unpleasant and sad, but it's true. You could. But you didn't." She shrugged. "You're his son, and you hate him. But perhaps he's not the worst father. He's rational. Strict. Effective."

"*What?*"

"Perhaps he even loves you, in his own way. Perhaps all the fathers in the world are projections of one single entity. It's just that their method of transformation is different. A ballerina's shadow is a monster with a tiny head and massive legs . . . Can you imagine how badly any entity can be distorted by an intricate type of projection? If this pile of muck is a projection of a blooming garden onto an infinite time frame, onto rain and cold . . . If my father—who left my mom with a baby in her arms—if he's a projection of a magnanimous and loving man, but the sun went down, and the shadow got distorted . . ."

Sasha spoke, realizing to her surprise that she no longer thought in words. Words—only later, but in the beginning—supple and firm . . . images? Pictures? Live creatures? The necessity of converting these thought-sensations into the familiar verbal form was becoming a burden to her.

Kostya must have noticed this, because he held her hand like an attentive nurse. "Sasha . . . Are you all right?"

"Me? Oh yes. Poor Juliet was mistaken. Remember? "Tis but thy name that is my enemy; / Thou art thyself, though not a Montague. / What's Montague? It is nor hand, nor foot, / Nor arm, nor face, nor any other part / Belonging to a man. O, be some other name!' This is a common misconception, not unlike the 'world is flat' belief. 'And whatever your ship is named, that is how it will sail.' Yes, that's it. That is exactly right."

"Sasha . . ." Kostya seemed nervous.

"Listen." She closed her eyes to avoid seeing Kostya and her room, in order to feel the full extent of the strokes and trills of her new thoughts, thought-images, thought-creatures. "I can construct/materialize/actualize/objectify/depict for you and Zhenya this 'Love,' the same as Romeo and Juliet's. You will feel, live, experience, burn with this love, the only one in the whole universe. I will *manifest* it for you."

Sasha stumbled and opened her eyes to see Kostya watching her with growing tension. The firm shadows dancing in Sasha's consciousness slowed down, and familiar thought-words jumped out to the foreground like a teleprompter line.

"Forgive me, I made a bad joke about love. I am talking too much. I . . . you see, I am continuing, flowing, swelling—I cannot stop. I am forced from inside, I am like yeasty dough, sooner or later I will crack, and then Kozhennikov . . . Sorry. And then *he* will look at me like this, over his glasses, and say: 'This will teach you some discipline.' And then I shall not bear it, Kostya. I will do something terrible. I will kill. I will *manifest* a bullet in his heart."

Kostya's pupils widened; Sasha knew something was about to happen. And it did—gritting his teeth, Kostya lightly slapped her cheek. Sasha felt Kostya's insides twist and resonate from this slap.

"Don't worry, it's fine." She tried to smile. "No reason to worry," she repeated, "it did not hurt. Here's the thing: if entities can be *manifested,* then they can probably be formed anew. It must be possible to create new entities, rather than simply project ideas. I am a projector, a motion-picture camera. Right now, I project shadows on the screen. But can someone make entities out of nothing? What do you think, can one create something out of nothing?"

"You need to drink some water." Kostya was becoming paler by the minute. "They have driven you insane. Sasha, there was this one girl, a third year; she went mad . . . just like that."

"All girls are mad. Each in her own way. Listen, I think I am omnipotent. I broke out of our text and can view it from the outside. And I can see—it's just letters. Every person is a word, simply a word. And others are punctuation marks."

"Listen, I can call someone . . . or . . ."

Sasha drowned in silence. Kostya's lips were moving; he was worried, close to despair. Sasha blinked; she saw Kostya as only half-human, and half—a shadow, a projection of something imperative, much more fundamental than the entire human race. However, Kostya was still human, while Sasha—no matter what Sterkh said—struggled, slid out of her shell, losing her form and losing the ability to think. The professor's exasperated words dangled at the edge of her dimmed—or just beginning to burn?—conscience: "Have you ever turned a dirty sock inside out?"

And then the door flew open, and *it,* which stood outside, stepped into the room.

"What happened to her?"

Kostya stood leaning over the wall. The door to the bathroom was ajar. Water poured out of the faucet. Farit Kozhennikov's voice answered something, but Sasha could not distinguish the words.

She sat behind the writing bureau. She had not fallen on the floor unconscious, as could be expected. Instead, she sat moving her pencil over the sheet of paper, and the entire paper was covered with scribbles, strokes, and spirals.

"What is going to happen to her?" Kostya asked again.

Again she missed the reply. The sound of water stopped. Farit Kozhennikov stepped into the room, and Sasha shut her eyes for a second. Only for a second: Farit wore light-gray glasses—almost transparent, but still opaque.

"Should I go?" Kostya's voice sounded hollow.

Kozhennikov placed two washed cups on the shelf. Sasha recalled drinking kefir yesterday morning, and not having a chance to do the dishes before classes.

"If you are not busy, son, you can run down to the corner store and get some tea, biscuits, and instant coffee. That is something Sasha Samokhina truly needs right now. Can you do that?"

"I will," Kostya said after a short pause.

"Here is some money." Farit put his hand into the pocket of his leather jacket.

"I don't need any, I have my own money." And Kostya left without looking at Sasha.

She glanced at the sheet in front of her. In its center, almost hidden by her scribbles, an unfinished symbol twitched slightly. While she watched, the symbol lost its volume and flattened, until it finally froze. Farit carefully pulled the paper from underneath Sasha's clenched fingers and brought over his lighter. The paper went up in flames. Kozhennikov opened the screen of the tiny fireplace and put the wisp of flame onto the sooty bricks.

He opened the window a little wider.

"Omnipotent, are you?"

Sasha rubbed her eyes; they burned as if from a long look at the sun. Cloudy tears poured down her face, finally washing off the meticulously applied mascara.

"They worry about you," Kozhennikov murmured. "But they don't know everything about you. If they did . . . they would kill you to avoid a universal catastrophe."

He may have been speaking with irony. He employed a bit of sarcasm. But she didn't think he meant anything but what he'd just said.

Sasha stared at her pencil. Kozennikov picked up a stool and sat in front of her—very close. She could have touched him if she wanted to.

"Do you feel like a genie fresh out of the bottle? Ready to build castles and destroy them? You can do anything, anything at all?"

Now he seemed serious. Or, perhaps, he was making fun of her.

"I can't stop," Sasha whispered. "I cannot—not be."

"You *can,*" Kozhennikov said, and the sound of his voice made Sasha flinch. "Because I *demand* that you remain within the academic limits of this program. That you don't draw live pictures without your professors present. That you don't fly like Peter Pan, and don't try to enter all the visible openings. This is my condition, and I never—remember, never!—ask for the impossible."

He placed a cellular phone in a soft pink case in front of Sasha.

"This is for you. Call your mother right now and tell her your new number."

Sasha swallowed.

"Do what I say." Kozhennikov put a plastic card with a long number on the table.

The phone worked. The keys sang gently when pressed.

Beep. Beep.

"Hello . . . Mom?"

"Sasha? Sasha, hello! Where are you? I can hear you so well!"

"Mom, I have a cell phone now. Write down the number."

"Seriously? Isn't that something! Listen, it isn't too expensive, is it?"

"No . . . not really. Write it down."

Kozhennikov sat, one leg thrown over the other, and watched Sasha through a pair of smoky glasses.

"So can I call you on this number?"

"Well, yes. At least if you urgently need to talk to me."

"That's great."

"Mom . . . sorry, I just wanted you to have the number. I can't talk for a long time . . ."

"Bye! Good luck! We're fine, the baby is doing well . . ."

"Say hello to . . . Valentin. Good-bye."

She pressed the Off button. A picture lit up on the display: a globe, or perhaps a stylized clock. Sasha took a deep breath.

"Good." Kozhennikov nodded. "Now look me in the eyes and listen carefully." He took off his glasses. Sasha blinked; Kozhennikov's brown eyes, ordinary, with normal pupils, stared her in the face. "Always carry this phone with you. Don't you dare turn it off. Make sure the battery is always charged. Got it?"

"Yes."

"If you commit any offense, this phone will bring you bad news. You, genie fresh out of the bottle, remember: for each attempt to build yet another castle, you will get some very, very sad news. And you will find out immediately. Carry your telephone with you at all times."

Sasha looked down at the phone.

It was small and delicate. In a pink fuzzy case with—as Sasha now saw—little pig ears. The case was shaped like a pig, with a drawn piggy snout; it was cute, almost childish.

Everything had just changed.

If she was a genie, then it was as if she had been flying up to heaven and was then suddenly jerked by her beard and her face smashed into the concrete wall. And then locked in a cell, three meters by three meters. Without windows or doors.

Only a few minutes ago she'd felt omnipotent. Only a few minutes ago she'd felt how the new reality grew around her—it was slightly uncomfortable and a little terrifying, but the process was preeminently fascinating!

Now, though, she was withering. Shriveling into a tiny blob. It happened when synthetic fabric was set on fire: a full-size elegant dress would shrink into a minuscule globule of black tar, and in only a couple of seconds. Sasha, omnipotent just a minute ago, Sasha who could fly, who could transform the world—was now turning into a dot on a flat surface.

The doorbell rang. Kostya came back, carrying a pack of tea, a jar of coffee, biscuits, and a chocolate bar; out of the corner of her eye Sasha saw him place the groceries on the shelf, but she did not turn her head.

Kozhennikov said something to his son, who replied in a low voice, then in turn asked something. Sasha did not discern any words.

The door closed. Kostya left. Sasha remained immobile.

"I don't see anything tragic," Kozhennikov said softly. "You are going to continue all your previous activities, but only under the supervision of your professors. I think they might schedule additional sessions."

"I won't be able to study," Sasha whispered.

"You will be able to. On the contrary, you will make a bigger effort. But discipline, Sasha—discipline and self-control—are very important things, sometimes crucial. Tell me, am I wrong?"

Sasha was silent.

"It is in your power to make sure it never rings," Kozhennikov said gently. "It all depends on you. As usual."

"I saw you," Sasha said. "When you entered the room. I went blind almost immediately. Farit, it's impossible to live in the world where you exist."

"It is impossible to live in the world where I do not exist," he said after a short pause. "Although it's hard to resign oneself to my existence, I understand that."

"Don't bend your knee, Sasha! Stretch, like this . . . just a little bit more, and you'll make it!"

Lisa Pavlenko stretched into a split, bearing her hands down onto the floor, but maintaining an absentminded facial expression. Sasha groaned and got up.

"I can't. My muscles hurt too much."

"Because you must stretch every day!" To strengthen his argument, the gym teacher pressed his hand to his chest. "Lisa stretched—and she did it, see?"

"I'm delighted for her," Sasha said.

Dima Dimych sighed. Yulia Goldman had been in a bridge position for the last five minutes, curved like a triumphal arch, and the tips of her hair brushed the wooden floor.

"Sasha, you must at least pass the somersault. And put away your cell phone—didn't I ask you not to bring cell phones to the gym?"

Sasha hesitated, but then took the pink cord off her neck. She put the phone into the pocket of her sweatshirt and zipped it up. Dima Dimych looked almost annoyed.

"Is somebody going to steal it? Can't you put it down for a second?"

Sasha's stare was grim enough to make the young gym teacher shrink in embarrassment.

At three forty, Zhenya Toporko exited auditorium 38. She threw a haughty glance at Sasha and, without saying hello, sailed away down the corridor.

"Ah, it's you," Portnov greeted Sasha.

She murmured a curt hello and sat down at her table in front of the teacher's desk—just a regular student. She pulled out the *Conceptual Activator*. Then the *Textual Module*. She stared at her hands.

The phone on the pink cord touched the edge of the table, a pink spot in her peripheral vision.

"At first I thought you were simply the kind of student who crams day and night," Portnov muttered. "Then I suspected you had a talent. But then I realized you are a verb. It happened when you regained your speech. When I made you silent, and you found the right word in a matter of only a few days. Remember?"

Sasha nodded.

"Then everything seemed to hang by a thread, and I thought I had made a mistake—and so did Nikolay Valerievich—and then you transformed in a single leap. It became obvious you were a verb, and I strongly suspected"—Portnov leaned forward maintaining eye contact with Sasha—"that you were a verb in the imperative mood. You are an imperative, Sasha.

"You are a command."

"I don't understand."

"You will." Portnov squinted. "It's the nature of our specialty: nothing can be explained. One can only achieve understanding on one's own. You are a command, a part of the Speech of Creation. A load-bearing structure. I told you once you were a projection. Remember? Here it is: You are a projection of the Word that is destined to *reverberate*. And every day you get closer to the original. You are a foundation upon which an entire universe can be built. And this cannot be explained, Sasha, it can only be understood."

Sasha shut her eyes. For a second she ceased thinking in words. Her thoughts seemed to be living creatures that resembled multicolored amoebas lit up from the inside.

"You understand everything," Portnov was saying. "You are just lacking experience and knowledge. It's your second year, and you have just started studying Speech . . . but already you are a Word, Sasha—a Word, not a human being. A command, an imperative. You have colossal value as a future specialist." He sat up straighter. "Well then—we will study in May, June, and part-time in July. Every day, and quite seriously."

Sasha glanced at the pink phone.

"Under professional supervision!" Portnov raised his voice. He slapped his pocket in search of a cigarette, then said in a different tone, very businesslike, "Get your pencil and paper. Open the *Activator*. Let's begin with the minor stuff."

▪▪▪

She felt like a balloon straining to go up. Her small pink phone pulled her down like an anchor, preventing her from breaking loose; like this, "at the edge of rupture," she lived through a long day, perhaps the most magnificent day of her life.

She left Portnov's auditorium filled with the picture of the world: brilliant, spellbinding, and terrifying. She carried that image until late at night, trying not to spill it.

Enlightenment surged over her like a tide and departed again. When Sasha perceived herself as Word, she felt serene like never before in her life. It was the tranquility of a dandelion blossoming for the first time on green pastures. It was a happy moment without wind, without future, and, of course, without death.

Then, just as suddenly, she would feel human. She would remember the existence of Farit Kozhennikov, remember the phone hanging from her neck. She would grit her teeth and wait for the word-sensation to sweep over her again, and having reached that point, she would freeze in warm numbness . . .

In the evening she had a really tough time. Having finished the *Module,* she went to bed and turned off the light. She closed her eyes—and immediately a magnificent anthill of meanings unfolded beneath her eyelids.

Conformities and associations. Projections and reflections. Sasha turned onto her other side, then one more time, and one more. She rumpled the sheets. She sat up: the clock ticktocked in the darkness. Streetlights burned along Sacco and Vanzetti. The accursed pink phone lay on the bureau. And all around her the accursed *eide* soared, whirled, and teased her. Sasha disliked the expression, but she could not find another *word* for the spinning colorful amoebas.

All one needed to do was to *manifest.* Everything already existed in the world. Everything that was the best and the most suitable. And happiness. The simplest thing—to grab this golden amoeba by its tail and *manifest* it accurately and clearly, without any distortions. Happiness is what Sasha felt when she perceived herself as Word. Happiness is what a man feels when he matches up his destiny. What would prevent Sasha from doing it? Because she could!

The human shell aggravated her like a too-tight suit. She longed to—had to—escape, but the pink phone lay on the table, and Sasha got up and went over to the window.

She opened a small windowpane. It wasn't enough: she unlocked the entire window frame. The spring night was fairly cool, a raw wind chased the clouds, in turn exposing the stars and then covering them up again. Sasha kneeled on the windowsill breathing deeply and feeling the wind creeping under her nightgown. The cold was fabulous, it sobered her up. Sasha was a human being.

"I am a human being. But I am a verb," she said out loud.

It was impossible to explain. Sasha, a second-year student who had lived through a disintegration and reconstruction, who had been forced to alter and who had been transformed, accepted her new status not with her mind, and not even with her intuition.

She simply was. She continued. She resided in space and time. She was getting ready to reverberate.

To be realized.

The pink phone lay on the table. Sasha wanted to turn it off. Better yet, to throw it down, onto the cobblestones. Let it break. Let the battery fall out. Let the display flicker out forever.

"I can't," she whispered. "I must not. I must not."

A dark whirlwind flew over the ragged cloudy sky. Sasha recoiled; across from her a shadow nestled on the slope of the tiled roof, shielding the stars like a storm cloud.

"Sasha, why are you not asleep at this late hour?"

She gripped the windowsill with both hands.

"Let's take it easy. And keep away from the streetlights; we have no need for sensationalism. We have forty minutes, let's not waste any time on warm-ups."

The cold wind impeded breathing. Below lay springtime Torpa: fog flowed over the streets as if over rivers, and the glow of the streetlights became hazier.

"Follow me . . . don't rush. Keep calm. And don't forget to breathe; you are not diving into the water."

They landed on the roof of the seven-story building. The fog flooded over the first floor and was creeping up to the second.

"Are you cold?"

"N-no."

"Sasha, I want you to know: this is not so much academic work, but more of a . . . um, process of adapting to the given situation. As our mutual friend would put it, we cannot ask for the impossible, and you, in your current state, require a certain relief. You must be allowed materialization. But as your professor, I emphatically forbid you to do the same when you are alone. And that restriction remains in full force and effect!"

Torpa was invisible far below, and only the rooftops swam over the cotton-wool surface of the fog.

"Sasha, we think very highly of you, your capacity for work, and your ethics. We understand how difficult it is for you. You won't give us a reason . . . to be disappointed, will you?"

Sasha opened her wings as wide as she could. For a second she became the town of Torpa—a sleepy town under a blanket of haze, floating in the clouds . . .

"I w-will do my best, I promise."

PART THREE

"Mom, hello. I am here."

"Goodness, Sasha! Are you at the station?"

"No."

"Where are you?"

Sasha laughed. "I'm downstairs, calling from the phone booth."

"Are you kidding?"

"Dead serious. I'll be up in a minute."

"You are unbelievable!"

When the elevator doors opened, Mom stood on the landing, happy, fresh, wearing a summer frock. "You are insane! Completely out of the blue! What a nutcase!"

And Mom hugged Sasha for the first time in six months. Sasha closed her eyes. Behind her the elevator doors closed and opened again, hitting the handle of her suitcase. And closed again. Sasha and her mother stood embracing a while longer, then Sasha reluctantly turned and picked up her suitcase.

The elevator doors snapped shut with an aggravated clunking.

"Listen," Mom said, greedily drinking her in. "You look . . . wonderful. Completely grown up."

They entered the apartment, and Mom pulled Sasha into the kitchen and sat her down without letting go of her hand. On the stove, steam whirled over a pot, where eggs hopped in the boiling water. Mom looked into Sasha's eyes, smiled, and shook her head.

"So big . . . so grown up. How wonderful that you came. You're just wonderful. But why didn't you use your cell phone?"

"It's a bit expensive." Sasha made a point to smile. "It's really for emergencies only."

"I called you a couple of times, but there was no connection."

"Yes, that happens in Torpa." Sasha's smile became even wider. "Is the baby asleep?"

"He just conked out, right before you arrived. We had a doctor's appointment yesterday, received tons of compliments." Mom was smiling. "It's so curious. Usually they try to scare you, refer you to specialists. But here we have a baby with the ideal weight, and ideal development, and he kept smiling at everyone. At this age babies are scared of strangers, but little Valentin is such a sunny baby. When he sees someone, he greets them. He sleeps like a bear. Eats like a piglet. And he's so beautiful! You'll see."

She finally remembered her pot, took the boiled eggs off the stove, and settled them under a stream of cold water.

"Valentin is working. He has so much work right now. But it does bring more money, you cannot imagine how expensive everything is these days." She looked at her daughter. "Sasha . . . have you got a boyfriend?"

"What makes you say that?"

Mom sat across from Sasha and touched her hand. "I just think so. You've changed."

"We just haven't seen each other in a long time."

"While the baby is asleep . . . we have some time. Tell me: how are you?" Mom asked. "Do you have friends? Boys are probably after you in herds—you're so beautiful."

"I study day and night. Not so much with the herds of boys."

"But still. You must like someone! What kind of boys are there in that Torpa? I can't even imagine. Are they nice?"

"They are nice, sure. Different . . . just like everywhere else. You say it like Torpa is some hole in the middle of nowhere!"

"It's not a hole." Mom caressed her hand. "I fell in love during my second year, I remember, purely platonically. I could not stop thinking about him, though. It was like an illness, it rolled over me and left just as quickly. But times are different now, aren't they?"

"At this point I have absolutely no personal life," Sasha confessed honestly. "The workload is too heavy."

Mom shook her head with a hint of distrust.

"You are a workaholic . . . and it's already the end of the second year."

"And I got straight A's."

"Straight A's . . . Sasha, let's start getting you out of there. It's the best time right now, after the second year. I made some inquiries—our university will accept you with open arms."

"Mom . . ." Sasha took away her hand.

Mom shook her head stubbornly.

"Sasha. Let's forget the past. You lived through . . . you did not accept Valentin. I mean, you accepted him to be polite, but inside . . . back then you were still a girl, a teenager. Now you are an adult, I can see it. And we can say all of those things, unspoken before, out loud. You can see—we are happy. The only thing missing is you, Sasha. Because you are also our daughter, you are a part of this family, and nothing and no one can replace you. Come home. Please."

Sasha's mouth was suddenly dry. Mom watched her from across the table and smiled.

"I have come back," Sasha muttered. "I . . . you're right. Now I've come back for real."

Mom got up, nearly toppling over her stool, and embraced Sasha, pressing her face to Sasha's shoulder.

"Your bedroom is still yours, of course—make yourself comfortable. Put your things away. Valentin are I are perfectly fine in our bedroom, and it's easier for us to get up with the baby right there. But he sleeps through the night now. He's such a sunny baby, calm and happy. You'll scc. People used to live in communal apartments, three, four people in tiny rooms, but these days we have our own apartment. Tomorrow we'll go to the university . . . or maybe you want to go by yourself? And then we'd have to go back to Torpa to get your documents. And pick up your things, you probably left some stuff there?"

"Uh-huh," Sasha said. "We can decide that later."

"Don't wait too long. Oh, the sink is clogged. I wanted to make sorrel soup, it's almost ready. I just need to add the sorrel. Want to do it? It is so cool when sorrel changes its color in the hot broth . . . Or do you want to take a shower first? Or put away your clothes? A whole night on the train, you're tired . . . Do you want to take a nap? In your room?"

"I'd rather help you," Sasha said. "Let me cut up the sorrel."

▪▪▪

She had spent the previous night in a blissful half-dream. Lying on the soft berth of a compartment coach, she'd listened to the rattle of the wheels and slowly, by sly degrees, she'd appropriated the train.

Her head had been a diesel locomotive. The wheels had spun along her stomach, sonorous and confident. The tracks had turned out to be smooth and cool by touch, like marble. In the morning they they had been covered by dewdrops. Sasha had felt the tiny particles fly all over, vaporize, and condense again; felt the fog slink away from her face; felt the wind dash behind her back, wagging like the tail of a dog. Green semaphores had risen over the horizon like stars.

She finished her second year and completed the so-called internship— almost an entire month of renovating the dorm. She liked working with the paint roller, liked the whitewash spray, and enjoyed walking around in work clothes stained with paint and chalk. She liked coming from the dorm back to her loft, taking a shower, and sprawling on her bed with a book.

She read nearly a hundred books that month. She read with a remarkable speed, read everything—classics, memoirs, travelogues, Harlequin novels, and mysteries. She had gone through the entire collection of the Torpa regional library with a fine sieve. The *Textual Module,* the *Conceptual Activator,* the exercise sets—all the Specialty books had been taken away from her by Portnov and Sterkh.

Sasha would read until she couldn't discern the letters any longer. Then she would brew some tea and sit on the windowsill without turning on the lights.

The sky would grow dim like a screen. The streetlights would come on, and Sasha's breathing would get labored. She would wait, watching the surrounding roofs. A rare passerby would glance at her curiously.

Quite often the waiting would be futile. At half past one in the morning, gloomy and disappointed, Sasha would slide off the windowsill and go back to bed. And lie there for a long time, listening to the rustling noises of the night, until falling into a deep sleep.

But once in a while—two or three times a week—an enormous shadow would conceal the stars over Torpa for a second, and a dark figure would land on the opposite roof. It usually happened on the border of evening and night, when the sky was still light on the west, but the streets were already dipped in a dense darkness.

Then Sasha, choking with joy, would leap from the windowsill out onto the street and unfold her wings—sometimes right above the pavement.

". . . Sasha, of course, you can go. But it will be difficult and unnatural for you. It would be best if you went for three days, just let your family know right away—a lot of students do just that; a couple of days at home, and the rest of the time with their friends on some trip. Why should you be stuck inside four walls the entire time? Careful, don't step on the shingles, they are broken . . ."

In the summer, even the nights above Torpa were hot and humid, so that steam rose up from the ground and the air trembled gently over the tiled roofs that retained the heat of the midday sun. During the short periods of rest Sasha would stretch on the tiles, absorbing their warmth, watching the stars, smiling vacantly.

During their nightly flights Sterkh did not so much instruct her, as—she understood it well—allowed her to materialize. He supervised and held her back with a great deal of tact; she slipped up only once—when she rose especially high over Torpa and suddenly saw that the town itself represented a phrase, a long complex sentence, and the comma could be moved easily.

Her right wing pressed to her side and the left one stretched out. Gritting her teeth with unexpected pain in hollow bones, Sasha went into a tailspin. The lights of Torpa melted, merging into concentric circles. Then the lights went dark. Sasha plummeted into the world of many dimensions, cold and dry like discarded snake skin. Somebody's will plucked her out of the darkness; again she saw the ground underneath, so very close, and expanded her wings right above the pavement.

Sterkh did not even reprimand her. Instead he said, "You skidded. Lost control. Nothing happened, but do you see how important it is for me to remain close?"

She calmed down incredibly fast. Perceiving herself as a Word made her forget the concept of fear, and even the wretched pink telephone did not cause her the usual despair.

Sterkh insisted her return home be that of a well-brought-up young lady: on foot and always through the front door.

"You are not going to crawl through the window like a cat into the birdhouse, are you? It's so aesthetically displeasing, don't you agree?"

Sasha thanked him profusely for each of those night excursions.

She did not know how she would have survived that summer without flying over Torpa's rooftops.

On the train on her way home Sasha recalled in minute detail the tiles and the waterspouts, the sparrow nests and the weather vanes of the old town; she thought of a boy who once saw her out his window. He was reading a book, *Karlson on the Roof*; Sasha laughed and waved to him.

The train rushed through the forest. Sasha dreamed of coming back to Torpa.

"Here we go, he's awake!"

A soft hesitant crowing could be heard from the bedroom. Wiping her hands on the way, Mom rushed into the room. At the door she smiled conspiratorially.

"You are not going to recognize him."

Sasha sat at the table, moving the tip of her knife over the wooden cutting board. She thought malapropos of the lifeless baby lying on that table, and of herself pressing the telephone receiver to her ear, accepting and absorbing the silence, wringing out fragments of somebody else's information. Thankfully, she had not had the pink cell phone back then. But then she'd had enough trouble without it.

In the past, coming home on vacation had meant Sasha was constantly afraid of something: of appearing insane. Of killing a man. Of turning into a monster in front of everyone. Now, with these fears behind her, or so she hoped, Sasha was afraid of the moment when she would have to tell Mom about the ticket that lay in the pocket of her bag.

The return ticket for the day after tomorrow, an evening departure.

"Come, baby Valentin, come, sweetie pie . . . Your sister came home . . . Sasha is here . . . Let's go say hello . . ."

Mom entered the kitchen smiling, a dark-haired, dark-eyed little boy with an intelligent—albeit sleepy—look on his face nestled in her arms. Sasha put aside her knife and got up.

How he had grown! From a little worm he'd turned into a human being, a child. He looked like Mom and like Sasha—the hair, the lips, the forehead. He had something of Valentin as well; sitting in his mother's arms, he gazed at Sasha with cheerful incredulity, as if asking—and who do we have here?

"This is Sasha, your sister. Sasha has come home. Our baby Valentin, meet Sasha . . ."

"Hello," Sasha said.

The baby looked at her with mistrust—and suddenly smiled.

Sasha understood why Mom called him "a sunny baby." His round face became even rounder, and the dimples on his cheeks lay in semicircles. Her brother watched her with sincere joy, as if he'd been waiting for Sasha for a long time.

As if he loved her.

"Shall we crack open the champagne?" Valentin rubbed his hands cheerfully. "In honor of Sasha's return?"

Mom had just put the baby to bed; he fell asleep soundly and without complaint. Sasha had a chance to notice that Mom's lullaby was different—not the one from six months ago, not the one that she had sung to Sasha. It was a new song.

One day of Sasha's time at home went by. One out of three days. Only two remained, but neither Mom nor Valentin—not even the baby—knew that yet.

"Sasha, for you, darling. Be healthy, and let all your dreams come true."

"Mom, it's not my birthday!"

"But we didn't get to celebrate your birthday with you! Tell me, how was it?"

"The usual. I bought a cake, a chocolate one, kind of like this one. Brought it back, some kids came over, so we had the cake, made some tea . . ."

"What, no wine?" Valentin asked suspiciously.

"No, we're not allowed to consume alcohol."

The moment Sasha said it, she bit her tongue. Valentin and Mom exchanged meaningful glances.

"What's so strange about it? It's the usual practice in many schools these days," Sasha lied.

"In our dorm we drank up to delirium tremens," Valentin said.

"You see—and was that normal?"

Valentin again looked at Mom, but she did not respond—she watched Sasha, propping her cheek on her fist.

"Since I moved into the loft," Sasha said to end the uncomfortable pause, "everything is really good. I get enough sleep. It's such a pretty loft, I have a flower box, even a small fireplace, not a decorative one, a real working one, and in the winter I can make a fire."

This time she bit her tongue hard.

"What do you mean—in the winter?" Mom asked. "You won't be there in the winter, you're going to transfer from Torpa, right?"

"Well, yes," Sasha said quickly. "I mean . . . It's still under consideration, right? They may not allow me to enroll as a transfer student, or something else may happen . . ."

"I thought it was decided," Valentin said.

"Yes, but there could be all sorts of circumstances. Who knows what could happen." Disconcerted, Sasha squished a piece of the cake on her plate. "What if some official wants to transfer his relative to the third-year group, for example? And then there is no vacancy left for me. It's not all that easy, is it?"

Mom was silent.

"Don't you *want* to leave Torpa?" Valentin asked mildly.

"Well." Sasha swallowed a piece of cake with effort. This was not the right time, not a good time at all for this conversation; she so desperately wanted to relax peacefully and not think of sad things, so desperately wanted to push this discussion to a later time . . .

"Well, I guess . . . I think it's better for me at Torpa. I have friends there . . . and I've formed connections with the professors, informal ones. I have an enhanced stipend. And I'm not even talking about the apartment . . . I mean, in Torpa I'm a star, and here I'd be just a dog's tail."

Mom was silent. Sasha did not dare look up.

"Aren't you exaggerating?" Valentin asked.

"No." Sasha glided her finger along the edge of her teacup. "I miss you, of course, and I would like to live with you. But I've gotten used to it in two years . . . and it's school, you know. I'm nineteen years old. It would be a pity to have to start all over again."

"Do you have a boyfriend there?" Valentin smiled encouragingly.

Sasha hesitated. This was a perfect opportunity to lie. They would believe in love.

"Well . . . what can I tell you . . . sort of. Yes."

"And what did you say your specialty is called?" Valentin asked, throwing a sideways glance at Mom.

"Professor of Philosophy." Sasha had made up this lie in advance. "And Theory of Culture. On a college level. Secondary academic institutions . . ."

"Is that what you wanted?"

"I'm nineteen—who knew what I wanted," she said with an easy laugh. "But why not? It's a good profession. And I might be asked to do some graduate work." Sasha tried to speak effortlessly and at the same time self-confidently.

Silence descended upon the kitchen. It was so quiet that she could hear the rustling of the bubbles rising in the glasses of unfinished champagne.

"I see." Mom's voice was hollow. "I'm going to bed. Good night."

She rose and left the kitchen. Sasha stared at the uneaten cake.

Sasha opened her eyes. Mom was standing at the door of her room, silent and still.

"Mom?"

"Shhhh . . . Did I wake you up?"

"No," Sasha said automatically. "What happened?"

Mom took one step. And one more tiny step. As if she did not dare getting closer.

"Nothing happened. I got up . . . I didn't want to wake you. Go back to sleep."

She turned to leave. Then stopped again in the doorway. "I had a dream. Remember how we went for a boat ride?"

"What boat ride?" Sasha propped herself up on one elbow.

"The boat ride around the lake. Don't you remember? We had these oars, bright yellow, plastic ones . . ."

"No. What time is it?"

"Half past twelve. You wouldn't remember, you were only three years old. I'm leaving, go back to sleep."

She left, closing the door behind her.

Sasha lay on her back. A boat ride? She had clear memories of herself at three years old, remembered the cubbies in her day care center, remembered the merry-go-round in the park . . .

But not the boat ride.

Mom must have dreamed it.

At half past two, still unable to sleep, Sasha tiptoed to the balcony. She struggled through the drying coverlets and swaddling blankets and stood in the fresh wind. She leaned over the railing.

She had two days left at home, and Mom had yet to find out.

Sasha desperately longed to walk into Mom's bedroom, hold Mom in her arms, and cry. She wanted it so much that she even took one step.

Then she stopped.

She looked down. She swung her legs over the balcony railing and perched on top, kicking her feet in midair. The pink phone stayed in her room, on the rug next to her bed, and Sasha knew—even though the evening was warm, and ascending streams rose up from the earth, and there, up above, the air was infinitely fresher and cleaner than here on this balcony—that she was not going to leap, was not going to soar, not going to rise above the city . . .

She felt sorry for Mom. She couldn't care less about Valentin; chances were he wouldn't be all that upset about Sasha's decision, but she felt so sorry for Mom that the pity made it hard to breathe. Her ribs hurt.

She closed her eyes. No, she was not going to fly, not going to allow for the temptation. But was she forbidden from sending up a tiny projection of herself? A reflection of Sasha Samokhina in the mirror of the August sky?

She did not have a chance to decide whether her actions were out-of-bounds. Everything happened by itself. She sat clutching the balcony railing, and she rose high above the linden trees; the street stretched into a yellow ruler, and only every other streetlight burned along the road. Billboards opened up like windows, brightly, even harshly lit. Sasha's shadow drifted, drawing slow circles in the sky.

"I'm sitting on the balcony, I'm not flying. I don't manifest anything, and I don't read forbidden books. I don't listen to extra tracks. I am not doing anything wrong . . ."

The dark spot of the park lay underneath her feet. Sasha inhaled its scent of grass and freshness through her widening nostrils. She slowed down, wanting to linger in that fresh stream, but the stink of hot asphalt and old exhaust gas made her suffocate, especially after the clean air of Torpa.

August. A sea of stars. A dull, dusty city below. One of the many shadows of the Eternal City that perishes and is reborn every second. Sasha's shadow circled and circled, and she herself sat on the balcony, as if hypnotized by the light of the distant flames.

She was Word; she was a verb in the imperative mood—no! Not yet. She was still human. But then . . . how could she *fly?*

Baby Valentin's smile.

He's also a word. Mom says gently: "Sunny baby."

And somebody says: "Moron, creep, idiot!"

And that is what will happen.

And somebody says: "Get up! It's already half past seven!"

And somebody says: "Go away."

There are words that are simply trash, refuse, they turn into nothing immediately after they are spoken. Others throw shadows, hideous and pathetic, and sometimes gorgeous and powerful, capable of saving a dying soul. But only a few of these words become human beings and pronounce other words. And everyone in the world has a chance of encountering someone whom he himself spoke out loud . . .

The sun was rising.

Sasha sat on the balcony railing like a parrot on its perch, and stared straight ahead with unseeing eyes.

"When are you planning to return to Torpa?"

"I have a ticket for tomorrow night."

The answer burst out of her with suspicious ease. Perhaps Sasha's shadow still soared over the city and park, while Sasha herself sat in the kitchen, smearing a pat of butter on a slice of white bread.

"What do you mean *tomorrow night?*"

Mom's face looked exactly the way Sasha feared it would look last night.

"You got tickets for tomorrow—in advance?"

Sasha pressed the butter onto the smooth wheat fabric, flattened it out, and then pressed it again.

"I have extra classes, the summer sessions. Even during vacation."

"You are lying," Mom said sharply.

Sasha looked up in surprise. "I'm not lying. I know it sounds strange, but it's true."

Or, at least, partially *true,* she added to herself.

Mom seemed pensive, as if she were calculating something in her head. Coming to some sort of conclusion, she said, "When you are done eating, could you please run out and get some milk?"

"Sure." Barely containing her relief, Sasha placed her tortured slice back onto the plate. "Be right back."

When she came back, her brother was already awake and lying on his back, thoughtfully studying the merry-go-round horses that swam slowly over his crib. Mom had already cleaned up the kitchen and was now pushing her iron over the ironing board. Steam rose over the baby's blue shirt.

"I'm coming with you."

"What?" Sasha almost dropped the bag of groceries.

"I'm coming with you. Valentin can watch the baby for a couple of days."

"But what are you going to see? It's vacation time right now. There is no one at the institute."

"Then who is going to teach the extra classes?"

"My professor . . . Mom, wait—are you going to check up on where I live, who my friends are, what I do there?"

"That's exactly what I'm going to do. I want to see with my own eyes who's teaching you, and what is going on there."

"It's a typical learning institution."

But Mom shook her head. "No. You're hiding something."

The iron pressed into the shirt stretched over the board aggressively, like a tank. Mom kept pushing the iron over the same perfectly smooth spot.

"At first I didn't want to humiliate you with my nurturing: beginning of independence, friends, boys. Then, to tell you the truth, I had other priorities. But now . . . Sasha, tell me: Have you been threatened, and now you are afraid of confessing?"

"What am I supposed to confess?"

"Is it a cult? Do they make you pray?"

"No, of course not!"

"I am going to Torpa." Mom's voice was full of metal. "I am going, and . . . if need be, I will raise hell. I'll get the police involved, the public prosecutor's office. I will find out what's going on, and they will have to answer to me!"

A year and a half ago Sasha would have wept upon hearing such words and thrown herself into her mother's arms. She would have asked, *begged,* her to come to Torpa, to help her, to save her. Back then she would have believed that her furious mother had power over Farit Kozhennikov. But now . . .

"Kind of late, don't you think?"

"Excuse me?"

"Mom, I don't want to change anything. I like it there . . . and I'm not going to allow you to interfere."

"What?"

Mom let go of the iron. It stayed on the ironing board, steam hissing underneath the platform, making the iron resemble a steam train.

"So it *is* a religious cult?"

"No. I just don't want to change anything."

"You promised to return!"

"I never promised anything."

"What have they done to you?"

"Nothing."

"I'll write a statement for the police."

"On what grounds? I'm over eighteen. And there's nothing going on, besides."

"Have they drugged you? Hypnotized you? Is it some sort of conspiracy?"

"Mom, it's been going on for two years. In all that time, you've never said anything. Didn't seem to care. Two years, and you haven't been concerned about *anything* until now?"

Mom stepped back. A few minutes ago she was ready to attack, fight, defend. Now she looked as if she had been hit on the head with a stick.

"Two years," Sasha repeated ruthlessly. "Nothing can be done now."

Mom stared at her as if through wet glass. As if the outline of Sasha's face wavered in front of her, melting and flattening.

Black smoke rose from underneath the iron's platform. Sasha forced the iron off the board; a burned hole gaped in the blue baby's shirt.

"You have a new life," Sasha continued without remorse. "A new husband, a new baby, new happiness. And I have a new life, too. I'm not leaving forever, but you should not try to force anything on me. Don't try to find out what's going in Torpa. Some things I will share, but some things need to be all my own. But things are perfectly fine, believe me."

The baby cried in the bedroom. Perhaps Sasha had spoken too loudly. Perhaps little Valentin felt the tension filling the apartment. Mom flinched, but continued staring at Sasha.

"I feel badly about the way things worked out," Sasha said, looking at the hole in the baby's shirt. "But Torpa is where I belong, and there is no way back. I am sorry."

▪ ▪ ▪

"Miss! Torpa in fifteen minutes!"

"Yes, thank you. I'm awake."

She'd never before returned to Torpa this early in the summer. The night was stuffy, windless. The train departed. Sasha walked ten meters along the platform and found herself knee-deep in fog.

The birds began waking up. The bus came on time.

The linden trees were green on Sacco and Vanzetti.

Sasha dragged her suitcase up to the third floor and unlocked the door of her loft. She placed the suitcase by the door, poured some water into a cup, and watered the ivy in the flower box outside her window.

She lay down on her bed, stretched out—and realized she was home. She knew that the dark shadow circling over the city had melted. And she, Sasha, was once again a singular entity.

"Greetings, third years."

September first in Torpa was always filled with sunshine. For the third time Group A was greeting the new school year, and for the third time outside the windows of auditorium 1 Indian summer showed itself in the green linden trees, in the dark shadows on the pavement, in the heat and dust.

Portnov remained true to himself: a wrinkled checkered shirt, old jeans, straight blond hair pulled into a ponytail. His glasses, long and narrow like razors, were designed to allow him to look over the lenses.

"Biryukov, Dmitry."

"Here."

"Bochkova, Anna."

"Here."

Once he called a student's name and heard his or her answer, Portnov would allow for a short pause in order to bestow a significant glance upon the student. Occasionally the glance would last three or even four seconds.

"Goldman, Yulia."

"Here."

Somewhere in the assembly hall terrified first years listened to "*Gaudeamus.*" The dorm, filled with new residents, smelled of paint and fresh whitewash.

"Korotkov, Andrey."

"Here."

"Kovtun, Igor."

"Here."

"Kozhennikov, Konstantin."

"Here."

Kostya sat next to his wife. Clean-shaven, ascetically skinny, slouching slightly. Sasha's heart skipped a beat when he walked into the auditorium; they said hello as if they'd parted only last night, but did not say another word to each other.

"Myaskovsky, Denis."

"Here!"

Denis was smiling. The euphoria he experienced after he'd passed Sterkh's test had put a stop to his prolonged depression. Sasha noticed that Denis looked suntanned and that he sat sprawling at the table, one leg thrown over the other. Judging by his looks, he was not afraid of anything.

"Onishhenko, Larisa."

"Here."

"Pavlenko, Lisa."

"Here."

Dressed in a black T-shirt and black jeans, completely devoid of makeup, Lisa resembled a monochrome photograph. Smooth blond hair appeared to be glued to her head.

"Monastery style," Portnov said. "You're missing a wimple."

Lisa did not reply.

"Samokhina, Alexandra."

"Here."

They glared at each other for five seconds or so—Portnov over his glasses, Sasha straight back at him. Portnov was the first one to look away.

"Toporko, Zhenya."

"Here!"

Zhenya had gained some weight, and Sasha thought that her face had grown harsh. Zhenya pushed her pencil over an empty page in her notepad, as if scared of looking up at her professor.

"Very good." Portnov leaned back in his chair. "Congratulations on the beginning of your third year. This semester we will concentrate on studying Speech as a multilevel system of efforts that either alter the world or prevent it from changing."

The third years of Group A resembled a garden of stones. No one moved. It seemed that no one even blinked.

"The starting pistol has just gone off, and the date of your placement exam has been made public: January thirteenth. During the exam each one of you will have a chance to apply the knowledge you have absorbed in these two and a half years, as well as demonstrate the practical skills built upon that foundation. In case you successfully complete your mission—and I am convinced that will happen—you will face a radical change to your existence: you will have an opportunity to become a part of Speech . . . Yes, Pavlenko?"

"Will we be using Speech in practice? Are we going to use Speech?"

"No." Portnov stared at Lisa over his lenses. "Speech will be using you. Any more questions?"

Yegor stood in front of the bulletin board, tilting to the side, pressing his right hand to his chest, swaying as if losing his balance—and regaining it at the last moment.

"How are you?" asked Sasha, just as a simple greeting.

Yegor's hair was bleached by the sun, and his eyes appeared even darker and deeper. He stared at Sasha for a long time, and once she stopped expecting a reply, he finally moved his lips.

"I had a practice session. Just now."

"Did you succeed?"

"You were right," Yegor said. "Listen . . . I'm scared."

"Nonsense," Sasha said. "Just study, and don't be afraid. You'll learn things, pass the exam, get your diploma, then you'll become a Word. Perhaps, you will even become a fundamental concept. They say it's a big honor—"

"I'm a verb," Yegor said.

"How do you know?"

"I was told. Irina Anatolievna, she said that I'm a verb in the subjunctive mood. I express a wish, or a condition, the 'if it were true . . .' Do you understand?"

"Yes," Sasha said. "Your professors have quite a technique. Ours dragged their feet up until the last possible moment, they never told us anything."

"But I didn't get it," Yegor said. "*If* I bought those skis—then everything would have turned out differently, right?"

Sasha took a step back. "I don't think so. You see . . ." But then she fell silent.

A horde of first years showed up, stunned by their first lecture.

They gathered around silently, hesitant to get closer to the bulletin board, made nervous by the spooky crippled second year and the third-year girl, normal-looking on the surface and thus even more terrifying.

"I am a verb as well," Sasha said. "But I'm a verb in the imperative mood. I suppose nothing would have worked out for us anyway . . ."

She was silent again. She didn't want to continue this conversation surrounded by a bunch of frightened children. There was really no point in continuing it—she had told no one about the "loop" that Farit Kozhennikov put her in for pedagogical reasons, no one but Kostya.

So she turned to the first years. "Hey, what do you want? Do you need to copy your schedule? Then go ahead, copy it down, the bell is about to ring. Do you know what happens if you are ever late for class?"

Pencils began to rustle. Girls started whispering to one another. Sasha took hold of Yegor's sleeve and pulled him aside; they hid in the shadow of the bronze equestrian, but Sasha was not in a rush to let go of his sleeve.

"You see, Yegor, one's own experience is an individual method. When you understand something, when you know it for sure, but cannot explain it to someone else who has not had the same experience . . . well, it's a very unpleasant feeling. I can only imagine how Cassandra felt."

"I don't understand," Yegor said. "I'm a little slow these days . . . after this summer."

"It'll pass. Everything will pass, in the grand scheme of things. Where is that girl Natasha, the one who lent me her sweater?"

"She failed the summer finals."

"How?"

"She failed Specialty. She took it three times. And failed. Where do you think she is now?"

"Same place as Zakhar," Sasha's voice sounded hollow.

"Who's that?"

"You won't remember him. It doesn't matter, Yegor. But how are you? How do you feel . . . after all this? And who's teaching Introduction to Applied Science, how is it?"

"You sound like my mother," Yegor said.

Sasha smiled wistfully. "Is that bad?"

"It's weird." He shrugged slowly. Just as slowly, he said, "But if we are Words, we couldn't have had a relationship anyway."

"Except for a grammatical kind," Sasha forced a smile.

Yegor looked down.

"Forgive me. When I was still a human being . . . I was wrong."

***All of them are to blame, and everyone has admitted his guilt, and** now I'm drowning in their apologies,* Sasha thought grimly, sprawled on her bed and thumbing through the *Textual Module.* She learned to *scan* the paragraphs, skimming the surface, without diving into the grinding chaos of words. This method did not replace her usual meticulous study technique, but its value was undeniable. Unlike Portnov's exercises and Sterkh's trials, no restrictions were imposed on the paragraphs: Sasha was allowed to read the entire textbook if she wanted to, which is exactly what she was doing at the moment with a sense of serene pleasure. In moments like these a magnificently curved fragment of a sphere that enveloped the planet appeared in front of her eyes, so very close; the sphere was pearly-gray, the color of smoke, and it teemed with ideas and meanings, images, bits and whole impressions. All was accidental and all was interdependent, and it seemed that all she needed to do was to reach for a fresh meaning, grab it, process it, comprehend it—and everything would change. The *world* would change.

This is where geniuses scoop up their ideas, Sasha thought, almost without envy. They don't understand how it works, they rely on intuition: reach out with your hand—and here it is, your idea.

What a depressing way to go through life, hoping for ideas.

She had ten minutes left until her lesson with Sterkh, the first one this year. Sasha closed the book and put it in her bag, then checked to make sure she had her pens and pencils.

She sighed, put the pink case with her telephone around her neck, locked the door, went outside, took two steps in the direction of the institute . . .

And froze, as if her feet had been glued to the cobblestones.

Mom was walking down Sacco and Vanzetti. She swiveled her head, peering at the numbers of the buildings. For an entire minute Sasha wanted to believe that it was a mistake, that the woman moving along the paving stones only resembled Mom, but was really somebody completely unfamiliar.

In an instant, two alien worlds collided. Torpa, the institute, Sasha's metamorphosis, words and meanings. Mom, home, previous human life. The worlds that had never before come into contact now overlapped, and Sasha felt a dull pain in her temples at the thought of how this meeting would turn out.

Her initial impulse was to run over to Mom, shout, curse, scream in her face. "Leave! Go away from here!" However, Sasha restrained herself, only to have her second impulse flow through her: hide. Bury her head in the sand like an ostrich. Once she managed to overcome that temptation, she realized that there was nothing she could do. She had no idea what action to take, and the time before her lesson kept shrinking, Sterkh was expecting her in seven minutes . . . no, in only six, now.

Mom stopped in front of the institute. A cluster of first-year girls whispered among themselves, heads close together, throwing quick glances at the second-story windows. Mom had to ask them a question, but she also clearly wanted to know what the students were saying before she interrupted. Sasha could understand that: sometimes you can understand more about a school by listening to a chance conversation.

Mom stepped from foot to foot. She clearly felt lost and stupid. Sasha could imagine Mom had taken a long time to make the decision to come to Torpa, and had no idea what she was going to see, and now here she was: a charming provincial town, strange but very beautiful. A four-story institute building on Sacco and Vanzetti Street. The girls, perfectly lovely on the outside, clearly anxious, but what young students wouldn't be in the beginning of September?

"Girls, excuse me, are you students here?"

The group separated.

"Yes, we are," a tall, beautiful girl in a very revealing outfit, more appropriate for a beach, replied cautiously.

"Do you know Sasha Samokhina?"

"Is she a first year?"

"Third."

The girls exchanged glances.

"We don't know any third years yet . . . almost no one. We've just started."

"I see. I'm sorry."

Mom marched over to the entrance of the institute and took hold of the door handle. She disappeared inside.

Sasha bolted toward the alley. Flew into the yard and over to the dorm. *Please let him be home. Let him be home . . .*

She banged on the door to room 3 with her fist. This double room was given to the newlyweds Kostya and Zhenya last semester.

"Come in," said Zhenya's annoyed voice.

Three minutes remained until her session with Sterkh. The pink phone hung on her neck.

"Sasha?"

She turned. Kostya was walking down the corridor, two steaming mugs in his hands.

"I need your help," she said without preamble. "I have a session with Sterkh at twelve oh five. And my mother just arrived."

"Your *mother*?"

"I forbade her, but she came anyway, without warning. What the hell am I going to do? Go see Sterkh, please, and I'll take your slot . . ."

Kostya placed the cups on the floor and looked at his watch. "My slot is right after yours. Twelve fifty-five." And without looking back, he rushed to the exit.

The door opened. Zhenya peeked out, dressed in a bathrobe, sleepy-looking. She glared at Sasha.

"Samokhina?"

"Kostya made you some tea," Sasha said pointing to the floor.

Then she beat a hasty retreat.

Mom stood in the middle of the vestibule, skeptically observing the bronze equestrian under the dome. The dome lit up when the sun came out and faded when a chance midday cloud floated by.

"Hello, Mom."

Sasha's voice made Mom jump.

"Sasha?"

Mom was uncomfortable. She clearly felt guilty, and at the same time she was very happy to see Sasha.

"Who are you looking for?"

"For you, of course." Mom's cheeks flushed.

"Did something happen?"

"No . . . it's just . . ."

"You decided to check up on what they are teaching me here?"

"No." Mom looked away. "It's just . . . I wanted to see you."

"Then should we go to my place?"

Students watched them with curiosity. Parents *were* a curiosity here—she remembered Kostya's mother at his wedding; she couldn't remember another one. Sasha led Mom out of the institute and farther down the street; they passed the lions. She used the lighter key to unlock the front door, the darker one to unlock the door to her loft.

"Come in."

Mom looked around at the tiny, almost doll-like apartment with its antique bureau and ivy outside the window.

"Nice place you've got yourself here."

"Make yourself comfortable." Sasha maintained a casual, confident tone with ease. "You can rest after your trip. How was your journey?"

"Sweetheart . . ."

Mom faltered. Sasha gazed at her, simply and guilelessly, without offering any assistance.

"We said so many things to each other . . . so much. I know you did not want me to come. But I simply cannot live with all this—with everything we've said to each other."

Sasha stretched her lips in a polite smile. "Mom, they were just words. They didn't cost anything. La-la-la, blah-blah-blah. We said some words, we threw them away, we forgot them. I'm sorry, I have to go to class. There is a teakettle, biscuits, kefir. Wait for me, will you?"

Mom's eyes followed her to the door. Only now did Sasha notice how bloodshot, anxious, and haunted her eyes were.

She ran up to the institute's porch, jogged up to the fourth floor and higher, to the attic. She stopped in front of the dusty round window and considered the situation.

How much of a problem was Mom's visit?

Actually, it was not that threatening. Not that Sasha could see. Sasha did not break a single rule dictated by Kozhennikov. Maybe only her session with Sterkh, because Sterkh always made the schedule himself, and hated it when students shuffled things around. But then Sterkh did not normally write reports because of small indiscretions. Sasha would explain the situation to him; it was a force majeure, a special circumstance, after all.

She'd done the right thing by leading Mom away from the institute. But theoretically, what would Mom even see there? What sort of compromising thing? Limping, wretched-looking second years? But don't cripples have rights to higher education?

The institute was encased in a thick layer of informational insulation, and in two years Sasha had had plenty of chances to be sure of that. A protective layer of stable living conditions, coupled with tangible provincial mediocrity. A casual bystander wouldn't see anything suspicious. Just like Kostya's mother came for his wedding and saw nothing unusual. Students, lectures, exams. Love, the wedding. The difficulty of getting the superintendent to assign a room to the newlyweds. Striped mattresses in dorm rooms. A student dining hall.

Gradually, thickening with every year, the same informational vacuum enveloped everyone who ended up here for a long period of time. It was simple, ordinary, provincial: "a student in Torpa." And no one cared. The world is full of someone's acquaintances and relatives who exist—and yet they don't. People don't write or call for years, and no one really cares. But they *do* exist—somewhere.

Sasha drew a deep breath. Mom had come—this was out of character; no one had expected this turn of events. Yet there was nothing tragic about it. One thing was certain, though: Mom had to return home tonight!

She waited. Kostya was with Sterkh in auditorium 14. She hoped his session was going well . . . the first session this year. Kostya had taken off immediately, without asking questions, had just ran—to cover for Sasha. She wondered if he had been prepared.

She wondered about Mom.

Sasha squeezed the pink phone in her hand. She could see the street out the round window: if Mom decided to sneak out of Sasha's loft and turn up at the institute to hold some sort of an inspection, Sasha would notice.

A minute before her—or Kostya's—official time slot, she went down to the auditorium. Kostya came out; Sasha scrutinized his face, trying to discern: Were things normal? Good? Did everything work out?

Kostya was smiling. "Everything is fine."

"Thank you," Sasha whispered gratefully and, holding on to the phone case on her chest, she entered the auditorium.

"Good afternoon, Nikolay Valerievich, I apologize for rescheduling, it's my fault, there are circumstances . . ."

"Calm down, Sasha, no need for such excitement. It's all perfectly fine. Kostya and I had a terrific session. Just don't do it again. What happened?"

Sasha sat down and laced her fingers together. "My Mom came to Torpa."

Sterkh raised his eyebrows. His triangular face remained impassive, but Sasha could tell right away that her news made a much bigger impression that she had anticipated.

"She's leaving tonight," she rushed to say. "I'll take her to the station."

"But do you know why she came?"

"We had a fight in the summer, before I came back. She . . . well, I convinced her to change her mind. At least I thought so. Anyway, she really wanted me to drop out, to transfer." Sasha lowered her eyes.

"Does she still want that? Why did she come—for what, exactly? Did she tell you?"

"She wants to make sure that I haven't been involved with some religious cult," Sasha admitted after a pause.

"It is strange," Sterkh said pensively. "Are you two very close?"

"Yes. I mean, no. I mean, we used to be. It's different. She got married, had a baby . . ."

"I know. Sasha, there is no reason to worry and no reason to upset her. You can introduce her to Oleg Borisovich, to me . . . to other professors. Give her a tour of the institute. But the sooner she goes back home, the better it will be for her and for you."

"Right," Sasha said. "Nikolay Valerievich . . . I have one more question."

"Yes?"

"What is a verb in the subjunctive mood?"

"Do you have a young man named Yegor Dorofeev in mind?"

Sasha sat up straight. "Yes."

Deep in thought, Sterkh touched his sharp chin.

"It is a fairly rare specialization. All verbs are extremely valuable, but the subjunctive mood has its own specific nature. When it comes to Speech, it specifies projecting structures that unfold a fan of possibilities. You and Yegor are no longer together, am I correct?"

Sasha frowned. "Is that important?"

Sterkh stretched, rearranging his folded wings. "You don't think that is any of my business? Then maybe Yegor isn't any of *your* business . . . just as you wish. Let us repeat the step-by-step inner transformations—"

"Yes, we broke up," Sasha said through gritted teeth. "And so we have nothing in common any longer."

"You are on edge." Sterkh sighed. "You are worried about the situation with your mother. Fine, let us continue this discussion. Verbs in the subjunctive mood are very vulnerable. The uncertainty of such verbs . . . no, let me try something else. Sometimes—during the formative period—a person like that, especially a young person, may become a shadow of another verb. A verb in the imperative mood. The imperative entity leaves imprints, the subjunctive entity accepts them. Like stamps and sealing wax, like molds and putty, like two DNA strands. Thus, the subjunctive entity lives and acts the way the imperative entity wants it to, whether consciously or subconsciously."

Sasha's jaw dropped.

"I said 'may become,' I did not say 'that is what always happens.' But this much is certain: the boy fell in love with you when you needed it, and broke up with you when it was necessary for you."

"But I didn't *want* him to break up with me! It's just the opposite, it was important that he stay with me! Because at that moment—"

"I understand perfectly. You did not want him to. But you *needed* for him to break up with you. You had to be alone."

Sasha was silent for a long time. Sterkh did not rush her; he leafed through his daily planner, rubbing his chin. Only a year ago Sasha might have had a breakdown over such news. She would have tried to not believe it. She would have surrendered to despair.

Now she found herself perfectly calm. As if everything Sterkh was talking about she knew or had predicted in advance.

"Nikolay Valerievich. Are you sure I influenced Yegor?"

"I am not sure." Sterkh looked her in the eyes. "But I cannot exclude such a possibility."

"Is this . . . Will this have an impact on his fate?"

"He's long been removed from under your influence. I spoke with his Introduction to Applied Science professor, she consulted with me. He is a talented but a very complex student. Unfortunately he is not particularly diligent. He needs to study harder; he missed a lot during his first year."

"He will study," Sasha said firmly. "I will talk to him."

Mom sat at the table, half-turned to the window, at the same place where Sasha loved to spend her evenings. The cardboard silhouette of Mom's face stood out against the background of the pink sunset.

Sasha stood still. For a second she thought that Mom was a wax sculpture placed in front of the window. Even her eyes appeared dull and immobile.

"Mom?"

Mom turned her head.

"It's so beautiful here. The pavement, these buildings, even the lanterns are so picturesque. Did you have your class?"

"Yes."

"What did you do?"

"The usual student stuff. Textbooks, notes. Let's go downstairs to the café and get some food."

"I am not hungry. I had some tea, washed my cup. Sasha . . . you are doing so well; everything looks so neat. Such a nice apartment." Mom spoke while looking at Sasha—and at the same time not seeing her.

"Did you call home?"

"Yes. Everything is fine, but it's hard for Valentin, obviously. He has some issues at work, he's missed quite a few days, and taking time off right now is not very convenient. And I feel so anxious."

Sasha took the opportunity that presented itself. "You should go home tonight. I will take you to the station."

"Sasha . . ."

"You came to see how I live and where I go to school, right? Well, now you have seen that I live well, and I study like any normal student. Or are you planning a full inspection?"

"Sasha . . ." Mom faltered.

"Let's not fight anymore," Sasha said firmly. "Forget everything I said—it's all nonsense. Just words. You should go tonight, otherwise who knows what could happen while they are at home by themselves." She smiled, hoping to indicate she was joking.

Mom took a deep ragged breath. Not letting her say another word, Sasha picked up her overnight bag. "Come on—let's go. It takes time to get to the station, then we have to get you a ticket, get some supper at the café . . ."

Sad but determined, Mom shook her head.

"Sasha, I made a decision. You are coming with me."

Sasha dropped the bag on the floor and exclaimed, "I can't! I'm a student here. I have classes tomorrow!"

"Who are you trying to deceive?" Mom asked gently. "Your endless and very complex studies, additional lectures—even in the summer—all for what? To prepare you for teaching philosophy at some vocational school?"

Sasha found herself at a loss. She had an unshakable belief in the informational "fog" surrounding the institute and everything connected to it. Mom's calm logic practically disarmed her, because she wasn't wrong: What *was* the purpose of Torpa? And, even if she could explain it, would it even make sense to Mom?

"Sasha, I bear all the guilt here. But you are my daughter, and I am not leaving you here. I don't know what is going on at this school, but I feel that something is wrong. I don't want you to have anything to do with Torpa. If it is necessary, I will find a lawyer. Or a doctor. If I need to, I will sell our apartment, I will withdraw all our money from the savings account, but if you are in trouble, I *will* help you!"

The pink phone on Sasha's neck rang sharply.

She had never heard its ring tone before. "Pop goes the weasel . . ." It was loud, shrill, reedy.

It was the most terrifying sound she'd ever heard.

Mom stopped talking and looked at Sasha in surprise. The ringing continued. Finally Mom said, "Answer it. What's with you?"

Everything had already happened. Everything just happened. Holding on to the edge of the bureau, Sasha lifted the phone to her ear. "Hello?"

"Sasha! Sasha, it's Valentin!"

The screaming voice was full of terror.

"Is your mother there? With you? I can't get ahold of her!"

"She's here," Sasha said. At least she tried to say it.

"Hello! Can you hear me?"

"Yes," she said, firmly. "She's here."

"Give her the phone!"

Moving her dead fingers, Sasha pulled the pink cord off her neck and gave the phone to Mom.

"Hello, Valentin? My battery went . . . What? *What!*"

Sasha clutched the bureau with both hands.

"There were nine! I took one yesterday . . . yes . . . God, how could you . . . Nine, count them, there should be nine pills . . ."

Mom choked. Her face went white in the light of the setting sun. Sasha shut her eyes.

"Nine," Mom exhaled. "Did you count them? Nine . . . I'm sure. Yes, I took one, I am positive. There were only nine. Are you sure? Oh God . . ."

Mom caught her breath. Inhaled deeply—exhaled. And one more time. Valentin kept talking, rapidly, almost choking.

"Calm down," Mom said finally. "I'm leaving now. Relax, everything is fine. You can explain in the ambulance. It's a lesson for both of us. I left it there . . . I just didn't think he'd reach as high as the shelf. It's all right, wait for me, I'll be home in the morning . . . I love you."

The pink phone fell onto the bed. Mom sat down next to it and went limp like a snow pile in the spring.

"Mom?"

"The baby got hold of my sleeping pills. They are so brightly colored, you know, those pills. He tried to pluck them out, one after another. And then he put them in his mouth, but Valentin caught him. He did not know how many of the pills were in the jar, and he called the ambulance right away. The baby just didn't have enough time to swallow any, thank God. Simply not enough time. It was sheer luck. I'm leaving, Sasha, leaving right now."

Sasha bought a compartment carriage ticket and refused to take money from Mom.

At the station cafeteria they bought hot dogs, two portions of cabbage salad, and a couple of pies that were still hot and smelled really good. Mom called home a couple more times using Sasha's phone. Baby Valentin was doing great. The ambulance team reprimanded his father for being absentminded and confirmed that the baby was just fine. "Shaken but unhurt," Valentin said, making an attempt at being lighthearted.

Sasha and her mother came out of the waiting room toward the platform and sat down on a bench. The night was warm, filled with a cool wind and the scent of grass and moisture—an autumn and at the same time summer night.

"How are you getting home? It's so late . . ."

"Cars go back and forth here," Sasha said with as much confidence as she could muster.

"It must be expensive . . ."

"Don't worry about it, I'll be fine. Trust me, I'm all grown up!"

Sasha made a feeble attempt at smiling.

She was still shaking, though, and she worked hard to conceal the tremor. The fear refused to back down. Sure, everything was fine—Mom repeated every ten minutes—but the phone was still there, hanging from her neck, and the little stylized globe rotated on its display.

The fear suspended over the universe.

It's impossible to live in the world where you exist. It is impossible to live in the world where I do not exist.

Although it's hard to resign oneself to my existence, I understand that.

Crickets sang.

A freight train rolled by drowning out all the sounds, but as soon as the roaring subsided, the crickets started up again.

"You were right," Mom said. "They need me. It's as if you knew. 'Who knows what could happen while they are at home by themselves . . .'"

Sasha looked down.

"It looks like I jinxed them."

"Nonsense."

"But everything is fine now, right?" Sasha nervously touched the phone on her neck.

"Everything is fine."

Forty minutes remained until the train's departure. Mom spoke in short declarative sentences.

"It is a very nice town. I didn't expect it to be so old. It is strange that no one really knows about Torpa. Although there is a tourist center. I saw it. There is a tourist center. And the little shop sells landscape photos . . ."

A local train arrived. The doors opened and women with large checkered bags came out, then an old man with a sheathed scythe. The train started and melted into the dark.

The semaphore went green.

Three bright lights came on in the darkness: the long-distance train was approaching the station.

"Mommy," Sasha whispered. "Don't leave them alone for long. Don't leave them alone at all. Stay with them, I will be fine. I . . . I will come and visit during the break."

The train stopped. The locks slid open with a grating sound, the doors opened one after another, and the train attendants stepped down onto the platform, pushing back the curious passengers.

"Standing for five minutes! This stop is five minutes only! Don't let children get off the train! Don't go too far!"

A man in sweatpants and a wife beater looked around, inhaled deeply, murmured "Such air!" and immediately lit up a cigarette.

Mom handed her ticket to a fat uniformed train attendant, who nodded. "Come in . . . Seat number fifteen."

Sasha stepped inside with Mom. For one minute she dove into the smell, the life, the temporary nature of the train—but this time the train was somebody else's. It was transitory, this ghostly, dreamlike way of life was about to take off, and Sasha would remain here.

Here where she belonged.

They went back onto the platform and stopped, not knowing what else to say.

"Departing in one minute," the train attendant rushed them. "Take your places."

Then Sasha hugged Mom's neck just like she had when she was a little girl.

"Mommy, I really, really love you."

The cursed pink phone, stuck between them, cut into Sasha's chest.

"The train is departing! Everyone back on the train!"

They did not let go of each other's hands. They could not let go.

"Ma'am! The train is leaving."

"I love you," Sasha whispered, choking on her tears. "I love you . . . Good-bye . . ."

The train started moving. Sasha ran alongside it, waving, and for a long time she kept up with the train. Mom waved out of the open window in the corridor, and Sasha saw her hair flowing in the wind. The train gathered speed, Sasha ran faster, Mom leaned farther out of the window, and kept waving, and shouted: "Good-bye!"

And then the platform ended.

The windows of the moving train merged with the faces. The roaring was replaced by a distant noise. Sasha watched the train until she could no longer see the last of its lights.

Then she walked over, moving her aching feet, and sat down on the tracks.

"Sasha?"

The moon was high up in the sky. Farit Kozhennikov stood over Sasha.

"It's late. You have classes tomorrow. Shall we?"

"Please, Farit . . . Leave me alone."

"You need to control yourself. You have to get back to town somehow. It's very late and very cold. Let's go."

He spoke so calmly and with such authority that Sasha could not resist. She got up and followed Farit, dragging her feet slightly. The heels of her shoes broke, the heel taps were lost. The shoes would have to be thrown away. No matter.

Kozhennikov opened the door of his white Nissan for her. Sasha shrank into the seat.

"Are you cold?"

"Why, Farit? What did I do wrong? Did I break any rules? Why?"

"You could not solve the problem on your own. I agree, it is not your fault, or at least not entirely. But remember: the baby did not swallow the pills, he only played with them. It's only fear, Sasha. Fear the General. Fear the Emperor who shapes the reality. You should buckle up."

The car rode onto the highway surrounded on both sides by the forest. The road signs flashed in the lights and rushed backward, like smeared spots of white fire.

"Fear is a projection of danger," he continued, "genuine or imagined. The thing you wear around your neck is a phantom fear, the kind you get used to . . . kind of like a familiar sprain. Nothing happened. But you believe in trouble, and that is why you lived through these minutes as if through a real tragedy."

"*You* taught me to be afraid," Sasha said, gripping the phone.

"No. You knew how to be afraid without me. Everyone knows that. I simply directed your fear, like an arrow toward the target."

"And you have achieved your goal?"

"Yes."

Sasha turned her head. Kozhennikov watched the road, the speedometer arrow inching toward 120.

"The first years," Sasha said slowly. "Do you select them somehow?"

"Yes."

"Don't you feel sorry for them?"

"No. They are Words. They must realize their preordained purpose."

"And other people? They . . ."

"They are different. Prepositions, conjunctions, interjections . . . expletives." Kozhennikov smiled. "Every man carries a shadow of a word, but only Word in its entirety, firmly imprinted into the fabric of the material world, can return to its beginning and grow from a pale projection to an original entity."

"And your instrument is fear?"

"Sasha." Kozhennikov slowed down at the turn of the road. "For a while now you have been working hard not because somebody forces you to, but because you are interested in it. You have tasted the honey of that knowledge. To be Word—do you understand what it means?"

Sasha didn't answer. She was silent until they reached Torpa; finally the Sacco and Vanzetti cobblestones clattered under the tires. The car stopped near the porch guarded by the stone lions. The streetlights were on, but none of the windows were lit.

"Thank you," Sasha said in a strained voice. "Good-bye." She opened the car door.

"Sasha?"

She froze.

"Give me the phone."

Sasha turned to face him. A streetlight reflected in Kozhennikov's glasses made it look as if two burning white eyes stared at her.

With difficulty she pulled the pink cord off her neck. Kozhennikov weighed the phone in his hand.

"Do you understand what it means to be Word? The verb in the imperative mood? Do you know what it is?"

Sasha was silent, having lost the gift of speech.

"Good." Kozhennikov carelessly dropped the phone into the glove compartment. "Good night, Sasha."

He drove away.

"Yegor, may I speak with you for a minute?"

The dining hall was full of noisy conversations and the clanking of dishes. Students carried hot borscht, in which floated white commas of sour cream. Sasha waited until Yegor finished eating; when he was walking out with a bunch of his classmates, pulling his cigarettes on the way, she placed herself in his path with determination, but without theatrics.

"I'll catch up with you," Yegor said to his classmates.

They went up to the hall. First years sat in the row near the bronze equestrian's hooves. Sasha led Yegor a bit farther—toward the deep window niche.

"Here's the thing. Are you having problems with Applied Science?"

"I wouldn't put it that way. I mean, everyone is having some issues, and so am I, but—"

"I don't care about 'everyone.'" Sasha's voice was harsh. "You are a verb in the subjunctive mood, and that makes you special. *If* you don't study hard, *then* . . . Do you have any idea what could happen?"

Yegor stared at her with empty, static eyes.

"Don't you understand what I'm saying?"

"I understand. They say this to us in every class. 'If you don't tie your shoelaces, you will fall down. If you don't eat your oatmeal, you will grow up a loser. . . .'"

"Yegor—"

Sasha stopped herself short. Yegor was clearly at the most complicated stage of the informational reconstruction: he had almost completed his deconstruction period as a person, but he had not yet formed himself as a word. She remembered herself a year ago: they had met around the same time, and back then Yegor was a confident, strong, and kind man. Yegor had pulled his classmate Stepan out of the water; back then Sasha would freeze in the middle of a movement, staring at a point in the distance, and she had been convinced that she was going to fail the Applied Science exam . . .

She held Yegor's hand. One more second—and she would have *claimed* him, making him a part of herself.

She restrained herself, remembering her tragic experience.

She carried a tray of dirty dishes to the sink. Kostya pushed aside a stack of plates, freeing up some space on the long white zinc table. Sasha nodded gratefully.

"You can't help him," Kostya said. "And stop thinking about it; it's their business, let them work at it. Like we had to work."

"We helped each other," Sasha said softly.

"We are classmates. And they—he won't understand you. It's not time yet."

Kostya went toward the exit, and Sasha thought that he was right. Certain things could not be explained. Isn't it what Portnov and Sterkh had been saying from the very beginning?

Fall came suddenly in the middle of September, and it became very cold very fast. The rain continued up until the arrival of the first snow. Sasha made a fire in her tiny fireplace using coals from a paper bag and wood that she bought at the market. The kindling crackled, sending sparks flying; Sasha spent hours in front of the fireplace with a book in her lap. She went to bed, covering herself with a sheet; in the middle of the night she would pull a blanket over, and in the morning she would wake up because the room would get cold, and, yawning convulsively and wearing a jacket over her nightgown, she would make another fire in the fireplace.

Smoke rose over the roof. The first snow fell softly, landing on the heads of the stone lions, burying the town of Torpa.

"Mom?"

The landlady's phone stood on a shelf on the first floor near the front door. An antique telephone apparatus with tall horns for the receiver. Sasha leaned over the brick whitewashed wall.

"Hello! Mommy! Can you hear me?"

"Hello, Sasha darling. I'm so glad you called . . ."

A distant voice. A deliberate vivacity, even vigor.

"How's the baby?"

"He's well. He's coughing a little. In the summer we tried to boost his immune system a bit, but it's not working all that well. It's one obstacle after another. But everything else is fine. We want to change the wallpaper in your room, the old wallpaper is simply atrocious. I might go back to work, just part-time. Not yet, of course, in about six months or so. I miss working. We may get a nanny; pay her by the hour . . ."

Mom spoke easily, and her tone more than her words were intended to convince Sasha of her complete serenity, stability; it was telling Sasha gently that they were just fine without her. Sasha imagined Mom standing over the stove, holding the receiver, stirring rice cereal in a little pot, all the while smiling and talking and talking and smiling . . .

Sasha closed her eyes. The telephone receiver warmed up with the heat of her cheek. The membrane trembled, turning her voice into a current of sound waves. A curly cable extended from the receiver, but the words stretched farther, and Sasha stretched with them—from her house to the metal telephone box, farther along the wires, into the frozen ground, under the fields and snow piles, under the roots and concrete plates, farther, farther; Sasha felt extending her arm so very far, stretching it to the point of a spasm.

Mom was not standing over the stove. She sat in a chair, her eyes closed, clutching the armrest with her left hand. Her fingers were clenched tightly as if in pain, but Sasha, who *claimed* Mom at this moment, knew that there was no pain.

Her throat felt tight. And both Mom and Sasha froze, very still, and silence reigned on both telephone receivers.

"Mommy . . . I am doing great, too, I am studying hard, and they are feeding us well . . ."

Like an almost-empty can of dry peas, words that meant nothing rolled around—back and forth along the wires. With every word, the distance between Sasha and her mother stretched farther and farther; they had nothing to say to each other anymore, they could not hear each other, not a single sincere word between them . . .

"Mom!"

The scream rolled down the telephone cable—under frozen streams. Under snowed-in meadows. Echoed in the plastic receiver.

"Sasha? What's wrong?"

This is it, these were the words of the true Speech. *Eide,* meanings. Must *manifest*: "None of it is your fault, drop this weight, live and be happy."

But to say this in human terms, out loud, would be hideous. It would be nonsense and a lie. And nothing would change, things would only get worse.

"Mommy . . . give the baby a kiss for me, everything is just fine."

"I will. Good-bye, Sasha darling, talk to you soon."

Short beeps.

"Time is a grammatical concept. Is that clear, or do I need to explain?"

"It's clear."

"Before you start manipulating time, you must set up an anchor. 'Now—Then.' Represented graphically, it looks like this. A bobber with two poles, red and white. Don't rush, Sasha! We're already getting ahead of the program, and we don't have to—"

"I know. I *do* have to, though. I can feel it. *Now.*"

"Good. The anchor shifts into the Then condition as soon as you change the grammatical construction. Aside from the basic vector—past-future—you must consider the overall duration of the action, the periodic nature of the action, the finality or incompleteness of the action, the relationship between the beginning and the end of the action and the Now point—Sasha, put down the pen! Don't rush! It's an extremely complex exercise; very few third years are brave enough to approach it, let alone master it!"

"I am ready."

"I see. Well then. Let us take half of the grammatical measure, half a measure backward. Concentrate. Time is a grammatical concept. Is that clear, or do I need to explain?"

"It's clear."

"Before you start manipulating time, you must set up an anchor. Now—Then. Represented graphically, it looks like this. A bobber with two poles, red and white. Don't rush, Sasha!"

"Nikolay Valerievich, we've done this already. If we don't shift the construction one minute back . . . I mean, half a measure back, we are going to continue moving in circles!"

"Practice makes perfect. Relax, Sasha. Calm down. The reverse reconstruction is a little bit more complex. Now the bobber changes colors . . . Now—Then. Recognize this."

"I got it! I . . . will try. It was, it went on, it repeated, it ended. Ended. *Now.*"

"Bravo! Want to try again?"

"Yes."

"Let's begin. Time is a grammatical concept. Is that clear, or do I need to explain?"

She would go to the riverbank. She would make a snowball and press it with her hands to make sure it stayed firm. She would throw it straight up. Time after time. A janitor who was shoveling snow on Lugovaya Street probably thought she was skipping classes, openly loitering.

The snowball separated from her palm. It went up into the zenith and froze for a moment. It flew down, but did not fall. Again, it went up into the zenith. Flew down. From "is" it shifted to "was," then went into the "had been" loop, and Sasha's heart kept repeating the same beat.

The janitor pausing for a smoke break watched the girl juggling a snowball. The smoke from his cigarette stood motionlessly in the air, glimmering like a television screen.

Now. Sasha did not say or think it. Sasha *did* it, returning herself into the previous grammatical tense, to the point of Then, where she'd set up the anchor.

The snowball fell and drowned in a snow pile. A streetlight lit up at the corner of Lugovaya Street. It was getting dark very fast. Sasha's hands, red and frozen, burned like fire.

A person needs two eyes to determine the exact distance to objects. Two points of view that form an angle. That's what Portnov was telling them during lectures: your projections onto the nearest future and your projections onto the nearest past are set closer than the eyes on your face, but they guarantee stability to your personal time frame. "Was" and "will be"—two bearings, two legs, when you walk, you can shift the center of gravity a bit forward, or a bit backward . . .

Sasha ran over the snow—slightly ahead of herself, then slightly behind. I was! I will be! Snow flashed white sparkles; Sasha's shadow became short and fell under her feet, then crawled forward and became longer the farther Sasha moved away from the streetlight.

The janitor watched her run.

"The language of creation knows no grammatical tense. It has only one mood—the imperative. The first derivative from creation uses the subjunctive mood. The second derivative uses the narrative."

"But does name exist in time?"

"Yes. Realized name becomes a process."

"If Name is a process, then what is the connection between names and verbs?"

"Do you remember high school physics? Remember the wave-particle duality?"

"Well . . . in principle."

"Abysmal ignorance," he said, but without rancor. "There is motion and static. Action and its object. The speed, mass, and length of a wave. Names are building blocks of creation. Verb is a command to build, a will in its purest form. An impulse. Concentrated action. Verb can pull a name out of nonexistence, and it can send it into nonexistence by a single command. All the verbs I've ever known were egocentric, narcissistic, and meant to succeed. Geared toward creation at any cost."

"I see. Then how . . ."

Sasha looked up at Portnov and promptly forgot her question.

Portnov wore jeans and sweaters. He had blond hair that was beginning to go gray, glasses with narrow lenses, and cold blue eyes. He was not a particularly pleasant person, he could be quite rude; Sasha never thought of him as a man, never wondered whether he had a family, a wife, a mistress, any children. Portnov was a teacher, a whip-cracker, an animal tamer. Portnov was Portnov.

But now, it was clear that whoever was sitting in front of Sasha was not human. Moreover, it had *never* been human. For the first time in her life Sasha saw—recognized, understood—what exactly an "embodied function" was.

"What happened, Samokhina?"

Sasha stared at him, forgetting to breathe, completely in awe. A glossary? An activator? A textbook? A textbook that was given a human name?

"Oleg Borisovich . . . ," Sasha whispered.

She saw him again: hair pulled into a ponytail. A gray sweater with blue stripes. An attentive glance over the lenses.

"What?"

"You . . ."

"What about me?"

Sasha swallowed bitter saliva.

"You've just seen me?" Portnov sounded surprised. "You manifest entities, read highly complex informational structures, and you've *only* just seen me?"

Sasha managed a shallow nod, and then shut her eyes, trying to drive the tears back into her eyes.

"What's the matter?" Portnov actually sounded worried. "Sasha?"

"You are not human," Sasha whispered.

"So? Neither are you."

"But I *was* human. I was a child. I remember that. I remember being loved."

"Does it matter to you?"

"I remember it."

"Trust me, I can remember anything you want. I remember being a child. Being raised by monkeys. Being a girl. Working as a cabin boy. Saving a baby out of the fire, scoring the winning goal during the World Cup. Memories are projections of events, and in this case it is much less important whether the events are real or not."

Sasha's tears rolled down her face, smearing her makeup, leaving black traces on her cheeks and fingers.

Portnov took off his glasses. "Are . . . are you feeling *sorry* for me?"

Sasha shook her head.

"Are you lying because you are afraid of hurting my feelings?"

He knows everything about me, Sasha thought. *He spent so many years turning people into Words that it is possible he knows more about us than we know ourselves.*

She located a handkerchief in her bag and began to dry her eyes with so much effort, as if she were trying to rub them entirely off her face. Portnov watched her with surprise and sympathy.

"Are you scared? Is it such an unpleasant idea? Are you simply that used to considering me a human being?"

Sasha sniffed and shook her head.

"Emotional memory," Portnov murmured. "You have already become a butterfly, but are still trying to crawl. You remember being a caterpillar. Samokhina, get ahold of yourself. We are losing time, and this session has a time limit, don't you agree?"

First years crowded the dining hall. Their first winter exams were coming up, but the queue was animated by their laughter and lively conversations. First-year girls flirted with the boys, the boys cracked jokes. Sasha thought that any first-year student at any dining hall of any given institute would behave in the same manner.

Second years sat hunched over their plates—some wearing gloves, some wearing glasses, some sporting nervous tics. Even in the dining hall most of them couldn't part with their books, printouts, and headphones. These students had already lived through the destruction and re-creation, and now they faced their first exam in Introduction to Applied Science. Sasha mentally wished them luck.

Yegor was not there. Sasha took another good look around, but it was in vain.

From the entire lunch menu she chose fruit compote, pale pink, with a slice of apple on the bottom of the glass. She sat in the corner of the dining hall facing the entrance—to make it easier to observe the room.

Here they are, eating and drinking. They are still almost entirely human; they have human psyches and human bodies. With time, during the learning process, they will come out of their human skin and become Words, tools of Speech, the bones and tendons of a highly complex text that is called reality. Words know no fear, and no death. Words are free and conform only to Speech. And Speech—Sasha knew this!—is the core of harmony.

"Dear third years, I'm so used to the individual sessions with each of you that it feels a bit strange—and all the more pleasant—to see the entire group in one room. I'm glad this small auditorium fits every one of us. Am I right—is everyone here? Do we need a roll call?"

"Everyone is here," Kostya said with a quick glance around the room. The third years of Group A sat behind the desks, chilly air wafted through the open window, and the heat from the radiators made the air above them tremble.

Sterkh was smiling. His sharp chin nearly touched his speckled tie, arranged in a soft romantic knot. His black suit puckered on his back. Sasha always wondered why Sterkh insisted on wearing his wings even while in his human appearance.

Maybe it was because, unlike Portnov, Sterkh used to be human. Yet that was a very long time ago. Now he represented a combination of two concepts: two poles, two energy flows, intertwined under the direction of one will. Perhaps the wings were a nod toward his dual nature; perhaps it was too dangerous to require such a complex organism to go through an additional metamorphosis. It could be Sterkh's personal whim. Or maybe it was something else, something way beyond Sasha's comprehension.

The thing that Portnov called "emotional memory" flatly refused to weaken. For some reason, Sasha was pleased to know that Sterkh used to be human. Even though whatever he was now was just as far from human nature as an electronic microscope from a tortoiseshell comb.

"Why did I want to gather you today? Today is December thirteenth, and that means that exactly one month remains until the placement examination. This month will require all your strength. Unfortunately, there is no makeup date for this exam: you have exactly one chance."

Sasha sat by the window, looking askance at the snow-covered street. With the arrival of the cold weather Sterkh forbade her to fly at night; in response to her pleading that she was not at all afraid of the cold, he shrugged his shoulders in surprise: "What does it have to do with the cold, Sasha? You have so much work now, such a heavy load! Not to mention that footprints of bare feet on the snow are so aesthetically displeasing!"

Large snowflakes fell onto Sacco and Vanzetti.

"Today I will tell you in detail what it is like to take the placement examination. It will help you keep it together and be prepared for the challenge at the defining moment. On January thirteenth, at noon sharp, both groups, A and B, will enter the large assembly hall and take their seats. You will be introduced to the examination committee.

You will not be nervous, will not feel anxious, you will not have anything with you—under no circumstances are you to have any paper or pens. Nothing! The head of the committee will read out the names, and those called will go up to the stage, choose an examination sheet, and sign for it in the ledger. You will have three assignments: the first two are standard; the third one is individual, selected for each one of you according to your future specialization. In the process of completing this assignment you will cease being a human being and commence as Word; for the first time you will *reverberate,* my dears, and this is quite fundamental."

Sterkh surveyed the audience as if searching for expressions of rapture on the faces turned toward him. No one was smiling: everyone looked at him intently and attentively, fans watching a penalty kick going toward the favorite team's goal.

"You should not pay any attention to the drastic changes in your condition, time, space, and internal state. This is going to be quite a shock. It is *supposed* to be a shock, and you should prepare yourself for a shock. The subjective time of the examination may stretch from one minute to several hours. Don't worry if things happen fast. Don't be afraid if the examination seems too long. Remember: the goal of the examination committee is to help you, not to fail you. Remember also that you get only one chance."

Wind beat into the glass. Snowflakes rustled. It was getting dark pretty fast; Sterkh clicked the switch. The overhead light exposed a small dusty auditorium and nineteen third years silently watching their professor.

"So." Sterkh moved his shoulders, settling the wings in a more comfortable position on his back. "Any questions?"

"Mommy? It's me! Can you hear me?"

A very distant voice. As if through a blizzard, something rustled and howled thinly in the receiver. As if from a distant galaxy, as if through a thick layer of water, as if through cotton wool.

"Mom! I'm doing great! How are you?"

"Depends on the day, Sasha, but we're hanging in, bit by bit. The baby has a cold. I have to take more time off. It's because I did not nurse him, and his immune system is not as strong as it should be—"

"Stop it! That's just superstition. It is not your fault! Don't worry, he'll be fine!"

"Of course," Mom said, but she still sounded anxious and tired.

"Mom, I'm not coming home for the winter break this year . . ."

That's it. It was out. It just slipped out.

A pause.

"That's a shame. Such a shame. But what can you do?"

The phone line filtered emotions like blotting paper absorbs tea leaves.

"Mom, don't be sad. Everything will be fine. The baby will feel better soon. And I will call you soon."

"That's good. Call me, Sasha. Call me."

"I will. Good-bye!"

She placed the receiver on the horned cradle. Sasha stood still for a while staring at the wall.

Portnov called it "emotional memory."

One month remained until the placement exam.

On the morning of December thirtieth, drunken first years danced in the fresh snow singing "A little tiny fir tree born in the forest!" Nearly hysterical with glee, the third years joined them in groups and one at a time. The second years wandered around, thin and quiet, like shadows.

A poster decorated with gouache paints and tinsel invited everyone to the holiday roast. The assembly hall was filled to capacity. Vika and Lena, Sasha's former roommates, sang racy ditties, a bit stupid, a bit vulgar, but still funny.

Sasha sat in the assembly hall, in the very midst of a laughing audience, and close to the end of the show she suddenly thought of Zakhar. She recalled how two years ago he, a second year back then, stood at the edge of the stage wearing Portnov's glasses spouting complete nonsense, but so courageously and confidently that Sasha, who always cringed in the presence of bad actors, did not feel any discomfort, only fear—*what if Portnov mistook the quick parody for ridicule . . .*

In two weeks Sasha's classmates would enter this assembly hall and never return to their previous lives.

She left before the concert ended. Among piles of coats and jackets in the coatroom she found her own, the little hanging loop already missing. She got dressed and left, planning to get home and go to sleep, but the evening over Torpa was clear, quiet, and not too chilly. Sasha decided to take a walk; she strolled down Sacco and Vanzetti away from the center of town, toward the outskirts.

Fireplaces and woodstoves had been lit. Smoke rose over the roofs, white in the moonlight, and went straight up in promise of good weather. Sasha's back itched: she imagined how lovely it would be to fly in this transparent world between snowy roofs and the sky propped up by the silvery pillars of smoke.

The moist cobblestones made the pavement black. A car rode by—Sasha moved to the side. A holiday garland noiselessly blinked on the facade of a dark—closed—café, alternating red and yellow and blue and green flashes.

And nearby stood a man, so still that Sasha had not noticed him right away. Only when he said "Yes, I understand that," did Sasha flinch and stop.

The voice was familiar to her.

Kostya stood leaning over the pink brick wall, pressing a cell phone to his ear. He stared at the lights without blinking and did not see Sasha.

"I understand that as well. Yes, you are right, it does not matter. But is there anyone who is not afraid of that? I mean, anyone human?"

Pause. Sasha stepped back, about to leave.

"I got it. Yes. It's a deal. Good. Good-bye, Dad."

Sasha moved to turn around, but she slipped and fell into a snow pile pushed over to the edge of the sidewalk by the street cleaners. Kostya turned sharply.

"I'm sorry," Sasha said. "I was just walking."

Silently Kostya gave her his hand and helped her up.

"Did you know that I'm a pronoun?"

"You? No . . . I didn't."

The garland blinked. Kostya put the phone inside the pocket of his jacket.

"And you are a verb?"

"Yes."

"I knew that. Guess who I was just talking to?"

"I heard you say good-bye to him."

"Of course. You were right: in his own way, he's a good father. Rational. Strict . . ."

"You remembered my stupid words?"

"Why wouldn't I? And they weren't stupid. Anyway, I asked him once: How did he, not at all human, and not even close to a protein-based entity, manage to produce a son? I suspected something was off, but do you know what he said to me?"

"What?"

"Do you really think that controlling the informational space of Hypertext is easier than producing one effective sperm cell?"

They faced away from the blinking garland and walked back along Sacco and Vanzetti toward the humming, singing, celebrating New Year's Eve institute.

"What did he say to you?" Sasha took the risk of asking. "What were you talking about?"

Kostya exhaled a long cloud of smoke.

"I think he was trying to cheer me up before the exam. And the funniest thing is that he's succeeding."

"Really?"

"There is nothing impossible. When he says it, I believe it. And then it turns out that only I am at fault for my grandmother's death."

"Kostya," Sasha said softly. "Unlike words, people actually die . . ."

"I noticed," he replied drily. "What kind of verb are you?"

"Imperative mood."

"No way!" Kostya stopped for a second. "That explains why they've spent so much effort on you lately, Portnov and Sterkh. A verb in the imperative mood . . . Of course you are! I'm a pronoun. A substitute. My place has not been chosen yet. Or perhaps it's the other way around, it's been chosen in advance. Unlike words, people actually die, but Farit Kozhennikov is not a word! He's a rule, a grammatical rule. When *he*—his external shell—becomes old and dies, I will become *him*."

Sasha gasped. "Is that what he told you?"

"No. It's . . . forget it. I never said that."

They continued walking in silence, passed the institute and in about fifteen minutes they came out to a square where a fir tree market was open—exactly the sort that Sasha remembered from her childhood. A green fence, old pictures on plywood poster boards: decorated trees, gigantic bunnies, red-and-white Father Frosts. Hundred-watt lightbulbs painted different colors and soldered into a single garland. Stomped-upon snow, red-cheeked customers, children with sleds—a small, animated crowd.

"All of them are words," Kostya said behind Sasha's back. "All people have been manifested out loud some time ago. And they continue saying words, having no idea about their true meaning."

Sasha thought that Kostya repeated almost identically what Farit Kozhennikov had talked about before. But she did not say anything:

somewhere in the depths of Hypertext her unspoken words turned into gold coins with a round symbol on their faces.

"Should we buy a tree?" she thought out loud.

Kostya glanced at her—and marched determinedly toward the market.

An antlered fir tree with floppy wide branches touched the white ceiling; it rested in a pail in the corner, at the lowest point of the room. The tree had no decorations aside from a single gold garland. The tree appeared to be holding the gleaming train of a nonexisting dress with its many hands.

Fire burned in the tiny fireplace.

Sasha and Kostya lay close, arms and legs intertwined. Kostya dozed off. Sasha watched the sparkly reflections of the fire dance on the gold tinsel.

Two weeks remained until the placement exam. If she was sorry about anything, it was about words that lingered unspoken. And especially sorry about the others, the ones that had flown off her tongue.

If somewhere, at some point in time, in a different text, her words became human beings, they had a reason to reproach Sasha. But then they had a reason to thank her as well.

At least, that was what she wanted to believe.

In the morning she got up to make a fire in the cold room. Kostya was asleep. Sasha couldn't go back to sleep; slipping a jacket over her nightgown, she sat at her desk.

She opened *Textual Module* 8. As she was accustomed to. Without thinking.

> . . . when they had suddenly obtained a sight of the land and seas and sky, and had marked the vastness of the clouds, and the force of the winds, and had beheld the sun, and had marked not only its size and beauty, but also its power, since by diffusing light over the whole sky it caused day,—and when, again, after night had overshadowed the earth, they then perceived the whole sky studded and adorned with stars, and the change in the light of the moon as it alternately waxed and waned, and the rising and setting of all these bodies, and the fixity and unchangeableness of their courses through all

eternity,—when they saw those things, they would assuredly believe that . . . *

Noise. Rasping sounds. Similar to the breathing of air full of whistling and music, conversations, radio news, frequencies and waves, overflowing and dissolving.

The fire was flaring up and warmth filled the room.

A week before the examination Sasha stopped sleeping. Every day she thought that her fear and anxiety had reached it pinnacle, but one more sleepless night would pass, and Sasha would discover that her pre-exam fever jumped another two or even three degrees.

"Sasha, calm down." Sterkh reassured her. "You are too emotional. In combination with certain peculiarities of your gift all this passion evolves into a rather explosive mixture. Calm down, relax—you will pass with an excellent grade."

It was easier said than done.

On January eleventh, second years were taking their Introduction to Applied Science exam. In the morning, around half past seven, Sasha looked out the window and saw Yegor sitting on her porch, between the stone lions.

He was just as still and white as the sculptures. Two white piles of snow lay on his shoulders.

"What's wrong?" Sasha opened the door; the drifting snow licked her fur-lined slippers. "What are you doing here? Did they kick you out of the dorm?"

"I was reading the *Module,*" Yegor rose awkwardly from the steps. "Has it ever happened to you . . . Have you ever read your future in the *Textual Module*?"

"Yes," Sasha said, stepping back inside the entrance hall. "Come in, I'm freezing."

Yegor stepped in. A yellow lightbulb burned on the landing of the first floor.

"I am going to fail the test," Yegor said.

"Wait. Did you read it in the *Module*? But it refers to the most probable future, not the one that's been established absolutely and irrevocably!"

---

* Cicero, *On the Nature of the Gods.*

Yegor shook his head. Two small snowballs fell on the floor.

"I'm going to fail. The test is at ten. I won't pass!"

He stood in front of her, hunched over, small, and pitiful. Sasha analyzed her sensations: she was sorry for Yegor and a little uncomfortable on his behalf. As if a child, scared, crying, came to tell her about a boogeyman who lived in the closet.

Yes, he used to be her man. She'd worn his sweaters and shirts, she'd walked around with him, never letting go of his hand. Only a year ago . . .

A year ago, Yegor had come out of the examination room and she'd held him, congratulating him on his success. He'd smelled like someone close to her, but his arms had hung lifelessly along his sides, and his response to Sasha's muddled words had simply been, "I'm sorry. I have to get ready for the English exam."

Sasha had survived that day, and many days that came later. And now she looked at Yegor and felt only compassion. And a little awkwardness. He was still a human being, and Sasha was not. She knew what they were taught. And he was stumbling around in the dark, like a frightened puppy.

She held his hands gently.

"Listen. It's only fear. It's your materialized fear: get rid of it. You can do it. Farit . . . I mean, Liliya Popova. It does not matter what he's called, but *he* never asks for the impossible. Concentrate. You will pass the test. In the worst-case scenario you can have up to three makeup dates."

Yegor blinked.

"I have a mother, my dad . . . a younger brother. Three makeup dates, you say? *Three makeup dates?*"

He wept.

On the way up the stairs she had a brilliant idea. Letting Yegor in and shutting the door, she looked around in search of a shiny object.

She shook the puff out of a powder compact and wiped the mirror.

"Turn your face to the light."

And when Yegor silently complied with her request, she sent a flash of light into his eyes.

His pupils did not contract as a normal human being's, but widened. For a split second a dismal, dwindling, airless world opened up to her. Then Yegor squinted.

"Don't close your eyes!"

She tried again, and this time she saw him from the inside: man-word halfway to his actualization, highly complex transformation processes, and everything was drowned by sticky gray goo. Fear? Despair? But no matter how hard she tried to see, it was clear that she, a third-year student who still hadn't passed her placement exam, wasn't going to be able to figure it all out right there and then.

"Hold on . . . we'll get through this. We can do it."

Sasha squeezed his hands, *claiming* Yegor, making him a part of herself.

"Listen to me, only to me. We progress from human being to word, and right now you are at the steepest point of the road. When you overcome this obstacle, when you finally realize what you are being taught, you will become absolute. Do you understand? You will be eternal. You will become Word and will accomplish your mission. You are a tool of Speech, an instrument of divine harmony. You are a participant of creation, and that means you will *be*. But right now you are a little human being. So you must fight your fear. I will go to your test with you, I will wait . . .

"And I will help you."

The second years took a long time to reappear. Sasha waited under the hooves of the bronze horse.

She was a lousy teacher, but she'd "claimed" Yegor more deeply than she'd ever dared to claim another human being. Now she knew him better than her own mother. She understood him like no one else; but this morning, when Yegor convulsively embraced her and found her lips with his own, Sasha had pulled away.

"Not right now," she'd said in Portnov's voice. "Focus."

She'd spurred him on, pushed him and urged him on; like a blood donor, she'd transferred her confidence and her own will to win into Yegor. She'd brought him to the exam, nearly leading him by the hand.

"There is nothing impossible. There is no reason you cannot pass! Go!"

An hour had passed since the door closed behind him. Then another hour. Students came out one or two at a time. Some immediately lit up cigarettes, others threw their arms around their friends. Somebody was laughing hysterically. Gradually the corridor became noisy, second years chased one another around in the hallway, and Sasha recalled the half-forgotten, "What are the sparrows singing on this last day of chill? We live, we breathe, we made it, and we are living still!"

They resembled small, funny critters at a veterinarian's office. Sasha had no idea where this comparison came from. Animals don't understand what is happening around them, they are controlled by animal fear. And then, when they are let go and allowed to roam free, they express their joy just like that.

One more year had to pass before the gray fog in their consciousness would be dispelled and they would see Hypertext in all its splendor and perfection. Then they would understand their place in it, and would be overwhelmed by their ecstasy.

Sasha closed her eyes. Joy, ecstasy—the human emotions were too shallow; what she experienced facing Hypertext could only be expressed by the word of true Speech. This word, sharp and dazzling, emerald-green and opal, and graphically . . . Where were her pencil and paper?

Keeping in mind the limitations, she would draw only sketches. Only the most elementary ones, not the ones that could be *manifested*. Only drafts of words and concepts. She became so involved that she nearly missed the end of the exam.

Yegor was the last student to come out of the auditorium. He took a few steps along the corridor and stopped. Sasha saw his face and knew right away.

"Makeup exam is the day after tomorrow." He stared straight ahead. "But I cannot. I cannot."

"Time is a grammatical concept. Is that clear, or do I need to explain?"

Sasha left an anchor in "happening right now" and rushed into "happened today." As far back as she could.

. . . The second years took a long time to reappear. Sasha waited under the hooves of the bronze horse. Let's see: she'd leapt only one activity back. If we assume that one "exam" equals one "activity."

Students came out one or two at a time. Some immediately lit up cigarettes, others threw their arms around their friends. Somebody was laughing hysterically. Gradually the corridor became noisy. "What are the sparrows singing on this last day of chill? We live, we breathe, we made it, and we are living still!"

Watching them, Sasha pulled a pencil and a piece of paper out of her bag. She drew a few graphical concepts. It is difficult for a human being in a human body to process thoughts using words of true Speech. They transform into bulky images, breathtakingly beautiful, but that have a fatal influence on the speed of cogitation . . .

Yegor was the last student to come out. He walked a few steps along the corridor and stopped. Sasha saw his face and bit her lip.

"Makeup exam is the day after tomorrow." He stared straight ahead. "But I cannot. I cannot."

Now. Then.

Again Sasha sat by the hooves of the bronze horse. She must have done something wrong with the concept of "activity." Perhaps whatever was happening to Yegor was more intricate than a regular exam with a starting point of ten o'clock in the morning and an estimated ending point at two o'clock in the afternoon. Or perhaps Sasha simply lacked the experience and skill: returning to the past again and again, she kept showing up in front of a closed door.

"Sasha, what are you doing?"

Sterkh came in through the front entrance. The tails of his long black coat were whitened by the snow. Sasha was well aware that Sterkh was not present in her initial "tests."

Did that mean that the false hunchback lives—exists—outside of general time limits?

"Sasha, I did not teach you to operate grammatical tenses just so that you could float like a flower in the ice hole. Please take that into consideration: no independent acts during the exam. Do only what is written on your examination sheet. Are you guarding this boy, Yegor Dorofeev?"

"Yes. He . . ."

"Verbs in the subjunctive mood often suffer from weak willpower," Sterkh looked concerned. "And in our line of work, lack of will is a death sentence."

"Nikolay Valerievich, can you help him? Right now? Just let him pass this test? Just this one?" Sasha struggled to speak, dizzy from the nonstop time iterations.

"A verb in a subjunctive mood is a possibility." Sterkh unbuttoned his coat, and drops of melted snow fell on the dark parquet floor. "Occasionally a brilliant possibility. But more often than not it is a lost possibility, Sasha. I wanted to tell you before . . . but—I just didn't have the heart to upset you."

▪▪▪

Sterkh left. Sasha watched him walking away.

She already knew what she had to do. Up to the minute detail. The pink phone on her neck probably would have prevented her. However, Farit Kozhennikov had taken away her phone, thus letting her loose.

She flipped over a page in the half-filled notepad. And one more empty page. A white field.

This was where she'd made a mistake. She should not have considered an "activity" equal to taking the exam; an activity was a lot less obvious, intermittent, a dashed line. It was fractioned and simultaneously viscous. And *that* was not called "love," not at all; this activity had its own verb, its own symbol, and its own notation.

As long as the pencil did not break.

Now. Then.

In the morning, around half past seven, Sasha looked out the window and saw Yegor sitting on her porch, between the stone lions.

He was just as still and white as the sculptures. Two white piles of snow lay on his shoulders.

"What's wrong?" Sasha opened the door; the drifting snow licked her fur-lined slippers.

For the first time in her life she stepped that far into the past. A few hours. She felt a little frightened.

She let Yegor into her apartment, opened the fireplace and placed an old crumpled newspaper onto the coals.

"We'll take care of everything. Don't worry."

She put a couple of dry logs on the newspaper and lit a match.

"We'll get warm in a minute. Just wait."

She picked up her bag, which had been left on the coat hanger overnight. For a second she was confused: it was the same notepad, only the page that was supposed to be covered with signs and symbols was still white and empty . . .

She should sharpen her pencil to make sure it did not break.

"Yegor, don't be surprised, promise? I know what you want to tell me. I know you will pass this exam. I know *how* you will pass it. Look at me. Look at me . . ."

She placed a piece of paper on the table. *Don't forget to sharpen the pencil . . .*

"Will." One of the essential symbols with multiple meanings, everything depended on the nuances, on the added meanings. In five dimensions, plus an occasional glimpse of the sixth. Perfect.

"Sasha . . ."

"Be quiet and keep your mouth closed. I am working on something important, just be quiet . . ."

Projection of will onto the identity: will-dash, plus Yegor's own willpower, which she must take into account, will-two dashes . . .

The symbol glimmered, unfolding in time. She planted the fourth dimension within the time loop—no one had ever taught her that, she'd never even heard of this complicated paradox, but it just made sense to her, and now it was too late to back out, no matter what the side effects would be.

The clock's *ticktock* slowed down. The pendulum hung for a second, then swayed again. Sasha smiled happily.

She *could*.

Taking Yegor's hands, she *claimed* him, merged with him. He was such a nice, strong, kind man. This is what the institute had done to him; Sasha fought a sudden and unnecessary feeling of pity. On the way to becoming a carved sculpture, wood goes through the aesthetically displeasing stage of being a stump; half-finished work is not usually displayed in front of half-wits, but lately Sasha was anything but a half-wit.

Here is the second-year Dorofeev. And here is his folded-in entity. Like a letter in an envelope. Receive and sign for it.

Yegor's hands twitched in her own.

"Sasha . . ."

"Don't be afraid," she said softly. "Let's go, it's time. It's already half past nine. Time went so quickly! And the same two logs are still burning, but never mind that. Let's go, do not worry. It is my imperative. It is my command."

An hour had passed since the door closed. Then another hour. Students came out one or two at a time. Some immediately lit up cigarettes, others threw their arms around their friends. Somebody was laughing hysterically. Gradually the corridor became noisy, second years chased one another around in the hallway: "What are the sparrows singing on this last day of chill? We live, we breathe, we made it, and we are living still!"

Yegor was the last one to come out. He staggered. Grabbed the wall with his hand.

"Well?"

He stepped forward and embraced her. He staggered, holding on to Sasha like a drunk holding on to a tree. Sasha gritted her teeth and replanted her feet firmly on the ground.

"How did you do it? How did you manage? *How?*" Tears rolled down his unshaven hollow cheeks. "You did it . . . You . . . thank you. Thank you. Thank you."

Yegor's classmates slowly tightened the circle around them. Sasha's "anchor"—the one she planted in Now—was approaching with every minute, and she suddenly realized with dread that she had no idea how to get out of the loop. Time is a grammatical concept; in a few minutes Sasha would again look out the window and see Yegor sitting on the steps between the stone lions. And everything would repeat itself again, only this time Sasha, burned-out and frazzled, would not be able to replicate her heroic deed, and Yegor would fail yet again . . .

And fail again . . .

And again.

"Everything is fine," she whispered. "You need to rest. Go, wash up . . ."

Her gentle voice exuded power over Yegor. He straightened up and, squeezing Sasha's hand one more time, shuffled through the crowd of his classmates toward the men's bathroom. Sasha did not have to look at her watch to sense the "anchor" drawing closer.

The front door opened. Sterkh stepped into the hall; snow melted on the long tails of his black coat.

"Hello, Nikolay Valerievich."

"Hello, Alexandra. Congratulations, you are in the loop with variations. In the old times it was used as a punishment for disobedient slaves."

Sasha was silent. Everything that had happened in the last few hours (or minutes?) took so much of her strength that she was now ready to fall down—or burst out crying.

"I am kidding," Sterkh's voice was a little softer. "Get some paper. Concentrate. If a sum of realities is expressed through a subjunctive mood, then in order to come out of the loop, we must first of all define the actual reality—the current one—then express it through the narrative and lock it in with a command. Go ahead!

"Oh—and if you make a mistake, I'll write a report to your advisor."

▪▪▪

The next day, on January 12, Sasha carried the fir tree outside and fixed it in a snow pile across from the stone lions. The tree looked alive; the wind stirred its gold garland.

Portnov and Sterkh held her in a consultation from noon to two in the afternoon. Sasha returned from the institute, lay down on top of her comforter, and, surprising herself, fell asleep.

She dreamed of Zakhar. He was sitting in an underground vault filled with gold coins with a round symbol on their faces. In her dream he seemed very happy to see Sasha. "Are you here as well? That's cool. I'm bored here all by myself. I have been sitting here for a thousand years, cleaning sticky dirt off these words. Help me."

And Sasha sat down—in her dream—next to Zakhar, picked up a small moistened rag, and began to clean the dull coins, one after another. Her efforts would alter the zero on the face of the coins—change it into fives, tens, eights—and when the figure eights fell down on their sides, Sasha would detect the sign of infinity . . .

"Have you been here long?" she asked Zakhar.

"There is no such thing as the fourth dimension here. And no third dimension, either." And then Sasha realized that the coins, and Zakhar, and she herself were drawn on a flat surface, and the time in the picture was not moving . . .

She woke up when it was already dark. Snow fell outside her windows. Somewhere on Sacco and Vanzetti a street cleaner's shovel made scraping sounds.

Less than twenty-four hours remained until the placement exam.

That night Sasha said good-bye to her landlady and called Mom. Baby Valentin was sick again, and Valentin senior had left for a business trip and not returned yet. Mom's voice sounded tinny, detached, as if from another planet. "Everything will be fine," Sasha said, knowing perfectly well that Mom did not believe her.

Her suitcase was half-packed. Sasha thought that she had no clue where she would unpack it, and whether she would have to do it at all. With pleasure she realized that this thought did not frighten her in the least.

She gathered the trash—old drafts, notes, slips of paper—and made a fire in her fireplace for the last time. Paper covered with ink did not burn well.

Someone rang the doorbell. Sasha saw Farit Kozhennikov in the window—and for the first time in her life she felt no fear.

He walked in and looked around. Straddled the chair. Sasha had not finished cleaning up; plastic bags lay around, in the corner stood a broom, a dustpan, and a mop.

"Ready for departure?"

"Farit," Sasha said drily. "I'm very busy. If you have something important to say—say it. If not . . . As you can see for yourself, I'm not exactly relaxing right now."

He swayed back and forth.

"Important . . . yes, I guess you can say that. Let me ask you something: How many of your classmates would decline taking the exam if they had the option?"

"All of them."

"Are you sure?"

"Absolutely. Of course, we can cheer one another up, we are sure of our success. We are words, we must reverberate, must fulfill our destiny. But if somebody could slip out, scamper, do a vanishing act with impunity—he would flee so fast only a clean pair of heels would show."

"And how about you?"

"What about me?"

Kozhennikov adjusted his glasses on the bridge of his nose.

"As your advisor, I am officially offering to release you from the placement exam. To release you from your tenure at the institute. Officially. According to the 'it was only a dream' method."

The fire burned in the fireplace. Old notes, papers, and drafts were dying down. Sasha sat at the table—her back very straight.

A minute passed.

"Are you joking?"

He took off his glasses. Sasha met his ordinary, average brown eyes.

"No."

"Farit, are you making fun of me?"

"No. I will tell you right away: none of your classmates has received such an offer, and none of them will."

"Why me . . ."

"Because."

Sasha squeezed her hands. A second ago she was sure of herself, calm, even detached. A second ago she was a grown-up, devoid of fear and ready to look straight into her destiny's face.

"Once again you will be sixteen years old," he said. "Everything that happened later would turn out to be a dream and shall be forgotten."

"That's impossible."

He sniggered.

Sasha stared at him. His face was hazy before her eyes. Sasha hadn't cried in a long time. She had forgotten how to cry. She did not believe something could shake her so violently before the placement exam.

"Think about it. 'It was a dream.' Say it—and you will wake up. Back there. And nothing will happen again. There will be no me. There will be no institute. You will be accepted at the School of Philology—if you don't fail the entrance exams. Well, have you decided?"

Sasha bit on her fingers.

Mom . . . Valentin . . . and the baby. They wouldn't be there. And what *would* be would possibly—most likely—be completely different. Absolutely different. Would Mom be happy? Of course she would, she would have Sasha . . . even without Valentin, without the baby. Mom would have Sasha! She would do everything to . . .

Word. A verb. Harmony of Speech. A crystal termite nest of meanings. Inhuman beauty. Infinite cognition. Page after page, and the book does not end, the most fascinating book, is it possible that Sasha would not know what happens next?

Minus three and a half years. Difficult, terrifying years. It was a dream. How simple. *It is only a dream* . . .

Kostya. He wouldn't be a part of her life; that was for the best. Yegor . . . They had no choice, they would never have to choose.

HOW LUCKY THEY ARE!

"Farit, why?! What have I done to you? Why do you constantly pick on me? *Why?*"

"Sasha?"

"Why do I get to choose? I can't . . ."

By then she was sitting on the floor, hunched over, pressing her palms to her cheeks. Kozhennikov lowered himself next to her.

"I pick on you? On *you*? Not a hair fell off your head! All your relatives are alive, more or less healthy, happy . . ."

"I cannot choose! I can't—like this—I can't choose, do you understand that? Why . . ."

"Cut it out. Any of your classmates—any of the third years who had ever existed—would give their right hand for such an opportunity. You said so yourself."

"Why, though? Why like this?" She lifted her tear-filled eyes up to him. "Why through fear? Why not . . . Why wouldn't you explain things? I would study. I would work hard if you were nice to me!"

He shook his head. "You wouldn't have, Sasha. Only a strong incentive takes you over the edge. Only motivation."

"But there are other stimuli. Love. Ambition . . ."

"There are none equal to fear," he said, almost with regret. "It is the consequence of objective, unyielding laws. To live is to be vulnerable. To love is to fear. And the one who is not afraid—that person is calm like a boa constrictor and cannot love." He held her shoulders. "Well, have you decided?"

She pushed his hands aside and got up. She bit her lip. Tears streamed down her face—but it did not matter. What mattered was her jagged breath that made her voice sound so piteous.

"I have decided. I want to finish the institute. Become a part of Speech. To reverberate. Be admitted to graduate school. That's why tomorrow I am going to take the placement exam." She staggered but stayed on her feet.

Kozhennikov's pupils narrowed. Only for a moment. His eyes looked as if they were lit up from the inside. Sasha recoiled.

"Is that your final word?"

She shut her eyes.

"Yes."

"Good afternoon, third years."

Both the assembly hall and the stage were brightly lit. Portnov and Sterkh stood below the stage, near the first row of chairs, and two men and a woman sat behind the long table placed near the front edge of the stage. The woman's name was Irina Anatolievna—she taught Specialty to Yegor's year—but the men were unfamiliar to Sasha. At least she thought so, until one of them, the one sitting on the far left, raised his head. Sasha's mouth dropped open: it was the gym teacher, Dima Dimych. Wearing a suit and tie. With an unusual look on his face: it seemed frozen. As if all the muscles responsible for facial expression had turned into plaster of paris.

The third examiner, blond, about forty years old, had never been human. Like Portnov, he was a function.

The old wooden chairs squeaked mercilessly. Sasha took a seat in the middle of the second row, with Denis Myaskovsky on her right and

Lisa Pavlenko on her left. Kostya sat in the front row, two seats to the right of Sasha. If she wanted to, she could reach for him with her hand. But Kostya stubbornly avoided looking at her.

"Dear third years!" Sterkh stayed below the stage, not coming up. "The big day has arrived. You will now receive printouts with your assignments. You will have time to prepare. Do not rush and do not be nervous. When you hear your name, approach this table, sign, and receive your examination sheet. Is everyone ready? Can we begin?"

Dead silence was his answer.

"Biryukov, Dmitry. Noun."

"Bochkova, Anna. Noun."

"Goldman, Yulia. Adjective."

Staggering in her high heels, Yulia stepped onto the stage. The blond function sitting at the corner handed her several stapled sheets of paper. Unsmiling, Dima Dimych offered her a pen. Yulia managed to sign, her hands shaking; she started reading her assignments on the stairs that led down from the stage, and Sasha saw how the expression of panic on her face was replaced by surprise and then joy.

"Kovtun, Igor. Adverb."

They rose one after another. The procedure was running smoothly and clearly had been run before; the established routine had a calming effect.

"Kozhennikov, Konstantin. Pronoun."

Sasha watched Kostya move toward the table. He was handed the stapled sheets by the blond teacher, and the former (false?) gym teacher offered him a pen. Sasha saw Kostya's eyelid twitch.

Walking down the steps, Kostya tripped up.

"Calm down," Sterkh said gently, steadying him. "All your emotions stayed outside. All your fears are buried underneath this threshold. Concentrate."

Sasha watched Kostya read his assignment. At some point he paled, his lips shook; then he relaxed and Sasha felt his instant relief. He will pass; he will get through this. He was confident, he managed to regain this confidence. Pronoun . . . let it be so.

"Samokhina, Alexandra! Verb!"

Sasha jumped up, making the wooden row shake. Already? So fast?

She climbed out from the row, stumbling over someone's feet and knees. She rose up to the stage: the room swayed like the deck of a ship. The six eyes of the people sitting at the table watched her. The stack of examination sheets under the blond man's hand had become much thinner.

Dima Dimych's lips formed a faint smirk, so unlike the sincere and sparkly, toothy smiles he so generously gave to all the girls at the gym.

"Good luck . . . *verb*."

"Sign here," said the blond man.

She picked up the fountain pen with a gold nib. The nib scratched the paper. Sasha barely managed to write "Samokhina" in black ink across from the blue check mark. She turned and began walking away from the table.

"Sasha, you may want to take the examination sheet—just in case."

She turned around. Dima Dimych watched her ironically, but without mockery.

She accepted three thin sheets from his hand. Clutched them with her moist hand. Made it back to her seat and only then took a look.

On the top of the first page she saw the round symbol for "Word." And one more—for "verb." And the third one, the meaning of which Sasha did not understand and so became frightened, but then immediately realized that this was not an assignment. It was the header, the legend, the identification symbols; underneath printed text read: "Alexandra Samokhina." There was today's date and her crooked signature.

She looked down. Here was the first assignment; Sasha tensed up and immediately relaxed. Piece of cake. She'd done hundreds of these last year.

Second assignment. Yes, Sterkh was right. This is simple, a cakewalk.

The distribution of examination sheets continued; now they had reached Group B. Oksana, Sasha's former roommate, was walking toward her seat, pressing the papers to her generous bosom . . .

Third assignment. Sasha turned the coarse paper over.

On the third page a black "fragment" displayed an "anchor" of three white circles in its center.

At first she froze. Then she smiled.

She could do it. She'd done it before. She must focus her eyes on the "anchor" and hold her breath. There stands a black city, where a monster lives in the tower. Fragment number one hundred. On the other hand, why exactly one hundred? What if it is number one hundred and one? Two hundred? One thousand?

". . . by now all of you have received your assignments. I repeat, you have enough time to prepare. Do not rush. As soon as you are ready I would like to ask you to raise your hand and . . . what's wrong, Sasha?"

Not giving herself time for reflection, she cast up her shaking hand.

"I am ready."

"Already?"

The three examiners stared at her: the function, dispassionately, the woman, anxiously; only the gym teacher, whose new identity Sasha could not get over, squinted with obvious pleasure.

At the foot of the stage Sterkh nervously moved his shoulders. "Are you sure, Sasha?"

"Yes." She got up.

She caught Kostya's eyes. A long, heartrending glance. She recalled the fir tree with a single garland, the flames in the fireplace: this is where she should have placed the time loop. She hadn't thought of it . . . or was too scared. Because she had already had a bitter experience, there was already a day in her life when Yegor repeated time after time: "Let's get married . . ."

Yegor had never found out the truth about the infinite day. Thinking about it made Sasha almost proud.

What am I doing? she thought, making her way along the row. I am a verb in the imperative mood, and I am about to *reverberate* for the first time. I am going to become a part of Speech. Become a command. And here I am, thinking about . . . garland.

At the foot of the stairs leading to the stage she was met by Portnov and Sterkh.

"Good luck," Portnov said solemnly, looking over his glasses. "You are the best one."

"Everything will be fine." Sterkh offered her his hand helping her up the stairs. "Good luck, Sasha. We will fly together again."

In front of the table she stopped, not knowing what to do next. Dima Dimych rose and beckoned her with his finger. At the far end of the stage stood tables, just like in the auditorium. A cup filled with sharpened pencils, a stack of white paper, and a bottle of mineral water surrounded by glasses were placed on each table.

"No need to be nervous"—the false gym teacher moved a chair toward Sasha—"we are old friends. And we will be working together during your fourth year. Then during your fifth. Then, I hope, you will be accepted to graduate school. Right now, though, we only have a placement exam, and you must pass beyond the limits. Jump over your own head. As usual."

Behind Dima Dimych she saw a highly complex structure, terrifying and powerful—it was hard to imagine that some time ago Sasha had *that* as her swing partner. She forced the corners of her lips to lift slightly. The examiner nodded, encouraging her.

"The first two assignments we can deal with quickly, agree?"

"Yes."

"Go ahead."

She tested the tip of the pencil with her finger and pricked it. Licked off a drop of blood. Without stopping, without checking herself, she drew a chain of associations on the paper—from memory.

"Excellent. Next."

Sasha took a deep breath. Five cognitive processes begin at one point of time, each is periodical, the periods are multiples . . .

"That's enough, thank you. I knew it wasn't going to be difficult for you. I am interested in the third sheet."

Sasha licked her dry lips.

"Water?" the former gym teacher opened a bottle of mineral water. He poured some into a glass: the bubbles hissed and stuck to the walls of the glass. "Here you go."

Sasha took a sip and coughed. She drank the whole glass. The examiner immediately poured her another one.

"Keep drinking. I assume you know how to complete the tests with the black fragments?"

"Of course." Unintentionally Sasha spoke in the same tone.

"Good. If you are ready, let us not lose any time. Begin."

Sasha pulled closer the page with a black rectangle and three white dots in the center. Took a deep breath.

Behind her she heard the anxious rustling of paper. Her classmates were preparing for the test. She wanted to turn around for the last time to see their faces, but she did not dare.

The stage of the assembly hall smelled distinctly of dust. One of the windows let in a draft. And everything was drowned in sharp light; even through closed eyelids Sasha saw the glow.

"Right now?"

"Yes. Verb, you may begin."

Sasha focused on the three white dots—three luminous eyes. She held her breath. One, two, three, four, five . . .

▪▪▪

. . . one hundred sixty-eight, one hundred sixty-nine, one hundred seventy.

Out of the blackness emerged—jumped out, revealed itself—a city surrounded by a wall high enough to reach the sky.

She saw it in minute, most explicit, most authentic detail. The city was the color of coal, graphite, the color of dark steel, faultless in its monochrome harmony. Sasha felt marble under her bare feet. Cool stone, and warm stone, smooth and rough, soaring walls, slender windows, spires rising into the sky . . .

It's happening. She will do everything right. There, in the tower, a monster is waiting for her. Sasha must meet it face-to-face and not feel fear. A year ago it seemed impossible. But not anymore: having recognized her power, Sasha threw open her arms, unfolded her wings, and flew.

She grew.

She billowed. She swelled. She absorbed outlines, smells, the texture of stone. In those places where Sasha stretched enough to reach the city, it ceased being carbon black and became softly gray, like an antique photograph. She claimed this life and this happiness. She inhaled the smoke, and the curve of a roof glistening in the rain, and the wisp of fog, and a majestic spire. The more she took, the more powerful and multidimensional she became. Multicolored thoughts, so heavy and reluctant in a human brain, now flowed like a stream. No—like the sea.

She embraced the tower. It flinched, tensed up like an egg a split second before the birth of a baby bird, but Sasha squeezed it softly, buried it under her will like under cement. The tower failed to open, and whatever was hidden inside was now buried forever, and Sasha continued to grow without obstacle.

She claimed the city. She sensed it within herself like one senses one's heart in the moment of powerful joy or fear. She flowed farther, claiming the dark sky with two dull stars. These stars were superfluous in her picture of the universe.

Superfluous.

Extinguish?

She appeared—she was—a dark empty space. And she was also sitting at the table on the stage of the assembly hall, and in front of her lay a black "fragment." Examiner Dima Dimych sat across from her at the table. His face was no longer cast in papier-mâché. He frowned and grew visibly more anxious with every second.

"What's happening?"

Sasha hung between the points of "was" and "will be." At this moment—for the first time since she'd opened the fragment—she had the feeling that something was not quite right. Something was wrong.

But she was doing everything correctly!

"Stop her! She's broken loose again! Stop her, she's uncontrollable!"

The door opened with a long screech. Simultaneously the heads of people sitting in the assembly hall turned: a man in very dark glasses walked down the aisle, stepping slowly, heavy-footed, over the old, dull parquet floor.

The suit jacket on Sterkh's back ripped open along the spine; steel-colored feathers peeked through the jagged slit.

"What is the matter?"

"Calm down. Continue the examination."

Sasha sensed but did not see them around her. Not people—structures, diagrams of processes and human beings; the examiner who was a function. The matronly Irina Anatolievna. The gym teacher, Dima Dimych, with his strange and terrifying metamorphosis. Sterkh stood with his angular twitching wings thrown up in the air. Next to Sterkh was Portnov, so tense that he was constantly changing, pulsating like a garden simultaneously undergoing both spring and fall. Something was wrong; she had gone too far. According to the planned examination she was supposed to stop near the tower . . .

She felt as if a page from the *Activator* opened in front of her—enormous, multidimensional, encompassing all that could be represented in the universe. She saw herself—a mute word ready to reverberate. She saw many layers of reality—bright, textured, dull, vague, they gathered into surreal folds at the edge of her field of vision. Probabilities and rearrangements: she was supposed to stop at the tower, meet the examiner, select a point of application—she was a verb—and *reverberate;* it was similar to throwing a bowling ball into the midst of immobile pins or swinging a still pendulum. Chip the neck of an ideal and thus nonexistent pitcher. The dominoes would collapse, cars would run along distant roads, raindrops would fall, and Sasha would materialize for the first time.

She, the Imperative, an instrument of Speech.

But something had gone wrong. She could no longer go back—not because the fourth dimension was irreversible. Because her nature, her inner essence, led her here, to this dark space with two stars above her head, and here she was subject to different laws that did not fit into any reality known to her. Laws alien to any dimension.

"Stop!"

"Stop her! It's not a verb, it's a . . ."

"Yes. She is Password."

Sasha, who was the dark space, shuddered. Two stars leaned over above her head—they were eyes, very intense, unblinking, and now black lenses no longer remained between them and Sasha.

"Greetings, Password."

That, which came from the darkness, spoke without words, in bare meaning. Sasha knew how to communicate, but she did not answer. She lost her . . . no, not her tongue. She lost that place in her soul where words are born.

"Do you hear me, Sasha?"

She was still sitting behind the table. In the empty and dim hall without ceiling, without walls. Fog curled above her head. Across from her, in the examiner's chair, now sat Farit Kozhennikov.

"Can you hear me?"

She nodded, overwhelmed for a second by the pain within her enormous, heavy head.

"As I'm sure you've gathered, you are not simply a verb in the imperative mood. You are Password—a key word that opens a new informational structure. Macrostructure. Do you understand what it means?"

Essences around her shifted, remaining in place, flowing, turning different facets. Meanings followed in a single file. Sasha managed to grab the simplest definitions, the ones lying on the surface.

"Reverberate. Beginning."

"Mistake—no. Act of creation—important."

"All the subtleties and finesse will be taught to you during your fourth and fifth year, and in graduate school. The Introduction to Applied Science is over; your applied science is here. Your most important applied work."

"Password. Name, new essence, Creation.

"Creator . . ."

Concepts moved like a triumphant procession. Like a large ship going by. Sasha recognized them sequentially—and simultaneously.

"Sasha." Kozhennikov's voice interrupted the stream of information like a wave breaks into the surface of the water. "Stay conscious. The transformation has not yet been completed. When you reverberate . . . do you know what will happen?"

"I . . ."

"You are Password. You will align fragments of reality—and open a new informational expanse. Do you understand what is happening?"

Farit Kozhennikov spoke, his lips moved. Reality again split and faded. Sasha found herself in the assembly hall, a bottle of mineral water stood on the table, bubbles hissed, each reflecting the assembly hall, the professors, a cup filled with pencils, Sasha leaning over the sheet of paper . . .

"Pick up your pencil. Concentrate. Are you ready?"

She complied—but did not feel the pencil in her numb fingers. She blinked—and lost her human body, hanging in the middle of the empty dark space. Empty and dark. And only two stars watched her from above—the white eyes.

"Your will. Create. Reverberate."

The order was so authoritative that she immediately felt relief.

It was simple—like flicking a switch in a dark room. Digits on the display would coincide. Grooves would align, template and print would line up. The darkness would be broken by the light.

"Reverberate!"

She held her breath under the petrifying stare of the two distant stars.

Silence can be unbearable—a moment before the Word finally wrenches itself free.

Darkness—a second before the appearance of the first spark.

In the beginning was . . .

Silence. Stillness.

In the beginning was . . .

"No."

Two yellow eyes inched closer.

"Why?"

To live is to be vulnerable. A thin membrane of a soap bubble separates one from impenetrable hell. Ice on the road. The unlucky division of an aging cell. A child picks up a pill from the floor. Words stick to each other, line up, obedient to the great harmony of Speech . . .

"Everything will be different for you. Your will. Your power. Let the sun shine always. I believe in the world without evil. Let a hundred flowers bloom. You are the favorite instrument of Speech . . . Reverberate!"

Sasha flinched from the force of this command. But she didn't flinch from her response.

"No."

"No?"

"No. Because for me to love is to be afraid."

There, in the assembly hall, a glass pitcher fell off the examiners' table.

"I will reverberate, and the fear will reverberate in me—in the First Word. And all the love that I carry will forever be poisoned by fear. I refuse . . ."

Shards of glass flew up.

"Word is spoken."

"The end. She failed."

"She did not pass."

"Failing grade."

The empty dark space around Sasha lit up with a multitude of stars, and the stars turned into gold coins. Dull, heavy, they flowed and overflowed, threatening to bury her underneath.

"I refuse to be afraid!"

And at that moment she reverberated, and knew she was *heard.*

"Sweetheart? Honey?"

The baby was asleep. He breathed heavily. He coughed in his sleep and tossed and turned. The woman lay next to him, her hand squeezed between the beams of the wooden crib, pressing her palm to the hot little head.

"Baby . . . sweetheart . . ."

The other side of the queen-size bed was empty. Cold smooth sheets.

The baby had another coughing fit. The woman closed her eyes, sore as if filled with sand.

Several more hours until morning. Coughing. Crying. Long beeps in the receiver. "The person you are trying to call is out of reach." *Where is he, what happened to him? When will he come back? Will he come back at all?*

A strip of parquet floor crunched softly under a bare foot.

"Who . . . who is it? Who is there?"

Step. One more step. The woman was sitting up in bed. She was watching the darkness. Her shoulders twitched under the thin bathrobe.

"It's me."

"Sasha!"

"I haven't completely come back yet. I am in your dream."

"Sasha . . ."

"Mom, I have to tell you one very important and secret thing. I love you. I've always loved you, and I always will. Listen! I love you . . ."

The baby inhaled deeply—and breathed evenly.

In the morning, when the man returned and unlocked the door with his key, they were sleeping in a tight embrace—the baby was moist with sweat, but his forehead was cool and lusterless. And the woman was haggard, pale, with a weak smile on her lips.

Darkness.

"In the beginning was the Word."

Slow rotation.

"The light shines in the darkness, and the darkness has not overcome it."

Luminous dust folds into a flat silver curve with two soft spiral arms.

"Do not be afraid."

ACKNOWLEDGEMENTS

Fate brought us together and gave us more than twenty-five years of love, writing, and creativity, and we are eternally grateful for that.

We would like to thank our parents, relatives, and friends who blessed our union, sharing our joys and supporting us in our darker moments. Without you, this book would not exist.

We thank our daughter, Anastasia, a kind, intelligent, and creative girl who served as an exciting stimulus to write this novel. When we were working on *Vita Nostra,* our teenage Anastasia was on her way to becoming an adult, just like our heroine. Anastasia's trials and tribulations, along with those of her parents, grew into the metaphors upon which our story is built.

Our thanks to Julia Meitov Hersey, not just our translator, but also our loyal friend, for knowing all our texts inside out, and for lending us the tuning fork of her impeccable artistic taste.

Thanks to Josh Getzler, our wise literary agent from New York, for believing in our literary future. Josh's optimism, persistence, and cheerfulness make us believe in it as well.

Thanks to Soumeya Roberts, Jonathan Cobb, and the entire staff of Hannigan Salky Getzler literary agency for everything they do to ensure our success in the capricious world of literature and cinema.

Our sincere gratitude goes to David Pomerico, our incredible editor at Harper Voyager, who peered deeply into the soul of our novel and led the complex process of its adaptation to the American culture.

—*Marina and Sergey Dyachenko*

My deepest gratitude goes to Lev Grossman, who challenged and inspired me to transfer *Vita Nostra* from Russian to English, and to Marina and Sergey for trusting me with this process.

I would like to thank Kira Clingen, Susanne Kummel, Anatoly Belilovsky, Tom Crosshill, and Aliette de Bodard for reading and reviewing the novel in its rough unedited infancy, and for encouraging me whenever I felt like I was failing (which was more often than I care to admit).

Many thanks go to the awesome members of the HSG family and Harper Voyager's editorial staff for answering my neverending questions with infinite patience and grace.

Josh Getzler—Agent G—you are a masterpiece of a human being, a dear friend, and an extraordinary agent. Thanks for standing by me for nine long years, for introducing me to the magnificent David Pomerico, who made my translation rise as close to the original as possible, and for all those pictures of Layla to brighten my days.

Thanks to my family for patiently listening to my endless lectures on the finer points of everything that had been lost in translation. This work is dedicated to the memory of my father, Vladimir, who always said Sasha Samokhina reminded him of me.

—*Julia Meitov Hersey*